Delicious . . .

". . . is a book to be savored over and over . . . It totally satisfied my romance-loving heart."   —*Romance Junkies*

". . . is a nonstop powerhouse of suspense and sexy eroticism! *Delicious* is by far one of the best books that I have ever read."   —*TwoLips Reviews*

MORE PRAISE FOR THE WICKED LOVERS NOVELS

"Sizzling, romantic, and edgy, a Shayla Black story never disappoints."
—Sylvia Day, #1 *New York Times* bestselling author of *Bared to You*

"A wicked, sensual thrill from first page to last. I loved it!"
—Lora Leigh, #1 *New York Times* bestselling author

"Make[s] your toes curl!"
—Angela Knight, *New York Times* bestselling author

"Will . . . have you panting for more!"
—Susan Johnson, *New York Times* bestselling author

"Shayla Black . . . you rocked it!"   —*The Romance Reviews*

"Thoroughly gripping and . . . so blisteringly sexy."
—*Fallen Angel Reviews*

"Five-alarm HOT!"   —*Books-n-Kisses*

"Scrumptiously erotic, sensual, heady, and very arousing."
—*Affaire de Coeur*

"[A] fabulous read."   —*Fresh Fiction*

Delicious

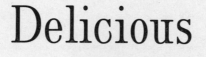

SHAYLA BLACK

HEAT, NEW YORK

THE BERKLEY PUBLISHING GROUP
Published by the Penguin Group
Penguin Group (USA) Inc.
375 Hudson Street, New York, New York 10014, USA

USA I Canada I UK I Ireland I Australia I New Zealand I India I South Africa I China

Penguin Books Ltd., Registered Offices: 80 Strand, London WC2R 0RL, England
For more information about the Penguin Group, visit penguin.com.

This book is an original publication of The Berkley Publishing Group.

HEAT and the HEAT design are trademarks of Penguin Group (USA) Inc.

Heat trade paperback ISBN: 978-0-425-26823-0

The Library of Congress has catalogued the previous Heat trade paperback edition of this title as follows:

Black, Shayla.
Delicious / Shayla Black.—1st ed.
p.   cm.
ISBN: 978-0-425-23242-2
I. Title.
PS3602.L325245D46   2010
813'.6—dc22
2009041102

PUBLISHING HISTORY
First Heat trade paperback edition / March 2010
Second Heat trade paperback edition / June 2013

PRINTED IN THE UNITED STATES OF AMERICA

10 9 8 7 6 5 4 3 2 1

Cover photograph copyright © Oliver Hoffman / Alamy.
Cover design by Marc Cohen.
Text design by Tiffany Estreicher.

Delicious

Chapter One

I'M going to sink inside you so deeply, you won't ever forget I was here.

Alyssa Devereaux shuddered at the memory of that growled promise, as she'd been surrounded by taut muscles and male need.

Luc Traverson. Even his name caused heat to stab her belly with want. He'd kept every bit of that promise; she'd never forgotten him for a moment.

The night he'd spent in her bed had been amazing, magical. Considering she'd long ago given up on fairy tales, that was saying something. Being enveloped in Luc's steely strength had been paradise. Under his stare that night she hadn't just felt like a desirable woman, but like the *only* woman. The intimacy . . . oh, God. Sizzling. Way beyond making her toes curl, he'd given her a whole new definition of pleasure. His endless dark eyes had burned as he'd slammed her with powerful strokes, his long, midnight hair draped around their faces, cutting off all reality but his whispered demands and rough breathing as he rode her from one orgasm to the next.

He'd brought her body to a fever pitch—to places she'd never believed a man could take her. He had done it again and again. For six hours. Never tiring, never satisfied. Greedy, rapacious, and amazing.

She'd had enough sex in her life to know they'd shared something more.

The next morning . . . gone. No note, no explanation. A few days later, he'd sent flowers with an apology for any discomfort or pain he might have caused. She'd been pissed off, a bit hurt . . . but not terribly surprised.

Still, she wasn't willing to give up. For the chance to see Luc again, Alyssa had broken her own rule and called him. Twice. He'd never returned her calls personally. Instead, his assistant had called merely to say that he would keep his terms of their arrangement. Nothing more.

She'd been nothing to him. Yes, she'd known before their night together that he didn't respect her. They'd first met when she'd stripped at his buddy's bachelor party a few years back. Somehow, she'd hoped opening herself completely to Luc would change his mind.

Stupid.

Still, he was everything she'd ever wanted in a man: attractive, successful, capable of deep caring, sensitive, sexy . . . She wasn't giving him up without a fight.

"Afternoon, boss lady." Tyler Murphy sent her a long, low whistle, his stare taking a meandering path down her body as she emerged from the back of the club and stopped before the stage. "You're looking very fine."

"Tyler," she greeted the sandy-haired giant. "Your job is to watch the patrons, not me."

"Since we're not open yet, there's no one here to bounce. Besides, I'm not into ogling drunken frat boys or horny married men. What color are your garters under that little black skirt?"

Her bouncer was former law enforcement of some variety—he'd

never said which kind—college educated with a degree in engineering. Tyler had a lot going for him. Why he'd taken a job here as a bouncer was anyone's guess. But in the few months he'd been with her, he'd proven himself indispensable. There were days her business *needed* him.

It was too bad, really, that her heart didn't need Tyler as well.

From beneath her lashes, she sent him a chiding stare. "I'll never tell."

"Aw, c'mon. Throw a guy a bone."

Alyssa glanced down at his crotch. "Looks like you've got your own."

Tyler winked and sent her a flirty grin. "All for you."

He was good-looking, built like something on the front of a bodybuilding magazine, smart, funny, dependable. But after long days of running Sexy Sirens—Lafayette, Louisiana's, most notorious strip club—and trying to start up a new restaurant, by the time she fell into her solitary bed at night, it wasn't thoughts of Tyler that made her ache. That honor was reserved solely for Luc Traverson.

And after a bit more than three months apart, he would be here today.

Feel me. Yessss. You're so tight, so good. That's it, sugar. Come for me. Again.

Luc's voice, sin wrapped in velvet, dipped in honey, wouldn't leave her head. Even the memory made heat rise inside her. Thoughts of that night always had the power to daze and stun her. She wanted it again. Him again.

"Hello? Earth to Alyssa."

Tyler. *Oops.* "Sorry. The restaurant is weighing so heavily on my mind these days."

He stared at her from green eyes that saw too much. "So clean plates and menus give you that flushed, wanna-get-fucked look?"

"Go find some drunken slobs to rough up."

"I'd rather be with you."

Tyler crossed his arms over his wide chest. His biceps bulged under his body-hugging black T-shirt. He really was gorgeous. And he wanted her; he'd made no secret about that. She could do worse.

"What's his name?" Tyler sighed.

"Who?"

"The man who put that needy look on your face. I don't know whether I want to bust him up or shake his hand."

"There's no one in my life." Which, technically, was true. Other than her hookup with Luc, she hadn't had sex in years.

"Liar."

At this point in the conversation, Tyler usually teased that he'd be more than happy to be that someone. This afternoon, he seemed to sense something was different.

"You're too good to be alone. The girls all worship you. You treat everyone fairly and work damn hard. You're sweeter than you give yourself credit for. You haven't resorted to murder when that asshole Councilman Primpton comes around, making trouble." He sent her a considering stare. "You've had it tough lately. You deserve a break."

If she wasn't careful, his caring would make her cry. A pity party would be marvelously easy to indulge in—and an utter waste of time.

Alyssa anchored her hands on her hips. "Not in the cards."

"Maybe you should postpone the restaurant opening for a few weeks."

"Why?"

Restraint left Tyler. He reached out to her, caressing his large hand down her arm in a soothing gesture. "Your mama has only been gone two weeks."

She tensed. "I hadn't seen her in fourteen years."

"Doesn't matter. You're still dealing with her loss."

She'd done so with mixed feelings. Anger, grief, sadness, rage, a need to rail at the woman who had done nothing to help or under-stand her. Pity that she'd been so self-absorbed.

And beside her grave had stood the blackhearted reason for the rift between them: Joshua. Even after a dozen years, beyond a hundred feet, and through a pair of two-hundred-dollar sunglasses, there was no mistaking the boyish-faced bastard. At least he hadn't seen her. If he had, Lord knew what he would have done.

She shook off the thought.

"Tyler, thanks for your concern, but I've put too much time and energy into this opening to put it off. I need to get it off the ground for cash-flow purposes. Besides, what good would wallowing about my mom do?"

He cupped her shoulders in a tender gesture. "You left here at three this morning, and Sadie told me you were back by eight. Baby, you've got to sleep and give yourself time to grieve."

She'd rather not.

Leaning forward, she placed a soft kiss on his cheek. "You're going to make some woman a great husband someday."

"You asking me?"

Alyssa snorted. "Do I look like the white-picket-fence type? Get your ass back to work."

"Yes, ma'am." He saluted her and turned away, only to turn back again. "Oh, I forgot to tell you, some guy is here to see you. Some chef."

"Luc Traverson?" she breathed.

"Yeah. He said you two had an appointment. He didn't look too happy. Is he the dude doing the guest chef gig this week?"

Tyler's question registered, but she didn't answer. Instead, she glanced around Tyler, to the club's front door.

Boom! There he stood, all six feet plus of him, his elegant, rangy body tense. The sight of him was like a visceral blow. She swallowed . . . and let her hungry gaze eat him up. Inky hair hanging

te here. Finally. She did her best to hide a sly
smile. There was no way he was going to ignore her anymore; she'd
make certain of that.

t was under that little skirt; he
knew. Sleek thighs surrounded by garters in some color designed to
drive a man wild. A lacy thong that would reveal far more of her
assets than it concealed. And under that . . . The feel and taste of her
slick, swollen folds dive-bombed his memory and revved him up, as
if he'd injected rocket fuel in his bloodstream.

And now he had to work beside her for a week. Hell. How was
he going to prevent a recurrence of the event he wanted to forget—
yet couldn't?

You're a professional. Cook and keep your hands to yourself. Besides, it wasn't as if he had nothing else to think about. Negotiations
for his cable TV show were nearly at an end. He had a bit of editing
to do on his latest cookbook. There wouldn't be that much down-
time this week, but what little there'd be, he would fill.

Clearly, Alyssa had a way to fill her time as well. The huge slab of
man at her side whose cheek she'd kissed a moment ago wore a Sexy
Sirens T-shirt stretched across his enormous chest. A bartender? A

bouncer? Whoever he was, the guy slanted a possessive glance at Alyssa that Luc couldn't miss, then glared at him.

Tamping down his irrational anger, Luc reminded himself that if Alyssa wanted to fuck her hired help, that was her business.

The violent urge to dismember her employee would pass.

Alyssa took a step toward Luc, then another.

"Mistress Alyssa," a female called over the speakers in a saucy vamp voice. "Your turn!"

She stopped. Closed her eyes. Sighed. Bracing herself?

Then, as if the hesitation had never been, she flashed him a cool blue gaze, pointed at a chair in front of the stage, then turned away and strode backstage. Luc couldn't help himself. He watched her walk away, the sway of those curvy hips a siren call. Damn.

If they had been alone, there was no way Luc could have prevented himself from touching her. Period.

Unless he wanted another brush with his uncontrollable wild side, he needed to forget his reckless promise to her and get out of this job. Now.

Reluctantly, Luc sauntered to the front of the stage and sat in the chair Alyssa had indicated. As soon as she finished whatever the hell she was doing and talked to him, he'd tell her all bets were off. Hell, he'd pay her for her inconvenience.

Because if he stayed, his dick would get him into trouble. He'd have her naked and be between her legs in two minutes. Or less. And that would be bad. He was looking for Mrs. Right, someone uncomplicated who wanted children as much as he did and would help him keep his beast at bay. Alyssa Devereaux, stripper divine, was definitely *not* that woman.

Suddenly, music pounded through the speakers, blaring with a naughty beat, a wicked slide of horn. Every note suggested sex—the hot, sweaty, no-boundaries variety.

The type he'd had with her and wanted again.

Pulling his loose shirt over his lap to cover his erection, Luc watched as Alyssa strutted onto the stage. She'd piled her straight platinum hair into some wild arrangement on top of her head and donned a sequined bolero jacket in red. He was dying to see what she wore underneath. The way she moved was an invitation . . . and a promise.

She planted her stiletto-clad feet in front of him with a decisive step, then swung her hips, making a sensual circle. She flattened her palm across the bare skin of her tanned abdomen—and began lowering it. She reached down . . . so damn slowly. Luc's breath caught in his chest until, finally, she touched herself. *Oh, hell.*

Her fingers glided between her legs, and she tossed her head back as if she were in utter ecstasy.

Luc swallowed. And started to sweat.

With a jerk of her head, Alyssa snapped her gaze back to him, her eyes like focused blue lasers jolting him to his toes.

Damn it, his nine weeks of dating church secretaries, interior decorators, and elementary school teachers showed. Not one of them had incited an erection. During that time, he'd awakened in the middle of the night more than once, sweating, his dick in his hand and Alyssa's name on his lips. Now, after less than five minutes in her presence, he felt ready to explode.

He had to think about the *right F* words—future and family. Unfortunately, with Alyssa near, the urge to fuck her again kept killing his good intentions.

In the next moment, she released the soft strands of her hair, which hugged her shoulders, clung to her breasts, flirted with her waist. Then she peeled off the little jacket and left it carelessly on the floor, exposing a tiny half top Luc could swear showed the shadows of her areolas. She stepped over the jacket and strutted toward the pole in the center of the stage. When she gripped it with both hands and undulated against it, pressing it to the juncture of her thighs, Luc damn near choked.

And still she continued to stare as if she danced just for him.

The music swelled, wailing with sensuality and suggestion. Alyssa upped her game, sticking a finger into the wet cavern of her mouth and sucking. More blood rushed to Luc's cock at the memory of her mouth around him, her tongue slick across the head, inciting a sizzle that burned his whole body. Even months later, he could feel the lash of her tongue, the hot silk of her mouth. He shuddered.

With a kittenish smile, Alyssa popped her finger from her mouth and drew the damp fingertip down her cleavage. Then her palm took over, smoothing her right breast with an invitation to pure sin on her gorgeous face.

Dear God, no wonder she'd built herself a little empire here in Lafayette. The woman was a walking wet dream and did her job well. No red-blooded, heterosexual male could withstand such intense teasing and stay sane.

Out of the corner of his eye, Luc saw Alyssa's employee, the one she'd touched earlier, sidle closer to the stage. With a quick turn of his head, Luc quickly saw that the mountain in the tight black T-shirt was tense, panting, and sporting a bulge that said he wanted to get busy.

Luc wished he could say that didn't piss him off. But he'd be lying.

Then, as Luc's stare returned to the stage, he damn near forgot his own name.

Alyssa turned her back on him and bent at the waist, staring at him over one mostly bare shoulder with a fuck-me look that stunned him. Luc gripped the arms of his chair, willing himself to stay in it, not charge up on the stage, lay her flat, and get inside her again this instant.

The spaghetti strap of her little top was falling down her arm. And that indecent skirt . . . With her bent over, the hint of the bare ass cheeks flashed from beneath the black silk. Her garters were a come-hither red. Her thong—he could see only a scrap of it—matched.

Soft fingers teased their way up her shin, her thigh, and disappeared under that little skirt. Her eyes half closed, her sultry mouth parted on a silent moan of seeming self-pleasure. His entire body tensed.

He had to get the hell out of there.

Her hands swept up her undulating hips, gathering the skirt with them. She tugged at the little black garment, and it fluttered to the floor. The tanned halves of her backside, bisected by a bit of red lace, crashed fresh lust into his chest, making it damn hard to breathe.

Alyssa had a gorgeous ass. But he'd known that. Luc squeezed his eyes shut so the visual temptation of her bare flesh didn't taunt him. Memories of tunneling into her ass pounded him instead. Her perfect willingness to take him any way he'd wanted. The tightness of her damp, musky body clasping him. The sweat dripping off of them as he'd thrust deep. Her moans.

Christ, the burning lust had to stop—at least long enough to tell her that he wouldn't be staying.

Praying the torture would end soon, Luc opened his eyes. And sucked in a breath.

Alyssa flashed him a naughty smile of invitation as she ripped her small top right down the front to reveal a red demi bra that barely covered her nipples. Hard nipples. Pink, melt-in-his-mouth nipples he remembered all too well.

Luc squirmed in his chair—and nearly went off like a teenage boy. Beyond aroused, his cock was so sensitive, the feel of denim sliding against the head nearly had him coming.

He had to leave. Forget the polite conversation; he'd send her an e-mail with an explanation. Because if he stayed, he would shove his long-term goals aside and fuck her senseless.

As he stood, Luc mentally reviewed a list of chefs—female ones—he could pay to assist Alyssa this week. A short list, but a few durable names. He'd send idiotproof recipes . . .

The red bra dropped to the ground at Alyssa's feet.

Her large breasts were as golden as the rest of her body and swayed gracefully with her every undulation, every step. Those nipples he remembered so damn well beckoned, *Taste me.*

Turn away! he demanded of himself.

His legs didn't move.

Alyssa danced her way down the stairs, holding her breasts up in offering. She pranced past her aroused employee and shot the man a mirthful smile as she caressed the side of his face. Luc tensed when the beefy guy tried to snatch her up in his arms. But Alyssa was too fast and spun out of his grip, toward Luc.

The damp spot at the front of her thong kicked him in the gut. He clenched his fists as she danced closer, closer . . .

She dropped to her knees before him and looked up. Their gazes locked. She panted. Hard. Despite his jeans, her hot breaths caressed his cock. Release broiled in his balls, and he hadn't touched her once.

There was no way he could stop himself from reaching out to tangle his fingers into her hair and bringing her mouth closer. Except when he did, he grabbed air. Alyssa had already strutted away, that golden body of hers burned into his brain.

The music boomed one final time as she artfully fell to the stage, her body sprawled with legs parted, knees bent, hands half covering her breasts, her back arched . . . as if she were ready for him to cover her, take her.

Luc took a step toward her. Then he forced himself to stop and breathe deep.

Self-destruction wasn't his bag, and he wasn't going to get caught up in the trap now.

Beside him, the beefy bouncer clapped wildly and whistled like a man possessed. "That was hot, boss lady. Damn!"

Alyssa stood and smiled, her arms falling to her sides, as if totally unaware or unconcerned that she bared her breasts to her employee and her guest chef.

She did this for a living, he reminded himself. She displayed her body for strangers—and did who knew what else with them. Why should it matter to her who saw her tits?

"Thanks! I've been working on the routine for a while."

"Toward the end there, if you need to fall at someone's feet, I'll volunteer." Her bouncer winked.

"I'll keep that in mind."

She reached for the bolero jacket, thrust her arms into the capped sleeves, then covered her breasts with the lapels. Sort of. The garment had no front clasp, so it hung open, flashing cleavage and the generous swells of her breasts as she made her way down the stairs.

"Mr. Traverson, good to see you again." She held out her hand to him.

She expected him to touch her in a businesslike fashion? Luc steeled himself against the electric current that buzzed through him anytime he touched this woman. But no amount of bracing diluted the jolt that shocked him when he took her hand.

"Ms. Devereaux. We need to talk. Is there someplace quieter? More . . ." Luc glanced over at the bouncer's curious, intrusive stare. "Private?"

"Tyler." She snapped her fingers. "Back to work. It's four, right? Open the doors." Then she turned her stare back to Luc. "Follow me."

As if he could have resisted when she turned that gorgeous ass in his direction and pranced away . . . Impossible.

He followed her backstage, then down a hall that had been painted black. Red lights shined overhead, giving the back a Goth feel that contrasted with the public area's warmth. Then they ducked into a room at the end. White. Soothing with black-and-white photos on the wall. Splashes of red color in silk flowers and a desk chair.

Alyssa held the door wide, then closed it behind him once he'd entered. He realized that none of the club's other sounds could be heard. He cocked his head, listening to the crisp silence.

"Soundproof," she confirmed, perching her hip on the edge of the desk in a relaxed pose that somehow managed to scream sex. "Hard as hell to be bookkeeping at two in the morning with the Pussycat Dolls blasting out your ears."

That made sense, but had nothing to do with this meeting. "Listen, I—"

"Before we get down to business, can I ask your opinion of my number? I haven't danced around a pole in two years. I'm out of practice."

She hadn't danced around a pole in two years? Wow . . . He didn't frequent gentlemen's clubs; he found nothing gentlemanly about them, so he had nothing to compare her to. But if she thought her performance was out of practice, Luc decided he'd likely have a heart attack if ever he saw Alyssa in what she considered to be prime form. "Why ask me?"

She frowned. "Other than Tyler, who likes anything I say or do, you were the only man watching. I need a male opinion on this. Did it work for you?"

And then some. "Um . . . It was good."

"Good," Alyssa sighed. "I need it to be great. Damn! Tonight is Sexy Sirens' fifth anniversary, and I promised to perform. I don't really do it anymore. But I'll try harder when I take the stage later. Thanks for the opinion."

If she tried any harder, she'd incite instant orgasm in half the audience in the first thirty seconds.

"So how have you been?" Her smile lit up her whole face, the whole room. Hell, his whole body.

"Fine. Very busy. You?"

"Oh." She rolled her eyes. "Crazy busy! I had no idea the restaurant business was so tough. You'd know all about it, of course. But I'm still learning. Anyway, I'm glad you're here. I've been looking forward to watching you in action." Her smile was a tease in itself. "In the kitchen, of course."

His body temperature went up again. If he didn't leave soon, she would see action in the kitchen and anywhere else she would consent to let him fuck her. But how could he say this without upsetting her? He definitely owed her.

"I hear your cousin got married," she commented.

Luc tried not to wince. "Yes. Deke and Kimber were married a couple of months ago."

Alyssa paused, cocked her head, assessed him with those cool blue eyes. "You okay with that? I know you had a relationship with her, too."

Yes, one that had ended with the near death of his greatest dream. He'd engaged in a wild ménage with Kimber and his cousin, knowing that she loved Deke. Still, Luc had hoped to marry her, that Deke would get her pregnant, and they would all live as a happy family. All too soon, they'd paired off and left him alone. Possibly his last chance to raise a child with even a drop of his blood walked out the door with them.

He hesitated, then hedged. "She's still special to me."

It wasn't a lie, but not the complete truth, either. Kimber and Deke didn't need anyone but each other, and Luc had only been in their way. He'd accepted that because, while he'd adored Kimber, he hadn't loved her. He had, however, wanted the one thing they could have given him, wanted it so bad sometimes that yearning clawed a deep crater of longing out of his chest.

He wanted a child. And he couldn't father one.

"You all right?" Alyssa asked. "Can I get you a drink?"

No. What he had to do was get out of here before he let his dick lead him to stupid acts, like forgetting the fact that he needed to find an acceptable woman who wanted a child as badly as he did. Alyssa . . . She was sexy, determined, all woman, giving and mind-blowing in the dark. But she wasn't anyone's ideal mother material. If he ended up going the adoption route, case agents would take one look at her and run screaming. Even if she wanted children now—and why would she?—he didn't think she'd agree to dash to the nearest sperm bank or sit through rounds of in vitro fertilization. She'd want a man who could father his own children the normal way.

At thirty-five, Luc should be way beyond this blinding sort of adolescent urge for sex, the kind that obliterated all logical thought. Alyssa wasn't going to help him obtain what he most wanted in life. Somehow, he had to get the news flash to his dick.

Hell, he'd never before wished he were impotent, rather than sterile. Here was a fun first.

"No, thanks. Alyssa, I can't stay."

"Right now? I'm sure you're tired. No problem. I'll give you a tour of the restaurant and kitchen tomorrow morning. It's just a few blocks from here. I ordered all the food your assistant indicated and—"

"I meant this week. I can't do it."

"Another commitment?" Her sharp tone would have told him she was pissed off, even if her starchy expression didn't.

Luc wanted to lie, but he was already bailing on her. Lying would add insult to injury, and she deserved the truth. "It's what's between us."

"We had sex, and now you can't cook for me? What, exactly, does one have to do with the other?"

Luc shifted his weight from one foot to the other. Shit, this wasn't going well. "Look, I'm sorry for what I did to you—"

"You're sorry for making me orgasm so many times I lost count? I've got to hear the reason for this."

How the hell could she not get it?

Raking a stiff hand through his shoulder-length hair, he growled, "Damn it, I was in a frenzy. I plowed into you. I couldn't possibly have been gentle or considerate. And I apologize. I'm sure I didn't ask your permission before I . . ." God, he couldn't even talk about having anal sex with her without getting hard as concrete again. "It just wouldn't be a good idea if I stayed."

Alyssa pulled the lapels of her little jacket together in a useless attempt to cover her breasts. All she did was provide better shots of cleavage. And give him a harder cock.

"Did I seem like I minded that night?"

He swallowed. "Don't you understand? You probably begged me to stop. And I didn't. I don't remember hearing you. If I stay this week, I can't guarantee that I won't lose my head again. I don't want to hurt you."

"I'm not made of glass," she assured him, her whisper shivering right down his spine.

"There's someone else." Sort of.

Three dates didn't constitute a relationship. Looking at Alyssa's lush features and centerfold body, Luc could not summon up a vision of Emily's face to save his life. But he was going to marry her. Or someone like her. Alyssa simply wasn't the kind of woman he could see willingly playing mommy when he finally found a way to become a dad.

"Kimber? Still having ménages with your cousin and his wife?"

No, and he'd never go down that path again, but admitting that to Alyssa would only make her more determined. "Does it matter?"

She shook her head. "Whoever she is, I hope she can understand that you're here to do a job. I can put the past behind me and focus on work if you can."

Luc's hungry gaze skimmed down her body. "You haven't touched me, and I'm already unfocused."

He stormed across the room, grabbed her hand, and fitted it over his aching cock. Instantly, it was better—and worse. God, he wanted her to move on him, strip him bare, put his cock inside her mouth, her body.

Before he got carried away, he pulled her hand away. "You're a very sexy woman, and I am not myself around you. I can't stay."

Alyssa drew in a deep breath, and her chest expanded. Hell, he didn't need to see that. But he couldn't walk away as she slipped off the edge of her desk and sidled closer. "First, for your concern to be valid, I'd have to say yes to sex with you. Today, I haven't. Don't assume I would tomorrow, either. Second, *you* came to *me* three months ago, remember? In exchange for hooking up with you and your cousin, you'd cook for me during opening week. Even though Deke left before things got hot, I lived up to my end of the bargain."

"You more than lived up to your end. It's one reason I can't *not* think about you and sex in the same sentence."

In an attempt to show his cousin Deke that his now-wife was the perfect woman for them, Luc had arranged a threesome with himself, his cousin, and Alyssa. It had backfired on Luc. Deke left before the party started, which Luc had expected. What he hadn't anticipated was needing every sort of sex he could think of with the strip club owner—repeatedly.

"I'm sorry," he murmured. "I'll send you someone else who's totally qualified."

"I've already publicized the fact you'll be here. I have a year's worth of work and my entire savings riding on this place. I'd rather not have this restaurant fail and force me to dance around a pole again for a living. You gave me your word, and I trusted you. Are you really going to bail on me?"

Chapter Two

MUSIC pounded through Luc's ears. As the closing notes thumped and Alyssa struck a suggestive pose around the stripper pole wearing a thong—and nothing else—Luc's steel-hard cock stiffened again, now bordering on pain.

The moment the music died, the all-male crowd, squeezed into the upscale club, erupted into thunderous applause. Luc gritted his teeth. Every man in the room had a hard-on for the woman he was dying to get into bed again. And again. The woman he shouldn't touch.

After a full two minutes of standing O, the patrons finally sat again. Wearing a mischievous smile, Alyssa grabbed the microphone, halfheartedly slapping that little red sequined jacket on so that it covered her nipples—barely.

"Thank you for coming tonight, y'all," she breathed, still panting. "Your enthusiasm for the past five years has made Sexy Sirens a truly special place. I'm thrilled you came to spend your evening with me."

She batted her black lashes over her baby blues, working the crowd. Luc wanted to vomit. No, that wasn't true. He wanted to pick her up, throw her over his shoulder, and forbid her to ever return here or take her clothes off in public again.

He sighed. The caveman thing was Deke's style. And Alyssa wasn't his. Never would be.

Why the hell had he agreed to stay here and cook for the week? Oh, yeah. Guilt. She had agreed to help him three months ago. It wasn't her fault he hadn't—and still couldn't—keep his dick under control. Also not her fault that Deke had walked away and left her alone with Luc's regrettable dark side. Given how much of her life and savings she had tied up in her new restaurant, he'd be seven kinds of scum to skip out on her now. Her amazing breasts, her sharp, sugar-dipped questions, and his combustive memories had all worked against him. He hadn't stood a chance in hell of leaving.

After making a few more announcements, she sashayed her way off the stage and into a waiting throng of male admirers. Tyler, her bouncer, pulled out a chair for her and hovered protectively. With arms crossed and a menacing expression, he looked every inch a badass. Still, that didn't deter her ardent admirers. They fawned close. Some slipped bills right into her thong. She slapped hands away with a naughty smile . . . but that really didn't stop them.

A guy in an LSU shirt shoved his way through the crowd to Alyssa's side and planted a kiss right on her mouth. She didn't pull away, just placed gentle hands on his shoulders. A few seconds later, Tyler yanked the guy off her, shoved him toward the door with a mean motherfucker look, then hovered even closer to Alyssa. His stance screamed, *Mine!*

Refusing to watch a second longer, Luc cursed and swallowed a bitter truth. He'd been suckered. The night he'd spent with Alyssa, she'd sworn she hadn't let a man in her bed or her pussy for nearly two years. At the time, he'd believed her. She had been incredibly tight.

Faced with this foaming-at-the-mouth crowd, he didn't see how it was possible that her bed had been empty for even two days.

It didn't matter if she slept with her bouncer, all of her customers, and most of Louisiana's male population. He had made an agreement with her, and he would honor it. Furthermore, he'd keep his hands off of her for the week, no matter how alluring she was. He had a future—God willing, a wife and a child someday soon—to think about.

* * *

THREE in the morning. With the doors to the club shut and the dancers and waitstaff cleared out, she and Luc were alone. Finally.

She took a moment to savor the fact that, if all went well, she'd performed her last pole dance. Never again would she fill her belly by exposing her body. She'd done it to survive for the past fourteen years. The restaurant represented her future, her path to a better life. She'd work hard for a successful opening just to avoid showing complete strangers her tits again. Luc was a big part of her recipe for success. Thank God she'd convinced him to stay.

For her restaurant's sake—and her own.

Beside her, he stood tall, and so tense she could have bounced a quarter off him. Alyssa smiled. The scrumptious, skittish chef had no idea what was about to hit him.

"You sure you want to tour the restaurant now?" she asked.

He nodded. "Seeing your setup will allow me to plan stations, feel the flow of the food. Tomorrow I need to meet your staff. I've spoken on the phone with your sous and pastry chefs, as well as your assistant manager. They've all completed the training I sent along. We have the week's menu set. You said someone purchased the quantities of supplies I requested?"

Alyssa nodded and cast him a saucy glance. "You have expensive taste, Mr. Traverson."

"You'll make your money back, Ms. Devereaux."

Of course he'd make that promise. He wanted to be sure he didn't owe her a damn thing when he walked out that door. And she was dead determined otherwise. At the end of a week, Alyssa swore she'd own him, body, heart, and soul.

In separate cars, they drove the few blocks to her new endeavor. She refused to look at the fact that he'd declined to ride with her as a setback.

Once they arrived, Alyssa took the keys from her purse and unlocked the door. Just inside, she walked around the corner and flipped on the lowlights overhead. There was a brighter set . . . but why kill the mood?

Alyssa looked out over *her* creation. Simple elegance. A wall of floor-to-ceiling windows. Dark wood accented by walls of taupe and earthy gold, splashed with accents of burgundy and chocolate. The open space held an expectant air, as if waiting for guests. Chairs and crisply draped tables abounded, a few outfitted with china, linen napkins, and crystal so she could see the effect. The understated lettering on the foyer wall read BONHEUR, and the sight filled her with anxious pride every time she came here.

Out of the corner of her eye, she cast a glance Luc's way. Arms crossed over his chest, he scanned the restaurant, his gaze assessing. Her heart beat faster as she waited for his response. It made no sense, wanting his approval so badly . . . but that didn't stop her anxiety.

"Well?" she breathed.

"Bonheur," he murmured. "That's French for 'happiness.'"

"I thought it was fitting. Patrons should be happy here." *And I pray owning makes* me *happy, too.*

"I like it. Fine dining for large parties? Couples?"

"Either. Both."

He glanced out across the tables again. "If you're hoping to be a hot spot for romantic dining, you have too many tables for parties of four to eight, particularly in your cozy corners. The partition between the bar and the dining room . . ." He pointed halfway across the room to the half wall that separated the eating patrons from the merely drinking ones. "It's too short and too close to the bar. It will be hard to get any ambiance if people laughing, smoking, and drinking a lot are visible from the dining room. Raise that to the ceiling. Do you have vents to push the smoke back to the bar?"

She'd debated that, hating to close off the room. But he was right. "There's no smoking at all."

He hesitated. "Even in the bar? That will cost you money."

"It's worth it. I want to make my money from the bar because people are ordering drinks with their food or while waiting for their table, not because they're skipping dinner and loitering over a scotch, hoping to find a date for the night. I've got one bar; I don't need another."

Luc nodded, but didn't react otherwise. She made a mental note to drag more of the smaller tables out of storage and call her contractor to fix the wall in the morning.

"Where's the kitchen?" he asked.

Biting her lip, she led the way around a corner, flipping on more lights. Teasing and seduction, she understood. The restaurant business . . . That was his area of expertise, and now he was all button-down assurance. Alyssa was grateful for it. She'd tried hard to make Bonheur's kitchen optimal, a place a chef of Luc's caliber would be proud to cook in.

Winding down the hall, she was conscious of Luc's eyes on her. His gaze brushed her shoulders, hugged the curve of her waist, lingered on her ass. She could feel the burn.

"The kitchen isn't visible from the dining room. Good layout."

When they reached the large, mostly stainless steel room, she flipped on the lights. "I've heard people don't like seeing the kitchen when they eat."

Again, Luc crossed his arms over his chest, looking from one end of the room to the other, nodding slowly. "Very nice. Butcher-block prep area is well placed and large. Twelve-burner stove. Gas?"

"Of course."

His approval showed on his face, warming her. "A fair number of industrial ovens. Four sinks. Good placement of utensils along the walls. Warmers?"

Alyssa pointed to shelved space under the counters and another at the pass, where plates would be assembled.

"Good. You've got plenty of refrigeration space." He glanced around another corner and opened the door. "Great freezer. Ample storage."

"You can never have too much." She smiled.

"Hmm." He looked as if he was fighting the urge to smile back. "What sort of flooring is this?" He stomped a boot on the surface.

"Cork. Never slippery, easy to sweep or replace, and provides natural cushion for everyone's feet."

He finally turned to stare at her, the fact that he was impressed warming his features. "You planned all this by yourself?"

"Mostly. A bit of help from my contractor. Sexy Sirens has a few customers in the restaurant business, and I asked their advice. The rest . . . I did my homework. I wanted everything to be right."

Something on his face changed, closed. His body tensed as his dark gaze skittered away. "You succeeded."

Damn! What had caused the warmth on his face to chill? The mention of Sexy Sirens? Deke had told her once that she wasn't Luc's type because he was looking for a *lady*. Did his avoidance mean he saw her as one small step up from a whore?

She raised her chin. Alyssa knew men. Even if Luc was loath to admit that she was his type, she knew she made his dick twitch. It was a start.

Now he was all business again. "What time can you have the staff here tomorrow?"

"Noon work for you?"

"Perfect." He turned away.

"You've already approved the menus. Anything else you need to see tonight?" She gripped the keys in her hand, wondering how to recover the mood they'd shared just minutes ago.

Patience, she warned herself. *Stick to the plan.* The night was still young.

* * *

LUC followed Alyssa to the restaurant's empty parking lot. The ample lighting would make patrons feel secure. However, the illumination pissed him off because he could see every sway of her enticing hips as she sashayed to her car. It made him hard. Again.

He'd driven his SUV from the strip club, mostly so he didn't have to shut himself in a confined space with her, even for three blocks. He didn't think he could be responsible for his actions for even that long. In Bonheur's kitchen, the thought of laying her across one of those gleaming stainless steel counters and fucking her senseless gripped him by the throat. He should thank her for bringing up Sexy Sirens and the favors she'd likely had to give her loyal customers to obtain their advice. The thought made him grit his teeth and his dinner churn. His temper soar.

Alyssa was a stripper, for fuck's sake. Not the sort of woman who went without sex for two years. He'd been an idiot to believe that when she'd whispered the trembling lie as he'd tumbled her into bed three months ago. She was in the business of leading men around by their dicks. And she was good at it. He couldn't be angry with her for being herself; she'd never pretended to be anything different. But he could—and should—be furious with himself for caring.

Despite the lot being completely empty, he'd parked three spots from her. As he pressed his key fob to unlock the driver's door, he watched her do the same with her black sports car. Luc fisted his hands. She'd go home now, lose that little black skirt, white tank, red bra, and fuck-me shoes. Even though she played no part in the future he craved, he itched to follow her home . . . help her out of every garment, sink down into that perfect, tight body.

He swallowed. *Keep your dick in your pants. Cook, shut up, and get the hell out of Lafayette. Seven days. Think you can find some self-control?*

A feminine shriek zipped across the lot, shattering his thoughts. Alyssa.

Luc's heart stuttered, and he nearly leapt over his car as he rushed across the asphalt. She backed away—right into his chest. He steadied her, palms cupping her bare shoulders.

"What is it?" he demanded.

Alyssa drew in a shuddering breath. "Bastards!"

Before he could ask her who or what she meant, she reached into the interior and yanked on something. A moment later, she produced a long, serrated knife with a piece of paper attached. Under the streetlamps, it gleamed the word WHORE in bright red lipstick.

Shock crested, then quickly morphed into molten fury. It was ironic; he'd been thinking something similar only moments ago. But he would never have said it aloud, much less stabbed it to the front seat of her convertible.

"Who would do this to you?" His voice vibrated with rage.

She tossed the knife into her front seat and cast him a wary stare over her shoulder. "Who knows?"

Luc turned her to face him and clenched his jaw. "Who. Did. This. To. You?"

His tone took her aback. "Look, it's not new. Shit happens all the time."

All the time? That only infuriated him more. Luc drew her closer as a thunderous frown stole across his face. She wasn't afraid, and he was scared as hell for her. "What have the police said in the past?"

"Police?" She shook her head. "This is just . . . a prank or a pissed-off customer who thought I didn't pay enough attention to him, most likely."

And whoever did this could also be dead serious. That blade was no laughing matter. "What if someone really sick wants to hurt you? How long has it been going on?"

"Like I said, it happens. It's been a while but—"

"Get in my car." He was done allowing her to stand like a convenient target in a shadowy parking lot. He didn't provide personal security detail like his cousin Deke, but he'd spent enough time with the man and his business partner, Jack Cole, to know that remaining out in the open could be deadly.

"What?" She looked incredulous. "I'm not leaving my car here."

"I'm driving you home. You're calling the police and reporting the crime so they can investigate."

Alyssa hesitated, then softened. "Luc. Your concern is really sweet, but—"

"Get in the fucking car."

She blanched, and he cursed under his breath. He needed to get control of his temper. But the soaring sexual frustration, coupled with his alarm, had him on edge. Who thought they had the right to malign and scare her? Fists curled, Luc craved a chance to pound the asshole.

Alyssa sighed, and Luc readied his next argument, but she strolled toward his SUV. "Fine."

He opened the door for her and watched her slide inside, the strands of her platinum hair settling over her shoulders. She looked somewhere between placid and reserved, despite the fact that she'd just been threatened. Was she out of her mind?

Shaking his head, he dashed around to the driver's seat. When he slid inside, she was already on the phone.

"Sorry it's late, Remy. I thought maybe I should call y'all. Someone messed with my car . . ."

Quickly and unemotionally, she relayed their location and the event. Luc heard murmurs of the other man's conversation, his tone more good-ol'-boy than concerned, and he frowned. Didn't anyone take this seriously?

He grabbed the phone from her and spit out an introduction. "Dust for prints. She touched the weapon, but you may find other sets on the handle. Whoever did this *broke* into her car."

"Doubt it was much more than a prank. Boys down here get a little rowdy from time to time—"

"And stab the word 'whore' into her seat? That's funny how?"

Remy cleared his throat. "It's not. But I don't think no one meant no harm."

Luc gritted his teeth together. "Do you usually solve all your cases before you visit the crime scene?"

Finally, Remy got serious. "I'll investigate."

"Thoroughly."

Alyssa grabbed the phone. "Thanks, honey. I appreciate it."

When he ended the call, Luc could barely unclench his jaw as he sped away from the parking lot. "Honey? The man didn't even want to investigate, and you call him 'honey'?"

She shrugged. "It's a Louisiana thing. You'll catch more flies with honey than vinegar."

"Yeah?" he challenged. "Or is it a 'he's-my-customer' thing. Did he watch you strip tonight?"

She swallowed. "I asked all the local enforcement to come, including the sheriff. Keeps down the possibility of rowdies getting out of control and trashing the club."

Luc gripped the wheel tighter as he peeled out of the parking lot. "So that's a yes."

Fighting the urge to hit something in an unusual show of temper, he took a deep breath. The night he'd spent with her, it had been easy to pretend she had no other lover. They'd been alone, her house quiet. No phone ringing, no customers nearby, no psychos leaving menacing "gifts" in her car. Just the two of them, and hours upon hours of pleasure. God, he'd been so damn gullible.

She nodded. "Why does it matter if Remy and the boys were there?"

The short answer was that it shouldn't.

"If you should be worried about anything," she went on, "it's your hotel room. At nearly four in the morning, Homer has likely given your room away to one of those tourists come around for the arts festival that starts tomorrow."

He frowned. After everything that had happened tonight, she was worried about him? "I guaranteed that room with a credit card."

A Mona Lisa smile played at the corner of her mouth. That quickly, she made his dick hard again. Damn, how did the woman do it?

"Doesn't mean a damn thing to him. I'm sure when you didn't show up after the club closed, he figured your room was fair game. But if you don't believe me, call him." She punched a few buttons on the phone and handed it to him.

"You have the motel owner on speed dial?" He could think of only one reason why, and it horrified him. Did she turn tricks?

Hell, he was going to throw up.

"Out-of-town customers often need to sleep off their alcohol. Homer usually helps me out."

Luc liked her explanation much better. But still, he wondered. Didn't a lot of strippers earn extra cash on the side?

As the phone rang in his ear, Luc turned to Alyssa. Her face was golden under the streetlights shining through the windows as he raced down the quaint redbrick street, toward a neighborhood of older, still elegant homes. Odd that he remembered exactly how to find her house, despite the fact he'd been here just once. The image of the little craftsman with the Zen interior was burned into his brain.

Homer answered a moment later, muttering his words. Clearly, he'd been asleep and sounded none too happy about being awakened.

"This is Luc Traverson calling to advise that I'll arrive in a few minutes to check in. You still have my room?"

The man on the other end cleared his throat. "Well, when you didn't show, I thought . . ."

Luc waited, his temper rising again, for the motel's owner to finish that thought. "Thought what? You'd give my room away?"

"I waited until two thirty. You said you'd be here before midnight. Some road-weary folks came in with little ones and—"

"Do you have another room?" He closed his eyes and pressed the phone to his ear.

"Booked up. First time in a while, but this festival always brings 'em in. Some great zydeco bands playin' this year."

Luc resisted the urge to count to ten. "And tomorrow night?"

"Don't have a free room until Tuesday. Got a couple of those lousy chain hotels a few miles down the road . . ." Homer said with obvious distaste. "Bet they're booked up, too. 'Sides, I wouldn't let my dog sleep there. They don't clean nothin'."

His head was going to explode. Luc was accustomed to traveling to cosmopolitan cities. He stayed at Hotel de Crillon when he traveled to Paris, the Dorchester in London, the Peninsula in Tokyo, the Beverly Wilshire in Los Angeles. The fact he'd been stiffed on a room at Homer's Cajun Haven at four in the morning crawled on his last nerve.

He hit the end button on the conversation. Instead of giving in to his urge to throw the phone, he stiffly handed it back to Alyssa.

"You were right."

"Thought I'd save you the drive out there, since I know Homer too well."

And since he was, no doubt, another man who had seen Alyssa naked, Homer knew her awfully well, too.

Luc sighed. He had to stop caring who'd seen her bare. He'd want to rip the heads off most of the male population of this town for the next week if he didn't get himself under control. He'd fucked her for one night. What she'd done before—or after—was none of his affair.

So why did it bug the hell out of him? And where was he going to sleep tonight?

"I have an extra room at my place," Alyssa offered quietly. "It's clean and quiet and—"

"I couldn't impose." Because if he did, he'd get inside her again.

Last time he'd spent the night in her body, he'd been insatiable. For six hours. Nothing had been too searing, too depraved, too intimate. She'd wrenched the sort of desire from him that burned him, shamed and elated him at once. He'd taken everything she offered, then more—then come back again. He'd fucked her in every way a man could, repeatedly. Bareback. Something he hadn't done in more than a decade, except with Kimber.

And the memories of that incredible night with Alyssa were fraying his self-control.

"No imposition. I have the room; you need a bed."

She laid a soft hand over his as it gripped the gearshift. Her touch seized him clear down to his balls, igniting his blood.

"Besides," she murmured. "Maybe . . . you're right. If what happened tonight isn't a prank, then I'd feel better not to be alone. Do you mind?"

Yes. Very much. But he'd be every kind of a bastard if he said no.

He sent her a tight smile. "It will be my pleasure."

* * *

HE was lying through his teeth. Then again, so was she. She'd paid Homer very handsomely to give Luc's room away and she doubted that, despite the prank, anyone would try to hurt her tonight.

As Luc's SUV whipped down Lafayette's dark streets, exhaustion should have been weighing on her. Instead, she was filled with anticipation. She was finally going to be alone with the man she most wanted, in her house, where he'd made mad love to her before. Too bad Luc wasn't happy about it.

He was a puzzle. The lust in his eyes was unmistakable. Hell, every time he looked her way he damn near burned her. But his contempt wasn't hard to piece together. So his anger that someone else thought she was a whore intrigued her.

"If it's not a prank, who would stab such a note to the seat of your car?"

Sadly, the list was long. "Luc, let's wait and see what Remy comes back with."

"No." He flashed her an impatient stare. "If whoever did this drops by while you're sleeping, I'd like to have some idea who I'll be dealing with."

"Don't worry too much. If I thought I was in serious jeopardy, I'd call Tyler. Or Jack Cole. He and your cousin are the best, and he's an old friend. Because of him, the house has a top-of-the-line security system."

Luc ground his jaw. His knuckles were white on the steering wheel. "I said I'd keep you safe tonight and I will. Answer the question."

He wasn't letting this go, and that gave Alyssa hope. Maybe he cared, at least a bit. Even if it was against his good sense and his will.

"First, just about any jealous wife or girlfriend who doesn't like the amount of time her man spends in my club. That's common."

"Knives aren't usually a woman's style."

No. She'd had her tires deflated, her house egged, more ugly notes than she could count. Scorned women usually annoyed and rarely disturbed.

"What about past lovers?" He pinned her with a burning stare. "Current ones?"

She closed her eyes. Naturally, he'd assume there were many of both. She'd been down this road; it shouldn't hurt. But damn, it did. "The night you spent with me, I told you there hadn't been anyone in two years. There's been no one since you."

Luc shook his head, looking as though a hundred different thoughts blazed through it. "Alyssa, you could be in danger. I need you to be completely honest."

Jerking around in her seat, she faced him, trying to keep a lid on her temper. "I have been honest. Just because you don't believe me doesn't make me a liar."

"C'mon," he growled. "Not a customer who wanted just a bit more after seeing your gorgeous breasts naked? Not a contractor who did you a favor and wanted something in return?"

Anger seized her, gripping her chest in a steely fist. "I don't roll that way."

He hesitated. "So you didn't agree to fuck me three months ago so you'd have a guest chef this week?"

No, I was willing to say anything because I wanted you so badly . . . and hoped you'd want me back. And not for anything would she wear her heart on her sleeve now. He'd left her before dawn and pawned her off with flowers. Now he'd all but intimated she was a whore.

But if there was one thing she knew, it was men. He felt *something* for her. Her mission was to make it more.

"You were different."

"Of course." He snorted as he stopped at a red light.

Alyssa had had enough of his shit. She grabbed his chin and turned him to face her. "Maybe I was simply stupid enough to believe all your Southern gentleman charm and wanted to know what it was like to have sex with someone who didn't see me as a prostitute. Silly me. You were definitely more hard-core than anyone I've had, way more than your white-bread exterior suggests. You roll out that sort of red carpet for every woman?"

He tore away from her grip and clutched the steering wheel even tighter. He exhaled harshly, clearly trying to restrain his temper. So his behavior that night was a sore spot? Maybe he hadn't wanted to want her and was mortified that he had. And still did.

"I asked you about lovers. I'll take you at your word that you hadn't had one in two years prior to me."

"But you don't believe me."

"What about current lovers? Tyler?"

None of his fucking business. As far as she was concerned, this conversation was in the toilet. Logic told her to retire her stupid happily-ever-fantasies about Luc. He hadn't made love to her with such fervor because he felt the pull between them. He'd done it because she'd been his first real walk on the wild side and being bad flipped his switch. They probably should just have sex and not bother with emotions.

But her heart didn't want to give up.

"Tyler would never try to kill me. Whoever did this tonight isn't someone who's been in my bed. It's someone who's pissed at me."

He sent her a considering shrug, then took off as the light turned green. "Like who?"

"The kid who barged through the crowd tonight to kiss me. Peter. I don't even know his last name. He started coming around about six months ago. Real regular. Daddy is rich, and he drops a lot of money at the club. Seems to think that entitles him to special perks."

"You've advised him otherwise?" Even Luc's voice was dangerously tense.

"Absolutely. Tyler has made it perfectly clear as well. We've kicked him out, let him know his advances aren't welcome. But nothing fazes this kid."

Luc gripped the steering wheel even tighter. "He ever call you a whore?"

Alyssa shook her head. "He's usually real graphic about what he wants—nasty, dirty shit—but has never resorted to name calling. That's Councilman Primpton's speed."

"A city councilman? An elected official calling you a whore?"

How naïve was Luc? "Of course. His voting base is very conservative, so if he shut Sexy Sirens down, he'd be their hero. Even some middle-of-the-road folks would be thrilled to see me go. That's been Primpton's mission since he got elected eighteen months ago. The attempts started small, but with his reelection coming up, he's been applying more pressure."

"How?"

"Protesting in front of the club, scathing editorials in the local paper about the den of sin in the city's backyard and the 'trash' who runs it. Recently, he collaborated with a reporter to wear a wire and solicit me for sex." She snorted. "I can shove a lot of four-letter words into 'no.' "

Finally, they pulled up in front of her house. She hopped out and motioned for him to wait in the car. Juggling her keys, she unlocked the front door, unset the alarm, then ran around to the garage door and hit the button to open it. Luc drove in, then climbed out of the car, duffel bag in hand. He looked tense and nervous.

"I thought it would be better if you parked in the garage. Don't want anyone vandalizing your SUV or wagging their tongues. Come in."

He nodded, his stare glued to her. Alyssa closed the garage door behind them. She'd give anything to know what Luc was thinking. His tense demeanor and unflagging erection told her it was probably ways to avoid having the sex with her he knew he shouldn't want but desperately did. And after tonight's interrogation, she was in the mood to make him suffer.

Chapter Three

LUC shut the bedroom door behind him, breathing hard. It wasn't the climb up Alyssa's stairs that caused his respiratory distress; it was watching her in front of him. The short black skirt that hugged her ass. Those sexy red garters he had a flash of now and then. The hint of her bare cheeks visible with every step.

Damn it, he wanted to fuck her so badly he could hardly see straight. But messing with Alyssa was like dabbling in recreational drugs—stupid and potentially addicting.

Last week, he'd had his third date with Emily, a first-grade teacher at the local elementary school in Tyler, Texas. It had gone well. Sweet, hazel-eyed, and dimpled, she liked country music, couldn't stand profanity, and had great relationships with her family and pastor. A perfect wife. A perfect stay-at-home mother, just like his own. That's what he wanted. He needed to stay focused on her— and stay away from Alyssa this week.

Then never see the sexy stripper again.

Once inside Alyssa's guest room, he drew his cell from his pocket and thumbed his way down his contact list. Emily's name was there. He desperately needed the fortification of hearing her sweet, high-pitched voice, but it would be rude to wake her up at four thirty in the morning. She'd ask questions he couldn't answer. Instead of turning the conversation toward her school kids or her activities with the church, Luc feared what he'd say. Alyssa had scraped him so raw, he doubted he could exercise the verbal control necessary to deflect Emily's questions. The demands of his dark side juiced his bloodstream. Everything inside him screamed for a hard, pounding fuck.

So he was on his own.

Shower. He needed one desperately. Hot water dousing his skin, spray pelting his body, deep breaths . . . coming down off the lust high so he could sleep.

And not think about the sexy vixen lying in her bed less than fifty feet from him.

Grabbing his pajama pants from his bag, he made his way down the hall, toward the darkened bathroom. Soft light spilled down the hallway from her bedroom. *Ignore it,* he told himself. But when he turned for the bathroom and groped for the switch, he couldn't resist a peek over his shoulder at Alyssa's slightly ajar bedroom door.

And her very visible, delectable leg bathed in golden light.

Luc sucked in a breath as a million images of her in that bed bombarded him. Her arms and legs wide-open to him, her husky taunts and whispered encouragements drowning out logic. God, her mouth on his cock had been the most amazing experience . . . until he'd worked his way into her tight pussy and damn near lost his mind. Then she'd topped that by allowing him into that delectable ass, and he'd sunk into her with barely leashed abandon, amazed by the fit and feel of her. And the fact she opened herself completely to whatever he wanted for six undivided hours. No one had ever affected him that much before. Or since.

So being in the house with her now was as dangerous as bathing in gasoline before dancing around a bonfire.

Suddenly, she twisted on the bed. The perfect view he'd had changed as she moved her leg to the side, allowing him an unimpeded view of her taut calf and inner thigh.

A few inches to her left and, if she'd ditched her panties, he'd see every spectacular bit of her wet flesh. Even now, his mouth watered as he remembered the addicting taste that had kept him coming back to her again and again.

Alyssa moaned. Then thrashed again.

Holy shit, is she—?

"Yes!" she cried out, then gasped to catch her breath.

Masturbating. Hell.

Go in the bathroom. Shut the door. Stay the fuck away. The litany of good advice ran through his head, and he sucked in a harsh breath, trying to force himself to hear it over the pounding of his heart and the blood rushing to his cock.

"Oh, yes!"

Her hoarse, broken whisper fried his blood in his veins. He had to see her. Had to. Yes, she was bad for him, and he didn't want to be one of the many in her bed. But the woman was temptation personified. He'd never seen another woman more equipped to lead a man into sin.

Just one step . . .

Luc left his pajama pants on the bathroom counter and moved closer to Alyssa's bedroom, wincing when his jeans chafed his erection. But one step was enough to bring only her hip into view. Lovely, but he wanted to see her self-pleasure. How she was doing it, how seriously she pursued it, how her body bowed when ecstasy hit.

Damn, he felt like a sick bastard, but no way could he stop.

Another step closer, then a third, until he was hovering just behind the crack in her door.

Then he got an eyeful that lit him on fire. Alyssa wearing nothing but her red garters, sheer hose, and fuck-me shoes. She gripped
her breast in one hand and, with the other, dove into her very wet
folds.

Luc staggered back, gripping the wall beside him for support.
And he stared. Flames engulfed his balls, licked his cock. *Fuck, fuck,
fuck* . . .

Alyssa's fingers fluttered around her clit. Moisture gushed. Her
thighs tightened, her back arching. He panted, glued to the sight.
Seared.

She thrashed again, spreading her legs wider. Then she plunged
her fingers inside her drenched opening and bucked, whimpering.

Luc clutched the doorknob tighter. God, how badly he wanted
to go in there and give her relief, put his mouth right over her aching
clit until she came across his tongue, then plunge deep inside her
pussy with unrelenting strokes. Once she'd come a half dozen times
and taken the edge off his hunger, then he'd turn her over and use all
her delicious lubrication to slide into her backside and linger there,
thrusting slow, hard, deep.

Her muttering suddenly broke into his thoughts. She whispered,
and he couldn't make out her words. He wanted to—desperately.
Needed to know. What was she thinking while she fucked herself?
Whom did she think of?

Turning off the voice in his head that told him he was stupid to
court danger, he shoved the door open another few inches and eased
inside the shadowed corner. Her little bedside lamp spilled light
across her body, illuminating golden skin, the pale blond strands of
her shining hair—and her nearly bare pussy.

Again, she muttered something, and he still couldn't hear. The
suspense was killing him. The anxiety. Would Tyler's name fall from
her lips? Someone else's?

"Fuck me . . ." she cried softly.

Damn, he wanted to, so, so badly. He scrubbed a hand down his face, then fastened his gaze on Alyssa again. He couldn't stay away. Simply impossible. She was his weakness. His drug of choice.

Luc swallowed against the lust. He had to be strong. Once he married Emily—or someone like her—he couldn't think about Alyssa, only about the wife who would make his every dream come true. He had to keep his dick out of the equation.

Step back. Shower; sleep; forget Alyssa.

Gritting his teeth for strength, Luc lifted a foot and set it behind him. But still he couldn't leave. She had increased the tempo of her fingers over her clit. Now her hips thrashed. Her skin was flushed, and the air smelled like aroused female. Perspiration broke out between her breasts. She was the most beautiful, sexual creature he'd ever seen. And ever would. How was he supposed to walk away?

"Fuck me. Yes. Yes!" She moaned long and loud as she came. *"Luc!"*

She gasped *his* name? Shock burned him. Christ, he was about to come in his jeans.

Alyssa flopped back on the bed, eyes closed, breathing heavily. Luc stood still, transfixed, dick aching, heart racing.

Then she lifted her head and looked right at him. Heat arced between them for a heartbeat, two. Suddenly, an audacious smile shaped her lush mouth . . . just before she raised her hips to him in offering. "Please . . ."

Fire speared him. Leave or fuck her now—his only two options. Fucking her would be sublimely easy. And would do absolutely nothing to help him achieve the future he yearned for.

With a curse, he whirled out of her bedroom and raced into the bathroom, locking the door behind him. He leaned against it, every breath a harsh saw out of his chest. But the image of her self-pleasuring was burned into his brain, his name on her lips reverberating in his head.

How could he want someone so much who was so bad for him?

Shaking his head, he started the shower. One way or another, he needed relief now. If he was going to be smart and resist Alyssa, it was going to have to be by his own hand. Otherwise, he would never sleep. And be far too tempted to stalk into her bedroom and have her every way known to man.

Quickly, he dropped his clothes and stepped under the slowly warming spray without checking the water temperature first. He hissed at the cold, but his body was too overheated to care.

He rolled his shoulders under the spray, then grabbed his cock, trying to picture Emily—light brown hair, hazel eyes, apple-pie appeal. He knew she was kind and optimistic and eager for a family. But what would she look like without clothes? What kind of lover would she be?

Luc couldn't picture her sexually at all.

But sex wasn't everything. He enjoyed her sense of humor and friendship, her sweetness and . . . The idea of sex with her bored him.

A vision of Alyssa burst across his brain. His cock jumped in his hand, and he stroked it eagerly, hungrily.

Why her? Of course she was sexy. A man would have to be blind not to notice her beauty, the easy sway of her hips, those blue eyes that could tempt a man to sin. But today had shown him sides of Alyssa he hadn't known.

She was smart and determined. Bonheur proved that. She'd done a great job building the restaurant, despite not knowing a lot about the business. And she was brave—maybe too much so for her own good. That knife a prank? He didn't think so. But she'd taken it in stride. No drama, no tears, no hysteria. She was one cool customer. And she understood the people around her. Remy, Homer, Tyler, even the girls at her club. She seemed to know exactly what to say for maximum results.

All that only made him desire her more. Writing her off had been easier when he'd assumed she was just a good lay. Now . . . she revved him up on a whole new level. *Damn it.*

He stroked faster, tingles leaping up his cock. He swiped a thumb across the head and hissed in pleasure. His thighs tightened, and he clenched his jaw, picturing the way Alyssa had danced at rehearsal this afternoon, as if dancing for him alone. He envisioned her masturbating, fingering her way to orgasm, then lifting to him in invitation.

In his head, he again heard her beg him to fuck her. Pleasure soared. His hand moved faster on his turgid flesh, his rhythm and hold almost brutal. Need clawed its way from his balls, up his dick. Orgasm wasn't far behind . . . and thoughts of Emily were long gone.

In that moment, pressure built and heated. It burst, Alyssa at the center of the storm. Clamping his lips shut, he groaned as orgasm slammed him, clenching his balls, cramping his stomach. Semen spurted into the porcelain tub, then washed with the water down the drain.

Luc leaned against the tile, more relaxed, but vaguely unsatisfied. Yes, he'd gotten off, but need still keyed him up. His hand was a lousy substitute for Alyssa.

He dropped his grip from his cock and turned off the shower. Damn, he felt worse now. Not high on lust anymore, but confused. Depressed. What the hell was the matter with him?

You want something you can't have, the voice in his head taunted him. He'd tell it to shut up . . . but it was right.

Grabbing the shower curtain with an impatient fist, Luc thrust it back. To his shock, Alyssa stood three feet away, hip leaned against the vanity, a towel in her hand. She looked furious—and hurt.

"So, was that good for you?"

* * *

ALYSSA was still furious six hours later as she pounded on the punching bag hanging from the ceiling in her spare bedroom. With a grunt, she kicked it once, twice, then followed with a mean right hook.

What was Luc thinking? She'd offered herself to him—something she never did for any man—and he'd self-pleasured in the shower. Of

course he thought she offered herself to anyone with a Y chromo-
some and didn't understand that she'd invited him alone because he
was special, because she thought . . . maybe there was something
more between them than fabulous sex.

Stupid.

Another kick, another punch. Sweat rolled down her body. It
wasn't relieving her tension.

Before she'd guilted Luc into staying, he'd mentioned that he was
dating someone else. The thought of him with another woman made
her stomach tighten. Insecurity blindsided her. Was Luc sleeping
with this woman? Did he want his new girlfriend more than he
wanted her? Was he, God forbid, in *love* with her?

She had to know. Throwing herself at a man whose heart be-
longed to someone else was both pointless and embarrassing. For a
while, she'd been sure Kimber was it for him, but then Deke had
married her. Then Alyssa had heard through the grapevine that Luc's
involvement with the couple was over, and she'd had fresh hope.
Now . . . she didn't know what to think.

Lying on the table against the window, her cell phone rang
shrilly. With one last punch of the bag, she stepped across the room,
tore off a glove, then grabbed it. The display told her it was Tyler.

"Hey, I was just thinking about you."

"Yeah?" He sounded really happy about that.

"Punching the hell out of my bag and pretending it's your head,"
she teased.

"Funny," he intoned. "Look, I know it's early, but you should
come to the club."

Alyssa froze. "What happened?"

Tyler hesitated—something he never did. That man was as
straight up as they came. She trusted him with her life, so when he
hedged, it couldn't be good.

"Just come to the club," he said finally.

Something was absolutely wrong. "Shit. Give me an hour?"

"The sooner, the better."

She hung up, cursing as she made her way out of her exercise room and into the hall. She ran smack into Luc.

"Sorry." She backed away from him. It was either that or jump on him. She hadn't had the pleasure of "the morning after" last time, and Alyssa took one look at him, hair softly rumpled, eyes slumberous, and realized she'd missed something spectacular.

Her blood heated all over again.

"Good morning."

The words were polite . . . but lacked the passion she wanted to hear when he said those words, his head on the pillow beside her, just before he kissed her thoroughly and they welcomed the day together with pleasure.

Wasn't happening. Grimly, she remembered last night. Rather than depress herself again, she shook the thought away.

"Yeah. I have to run, grab a shower." She held up her phone. "Tyler called. I told him I'd be there in an hour. If you need more time to get ready, I'll have him pick me up."

"I'll take you."

"It's no problem for him to—"

"I said, I'll take you," he snapped, his stare roaming her flushed face and sweat-damp T-shirt.

Was he still pissed about last night or was this about Tyler?

"Fine. I'll meet you in the kitchen in thirty."

She spun away, wanting the sanctuary of her bedroom, the privacy of a shut door so she didn't have to shut away the pain of his rejection.

Luc grabbed her arm and held her back. "About last night . . . I'm sorry. I didn't mean to spy on you. The open door was—"

"Not an invitation," she lied. The truth would just get his back up. "Just like the guest bathroom door not locking properly, my bedroom door doesn't shut all the way. It's an old house. But I appreciate the apology. I'm sorry, too, for barging in during your shower. I only meant to make sure you had a towel and . . ."

He grimaced. "Look, I'm not going to lie. We share amazing chemistry. You turn me on more than anyone ever has."

Luc didn't look at all happy about that fact.

"But you're not into *me*, just my body. Got it." And it hurt like hell.

His grip on her arm tightened. "That's not it. Yesterday, I discovered great qualities I didn't know you possessed." He sighed, raked a hand through his long hair. "It's that . . . what I want isn't what I need. So if I'm cranky and irritable this week, it's because you have me tied up in a thousand sexual knots, and I'm trying to do the right thing."

The right thing being not having sex with her.

Did Luc think it was impossible to have an emotional attachment to someone who owned a club where women took off their clothes? Whatever. She still wanted him. Wanted him to want her. Burn for her. Because everything inside her yearned for Luc, his sultry smile, his talent, the way he'd made her feel more special in one night than any man ever had. She wasn't willing to give up.

"Does this have something to do with the woman you're seeing?"

"Yes."

Damn, how could one word hurt so much?

"If you picked her, I'm sure she's a great girl." She tugged her arm free. "I'd better get ready."

As she darted down the hall, Luc gave chase and pushed her against the shadowed wall. "She is. And that's not a reflection on you. You're just different."

In other words, she's not a stripper.

"Sure. Fine. See you downstairs in thirty minutes." She eased out from between the wall and his hard body, all but running to her bedroom, and slammed the door.

Once inside the bathroom, she shut that door—locked it—then leaned against it. And closed her eyes as tears spilled. She swiped them away with an angry fist.

Fucking hopeless. She sucked at relationships. No, strike that. She'd never really had one. From age fifteen on, her life had been a struggle to make ends meet, put food in her belly and a roof over her head. She'd learned how to read people over the years, but not in a romantic capacity. As far as she could tell, Luc was being honest with her. There was someone else he thought was better for him.

How the hell did she compete with that? Should she even try? Probably not, but something inside her kept screaming that she needed him.

Luc admitted to wanting her more than anyone. It was a start. Maybe they had more than great chemistry, and this was his body's way of saying so. It was possible this other woman was "better" for him because Luc *knew* her. With just one hot night between them, Alyssa realized he wasn't familiar with her as a person.

She needed to keep enticing him; that was a given. Using her advantage was critical. But she also needed to let him really know her. Not easy for her, letting down her walls. Trust in general was an expensive luxury—and a foolish one. But unless she wanted to lose Luc to this better-than-her bitch, Alyssa must figure out how to let him deep inside more than just her body.

* * *

THE silence in the SUV was choking. Alyssa kept biting her lower lip. Her sunglasses protected against the morning glare—and prevented Luc from reading her expression.

Whatever she was thinking shouldn't matter. But it did. Though she'd betrayed almost no emotion when he'd mentioned his relationship with Emily, he suspected that the words hurt. And he felt like shit. He wanted to say something . . . but why? He was leaving in six days and would probably never see Alyssa Devereaux again. It was better this way.

Except . . . she'd worn another short skirt—white with some curlicue pattern on it—and black garters. Her sheer black hose with a sexy seam down the back nearly made him swallow his tongue. The red shoes were pure fuck-me, as was the matching tank top that hugged her generous breasts and trim waist.

Right now he couldn't even remember what Emily looked like. And he was pretty sure that in the face of someone stabbing "whore" into her driver's seat, she would scream hysterically and cry.

Luc swore under his breath.

"With your job, you must have traveled all over the world," Alyssa offered.

As he cruised to a red light and stopped, he looked her way. She'd pondered a long time before asking him *that* question. Where was this going? "Yes."

"What's your favorite place?"

"You're seriously asking me about travel?" *Not our chat in the hallway?*

She bristled, eased back in her seat, looked away. "Just making conversation."

But why? She wasn't a talk-for-talk's-sake sort of woman.

"And you really want my thoughts on travel? Nothing else?"

"Never mind." Alyssa turned her head to look out the passenger window.

He winced. Maybe she'd extended an olive branch to show that she had no hard feelings. If so, he'd just squashed her offering without thought. He couldn't afford to be sexual with her—but he didn't have to be unkind.

"Barbados. I like warm weather. Their beaches are gorgeous. Swimming with the turtles is mind-blowing."

No reply.

"I went to culinary school in Paris. It's a great city. Winters are a bit too cold for me. But there's nothing like the street corner cafés and the culture."

She sent him a tight smile. "I'll take your word for it."

When she turned away again, he frowned. What did that mean? Travel conversation was suddenly boring . . . or that she hadn't been to Paris. The truth hit, and he sent her a lingering stare before traffic forced his attention again. How often did strippers travel overseas, especially ones who owned their own clubs? And now she had her savings tied up in Bonheur.

So why had she started this conversation? He didn't think it had anything to do with travel, really. Was she trying to get to know him?

After the way he had fucked her blind, left her, apologized with impersonal flowers, and distanced himself from her again just minutes ago, she could have been a raving bitch. Most women would have. Alyssa had simply asked a question.

Now he found himself intensely curious about the sexpot on his right.

"Tell me something about you," he demanded softly.

She shrugged, straight platinum hair sliding across her small shoulders. "You know the pertinent facts. I'm twenty-nine and opening a restaurant."

"You're a bit deeper than that. Did you grow up in Louisiana?"

Her gaze whipped to her lap suddenly. She bit her lip, looking pensive. "No. You grow up in Texas?"

He shook his head. "Clearwater Beach, Florida. You didn't say where you were from."

"I didn't," she agreed.

Luc wanted to pry more, but they'd arrived at the club. And he knew a closed subject when he heard one. Why the hell didn't she want to talk about her hometown?

As soon as he put the car in park, Alyssa jumped, race-walking for the club's back door. The late-morning sun glared on the chipped black surface, framing Tyler. The bouncer looked tense. He glared when he caught sight of Luc.

"What's going on?" she asked him as she approached and tried to brush past him.

Tyler grabbed her arms and pulled her against his body. Then he cupped her face in his hand, his mouth hovering a breath above hers.

Everything inside Luc railed at the sight. His mind screamed an order for Tyler to take his hands off Alyssa. Two facts hit him: First, she wasn't Luc's, so he had no say in who touched her. Second, she wasn't fighting Tyler in the least.

He whispered something Luc couldn't hear. In return, she nodded anxiously. Tyler hesitated, kissed her forehead, then took hold of her hand and reached for the door.

"What's going on?" he asked the bouncer.

Tyler glared at him over his shoulder. "I'm responsible for her safety, and I take it very seriously. Go back to your fryalator."

If he'd had any less control over his temper, Luc would have charged the bastard, despite the fact Tyler outweighed him by thirty pounds of muscle. Luc was sure he would have gotten in at least a few good swipes. But why give the asshole what he wanted?

"You give up your stand-up routine because you sucked?"

Alyssa jumped in between them, anger tightening her face. "Could you two stop it? Luc, someone broke into the club between last night's close and Tyler's arrival at ten this morning."

Luc went dead cold inside. Pure coincidence that someone had stabbed her seat with a knife, then her club had been broken into mere hours—or minutes—later? He'd spent enough time with Jack and Cousin Deke. Coincidences made them uncomfortable, and Luc agreed.

"They barged in through an upstairs window. Remy and the boys came over, but so far it doesn't look like anything was taken.

Tyler is trying to figure out how someone bypassed the security system. I'll have to call Jack and have him figure it out."

"Deke told me that Jack and Morgan are visiting her mother in California," Luc supplied.

Tyler clenched his jaw. "Shit."

"I'll call Deke and see when he can do it," Luc offered.

Her wary blue eyes flitted his way. "Thanks."

Before he could respond, Tyler dragged her inside. Eerie quiet reigned. No one else was inside. Luc didn't like the interior's vibe.

"Maybe someone who came for the anniversary celebration last night hid upstairs and let a buddy in after hours?" Alyssa suggested.

Tyler shook his head. "We always do a thorough sweep before locking up. And even if someone managed to elude us, opening a window from the inside would trip the alarm."

"Did you find anything out of place?" Luc asked. "Any . . . messages?"

"Luc, I doubt they're connected."

"But you don't know that they aren't."

* * *

JUST before eleven thirty, Alyssa followed Luc back outside to his SUV and they headed to Bonheur. The cloudy, muggy October day made the interior shadowy and stuffy. She hit the lights and started the overhead fans. Then she turned to Luc expectantly.

"The contractor is coming at two to fix the wall. Says he'll be done by sixish. What next?" She made her way to the kitchen, flipping on those lights. "You want to talk about opening day's specials? Tomorrow is coming fast."

Luc followed. "Why would someone break into the club?"

She sighed. "I don't know. Sometimes drunk frat boys get out of hand. I can't afford to put too much energy into thinking about it now. That's Tyler's job. Yours is to make opening day successful. What else do I need to do?"

"Take this threat seriously." He grabbed her by the shoulders and spun her around.

Alyssa raised a brow at him. He looked agitated, his breath coming fast. She blinked slowly, getting a long look at his erection on the visual journey down. Definitely aroused. She repressed a smile.

"I'd like to, but I can't afford to ignore the pending opening to focus on a few odd events. How did you phrase it earlier? What I want isn't what I need." She smiled at him, crossing her arms under her breasts and pushing her cleavage above her tank's neckline.

Predictably, his gaze followed. He swallowed hard.

"Don't ignore the danger because you're angry with me."

Alyssa wondered why she mattered to him at all. *Interesting question . . .*

"I'm not. Just stating facts."

With that, she pulled away from his grip and spun around. She had a suspicion that Luc was used to being in control and getting the last word in. He wouldn't like it if she turned her back on him now—especially if the view included her skirt clinging very low on her hips and exposing the rose tattoo on her lower back.

With a sway of her hips, she prowled toward the nearest stainless steel counter, stroked its sleek surface . . . and waited. She barely heard him cover the handful of steps separating them before he fisted her hair in his hand and forced her gaze up to his.

"Stop pissing me off," he growled.

"Stop telling me how to react."

Luc's mouth tightened, as did his grip on her hair. Alyssa merely sent him a challenging stare and a matching smile.

Something about this argument was getting to him, revving his blood. The gentlemanly Southern chef had a nasty side, and she was making him feel it.

"Damn you!" His mouth crashed over hers.

He shoved her against the counter as he pushed past her lips, into the hot cavern of her mouth, and inhaled her all at once. His tongue was everywhere, possessing, tasting—branding. In an instant, her body burned, blood tingling. She clutched at his starched white shirt, grabbing the collar to pull him closer.

Luc was everything she remembered—full of finesse, power, steel covered in silk, insistent—and more. Never had a man's kiss alone made her wet and aching, made her long to be closer to him in every way.

She ran her hands down his body, feeling every bulge of his shoulders, every ripple of his chest. Her palm flitted down his sixpack—and kept descending. Oh, so slowly, she dragged her hand over his erection. He hissed in a shocked breath, breaking the kiss, and hardened beneath her touch.

Smiling, she reached for his fly.

He groaned. "Alyssa, we—"

She palmed him again, squeezing his cock, then flicked the button of his pants open. His zipper went down, a bare rasp in the otherwise quiet. Then she ran her thumb over the sensitive crest.

"Dear God." He sucked in a breath. "We shouldn't . . ."

She said nothing, but simply sank to her knees.

Chapter Four

BEFORE Luc could stop Alyssa, she'd pushed his pants and briefs to his hips and taken his cock in her hand.

To be fair, he didn't try very hard to stop her.

The moment her palm wrapped around his erection, he sizzled, jolted as if he'd been pumped full of a thousand volts. God, everything about her was potent, overwhelming. He was drowning—the feel of her tight grip, the silkiness of her golden hair in his hands, the gut-punching sight of her licking her lips.

"Alyssa," he hissed.

Shit. He had to stop this. But how, when he wanted her so badly?

He'd eschewed sex for weeks. After his night with Alyssa, he'd pinned all his hopes for a child on Kimber and Deke, single-mindedly bedding the girl every bit as often as his cousin. But he'd be lying if he said Alyssa hadn't lingered in his thoughts. Being with Kimber had been absorbing. He realized later it had been the situation . . . not the woman. After that, he'd pushed aside his sex drive in favor of a future, a wife who would be the sort of devoted mom his own was.

Now the woman he'd ached for since that wild, dark night was on her knees in front of him, and God help him, he didn't have the willpower to stop himself from urging her mouth closer to his throbbing cock.

"You want this?" she whispered.

"Yes!" he bellowed, struggling for control . . . and failing. "Yes."

She opened her mouth, started to ease forward. Then she stopped. "You're sure?"

Now she was taunting him. That teasing allure had been his undoing three months ago, turned what should have been a normal night of sex into an unforgettable marathon in which he'd been determined to . . . He almost didn't have words for his urge. Put some sort of stamp on her. Leave his mark. If she wasn't careful, she was going to get the same treatment in her very own kitchen.

"Suck me," he demanded, his voice low and harsh.

Alyssa sent him another of those playful smiles. "Yes, sir."

Her words set his blood on fire. God, she was going to destroy him. This wasn't smart, and he knew it. At the moment, he didn't fucking care. He had to get her mouth around him, had to feel her tongue lash him, see her submissive at his feet.

Why now? Why this woman?

She moved in, parted her lips. Luc widened his stance, bracing himself for the first electric lick, his whole system jacked up on lust and need to possess. Then Alyssa exhaled on the sensitive head of his dick, and he shivered. Sensation rioted, and he held his breath. Trembled.

Her tongue peeked out. It was the most fucking erotic thing he'd ever seen. *Closer, closer . . .*

"Hello?" a woman called from the dining room. "Anyone here?"

Her heels clicking across the hardwood floors, toward the kitchen, finally registered in Luc's lust-saturated brain. *Shit!*

Alyssa rocked back on her heels, then stood. She cast a regretful glance down at his cock, then brushed a soft hand across his face.

Even her hand on his cheek sent sparks colliding inside him, and he cursed and pulled away, tucking himself back into his pants and righting his shirt.

As painful as this was, maybe he should be grateful for the reprieve. Whoever had arrived had just saved him from making a terrible mistake. Because no way would he have stopped at a blow job.

Regret softened Alyssa's face. "Luc—"

"See who it is," he barked.

She sighed and made her way out of the kitchen to intercept the new arrival. Luc stood behind a counter, panting, willing his cock to stand down. He couldn't be meeting his brigade for the week with an erection like this.

Why did Alyssa drive him to reckless acts he knew weren't good for him? Why did he let her?

Moments later, she returned with one of the sous chefs, Misa. He remembered her résumé, and she seemed both competent and excited for the job. A little starstruck, which always made Luc shake his head. Despite having a lot of bestselling cookbooks and a solid reputation in the culinary world, he found the whole "fame" thing odd. Thankfully, the petite Hispanic woman got over it quickly and took direction well.

The rest of the staff appeared in the next few minutes, and Luc talked them through the process. He assigned duties, and they cooked a few of the specials as a team to ensure that everyone knew what to do and they worked out any kinks before opening their doors. Tomorrow would be their mock service night, so they'd be open only to people Alyssa had invited, who had agreed to provide feedback.

She excused herself a moment later to confer with the waitstaff gathered in the dining room. As the smells of the kitchen wafted around Luc, and he looked around at the smart, proficient team of chefs Alyssa had assembled—without his help—he was impressed all over again. She was a damn smart woman.

And admiring her was only going to screw with his head more. Already, he wanted her so badly he could barely concentrate. Liking more than her body would only be a double dose of stupid. But he feared it was already too late. What would happen after her evening at the club, when they went to her little house—and they were alone?

* * *

MEETINGS concluded, Alyssa climbed into the SUV beside Luc in Bonheur's parking lot. The heavy silence between them jangled her nerves. He'd definitely put off the vibe that he didn't want to continue what Misa had interrupted. But his erection had risen again the minute they were alone, unmistakable and unflagging.

She tapped her toe, thinking. Everything inside her wanted to throw her arms around him and entice him again. The other half . . . Well, the off-putting vibe was strong, and she wasn't dumb. He was close to the breaking point. After she got him into bed, she hoped he'd relax and conversation would follow. Until then, all she could do was continue to tease him and deny her own needs.

She reached out, touched his shoulder. "The meetings went well. The staff seems very excited. Thank you for staying this week."

Luc jolted at her touch, then relaxed. "I needed to live up to our bargain. You had every right to call me on it."

"Actually, I'm sorry about that. I feel strongly about not forcing people to be where they don't want to." The truth, but it made her wince. Pray to God he didn't ask her why. "If I hadn't advertised the fact you'd be here opening week and had so much of my savings into the place, I would have let you walk."

He turned to her with a puzzled scowl. "After the way I— After that night, I don't deserve your compassion. I know I was hard on you."

"Luc, I'm not a hothouse flower."

"No," he agreed immediately. "You're far stronger than I suspected. But that doesn't erase the fact I wasn't gentle with you. I'm not proud of that night. I'm . . . sorry."

"I liked it. I'm not sorry at all." Her words came out in a passionate rush. "Don't you dare be sorry, either."

He didn't comment. Instead, he seemed to mull her answer over. "What if Deke had stayed that night? Would you have regretted that?"

Where was that question coming from? Luc was fishing for something. How much should she reveal?

Finally, she shook her head. "I still would have been with you."

Luc's jaw dropped. Then he closed his mouth, shaking his head as he sped down the road. "You barely knew me. We'd met . . . what, twice before that night?"

Three times, actually. But the first time, she'd been working—taking off her clothes. They hadn't been formally introduced. The other times had been casual gatherings. "I suspected right away we'd be good together. I was right."

Pasting on a smile, Alyssa turned away. Hopefully, Luc wouldn't dig any further into that topic. She'd have to keep playing it casual. He wasn't ready to hear that he'd rocked her to her core the night they'd spent together, that she'd loved his toe-curlingly intimate conversation.

No woman has ever given me such pleasure. I could drown in you forever. Touch me, sugar. Yeeessss . . .

As they approached the club, Alyssa filed the memory away. In silence, Luc stopped the car and shoved it into park. She reached for the door handle, and he grabbed her wrist, staying her.

"We're good together sexually, God knows. But that's it."

A dozen comebacks ran through her head, most on the theme that he couldn't truly know his statement to be fact because they hadn't tried anything beyond sex. But contradicting him would only make him more resistant. And that was counterproductive. She had to keep playing her trump card.

"I never said I was talking about anything but sex."

Before he could respond, she jerked from his grasp and exited the SUV. She burst into the club through the back door, Luc at her heels.

"Why do I get the feeling you're not being completely honest?"

Refusing to allow herself to be rattled, she kept walking. "I can't answer that. Nor do I have time to try. I have a business to run. If you'd like to go back to the house, I'll have Tyler give me a ride home when the club is closed."

Just then, her bouncer approached, wearing two days' growth of beard, a khaki shirt with Bettie Page in a bikini and fishnet stockings, and a mischievous smile. He stepped up beside her, slung his arm around her waist, hand caressing her hip. Then he buried his face in her neck and inhaled.

"Mmm. I'll be more than happy to give you a ride, baby."

Alyssa raised a brow at Tyler. But this shit was par for his course.

Luc gritted his teeth. "I'll wait for you and take you home."

Since showing annoyance at Tyler's display would not deter him, she simply smiled. "Great. I need to make sure everyone's got the right costumes and props. Last night was a mess. Thank God most everyone was too drunk to notice."

Tyler wrapped his arm around her again. "Wait. I came back here to tell you that your least favorite asshole is outside with his friends."

"Primpton? Awwww . . ." She sighed. "What does he want now? Obviously attention. What's his cause du jour?"

"The usual. Shutting you down in the name of morality."

"This is the city councilman?" Luc asked. "He protests your business?"

"With revolting regularity." She leaned against the wall and shut her eyes. As if she didn't have enough to worry about. The restaurant's mock service was tomorrow. Luc was surprisingly edgy. She had to be at the top of her game to get his attention. What she didn't need today was Primpton giving her shit.

"What do you want to do, baby?" Tyler asked softly.

He knew this crap bothered her. He'd caught her alone and crying once after Primpton had publicly called her some really ugly names.

"Ignore him and hope he'll go away or risk him swaying the public to boycott Bonheur?"

"That's the big question." Tyler smiled grimly.

"What exactly does he do?" Luc asked.

"He's just an ass." The last thing she wanted was for Luc to see an elected official calling her a whore. It would cement that as truth in his mind.

"It's worse today," Tyler admitted grimly. "He brought the local press with him."

Damn it! Fate had it in for her. "He's trying to scare people away from the restaurant's opening."

"That would be my guess."

"He hasn't had any luck in shutting down the club yet," Luc pointed out. "Maybe no one is listening to him."

"He's got his followers, and he's gaining power. Every time Primpton stages one of these protests, it hits me in the bank account. The married, over-thirty crowd is one of the most lucrative, and I'm guessing that men who've gotten an earful from their wives stay away, at least for a while. I recover eventually, but I worry the restaurant could be different. I'd been hoping for crossover business, but now . . ."

"You mean from men who might take their wives to Bonheur, hoping to see you?"

Luc caught on quick.

"Me or some of the other girls. Several of the dancers have elected to give up the stage and wait tables."

"Isn't that a pay cut?"

"Absolutely. But some of them are smart enough to know they can't dance around a pole for the rest of their lives, so they're waiting tables to make ends meet and going to school during their off-hours." She shrugged. "It's tough, but doable. If I did it, anyone can."

Surprise crossed Luc's face. "You went to college while . . . dancing?"

God, did he think she had no other aspiration than to take off her clothes? She lifted her chin. "Double major. Business admin and communications. Last year, I finished an MBA. I'm not just a pole dancer, Mr. Traverson; I'm a business owner. It behooves me to know what the hell I'm doing. Now, I'm off to discourage Primpton."

Alyssa turned toward the stairs, bristling. She shouldn't be surprised that Luc didn't see beyond her sexy façade. The first time they'd met, she'd been wearing a G-string and pasties. She'd had little opportunity to improve her image with him since.

"Isn't the city councilman outside?" Luc looked confused.

"Yes, but do you think I'm going to meet the man vilifying me in a mini and garters?"

* * *

LUC watched Alyssa, fixated, the front of his jeans expanding, as she disappeared to the private upper level of Sexy Sirens. His head was spinning.

A double major? *And* a master's degree? To say he'd had no idea would be a colossal understatement. He'd suspected that behind the woman's sharp blue eyes was a lot of intelligence. The ambition surprised him. Business owner or not, that was a lot of education for a stripper.

But now she was also a restaurant owner.

Was Bonheur part of some life change/self-improvement plan? And what about her waitstaff?

Though it chafed him, Luc turned to Tyler. The bouncer stared at the empty stairs, his tongue virtually hanging out of his mouth. Luc knew the bouncer wanted her. Hell, despite Alyssa's protests, he wouldn't be surprised if they were lovers. But Tyler's expression said he admired Alyssa, had feelings for her. Was it mutual?

A sudden pang of jealousy smacked Luc right between his pectorals. He fisted his hands. Could she actually love the mouthy slab of beef?

It didn't matter. He had questions . . . and Tyler had answers. Whether Tyler and Alyssa were burning up the sheets or having an affair of the heart was none of his concern—even if it bugged the hell out of him.

"Where did Alyssa go to school?"

"Why the fuck do you care?"

Luc shrugged, playing casual. "Curious."

"LSU, Lafayette campus. She graduated with honors, too. She's smart in a way that's so fucking sexy. It's hard not to think with your dick when she's around." Tyler pierced him with a laser stare. "Isn't that right?"

All too true . . . "And the waitstaff at Bonheur? Are they all in school and elected to wait tables?"

"Most. Every few months, Alyssa gathers the girls to talk about life after the pole. If they want to get an education, she helps them find tuition assistance and apply for scholarships. She encourages them to make more of themselves. A couple of the girls just want to keep better hours so they have more time with their kids."

Wow. He hadn't seen the caring side of Alyssa. This news surely brought her into a whole new dimension. "Couldn't these women make more money stripping and . . . taking customers on the side?"

"Turning tricks?" Tyler raised a brow. "You're damn lucky Alyssa didn't hear that. She'd skin you alive and boil you in oil. That shit doesn't happen here. Period. 'Course she can't stop a dancer willing to entertain customers after hours and off premises, but she usually ends up firing them since they're often trouble."

The answer floored Luc. *Educated and principled?* Had he failed to see past their scorching sex and her short skirts to the woman underneath?

As much as he hated to admit it, yes.

But did it matter? As much as he wanted her, he couldn't take her. She wasn't a mommy candidate. He couldn't even see her as someone's *wife.* Alyssa would be impossible to tame, and Luc wanted a woman who would be content to stay home and focus on children. He didn't see her as that type.

But her values went deeper than he'd believed. She worked damn hard and deserved a break.

"You said Primpton is out front?"

Tyler smiled tightly. "With all the local press. Someone needs to stop this prick. She doesn't need him, especially now."

"Because the restaurant is opening soon?"

"That, and her mother. Alyssa just hasn't been the same since the woman died."

Died? "When?"

"Two weeks ago. Damn shame."

Though they still lived in Florida, and Luc didn't see his parents often, they talked frequently. He loved them very much and would be devastated if something happened to them. Certainly, he'd be in no shape to open a new business.

"They were close?"

"No."

Tyler's answer was both automatic and adamant. And his face said he refused to say any more on the subject.

"So Primpton's latest stunt is one she doesn't need." Tyler gritted his teeth. "It's going to bug the shit out of her."

Not if Luc could help it.

* * *

A few minutes later, Alyssa emerged into weak sunlight. The muggy September air had an oppressive feeling, and she was glad she'd decided to forgo curling her hair. In this humidity, her do would be undone in no time flat. Plus, the sedate French twist looked classy.

With a hand above her brow, she shielded her eyes and scanned the sidewalk. *There.* Primpton and his oh-so-moral followers stood on the sidewalk mere feet away with signs and angry expressions. Among his followers were two men who had watched her onstage last night, then paid Sadie for a private lap dance. She arched a brow at them. They looked away—but held up their hateful signs.

Of course. Outside the walls of this club, she didn't exist as a real person. Just a whore.

Flashbulbs went off and a chorus of voices spoke over one another, all shouting. She frowned and looked at the cluster of people. Reporters. Then she gasped.

They were all gathered around Luc.

Primpton yelled at the press. "There's the jezebel! Take her picture. Tell the good people of Lafayette not to glorify a woman who reveals and sells her body to strangers."

Alyssa sighed. More of the same spiel. Didn't this moron ever get bored? Or give a shit about facts? Customers *never* got laid at Sexy Sirens.

At the councilman's shout, cameras swung in her direction. Shutters clicked. Alyssa hid behind her sunglasses and opened her mouth to address the reporters with her prepared press release in hand.

Instead, Luc spoke. "Thank you for coming today. I'm excited to be the guest chef at Bonheur. I have no doubt it will become Lafayette's premier fine-dining experience. I've personally overseen this week's menu, infusing it with the flavors from my books. You'll be in for a real treat. From décor to food and wine, it's top notch."

"How did you get involved with Bonheur?" called one reporter.

Alyssa bit her lip. Of all the questions the press could ask, that wasn't one he could answer honestly without making her bad public opinion worse.

"Ms. Devereaux and I have mutual friends and have been acquainted for some months. She was kind enough to assist me with a matter not long ago. When the opportunity to repay her kindness arose, I happily said yes."

"What sort of matter?" shouted one reporter. "Was it sexual?"

"It was a family matter, actually," Luc lied smoothly. "She helped me settle something between my cousin and me. She's quite sage. And that shows in everything she's created at Bonheur. The more I've been involved with the restaurant and its staff, the more impressed I've become."

Alyssa blinked. Luc was smooth. And that he'd said such things, press or no, amazed her.

"What dishes will you make for the restaurant's opening?" another reporter asked.

Wow, with a little charm and some misdirection, the press had suddenly focused on something besides publicly branding her a whore. Of course, having a celebrity like Luc in town was news for Lafayette, but still . . .

"Who cares what he cooks?" Primpton shouted. "She's whoring for him, and he's allowing himself to be led down the sinner's path. Pray for him; there's time to save his immortal soul. But her!" Primpton speared a meaty finger toward Alyssa. "Condemn the devil's mistress who's infiltrated the good town of Lafayette and seeks to corrupt our community and its morality!"

"I'll be cooking some new dishes I'm very excited about," Luc continued as if Primpton had never spoken. "There's an eggplant ravioli appetizer that's to die for. I have a pan-seared fillet with pearl onions, feta cheese, and a rich burgundy glaze that will melt in your mouth. Dessert is a surprise. The whole menu is amazing, and I urge you to attend in the next week and see for yourself how special Bonheur is. You won't be disappointed. The first hundred tables will receive a signed booklet with the week's recipes."

Alyssa did a double take. Booklets? That *was* generous of him.

Reporters shouted more questions at Luc after that, but he merely turned on the dazzling charm. Then he looked her way. With his first glance, his eyes nearly popped from his head.

Hmm. Was the pencil-slim skirt and white button-down blouse with classic pumps too ridiculous?

Though Luc's expression didn't answer her unspoken question, he recovered quickly and gestured to her. "Here's the lovely lady who can answer all of your questions. Alyssa Devereaux has worked incredibly hard to make Bonheur a reality. I don't want to steal her thunder. Why don't you tell them all the wonderful things about your new place?"

Something stung her eyes. Tears? Damn it! But there they were. Luc had done something . . . nice for her. And the press was transfixed by him.

She was no different. Alyssa blinked away her tears.

Out of the corner of her gaze, she caught Primpton and his followers fuming in silence. Rejoicing inside, she approached Luc, bursting with gratitude. For now, all she could do was mouth, *Thank you.*

Later, she'd show him exactly how much his support meant to her.

* * *

LUC had a headache, one that emanated from his clenched jaw and pounded in his temples. It clawed up the back of his neck and made his eyebrows throb. The source of the pain stood not five feet from him, dressed again in a saucy, up-to-there skirt and a come-hither smile.

After Primpton left in defeat, the action at Sexy Sirens started swinging. Now Alyssa smiled at a group of males all crowding around her. Luc couldn't hear the conversation, but there was no missing the way she crossed those long legs slowly, rubbing one against the other, then perched on the edge of her chair with a coy glance. The men—of all ages—nearly swallowed their tongues. So did Luc.

Tyler hovered behind her chair protectively. That was his job. But one of the other guys edged too close to Alyssa and tried to steal a kiss. In a blink, the bouncer grabbed his jersey and shoved him back. Before the guy finished stumbling, Tyler had his hand resting possessively on Alyssa's shoulder.

"No touching, boys. You know the rules." Tyler looked only too happy to remind them.

That didn't deter Alyssa's audience. One guy dropped to his knees, a breath away from her thighs, and got an eyeful of her legs— and took the scenic route to her breasts.

Now it wasn't just Luc's head throbbing, but his blood as well. The asshole was completely objectifying her, staring at a collection of her body parts. What the fuck did he know about her as a woman?

Haven't you been guilty of the same offense? Luc shoved the voice in his head away.

As Tyler dragged the trash at Alyssa's feet upright, the biggest of the younger men bent close. He braced one hand against the back of the chair and whispered in her ear.

She looked trapped against the chair. Tyler was still scuffling with the other scumbag. And Luc had seen enough.

Suppressing a growl, he stomped toward Alyssa, ready to bust heads. But Tyler got there first, knocking the would-be whisperer back with a snarled, "You know the rules. Back the fuck off, Peter."

Peter? The guy she'd mentioned after they'd found the knife in her car?

Then Tyler lifted Alyssa, sat in her chair, and set her on his lap. His hand rested high on her thigh, the other on her waist. And the bouncer's fingers weren't still. They roamed, his thumb brushing the curve of her breast, his other palm disappearing under her skirt, over her hip.

Alyssa didn't blink, much less fight him off.

This intimacy didn't look as if it was purely for show, since Alyssa seemed entirely comfortable with the asshole's touch. They looked like lovers.

Luc glanced at his watch. Shit. It was only 9:00. He couldn't see this for another five hours without puking. Or hitting someone. Or grabbing her and staking a claim he couldn't keep.

The phone in his pocket vibrated, and Luc grabbed it, thankful for anything to do. Deke.

"Where are you?"

"Hi to you, too, Cuz. I've had a great day; thanks for asking."

Closing his eyes, Luc tried to get a handle on his temper. "Sorry. Just edgy. I thought you were coming today to look at Alyssa's security system."

"Nearly there. I need to talk to you for a few minutes. Meet me at the back door?"

Deke wasn't the talking type. He'd almost rather cut his tongue out, so his request thumped into the pit of Luc's stomach. Whatever it was couldn't be good.

"On my way," he answered grimly, glad to be out of eyesight of Tyler mauling Alyssa.

Within minutes, Deke pounded a fist on the back door. It was almost impossible to hear with Muse blasting in the background, but Luc swung the door wide for his cousin. Deke entered the club, all tense mien and watchful gaze. *You could take the man out of the military, but . . .*

"What's up?" Luc demanded.

With an uneasy glance around, Deke asked, "Is there someplace we can talk?"

Luc hesitated. "Come with me."

Circling back across the club's floor, Luc was grateful that the crowd around Alyssa had swelled until he could no longer see Tyler touch her. He kept heading toward the front, then paused at the bar, sliding a fifty-dollar bill across the surface.

"Give me as many Heinekens as this buys."

The bartender, whom Luc had met only in passing, shrugged and deposited the money in the till, then slid eight longneck bottles across the smooth, well-worn surface.

Luc handed the first four to his cousin, then picked up the rest. "Come with me."

Deke raised a brow but said nothing as he followed Luc to Alyssa's private, soundproofed office. Luc kicked the door shut, slammed the bottles on Alyssa's desk, and tore one open. He drank the whole thing in three swallows.

"Jesus!" Deke stared in shock. "You okay?"

How the hell did he answer that? "Crappy day."

Deke set the bottles in his hands down, then lowered himself into a chair. He looked nervous. Damn nervous. Luc instantly regretted his behavior. Deke clearly had something weighing on his mind, far beyond petty jealousy for a woman who wasn't even his.

"It will pass. What did you want to talk about?"

Deke grabbed a beer, opened it . . . stalled for time. "Man, I don't know where to start. I meant to be out here sooner today." He swallowed. "But instead we dropped in on Kimber's family this morning."

Long drive for an impromptu visit. "Is everything okay with her father?"

"Yeah, Edgington is a tough old bastard." Deke took a long drag on his beer.

Luc felt ready to scream. What the hell did Deke need to tell him that he didn't want to? "Hunter? Logan?"

"Kimber's brothers are fine. We just thought we owed them— Damn it." Deke leaned forward in his chair, set his beer aside, and shot Luc a direct, apologetic glance. "I wanted to tell you face-to-face. Myself." He swallowed. "Kimber is six weeks' pregnant."

Chapter Five

"WHAT'S wrong?" Alyssa asked as Luc sped through the night, toward her house.

Three a.m. wasn't the best time for a heart-to-heart, but he exuded a fuck-off vibe like she'd never felt from him before. Something grim rolled off him in choking waves, and though she knew he wouldn't welcome the conversation, she felt his pain and couldn't remain quiet.

"Nothing." He bit out the word.

"So you always run red lights for the hell of it?"

Luc's body tensed. "Shit. Sorry. I wasn't paying attention."

"Did He-Man say something to upset you?"

His hands tensed on the wheel. "Deke is still looking at your security system. He'll call in a few when he's done."

A non-answer. Luc was good at evasion. Then again, maybe this had nothing to do with his cousin.

"Look, if your foul mood has anything to do with what happened in the kitchen earlier—"

"It's over, it's done, and it's not happening again."

Like hell. She crossed her arms over her chest. "I gotta tell you, Chef, I don't think your new girlfriend is keeping you satisfied."

"Keep her out of this."

"If there's one thing I know, it's men. And if you were happy, today wouldn't have happened."

"Nothing happened."

"Something *almost* did."

Luc was quiet for long seconds. Alyssa cursed under her breath. She'd pushed too hard. Maybe tomorrow would be a better time to talk.

"We haven't been seeing each other long. We haven't . . . Sex isn't the point of the relationship."

Translation: He hadn't slept with this woman. As sexual as Luc was, seriously? Alyssa was happier about that than she should have been.

"What? You two play Scrabble together?"

"Just drop it," he growled.

For now. "All right. Thank you for helping me with Primpton today. I didn't get a chance to tell you how much I appreciate you defending me."

"He's a disingenuous prick trying to stir up trouble to either elevate himself or his bullshit cause. I would have defended anyone he trashed."

Maybe that was true. But if Luc had nothing but contempt for her, he wouldn't bother. He must have some other feelings for her. She just had to figure out what and how to grow them.

"Which is part of the reason you attract me," she said softly. "You have a good heart."

"Alyssa—"

"Yeah, I know. I was a good fuck, and now you don't want to talk about it."

Damn it, she should have been subtler. She had to keep control of her emotions and use her head, or he would bolt.

Silent minutes slid by again; then he surprised her by asking, "What happened to your mom?"

"Who told—?" She sighed. "Fucking Tyler. He doesn't know when to shut up."

"Two weeks isn't long to grieve."

Alyssa hesitated. Answer him and open up a potential door of pain? Shut him out and end the rapport and another chance to show him that she was a real woman under the garters?

"We weren't close. Her absence doesn't alter my day-to-day life. She was my blood, and I know I should feel like part of me is missing . . . and in a way, I guess I do. When I first heard, I went through the shock and denial. Anger consumed me for a few days. Now I just feel . . . numb."

His gaze softened. "You're still processing."

"I guess. I've never really lost anyone before." She wrapped her arms around her middle.

When she thought of her mother's death, a tight emptiness cramped her gut. But she couldn't manage to cry. Maybe too many years had gone by. Maybe she was still too angry.

"Allergic reaction," she murmured. "My mother was violently allergic to peanuts. Somehow a trace of them made it into her food and . . . she didn't get medication in time."

"I'm sorry." He reached across the distance separating them and grabbed her hand.

She squeezed it. Now that she was talking about her mother, it wasn't *that* hard. "I think what bothers me the most is knowing that, because she's gone, we can't resolve what was wrong between us. It can never be fixed."

"And you regret the time you spent apart?"

Big, tough question. "Yes and no. I wish things could have been different, but they couldn't."

Luc released her hand to focus on driving again, and she felt the withdrawal of his touch like a pang. Why did she crave this man who wanted her far more than he liked her? And way, way more than he respected her?

"I know it's none of my business, but did she . . . disapprove of your career?"

Alyssa sent him a bitter laugh. "Dancing around a pole isn't a career; it's a way to make ends meet. And no. She didn't know. I appreciate you listening, but there's nothing you can do to change the fact we'll never have the chance to speak again."

"Is your mom one of the reasons you help the other dancers improve their lives?"

"No. I improved myself for me and me alone. I don't give a shit what other people think. But if these girls have the drive, I want them to better their own situations because they want more for themselves. They'll need the fortitude to manage a grueling schedule."

Luc nodded. "Sounds like eighteen-hour days."

"Often."

He sent her a measuring stare. "But you did it—more than once."

"As I said, I'm a business owner. And I have ambitions."

Alyssa saw the moment he understood.

"That's what Bonheur is about. You want . . . what? Normalcy? Respect?"

Luc was getting uncomfortably close to the truth, and it would probably make him laugh. Likely he thought her chances for respectability had died when Clinton was still president.

"It's just a restaurant," she protested weakly.

"No. Bonheur is *your* happiness."

She swallowed. He'd guessed that quickly, but she was afraid to admit he was right aloud. Would he laugh? What if the restaurant failed and she had to continue dancing? What happened when she got too old for even that?

"I'm not ashamed of myself," she snapped.

He understood her, but not completely—and she couldn't allow him to. She wanted to feel his body against hers, his heart beating with hers. She wanted his love, and yes, his respect. He could be as sexually demanding as he wanted, but he had no right to expect her to just hand him her soul on a silver platter. He was probing into a past she *never* discussed. With anyone. Blabbing about it wasn't going to change a damn thing. And who needed the pain of dredging it up when it did no good?

Luc turned to her, his expression startlingly solemn. "I'm sorry for your loss. I hope you find the happiness you deserve."

* * *

WHEN they reached the house, Alyssa hopped from the car before he could get her door or say a word. She was hiding something. Luc was beginning to understand her . . . yet there was a whole chunk of her he didn't grasp at all. It shouldn't matter. He wasn't staying, and he couldn't again be her lover—even temporarily.

Then why did he feel a driving urge to figure her out?

The pain. That note in her voice, the tightening of her sultry features. The past, her mother—something beyond normal grief—hurt her. Pride hit a note in there, too. Despite her pole-dancing ways, she'd taken the time to thoroughly educate herself. She helped others with the drive to do the same.

What the fuck did it say about him that, in this moment, he wanted to slay her proverbial dragons for her?

Luc stormed in the house, just a few steps behind her. The conversation should be done . . . but he wasn't ready to end it yet. He had more to decipher.

But the phone in his pocket vibrated, and he pulled it out with a curse. Deke.

He pressed the talk button. "Talk to me."

"It ain't good, man. Sophisticated shit. Someone who knew a thing or ten about security systems tampered with the sensors in her upstairs windows, then rigged the control panel to automatically bypass that zone."

So the culprit wasn't a drunk frat boy or a prankster. "Shit."

"I've fixed it again and put a trigger on it. If anyone so much as breathes on the device, it will sound an alarm. When Jack gets back, I'll have him look at it, too, see if there's anything else we can do to keep this place tight."

"Thanks."

"Keep a close eye on Alyssa. Someone wanted to get to her badly enough to screw with a top-notch security system. That's expertise or a shitload of money to buy the expertise. Makes me wonder just how hard this prick is for her."

Luc wondered the same thing and cursed.

"I'll stay close to her, especially until Jack returns." Wouldn't that do wonders for his restraint? But he couldn't worry about that now when Alyssa's safety might be in jeopardy.

"Need some hardware?"

Guns weren't his favorite, but Deke had made sure he was efficient and accurate. Luc wasn't registered to carry in Louisiana, but the situation was too serious to worry about technicalities.

"That's probably a wise idea."

"Give me a day or so. I'll be back with everything you need."

"I appreciate it."

Deke hesitated. "I'd do anything for you, man."

Except allow him to play daddy to this coming baby. Not that Luc should expect it. Or deserved it after the way he'd manipulated Kimber and his cousin.

"Same here," he said finally.

"You okay with the baby and everything?"

No. The news of Deke's pending fatherhood had nearly staggered him to his knees, left him unable to breathe. Deke now had everything Luc had ever wanted. Kimber and his cousin had barely tried to conceive and . . . Luc sighed. He was thrilled for them. For himself, he despaired.

And he didn't want to talk about it again. Think about it, even. His own failure as a man was sharp enough without the rehash.

This week he couldn't do a damn thing to move closer to his dream. Until he returned home, he had to focus on his promise to Alyssa and now on keeping her safe.

At the top of his list had to be figuring out who her stalker was. His best suspects were Primpton, a nut job if he'd ever seen one. Or Peter, the frat boy who had money and apparently hadn't learned the meaning of the word "no."

But what about Tyler? Would the bouncer manufacture terror so that Alyssa felt it necessary to be closer to him? He was shifty enough, but after tonight's display at the club, Luc couldn't see why he'd have to. Tyler could touch her any way, anytime, he wanted.

Finally, Luc answered Deke the only way he could. "You deserve to be happy. I'm thrilled for you both."

"Maybe you should . . . get tested again. It's been a while, right?"

Years, but nothing would change the fact he had a ridiculously low sperm count. Enduring the humiliation of jacking off into a plastic tube again made no sense. "There are other ways. I've read recently about a surgery that extracts sperm. I'm also looking into adoption. Or maybe I'll find someone with small kids or . . . There are options."

"Absolutely. All great ones."

"I'll work it out. In the meantime, take care of your sweet wife and give her my regards."

"Will do." Deke sounded reluctant, but he dropped the subject and ended the call.

As soon as Luc pocketed his phone, he swore and did his best to push aside the turmoil brewing in his gut. He had more pressing problems now.

He should have checked the house before letting Alyssa burst in. If someone had breached her car and her club, it seemed logical he might hit her house next—and perhaps make the attack more personal.

Thanking God that nothing in the house looked disturbed, Luc bounded up the stairs two at a time with a pounding heart. He reached the landing quickly. Light spilled from her bedroom door, and he eased inside.

A rumpled bed, feminine knickknacks scattered across the dresser, a book on the bedside table. Nothing out of place.

But a trail of clothing snagged his attention. Strewn across the gleaming hardwood floor, her tank top, filmy white skirt, silky hose, black garter belt, and lacy bra lay a step or two apart. Heart beating even harder, he followed the pieces to her half-open bathroom door. A barely there thong with a rhinestone-studded GODDESS hung from the knob. Luc leaned to the right and saw inside.

And lost his ability to breathe.

Alyssa had pinned her hair atop her head in a haphazard twist and filled her jetted tub with bubbles. She leaned back and sensuously soaped her gleaming skin with a pink loofah. Closing her eyes, she sighed.

Instantly, he got hard enough to pound steel.

Luc had ascertained that she was safe and no one had broken into her house. He knew needed to back the hell away now. But like last night when he'd watched her bring herself to orgasm, he couldn't seem to make his feet move.

Suddenly, she lifted her sultry blue gaze to him. "Need something?"

A loaded question. *Yes!* In fact, he feared he'd gone beyond wanting her to *needing* her.

Luc drew in a shaky breath. No. He just needed to get laid. His sex drive had finally reasserted itself after Kimber and Deke's deci-sion to become a couple—and exclude him. Alyssa just happened to be the first female in a fifty-foot radius.

Except . . . if he'd met her yesterday and she looked like she'd be the sort of mother he had in mind, he would have hustled her into bed and into a relationship as fast as he possibly could. He didn't just want her; he was beginning to *like* her. And that made her all the more dangerous.

Nor did her pretty pink nipples, hard and bobbing on the water's surface, help clear his thoughts.

"Alyssa, don't do this to me." God, he barely recognized his own voice. "Please."

She raised a brow at him, dragged the loofah across one breast, over her nipple, licked her lips, and let loose a little whimper. Luc staggered back, gripping the doorknob. The silk that had rubbed against her pussy all day filled his hand. She was everywhere, frying his brain, searing his blood. This had train wreck written all over it, and his craving for her was about to jump the tracks.

"Do what? You're in *my* bathroom."

He fisted his hands and counted to ten, eyes closed. "Shut the goddamn door next time."

"I'm used to living alone. If you don't like the view, don't come in."

She was being intentionally obtuse.

Swearing, he opened his eyes. "If you don't stop teasing me, you won't like what happens next."

Because he felt like a pressure cooker about to explode. What he'd done to her the last time he'd spent the night with her would look like gentle hand-holding compared to the need charging through his bloodstream. If he unleashed that on her, God help them both.

Alyssa merely sent him a calm, considering glance. "Then leave."

He exhaled roughly and stared at the ceiling. "I'm trying."

"Let me help you," Tyler offered, his voice mere inches be-hind Luc.

As Luc turned, the bouncer shouldered his way in, drifting farther into the little bathroom. He moaned appreciatively at the sight
of Alyssa bathing. "Damn, you look gorgeous, baby. Where's a camera when I need it?"

"What the fuck are you doing in here?" Luc demanded. "Get out!"

Tyler glared over his shoulder. "What are *you* doing here?"

"I've been staying here since Homer gave my room away." Luc
crossed his arms over his chest. "How did you get in?"

The bouncer sent him a gloating smile. "I have a house key."

Those five words jolted Luc. Yes, he'd suspected they were lovers,
but this sealed the deal.

If Alyssa was going to let Tyler barge in and stay, Luc couldn't
remain here, knowing they were fucking—or worse, hearing them.
Getting out was his only option.

Yet he couldn't make himself walk out and leave her to share her
bed with Tyler.

The other man reached around him and grabbed a towel off the
rack and held it up. "Out you go. I need to see you."

Alyssa speared him with an impatient glare. "Now?"

Tyler nodded. "I tried to call and tell you I was on my way."

"I think I left my phone in Luc's SUV." She sighed. "Can't a girl
get some peace?"

Despite her protest, Alyssa stood, water cascading down her
golden skin, nipples beaded and dripping. The sight charged Luc's
need for her again. Turbo-juiced and on fire, his sex drive overloaded his good sense.

"Let's go," Tyler demanded.

"She stays with me," he snarled.

Shaking her head, Alyssa sent him a smile of apology. "This
must be urgent. Hopefully, Tyler and I won't be too long."

What was urgent? Tyler's need to fuck her? Couldn't be more
urgent than his own.

Damn, Luc couldn't believe that Alyssa had chosen the beefy caveman over him. After she'd been relentlessly tormenting him, nearly giving him a blow job mere hours ago? After more than hinting all day that she wanted him? She was giving Tyler her attention.

Alyssa stepped out of the tub and allowed Tyler to wrap the towel around her, draw her body against his. He slurped water off of her soft shoulder and groaned.

Motherfucking son of a bitch! Luc grabbed the door, barely resisting the urge to punch Tyler in the face.

Why hit the man because the woman they both wanted had chosen? If he should be angry with anyone, it was himself, for wanting her in the first place.

"Do whatever the fuck you want. Looks like you're going to anyway." Luc slammed the door and stalked out into the night.

* * *

NOT at all proud of himself, Luc stood across the street from Alyssa's darkened house, whiskey bottle in hand, and waited. He'd been here for the past hour, and now that it was nearly four in the morning and he was well on his way to drunk and angrier than ever.

She'd chosen Tyler. Even now they were inside fucking like mad while he wandered the park, his proverbial dick in his hand, wishing like hell that he was in Tyler's place. This, after Luc had turned her down more than once, fucking idiot that he was.

To make matters worse, he'd picked up a message from Emily earlier. Instead of being relieved to hear her voice, the high-pitched, happy-happy tone had been like a red-hot steel rod shoved through his brain. She'd invited him to a church picnic next weekend, and his first reaction had been dread.

What was the matter with him?

Alyssa Devereaux.

It had taken Tyler's intrusion, Alyssa's subtle rebuff, and his own intoxication to realize that maybe the best course of action was to fuck her and get her out of his system. Of course, that option wasn't available just now since she was otherwise occupied.

Thank God he'd bought this bottle from Alyssa's bartender after Deke's visit.

What did Tyler do for her that got her off so satisfactorily? Was he an oral god? Was he exceptionally well hung? Luc made a face at the thought of Tyler's man parts. The one thing he very much doubted was that Tyler could surpass his stamina. Luc knew he had the bouncer—and just about anyone else—beat at that game.

Not that he'd ever been proud of the fact he sometimes went into a sexual frenzy and didn't emerge for hours . . . and didn't ask a lover about her comfort or pleasure. He took and gave to her relentlessly until she was a slave to the clawing need. In his altered state, he lived for her fingernails in his back, her breathy pleas, and above all, her screams.

Suddenly, Alyssa's porch light flipped on. The front door opened. Tyler stepped outside, and she emerged behind him, wearing a pale satin gown that flirted with her bare thighs, her hair spilling down her back like a shining beacon.

The bouncer reached the door of his truck, then turned. He cupped Alyssa's shoulders, brought her against his big body, stroked the soft crown of her hair. She laid her head on his shoulder, looking perfectly comfortable in his arms.

Luc looked away and took another swallow of whiskey. The liquid crashed to the bottom of his stomach, burning. Or was his gut on fire because he kept playing the vision of Tyler fucking Alyssa over and over in his head?

No avoiding the truth now. Luc was so damn jealous he could hardly see straight. Wasn't irony a bitch?

Alyssa straightened. Tyler murmured something, then kissed her forehead. She nodded—then stepped back.

Luc frowned. If they'd been burning up the sheets for the past hour, wouldn't they part with a lingering kiss?

Finally, the other man hopped into his sleek black truck and drove off. Alyssa watched him turn the corner. Then she clapped eyes on his own SUV.

"Luc?"

Fuck. He should have left, driven off someplace so he didn't have to see her with Tyler—and have her know that he'd been watching. But no, he'd been too busy drowning in alcohol and jealousy to think straight.

With a sigh, he pushed away from the tree, his gaze glued to her slender form, the breeze rustling her silky hair, her nipples poking the front of her shimmering low-cut negligee, the satin clinging to her hips.

Tyler had probably just crawled from between her thighs, and damn if Luc didn't want to crawl between them himself. He wanted her so badly, he didn't give a shit if he got sloppy seconds.

He was in so fucking deep.

Finally, he stepped into the streetlamp's pool of light.

Alyssa gasped, then smothered the sound with her hand. She peered down at the bottle he clutched. "You're drunk."

Luc wished that were true. He shook his head. "Not for lack of trying."

"Come inside the house and let's get some sleep." She turned for the front door.

He darted after her. Just inside the foyer, he grabbed her arm. "You have nothing else to say?"

She sent him a sharp glare. "No one asked you to leave."

"So I was supposed to watch him maul you?" Luc slammed the door, enclosing them in shadowy silence. Then something terrible occurred to him. "Oh, hell, no. Did you want us *both* to fuck you? Together? Never going to happen. I may not have exclusive rights to you, but I won't voluntarily share you ever again."

Alyssa wrenched her arm free from his grip and slapped him. "Goddamn you! I'm so tired of you finding every snide, roundabout way possible to call me a whore. Just grow the balls and say it. C'mon! You think I fuck everything in pants."

"Didn't you have sex with Tyler just now?"

Her mouth tightened. Pain crossed her face for a moment—until fury took over. "Since you left, you'll never know."

She stepped into the living room and turned for the stairs. And Luc couldn't stand it. He should let her go; this consuming sort of anger wasn't normal, wasn't him. But he couldn't do it.

He lunged and grabbed her around the waist, hauling her against him. She'd know instantly how hard he was, but what the hell? He was perpetually hard around her. And if she hadn't figured it out yet, he had more than a little clue for her.

"Did you let him fuck you tonight?"

Damn if his voice didn't break. Luc didn't want the answer to matter, but he was way past pretending it didn't.

She struggled to get free, but he held firm. When she gave up, he turned her to face him.

"Did you?" he demanded.

"You don't know a damn thing about me, and that question proves it. Even if I gave you the truth, you wouldn't believe it. You want to hear that I went down on him in the bathroom, then we moved to the bedroom so he could suck my tits while I rode him, then after a reverse cowgirl, he finished me off from behind. That enough detail for you?"

Luc closed his eyes against the image her words painted. God, he was going to throw up Jack Daniels everywhere.

He tightened his grip on her. "Is that the truth?"

"Wouldn't that make your life easier? You could quickly write me off. Oh, fuck me first, of course. Everyone else does, right? But then you could walk away because I'm nothing more than a whore. Well, you know what? Fuck you." Alyssa elbowed him in the stomach.

Luc grunted and doubled over, clutching his middle, as he glared at her retreating back.

"Damn it, Alyssa! I . . ."

"You what?"

What *had* he been about to say? Did it really matter? He'd insulted her utterly—and he still didn't know if he was right. He just knew that he had a terrible fear that if he let her go upstairs and into her bedroom alone, he might never have the chance to touch her again.

"I don't know," he finally admitted.

"You're right!" she screamed. "You don't know. You don't know shit about me. Did you ever think there was a woman under all this makeup and provocative clothes who had real feelings that had nothing to do with sex? Did you ever think that maybe I wanted you to see me as something other than a stripper and an easy lay? That maybe you meant something to me?" She shook her head. "Of course not."

Alyssa sniffed, then sobbed. The sound tore through Luc's chest. Jesus, he never meant to hurt her. "I'm sorry."

"Forget it. It doesn't matter anymore."

Her words incited a panic he couldn't fight. "Wait! I—"

"No." She stepped back, away from him. "Forget it. I don't get my car back from Remy until Wednesday, but I'll have Tyler drive me around until then. I'll get you a room with Homer in the morning. Shouldn't be too hard since I paid him to give away your room to begin with."

Oh, dear God. The bottom dropped out of his stomach, and he finally understood—too late. She'd wanted him to be with her. Spend time with her. See what was between them, sexually and otherwise. And he'd treated her with silent contempt. Like dirt. But even if he magically fell in love with her tomorrow, she didn't fit into his future plans.

Luc took another long swig from the bottle. "I'm . . . sorry."

"I get it. In your head, we're from different worlds. You've put me in my place, and I won't overreach again." She stiffened her spine and headed for the stairs, then turned back to him. "For the record, Tyler's visit was about the break-in at the club. At tonight's sweep, he thoroughly investigated the entire upstairs. Seems that my stalker left me another knife and 'love note' embedded in the pillow of my bedroom at the club. And this one not only called me a whore; he said he'd put a stop to me for good very soon."

Chapter Six

ALYSSA marched up the stairs. *One foot in front of the other. Get to your bedroom. Shut the door.*

No damn way was she showing Luc Traverson her tears. She'd already given him too much power to hurt her. And he'd used it thoughtlessly.

"What did you say?" he demanded. A moment later, he darted up after her and grabbed her, spinning her around to face him. "The same pervert who broke into your car broke into your club?"

"And threatened me. No need to trouble yourself with my safety. That's Tyler's job, which is why he came here tonight. Now, if you'll excuse me . . ."

She tried to jerk free from Luc's grasp. His heat and musky scent were getting to her. Those burning eyes, his tautly muscled body, were making her weak-kneed.

Never had she thought of herself as one of those stupid women who stayed in a destructive relationship with someone who held more contempt for her than affection. Apparently her heart was as susceptible as anyone else's.

It was a bitter pill.

"Luc, let go."

He shook his head, took her face in his grasp. "I can't."

On the shadowy landing, Alyssa saw the intent in his glittering eyes a moment before he lowered his head. God, she wanted his kiss so badly. Muscle, bone, blood, all strained forward to join with him. Touch him. Give him anything he wanted.

Why did he suddenly want her?

Because he fears Tyler just had you.

She turned away, biting the inside of her cheek against the pain of denial. A debilitating pang settled in her chest. As his lips fell to her cheek, tears stabbed her eyes.

"Don't do this," he begged in her ear, pulling her so tightly against him she smelled the park's freshly cut grass on his clothes and the whiskey on his breath. His touch was riddled with desperation as he wiped her tears away. Alyssa felt herself weakening.

God, how could she want a man so badly who held her in such low regard? She was supposed to be too smart for that game.

"You can't want me only because Tyler does." She sobbed. "I'm not a sexual trophy in some fucking competition. Just . . . let me go."

She tried to wriggle free, mentally flaying herself for the stupid hope that had encouraged her to seduce Luc in the first place, to lure him close with the silly idea that he might fall for her. He probably wanted someone like Kimber: wholesome, with a bright future and a squeaky clean past. Someone without a string of former lovers and a résumé in the sex trade.

If that was what he wanted in a woman, Alyssa was completely doomed.

He cupped her cheeks and brought her face back to his.

"You're not a trophy to me, I swear. I know I have no right to tell you what to do." He brought her even closer, and even in the dark, she saw pain contort his face. "I was jealous. So fucking jealous, it was eating me alive. The thought that you gave him what I so desperately wanted."

Jealous? Maybe he cared a little bit . . .

"I offered myself to you—more than once." The words came out like an accusation.

"I tried to be gentlemanly. Smart. Use my restraint and not ravage and plunder you again. I didn't want you to think I was a caveman or a madman. I didn't want to lose control. I have a specific future in mind, and I don't see how we fit together in that picture. But . . ." Pain laced his voice; then he exhaled raggedly. "I can't ignore or deny what I feel anymore. I'm worried as hell about you, yes. I'm terrified at the thought of this sick stalker getting his hands on you and hurting you. I'll do whatever it takes to keep you safe."

Whatever it takes. He sounded as though she really did matter. Yes, it hurt to hear that she didn't fit into his future, but for the right here and now . . . His words tugged at her heart, broke down the dam holding her emotions in. She was moments from a flood of tears. "Luc—"

"I can't live another moment without touching you. I need you more than my next breath."

Raw honesty ripped across his features as he leaned in again, thumbs brushing her jaw. His touch, like his stare, pleaded. Alyssa didn't have the will to refuse him.

She thrust her hands into his hair and pulled him to her. Their mouths met in a rush, a gasp, a melding of lips, a moan. The tang of alcohol and need burst across her senses. Luc threw his arms around her and lifted her against him, as if he could suddenly make them one.

Instinct guided her to wrap her legs around him. He was there to support her with a hand beneath her ass and another blistering kiss.

He sank deep, desire searingly evident in the way he fused their mouths together. Nothing had ever been so intimate. He kissed as if he wanted to savor every bit of her, memorize her. Alyssa kissed him back with the same fervor, though she'd memorized him long ago.

In her head she knew this embrace might not mean to Luc all it did to her. Clearly, he wanted her—at least for now. But what did he really feel for her? Anything?

Wasn't she too far gone to care?

Tomorrow would come soon enough, and with it, a load of recriminations. But from now until dawn was purely about pleasure. About connecting again.

Luc slanted another kiss across her mouth and stepped toward her bedroom, every move brushing their bodies together. Alyssa sucked in a breath at the incredible friction. He was really here. With her. She held him closer and moaned against his throat, stringing kisses up his neck, across his five-o'clock-shadowed jaw, until she met his mouth again. He was waiting, open and voracious. She melted under his onslaught.

Moments later, her world tilted; then the bed was at her back, and Luc was above her, propped on his arms. Breathing hard, he looked down at her through the moonlight.

"I've wanted you again since the second I walked in your club."

She met his gaze, which glowed with raw passion and truth. He meant every word, despite what else he believed about her. Despite what he thought she had done with Tyler tonight. Despite the empty months since they'd last joined.

"Me, too," she confessed.

In fact, she'd yearned for Luc since waking up alone three months ago, aching, and realizing he wasn't coming back.

"I've missed you," she blurted. "You probably don't want to hear that, and I know you have someone else—"

"Not tonight. Right now, it's just us." He stroked her hair away from her face. "I've thought about you so often . . . From the second

I got you beneath me all those months ago, you've been a fever I can't shake."

Not a declaration of love, but she'd take it. He did feel *something* for her. And honestly, she couldn't name her feelings for him. She'd never had a yearning to be in love . . . until she'd met Luc.

"Be with me," she whispered.

"Nothing could make me leave now."

Luc took her mouth deeply, longing in every crush of his lips, every swipe of his tongue.

Long minutes later, he lifted himself away to unbutton his shirt. Alyssa caught on quickly and helped, her fingers brushing his silk-on-steel skin. He blasted heat. In the shadows, she found the intriguing trail of hair that led down from his navel to his cock. She remembered tracing it with her tongue and making him moan and shiver.

She didn't even try to resist now. Instead, she pressed her mouth to him, low on his abdomen.

He stiffened, then hissed. "You're playing with fire."

A coy smile drifted across her mouth. "I like to burn."

With a moan, she licked her way up his treasure trail, savoring the spicy flavor of his skin, the hint of sweat, his utter maleness on her tongue. So addicting.

Tensing, he thrust his hands in her hair and pressed her closer. "The first time you did that to me, it nearly made me insane. This time, I want you so much more. Dear God . . ."

She smiled against his stomach, then nibbled her way up toward his chest, unfastening the rest of his shirt's little white buttons. Finally, she reached his brown nipples, small and male, already hard. She eyed them greedily.

"Don't," he warned gently. "My self-control . . . I'm hanging on by a thread."

"Let it go." She infused all her want into the whisper and backed it up with a hot stare—just before she closed her mouth around his nipple and sucked.

He cried out, the sound both broken and harsh.

Encouraged, Alyssa scraped his nipple gently with her teeth and sucked it again, even as her hands made their way to the fly of his jeans.

He grabbed her wrists and leaned away. "Don't do that unless you want me on top of you, inside you, in the next ten seconds. I'm a time bomb with a seriously short fuse."

"I would love to have you inside me now," she said honestly. "I've thought about you . . . Our night together was incredible. I need more of that feeling now."

Luc exhaled raggedly. "I don't want to hurt you. Last time, I was too rough, too demanding—"

"Too perfect. Do it again."

He stilled. Something crossed his face. Acceptance? Eagerness? Whatever it was made her heart pound in her chest in a crazed rattle.

Easing back, he stepped off the bed. She sat up, and anxiety clawed through her. Had she misread him? Was he leaving?

Instead, he shrugged out of his shirt, exposing miles of gorgeous bronzed shoulders, lean, rippling muscles, and a six-pack that made her gasp. God, he was . . . everything. Sensual, intense, so smart and engaging, not to mention talented. And he wanted her right now.

Luc tore open the button at his fly, jerked the zipper down, and shoved his jeans and underwear away with brutal efficiency, then stood naked. Fists at his sides, his chest heaved as he fused his stare to hers, piercing her with a desire that set her body ablaze, made her pussy ache.

No man had ever done this to her but Luc.

"If I hurt you, you *must* find a way to stop me," he said.

And that was another reason she had deep feelings for him. Whether he wanted to care or not, he did. Her safety was always a consideration. He might have taken her profession and life at face value, but he never treated her well-being as inconsequential.

The woman who landed his heart would be completely treasured, and Alyssa longed to be her.

"You won't."

A hard glint entered his chocolate eyes. "Stand up."

Shivering, her insides a jumble of anticipation and need, she did.
Luc bent to her and caressed his way down her legs, fingers tracing
a sensitive line from the curve of her ass all the way to her calves.

Just having his hands on her made her tremble, but his touch,
full of soft demand, made her knees weak. Her longing and impatience surged.

"Luc . . ."

Without warning, he grabbed the hem of her negligee and
pulled. A tear at each shoulder was her only warning before the gown
slithered down her body, to pool in a soft circle around her feet.

Suddenly, she stood naked.

At a brush of the cool night air, her nipples peaked. Or was that
caused by the sight of his rapacious smile? Her belly quivered as he
curled his hands around her calves and urged them apart. His mouth
followed, working hot and openmouthed over her shins, the insides
of her knees and thighs, until she was breathing hard, reaching
blindly for his hair, her fingers itching to feel its softness.

He rose to his knees and kissed the flat of her belly. "On your
back."

She complied as he lifted her and stood in a single motion, apparently too impatient to wait. She grabbed him tightly when he
crushed her mouth under his and kissed with a demand that robbed
her of breath and thought.

Then he laid her across the bed and looked down at her, naked,
his cock heavy with arousal. Those sinful dark eyes both threatened
and promised pleasure unlike anything she'd ever known as his gaze
latched onto her face. Slowly, his stare lasered its way down to her
breasts and lingered, before scraping down her belly and fixating on
her pussy.

"Spread your legs."

She'd seen his dominant side before. But Alyssa had a feeling she was going to experience it on a whole new level. His dark tone made her shiver. The commanding look on his face confirmed the gravity of his words—and stole her breath. Her chest could barely contain the chugging of her heart. But she did as he asked, parting her thighs a few inches.

"More."

His expression demanded that she make herself open and vulnerable to him in every way. Alyssa had no doubt he would take everything she was willing to give, then, like last time, coax more from her until she was hoarse and sore and sublimely satiated. She eased her thighs farther apart.

"More," he growled.

Breath catching, she hesitated. But despite her trepidation, she could refuse him nothing.

She parted her legs again, until the muscles of her inner thighs strained. Need was a pool of heat shimmering and undulating in her blood. Emptiness thrummed inside her. Everything cried out to be filled with his cock—and all the blazing passion that came with it.

He grabbed her hips, then slid his hands to the small of her back and pulled up. At his silent command she arched for him, bending her knees, thrusting her breasts toward him.

"Perfect," he murmured, then perched himself above her body, the rasp of his chest raking hers, making her tingle.

A hard press of his lips against hers morphed into a sweltering line of kisses down her neck, collarbones, then straight to her breasts. As he cupped one, he devoured the other, his mouth a hot shock to her system. He sucked hard on her nipple, and she felt the draw all the way between her legs. He thumbed the other simultaneously.

Moaning, she held Luc close to her, wishing the night would never end. Already, the man made her feel far more than any lover. More feminine, more natural, more ready for everything.

"I love these," he murmured, switching his attention to the other breast. "I remember how swollen your nipples became when I sucked them before. Were they tender afterward?"

"Yes," she cried out at the memory of his oral devotion—for nearly an hour—still fresh in her mind. "I still felt you there the next day."

"I want you to feel me here again tomorrow."

Quivering, she nodded. "Please."

Luc moaned as he dragged her nipple into his mouth once more and gave a hard pull, gently scraping her with his teeth. An electric want surged through her body. He bit his way down the side of her breast, then nibbled over to the other and repeated the process.

He was harsher than before, more demanding. Already the tips were growing tender, and he didn't show any signs of letting up. Even if she'd wanted to ask for mercy, she suspected he would show none. She sensed that he needed to find some way to brand her tonight, prove to himself that he had some part of her Tyler didn't. Rather than assure him that he had every bit of her, she embraced him, encouraged him with a murmured plea.

His free hand roamed over her shoulder, down the curve of her waist, across her hip . . . toward her parted thighs.

She nodded. "You wet?"

"A constant state when you're around."

His fingers flirted with her belly button, but that thumb drew little circles against her skin, so near her clit she wanted to scream.

"Touch me," she cried.

"Mmm, definitely. I'm looking forward to sinking into that sweet pussy. You were so tight last time, you grabbed me, milked me. Your arms around me, you screaming *my* name . . . So fucking hot. Unforgettable."

Alyssa could only whimper as she waited for him to finally touch her where she needed him most. Instead, he toyed with her.

Her ache multiplied, soared. Arousal gathered in her core. She felt swollen, needy, ready to beg if it would do any good. But he simply brushed his knuckles over her folds, giving her clit the barest touch.

Alyssa gasped. "Luc . . ."

"I want to hear you say my name a lot tonight. *My* name. No one else's."

She didn't think she could even remember her own name right now, much less anyone else's.

"Yes," she sobbed. "Yes . . ."

For endless minutes he cupped, laved, and stroked her breasts. He tugged on their tips, sucked them hard, murmuring his appreciation as they swelled, reddened, peaked even more. Her nipples were so hard, her want so sharp, that she fisted her hands in his hair, using him as her lifeline as she drowned in need.

Swiping his thumb over the taut bead of one, then the other, he stepped back and swallowed. "So tender and worked. Gorgeous."

Now without his touch, Alyssa craved more of the sensory overload and stroked her own breasts. But it wasn't enough to ease the relentless gnawing of her hunger. She slid her hands down her abdomen, toward her wet folds. Relief. She needed to curb the ache. Now.

Before she reached her destination, Luc grabbed her wrist. "No. I say how and when. It's not by your hand tonight."

"But—"

Alyssa never finished the thought. He crashed his mouth against hers and prowled inside, possession evident as he took the kiss deeper. Without warning, his fingers slid into her wet cleft, and he plunged inside. She cried out her pleasure into his mouth.

"Damn," he breathed. "You feel so good."

His fingers played her perfectly, as if he remembered her body and exactly how to make her scream. His devilish touch skidded across that sensitive spot inside her; then he alternated, pressing and rubbing, his thumb also strumming her distended clit. Fire converged inside, outside, tugging, drawing, swirling and growing. Again he smothered her cries with his kiss. She dug her nails into his shoulders, and he hissed. Then he sent her a predatory smile, a flash of sexual promise and white teeth in the dark.

"That's it. Ready to come?"

He didn't need to ask; he knew. But he wanted her to say it. Luc liked making her confess her desire. At the moment, she had no way of concealing it.

"Yes! Please . . ."

Instead of sending her over, he withdrew his fingers and raked them through her slit. "Very swollen. You'll grip me so tight."

He eased closer until he covered her, his chest pressing her deeper into the mattress, his thighs parting hers even more to accommodate his hips. His hands urged her wider still.

The anticipation suffocated Alyssa. She wanted Luc deep, so deep he'd never remember another woman and never imagine leaving.

"Tonight you won't have time to think about anyone but me," he vowed.

She never did anyway, but he didn't understand that. Yet.

"So many sinful things I want to do to you, but . . ." He cradled her head in his hands, and she met his stare in the dark, drowning. "I have to be inside you."

Alyssa tried to nod, but he held her too tightly, pinned beneath the lush heat of his body and her own desire. She panted, wanting, waiting . . .

"Look at me," he demanded.

She'd closed her eyes. She wasn't sure when. Didn't matter . . . Now she opened them. *Bing!* Their gazes connected, and her heart followed. That wild sense of connection, of belonging, slammed her. She could no more escape his glittering dark eyes than she could her own craving for him.

"I already feel you all through my body. How is that fucking possible? Again?"

He didn't answer his own question and didn't let her try. She merely marveled that he felt it as well.

Then she thought nothing as he grabbed her hips and surged forward, burying as much of his cock inside her as he could. She grunted at the delicious intrusion. Already, she felt full with him and knew he was halfway in—if that. His back stiffened. He cursed, wriggling his hips.

"Always so tight," he groaned. "God, you're killing me. You relaxed for me, sugar?"

His gaze was like the darkest syrup, sweetening her, melting her, covering her. She focused on loosening up, letting him in.

He eased back, then surged in again, this time a bit farther. She gasped at his steely penetration, at her pleasure-pain.

"That's it." Voice strained, Luc gripped her hips with biting fingers. "Relax. It's going to feel so good."

Alyssa sensed he was on the very edge of his control. And she couldn't wait for him to lose it.

Beneath him, she writhed, lifted up, taking him a fraction deeper. After months without sex, it burned . . . but felt oh so good. No one had ever made her love sex like Luc. No one else had ever made her feel her heart during the act, either.

"Yessss," he hissed, gripping her tighter still.

Finally, he slid deeply and completely inside her.

The feel of him buried in her body unleashed a fresh surge of need—and a flood of warmth in her chest. As their gazes connected again, she flashed back to their first night together and a rush of memories swamped her—all dripping pleasure.

But as he nearly withdrew from her body, she clung to him, tonight took sensation to a whole new level.

Luc eased his arms under Alyssa, up the length of her back, hands curving over the tops of her shoulders. Then with a roar, he thrust deep. Once. Twice. Then she lost count.

The sensation lit her up, then exploded through her body. She absorbed the power of his surge by moving with him, opening to him completely with a cry.

More warmth flooded her chest as the ache behind her pussy converged. Her legs wrapped around him as she tried to grip him tighter, keep him closer. He groaned, panted, sinking deeper, then deeper still.

Luc picked up speed, setting a hard rhythm. His stare drilled into her as his cock did, never wavering. Every thought and sensation flowed from his body to hers, then back again. And Alyssa knew he could read her every feeling, too. As soon as a reaction hit her body, he adjusted to take advantage of it, deepen it, exploit it.

Dear God, she was beginning to unravel. The fortitude and pain, caution and fear, that had held her together for years were coming apart. Yes, she'd come for Luc before, but this . . . this was reaching inside her to claw out something she never shared with anyone. He was going to take the pleasure from her, steal it right out of her soul without permission or apology.

She tensed. Could she give that much of herself to him?

"Luc . . ." Alyssa squeezed her eyes shut.

Too intimate. Too real. Too deep. He was everywhere. Why hadn't she had a lover in the months since him? Or in the years before him? Because no one else made her feel as if sex was anything more than a cross between an obligation and a bodily function. Even if she'd let every customer who came to the club have his way with her, Luc alone could take her apart, fill her with something so persistent and sweet and yearning, then remake her.

"Look at me!" he demanded under the relentless pound of his body.

And that compelling voice . . . No way she could ignore him.

Biting her lip and bracing for the rush of feeling, Alyssa did as he asked. She connected with his probing dark stare just as he rammed home.

Energy shifted, gathered, turned nuclear inside of her. Then she exploded.

Clawing at Luc, screaming his name, she burst into a million pieces, her heart beating for him, her soul scattered utterly by mind-bending pleasure. He rode her through the orgasm from crest to blast, pulling back as it coalesced into a tender ache that had her sobbing.

This time, like last, Luc used that as his cue to continue plundering her into the ultimate pleasure.

* * *

THE morning sun soaked the sheer curtains and hardwood floors. Gasping in a raspy breath, Luc pulsed up into the heat of Alyssa's pussy again as she rode him. She moaned and clung to him, her nails raking his chest. Above him, she looked like a sensual nymph, nubile, striking, built for pleasure. She'd long ago seared through his restraint and good intentions. Again, he'd lost every shred of control, and as he drowned again in the fierce ramp from pleasure to orgasm, he was caught in her trap. And he hungered for it.

Her mussed pale hair swung around her, some ends clinging to her waist. The shorter ones around her face flirted with her hard nipples, which he still hadn't been able to get enough of. Even now they beckoned.

Throwing his arms around her, he pulled her close, then anchored a hand at her nape. The other clutched the small of her back, controlling the arch. Yes . . . Right there. Again, he had the tempting little nipple on his tongue, his teeth scoring it just enough to sting. She hissed, then tightened on his cock.

"Come again."

He'd been demanding her pleasure all night, and she'd been giving it with utter abandon. It was never enough. He needed to see her again now, desire parting her lips and making her whimper. He craved the feel of her clamping down on him and hearing her scream his name.

She'd grown hoarse hours ago, her flesh swollen to the point that every thrust was work. Luc had driven her to orgasm so many times, he'd lost count. He'd fallen over the cliff into a fiery pit of pleasure three times, saturating her every time, reveling with a primitive need to mark her that he'd stopped questioning. An odd relief poured through him each time he spilled himself deep inside her. No, he couldn't get her pregnant, but damned if he wouldn't fill her up anyway.

"Luc." Alyssa sobbed *his* name.

Triumph spiked through him, followed by another insane urge to mark her. He laved one of her nipples again, then the other. Her pussy became sublimely, blisteringly tight. The fact she was so close urged him on.

He fit his mouth over hers, forcing her lips wide under his, and sank in as far as possible. The cadence of his kiss matched the rhythm of his thrusts as they strained together toward a cataclysm so powerful, it would likely devastate them both.

He pursued it with reckless abandon.

His body was about to give out, and he was furious. Hours upon hours he'd spent delving her, but he hadn't tasted her cream with his tongue until she cried out in surrender. Nor had he worked his way into that tight, perfect ass. Tomorrow. No, later today. He would do both. But tonight, once he'd gotten deep within her wet folds, he'd single-mindedly submerged himself and watched her come apart in his arms.

"Come again, sugar. For me."

He tiled her hips until they pressed completely against his, then rubbed her up and down his cock, forcing friction on her clit. Alyssa undulated with him, her groans becoming whimpers that turned to a plea, then . . .

"Luuuucccc!" She screamed his name as if it were a twenty-syllable word as her cunt clamped down on him. He used all the strength in his arms and thighs to keep her moving.

The pleasure was excruciating, scorching, beyond anything he'd ever experienced—or imagined. The sensations roiling around inside him melded into a tight ache in his balls. Then, primed, the orgasm began to explode.

Luc grabbed her tighter, clutching her hair, throwing an arm around her waist. *Oh, fucking hell.* This was going to bring him to his knees. Destroy him. It swelled and built and converged, big as a mountain, powerful as an earthquake.

"Alyssa," he gasped. "Oh, God. Shit. I can't . . . Oh, my—" To merge with her in every way possible; it was his most basic instinct. He slammed his mouth over hers and dove into the sweet heat.

The orgasm flattened him.

As everything inside him crashed around his heart, he held her tighter, burying his face in her neck while the storm raged inside him. "*Yes!* Lys, yes . . ."

His heartbeat thundered in his ears, and he felt nothing but blinding ecstasy. And Alyssa.

Long minutes later, exhaustion pounded him. Bitter reality roared in. She was still a stripper, likely with another lover. He still needed to find a suitable wife. And he wanted her more than he'd ever wanted any woman in his life.

Slowly, he lifted his head as Alyssa stroked his hair and tried to catch her breath.

"Look at me," he demanded.

She bit her lip, then glanced at him, her face flushed with satisfaction.

His gut clenched, even as a drugging call to sleep rolled through his veins. "What are we doing?"

Her mouth tightened. Her eyes grew guarded. "Just fucking."

Were they? Really? Because for long minutes—hours—he'd forgotten every other woman in the world. He'd wanted to grab this one and never let go.

Alarm bells went off in his head. Luc knew he should say something . . .

Before he could, exhaustion claimed him.

Chapter Seven

"ARE you going to tell me what the hell happened?" Tyler barked.

I'm falling in love with someone who can't love me back.

Alyssa winced at the thought. Lingering over the act of drawing back the blinds at Bonheur to let in the midday sun, she tried to decide what to say.

Finally, she turned to him. "Nothing."

It was a huge lie. The most shatteringly pleasurable night of her life reduced to one trite word. If she hadn't been going to hell already, the lie would have put her there.

He arched a tawny brow. "The shadows under your eyes have bags so large they could pack for a trip to Europe. As soon as we got to Sexy Sirens this morning, you shut yourself into your bedroom. I fucking heard you cry. I don't have to be a genius to figure out that since you spent last night with that short-order loser, maybe something went down."

"Tears are no big deal." Except Luc didn't love her. They were just fucking, and she'd just charged down the path to a big, ol' heartache with no idea how to backpedal.

"You didn't cry for your mother, but you cry for this prick? Baby, c'mon. You never call me at eight thirty in the morning unless it's an emergency. While you were getting coffee, I peeked in your guest room. The bed was perfectly made. Only other bed in that house is yours." Tyler crossed his arms over his chest, his glare pure pissed off. "Given that, you calling me not long after the crack of dawn is significant. *Now* do you want to tell me what the hell happened?"

The bastard was too observant. "No."

"You had sex with him."

Amazing, relentless sex. Why confirm the obvious?

Alyssa moved to the next window and focused on the blinds.

"Goddamn it!" Tyler spoke through clenched teeth. "Did he hurt you?"

"Tyler, just leave it."

"Hell, no! If he hurt you, if he *forced* you, I'll bust him up—"

"No. We were mutually consenting adults, and that is the end of this conversation."

Suddenly, Tyler was across the room and his arms were around her. He really was her best friend these days and it would be so easy to lean on him. But so unfair to him.

"You don't have to be strong all the time," he whispered. "Tell me. I'll help however I can."

She cupped his cheek in her hand. "You can't. But I appreciate you more than you know."

He sighed and tightened his grip on her, leaning into her until his forehead pressed against hers. It would be easy enough to slide into bed with Tyler, see if he could help her forget her overwhelming feelings for Luc. Alyssa had never played that game before, but she was pretty sure it would be pointless.

"Baby, you gotta give me something more. I'm dying here."

Before she could reply, the restaurant's front door slammed. Gasping, Alyssa whirled, ready to tell the interloper that the restaurant wasn't open to the public until tomorrow night. But it wasn't a stranger who stood there. It was Luc.

He looked furious enough to spit nails.

Tyler's preservation instinct must be nonexistent because, instead of backing off, he tightened his arms around her. She pushed against his chest and nudged him away. Reluctantly, he let her go, muttering a vile curse.

"What the fuck are you doing here?" Luc asked him.

Crossing his thick arms over his wide chest, Tyler looked pumped up on fury. "My job. You?"

"Since when is your job trying to get into Alyssa's panties?"

"She only wears thongs, actually."

Alyssa gasped. "Tyler!"

Luc ground his jaw, fists clenched. This situation was headed for the toilet unless she diffused it.

"Stop it, both of you. Tyler, can you leave us alone for a few minutes?"

"I'm not budging if there's any chance he'll hurt you."

Spine stiffening, Luc stalked across the room. "I'd never hurt her. Ever. You, I'd pound just for fun."

"Bring it on, asshole."

"No more!" Alyssa yelled. "We have things to do today that don't involve you two beating the shit out of each other." She looked at Tyler, eyes pleading. "I'll be fine. Please . . . You'd be doing me a big favor if you'd pick up my dress from the tailor."

Tyler clenched his teeth and seethed, ripping his keys from the pocket of his jeans. "If you need *anything*, if he harms one hair on your head, call me. You know I'm here for you."

She nodded. His devotion nearly brought her to tears. Why couldn't she love him the way he wanted her to love him? Life would be so much less complicated.

But easy was never her lot.

"Thank you," she murmured.

He drew closer, his face solemn, communicating both his dedication and concern. Then he cupped her face in his hands and placed a tender kiss on her lips. A second later, he was gone.

Now she was completely alone with Luc. The silence was deafening.

"You're here early," she said to break it. "The others have already done most of the prep work in the kitchen, so you should—"

"Stop it." He stalked to her, unnervingly close. "When I woke alone, I worried about you, but you left before the bed was even fucking cold so you could run to *him*?"

Alyssa paced across the room. How *dared* he imagine, after what they'd just shared, that she could possibly jump from his arms to Tyler's? Here she was, terrified that she'd lost her heart to a man who might never be able to truly love her back, and he imagined she'd run to another lover. That alone confirmed that, no matter how intimate last night had seemed, no matter how much her feelings had grown, his hadn't changed. She could not lose her heart to someone who didn't respect her. Someone likely to leave her in five days and never look back.

"Aren't we just fucking?" she challenged.

He stalked after her and grabbed her arm. "Goddamnit, answer my question."

"You think I'm *capable* of jumping from your bed to his? That I'm so insatiable, what we did last night and this morning wasn't enough?"

Luc didn't say anything for a long moment, just stared with blazing eyes. "I don't want to think that. God, woman. You singed my skin off. It was amazing. I looked forward to waking up this morning and having you again. But you never slept next to me, did you? I rolled over a few minutes ago, and you were gone. Now I find out now you've been with Tyler for the last . . ." He glanced at his watch.

"Three hours. I walk in, and he's holding you. He kissed you, for fuck's sake."

"A friendly peck!" she argued.

"Friendly, yeah," Luc grunted. "I'm sure everything on his mind is platonic."

"I don't control his thoughts, just mine. What's on my mind *is* platonic, whether you believe it or not."

"Give me a reason to believe it." His dark eyes beseeched her. "You look exhausted. The first words I hear out of his mouth are a plea for you to give him *more* because he's dying. Which implies that you were giving him something in the first place."

Alyssa closed her eyes. Maybe it was Luc's jealousy talking—at least in part. The other part . . . He was just never going to change his opinion of her, and no matter how much she cared, how sincere she was in expressing her feelings, how chaste she was with every other man, he'd never believe she was anything but a whore.

"I can stand here in perfect honesty and say that in the last three months, I've had sex twice, both times with you. Can you say the same?"

Luc paused, swallowed. His dark eyes flashed with guilt. His silent answer gouged her with pain. Bitterness flooded her mouth

"Three months ago, I was in a relationship."

Helping his cousin fuck the man's pretty wife. It burned her to know that Luc had jumped from her bed to Kimber's and never looked back until Deke had cut Luc from the action.

Suddenly, Luc paused, then frowned. "Are you and Tyler . . . dating?"

It didn't matter what she told him. He'd never believe the truth. "Tell you what—you give me all the details about your relationship with Kimber, then I'll spill my secrets. Deal?"

His face closed up. "There's nothing to tell."

Alyssa didn't have to know the whole story to know he was lying through his teeth.

"So you didn't fuck her after you left my bed?"

Luc closed his eyes, the uneasy tightening of his face making her insides bleed.

"This isn't about what I did or didn't do with Kimber."

"Then why is it about what I did or didn't do with Tyler?"

"Three months ago, we didn't make any promises or demands," he pointed out.

"We didn't make any last night, either," Alyssa flung back at him. "A night of sex doesn't entitle you to the details of my relationship with Tyler. And after this chat, spending last night with you was a mistake I won't be repeating."

His eyes flared with fury, and he stomped across the room. "Like hell. For whatever reason, you went to a lot of trouble to seduce me. Mission accomplished. Just because last night is over doesn't mean we're done."

Luc's words were spoken like a vow, and Alyssa's insides quivered. As much as she still wanted him, they couldn't continue like this. Even last night she'd realized that the longer she stayed in his arms, the more likely he would break her heart.

For months, she'd been romanticizing the connection between them. She wanted him for more than sex. Now she knew beyond all doubt that the yearning didn't run both ways.

"Wrong, Romeo. Last night was great, but you're already in another relationship and I don't 'fit into your future.'" She shrugged. "Itch scratched. Moving on."

"No way in hell," he snarled. "Are you saying that you have a new itch, this one for Tyler? Is that what this morning was about?"

Alyssa got how he might think that. If a man had disappeared so quickly out of her bed and she'd found him in another woman's arms, even if it was to be consoled, she'd be confused and hurt. Despite Luc's jealousy and whatever feeling he had for her, it didn't add up to anything lasting. And if she kept sharing her body with him, she'd never get her heart back. Anything less than full reciprocation on his part would crush her.

"This isn't about Tyler. Yes, I spent a lot of effort to seduce you, but you said when you arrived that sex between us wasn't smart. Allow me to admit that you were right." She checked her watch. "Misa will be here in five minutes and she'll be expecting direction. The rest of the staff will arrive in an hour. You'll need every minute to prepare. We're expecting a full house tonight."

A moment later, she heard a car door slam. Tyler was back in record time. She breezed past Luc, headed for the restaurant's front door.

He grabbed her by the arm and pulled her close. "Where are you going?"

She jerked free and lunged for the door. Luc didn't want her . . . but he didn't want anyone else to have her. Alyssa refused to play that game. Hopefully, dishing back some of his own medicine would put some distance between them.

Smiling tightly, she quipped, "Maybe it *is* time I let someone else scratch me."

* * *

THE mock dinner service was winding to a merciful end. The evening had been flawless. The muggy afternoon had given way to a cooler evening, and Alyssa had thrown open the doors to the patio, bringing the outside in. The food had been impeccable, the help she'd hired perfect. Not a hint of an undercooked steak or overcooked vegetables. The waitstaff had been deferential and efficient. Patrons all around smiled—and Bonheur had secured lots of future reservations.

Professionally, Luc couldn't be happier.

Personally, swallowing nails would be less painful than forcing down the fury inside him.

He stood just outside the kitchen, loitering in the hall, looking for a certain gorgeous blonde . . . *There*. She drifted from one table to the next in a graceful sway, her elegant black dress tastefully draping her gorgeous body. She'd swept up her hair in something classic and feminine. Understated diamonds winked at her ears and her wrist. Sophisticated, refined. A perfect match for her atmosphere.

And she still gave him a raging erection.

Smiling graciously, Alyssa paused at the next table, visited with guests, accepted a hug from a couple. Their toddler fisted her hands into the long sway of Alyssa's hair, and she smiled, kissing the little girl's forehead.

The sight of her affectionate gesture jolted Luc. He swallowed down a sensation he could term only pure longing. God, what an impossible wish. Just because Alyssa liked that child didn't mean she wanted any of her own. Or would be the sort of dedicated mother his own had been. Besides, even if she ended up having a huge maternal streak, she wasn't what he needed, and the road to parenthood with him wouldn't be easy.

Besides, Tyler was scratching her itch now. And Luc was alone— trying not to feel the confusion and pain crushing his guts.

A moment later, Alyssa drifted outside, under the external lighting, pausing to greet an older couple. Not five feet from her, Tyler watched her unblinkingly.

What had they spent the afternoon doing? If it was what Luc feared, that was his fault. Had he pushed her away with his accusations and behavior? Why the hell hadn't they just enjoyed their time together and had a week of uncomplicated sex?

Because nothing between them was uncomplicated. He couldn't touch Alyssa and feel nothing.

That scared the shit out of him.

Someone waving caught his attention, and he looked up to see Kimber standing with a hesitant smile and an upraised hand.

Pregnant.

Resentment jabbed him. Deke was living the life Luc wanted with a wonderful wife who would never refuse him her body or tell him that she had someone else to scratch her itch. She understood Deke's hang-ups and been patient until he learned to overcome them. Alyssa . . . What would she think if she knew he could not father children? Would she shrug—or think him less of a man?

With a sigh, Luc made his way over to Kimber and his cousin.

Deke stood and held out a hand. "Good work. Food was incredible. You always cooked fine meals when you lived with me, but you outdid yourself on this."

"Super delicious," Kimber added with a dimpled smile.

Luc shook Deke's hand, then slipped an arm around Kimber. "Thank you. And congratulations."

He forced himself to look at Kimber and mean the words. He *was* happy for her. For Deke. Somehow, someway, he'd find this ideal future for himself, and maybe he could get over the choking envy.

"Thanks," she murmured. "We're thrilled."

"As you should be."

Deke beamed with joy.

"I'll do my best to be a very committed uncle and spoil the tyke like mad."

Kimber smiled and hugged Luc close. "You're such a wonderful person, I have no doubt you'll succeed."

"Are you done cooking?" Deke asked.

Luc nodded. "The last ticket went out about ten minutes ago."

"Good. Sit. We've got hardware to discuss."

"On that note, I'll run to the ladies' room. I already spent three hours looking at the equipment on the trip over. Nice stuff. I hope Alyssa will be okay."

Without thought, Luc's gaze sought the woman in question. She was winding her way across the patio, the night breeze stirring the pale tendrils at her neck. Making him ache for her.

But he had to get his mind back on the present.

As if their sex life wasn't fucked-up enough, Alyssa had some prick threatening her. In that respect, Luc was glad Tyler was doing his job so diligently, even if he didn't like that the other man watched her as if she were dinner and dessert all in one.

Deke looked at him, then Alyssa. He brought his gaze back. "What's up with you two?"

Luc started to evade the question. But he stopped. Avoiding this . . . thing between him and Alyssa wasn't making it go away. And it needed to; he knew that. Why couldn't he work it out?

"I don't know. She's . . ." He rubbed his forehead, searching for the right words. "Under my skin."

"That guy her bodyguard?" Deke nodded at Tyler.

"Of sorts, yes."

Deke raised his brows. "He looks like he'd like to do more to her body than guard it."

"I'm pretty sure Tyler already does." Why else would she allow him to kiss her? Have a house key? See her naked? Touch her in public?

Leaning in, Deke stared at Luc long and hard. He swallowed, certain his cousin could see right through him.

"Unless I miss my guess, you've had an encore performance with Alyssa recently."

That obvious? "So?"

"So you don't care if she fucks him, too?"

Luc fisted his hands in the tablecloth. He knew it was telling, but hell, Deke saw through him anyway. "It infuriates the hell out of me. I've had moments lately where I wanted to break every bone in his miserable body."

"She's more than a fuck to you?" Deke sounded surprised.

As much as Luc wanted to avoid answering the question, he couldn't. In fact, he'd been asking himself the same thing.

"I don't understand it. She's everything I don't need. Shady profession, total lack of modesty, so damn independent. Probably multiple lovers," he snarled. "I can't see her being happy with a rock on her hand, kids in tow, living in suburbia."

"But you don't know that for a fact?"

"No," he admitted.

"Let me ask you something. Were you *ever* jealous watching me in bed with Kimber?"

Luc paused. But the answer was easy. "No. Though you two had a bond, for a long time I felt completely involved in the relationship."

"I couldn't stand watching you touch her," Deke admitted. "Every time you did, I thought it was going to fucking kill me. How is that different from how you feel about Alyssa being with Tyler?"

"I knew you weren't going to hurt Kimber," Luc hedged.

But did he really believe that Tyler would hurt Alyssa when he was trying so hard to guard her?

"Okay, forget this guy. What about Jack Cole? If Morgan was out of the picture, would you share Alyssa with Jack? He's a stand-up guy, and I'm pretty sure it wouldn't be the first time he'd had sex with her. Sure, it's been a few years—"

"Shut the fuck up," Luc growled.

The image of Jack Cole unleashing his challis and cuffs and commands on Alyssa was like running his guts through a meat grinder.

Truth was, he didn't want anyone else touching her.

"Okay." Deke held up his hands. "But take my word for it. When you've got feelings for a woman, jealousy comes with the territory." He stood as his wife approached. "Especially when the woman is beautiful. Everything okay?"

"Great." Then she frowned at Luc. "You all right?"

No. Leave it to Deke to throw the fact he felt more than lust for Alyssa in his face. What the hell was he supposed to do about it?

"Fine." He did his best to sound sincere . . . and knew he fell short of the mark.

"I have my next doctor appointment in a few weeks, and Deke will be out of town. Can you take me?" Kimber asked. "How much longer will you be here?"

A pity invitation, and he was desperate enough to grab it. Any small involvement with Deke and Kimber's baby was likely more than he'd ever have for himself, especially if he kept ignoring Emily and chasing Alyssa like a schmuck.

Bless Kimber for caring how he felt. He brought her close for a long hug. "I'd love to. I'm only here until Thursday."

"Oh, just a few days, then." She smiled. "That's great!"

Deke clapped him on the back and sent him a meaningful stare. "Make the most of them."

* * *

JUST after midnight, Alyssa shut the doors to Bonheur. A weight lifted from her shoulders. The evening had been a huge success, and everyone who'd come tonight said the food and service were spectacular. All wanted to come back, and she finally believed she had a future comprised of more than taking off her clothes for strangers. The evening really couldn't have gone better.

Except watching Luc with Deke and Kimber.

To say that the sexy chef still had feelings for his cousin's beautiful wife would be stating the obvious. He'd hugged her, looked into her eyes. The moment hadn't seemed sexual, but they were in public. And Deke supposedly didn't share anymore. Still, the embrace had unnerved Alyssa. Was the other woman the reason Luc couldn't give more of himself to her?

"You ready to go?" Tyler asked, hovering near her as he had all night.

"I'll take her home," Luc said, appearing behind her.

"It's my job." Tyler crossed his arms and donned his badass mien as tightly as he would leather pants.

Luc ignored him. Instead, he turned to her, face solemn. "I'd like to take you home. We should talk." She hesitated, and he pressed. "Please."

What did he want? If she went, she risked further heartbreak. But if she refused him, she'd never know. What if he wanted to renew their earlier argument? Or just have sex again. She winced.

"All right." She avoided looking at Tyler. "I packed up your things. They're in my foyer. Homer is expecting you."

At that, Tyler smiled. She also read the hurt on Luc's face. For her sanity, she had to sideline him to Homer's, but she should have done it when they were alone.

"Fine," he bit out.

Telling her that it wasn't fine at all.

"You sure you want to ride with him?" Tyler asked, clearly looking for any reason to get one up on Luc. "I can follow you, make sure he doesn't give you any issues."

She leveled him with a no-nonsense stare. "He's a chef, not a serial rapist. I'll be all right. We'll talk tomorrow."

Scowling, Tyler drifted closer, reaching for her. Luc was faster and closer, wrapping his arm around her waist. She ignored Tyler's not-so-silent curse.

Outside, she locked the restaurant's door and let Luc lead her to his SUV. His touch lingered at her waist, and she tried not to notice her quivering knees.

Once they were on the road and the beautiful night air sifted through her hair, she turned to Luc. "Spill it. What did you want to talk about?"

"Everything."

Alyssa had this niggling suspicion that Luc was going to try to talk his way back in her bed. And where he was concerned, she was so, so weak. Though she should give him brownie points for facing the conversation head-on, she really didn't know what to say that wouldn't lead to her admitting she had deep feelings for him and them undressed and entwined.

"I'm exhausted, and it's late," she begged off. "Can't it wait until tomorrow?"

"It shouldn't take me more than a few minutes to apologize."

She whipped her gaze around to him—and didn't say a word.

He swallowed, his long, dark hair whipping around in the night wind. He looked gorgeous, so capable and sensitive. She fell for him a bit more.

"Don't look shocked, please. I've had a few hours to think about what happened earlier. I was wrong to jump down your throat about your leaving this morning to be with Tyler. It's none of my business. You have a lot on your mind, and he works for you . . ." Luc shrugged. "I won't lie and say I like the way he looks at you. I have no doubt his thoughts are totally unprofessional. I also won't lie and say the thought of you with him doesn't make me crazy." Luc gripped the steering wheel tighter. "But that's between the two of you, and I have no right to interfere."

So he was past the anger and knew he'd pissed her off, and accordingly wheeled out an apology. But . . . "In other words, it's none of your business if I fuck Tyler, but you still think I am and will try not to growl at me about it?"

"It doesn't matter what I think. It's your life, and I have no right to tell you how to live it. I have four days and some change left here. I'd rather spend the time enjoying you than fighting with you."

"So let's put all the emotion behind us so we can fuck like rabbits for four days?"

God, why didn't he just slap her in the face instead of slowly stabbing her in the heart?

"I meant that you're right. I haven't been a monk since we first got together, and it's wrong of me to expect that you have no other life. I don't know whether you and Tyler have something going. I'm not passing judgment. All I'm saying is that I'd rather spend time with you, whatever we choose to do, than argue." He sighed, and shot an enigmatic dark stare at her. "You're a fascinating woman. I want to know you more."

Good guy or player? That was the problem. She didn't know Luc deep down. Either he was genuinely apologizing for allowing his misplaced jealousy to get the better of him or he was saying what he thought she wanted to hear, hoping that she'd be motivated to shed her clothes and spread her legs. Either way, he'd said nothing emotional . . . but this was the first time he'd pursued her. Could it lead somewhere?

"What I really wanted to hear was that you believed I didn't have sex with Tyler today."

Luc shrugged. "You don't owe me explanations."

"I don't," she agreed. "But I want to know what you really think."

It was probably pointless, but she couldn't stand him thinking she was the kind of woman who slept around.

He paused, seemingly lost in his thoughts, sorting through them. "You're too dedicated to your future to fuck away the afternoon the day *your* happiness opens its doors."

Tears hit her instantly. He got it. He got her! It was a start.

Alyssa bit her lip to hold it in. Damn exhaustion was making her weepy, and the shit had to stop.

She took a deep breath to compose herself. "Exactly."

"I'm sorry I put extra stress on you."

"I'm sorry I disappeared this morning. I should have left a note or something, explaining . . ."

What? That she'd been too overwhelmed by their time together and had lost her heart?

"That you were too keyed up?" he guessed.

It was as good an excuse as any. She nodded.

"I understand." He slanted a concerned frown to her. "Did you get any dinner?"

She sorted through her evening's events, then shook her head.

"Lunch?"

No, she'd been too busy making sure her appearance tonight was perfect to worry about food. "I skipped it."

"Breakfast?" He sounded incredulous.

Alyssa winced. She'd been curled up on her bed at Sexy Sirens, crying her eyes out.

"Damn it! You're not taking care of yourself. Did you sleep at all today?"

Because Lord knew Luc had made certain she didn't get any sleep last night.

Again, she shook her head.

A moment later, they pulled up in front of her house. He hopped out and rushed around his SUV to get her door.

Now that she'd been still for a bit, weariness crept up on her, and she stumbled out of the vehicle—into his arms. He brought her close, and she allowed herself to feel safety and warmth, pretend that she really mattered to him.

"That's it." He sounded fed up. "I know you're eager to throw me out, but you have to let me in to take care of you."

If she did that, she'd wind up naked with him again, letting him deep inside her body, deeper inside her heart.

"Luc . . ."

"You're not talking me out of it. Keys?" He held out his hand.

Alyssa wavered. How nice would it be to let Luc take care of her for a few minutes? She was always in charge of everything—had been since the day she left home. Right now, giving over her responsibility to him sounded like a ridiculously wonderful fantasy.

Fearing she would regret the decision but too tempted to care, she dropped her keys in Luc's palm.

Chapter Eight

As soon as Luc closed the keys inside his fist, he bent and swept her into his arms. She clung to his neck, and the masculine scents of pine, musk, and soap hit her system. It was a good thing he held her or her knees would have given way completely.

"Wh-what?" she sputtered. "What are you doing?"

He unlocked the door with one hand, shouldered his way in, and stopped her before the burglar alarm so she could disarm it. After the beeping stopped, he walked past her kitchen and stepped down to the den, depositing her on the downy-soft sofa. He lifted the quilt she usually kept across the back for chilly mornings and draped it over her legs.

"You okay?"

"More tired than I thought . . ." she mumbled. God, she wasn't even sure she could stay awake long enough to disrobe, even though sleeping in this dress would ruin it.

Groaning, she tried to push to her feet. Luc eased her back down.

Lacking the will to resist, she settled back into the cushions with a mutinous expression.

"You're not going anywhere."

"I have to change. Take off my makeup."

"Not right now, you don't. Give me five minutes. Just sit here that long. I promise to make it worthwhile."

She had no idea what he was up to and was too tired to argue. "'K."

As her eyes slid shut, she heard his footsteps retreat. The next thing she knew, Luc was gently shaking her.

"Alyssa?"

"Hmm." She'd fallen asleep on the couch while he'd . . . what? Watched?

Then the smell of food hit her, and her stomach rumbled in response. She opened her eyes to find eggs and toast and some fruit in yogurt on a plate beside her.

Before she could ask, he pulled the plate into his lap and sent her a stern glance. "You're going to eat. Furthermore, you're not going to go a whole day without eating or sleeping again. Now, open up."

Luc looked as if he meant business. Secretly, she was touched. Was the man trying to make her fall even more in love with him? Even in Tyler's most solicitous moments, he would never cook for her. He barely cooked for himself. And yes, this was Luc's profession, but the fact he'd done it after getting little sleep himself and being on his feet all evening melted her.

"I can feed myself." She reached for the fork.

"I'm sure you've been doing it since roughly your first birthday. But I'm at least partially to blame for your exhaustion and hunger. Let me."

She didn't agree with his assessment. She could have had someone at the club fix her a salad or could have found a few minutes to close her eyes, if she'd really wanted. She was a big girl. Yet Luc insisted on shouldering the blame.

Someday, he would make some woman seriously happy, and the fact it wouldn't be her nearly made her cry.

"Alyssa?"

Too tempted and tired to argue, she opened her mouth. Fluffy eggs with cheese and something spicy hit her tongue. Oh, then onions, tomatoes, and mushrooms so perfectly cooked they melted in her mouth. He followed with a buttery piece of toast, then a few spoonfuls of the yogurt and berry mix. Pure heaven.

"Why?" she asked between bites. "You're tired, too. Guilt?"

He paused, then lowered the fork and looked into her eyes. "I'm sorry if I upset you and ruined your day. But taking care of you isn't about guilt."

Insidious hope seared her. Alyssa opened her mouth to ask questions.

He placed his finger over it. "Shh. Not tonight. We'll sort it out tomorrow."

Luc was right. They weren't going to solve their problems or figure out what was between them while they were both this close to exhaustion. It wasn't in her nature to put off until tomorrow what should be done today, but she saw his logic. And wanted to live in this fantasy just a moment longer.

Nodding, she opened her mouth again, and he placed the next bite inside.

Once her plate was empty, he brushed her hair behind her shoulder, anchoring it behind her ear. "Still hungry?"

"What about you?"

"I ate before the dinner service. I'm fine."

Frustrating man wouldn't let her worry about him, but insisted on taking care of her. It was a guilty pleasure. Like eating ice cream, which she could never afford if she still wanted to fit into her clothes. But once . . . just this once, it was so damn delicious.

"Did you get enough to eat?" he asked.

Alyssa put her hand to her stomach. "Full."

He smiled tenderly, and her heart flipped. How easy it had been to fall in love with him . . . How foolish.

"Good." Luc helped her to her feet. When she wobbled, he looked down at her feet and frowned.

"What?" she asked.

Shaking his head, Luc bent to her and removed her shoes. *Ahhh . . .* The relief was nearly orgasmic. She hadn't realized how much her feet hurt. New shoes were the worst, but she'd gotten so tired later in the evening that the pain in her feet had ceased to register.

"That bad, huh?" Luc swore and lifted her against his chest once more.

"I can walk," she insisted.

He stared at her, and her gaze was snared by those dark, inscrutable eyes. "Yes, but you don't have to. Now, set the alarm."

As they passed the keypad, he stopped and allowed her to input the code. Once it was armed, he ensured the door was locked, then made his way up the stairs.

"I'm too heavy for this," she insisted.

Luc scoffed. "I once spent a summer hauling hundred-pound bags of grain up and down a loading dock, one bag on each shoulder. Carrying you around is a breeze."

Sweet liar. She smiled and closed her eyes, savoring his closeness and caring. God, this felt *so* good. But she had no doubt she'd pay for it tomorrow with every last bit of her heart.

* * *

LUC shifted, sinking deeper into a sublimely comfortable bed. Something smelled good, like peaches and cinnamon. *Hmm.* And a warm feminine body rested beside him, lax in a way only complete trust allowed. Experimentally, he moved a hand—and encountered a lush hip under his fingers.

His morning erection jumped from promising to demanding.

He opened his eyes and took in the pale walls, sheer curtains, shadows of late morning. Gorgeous platinum hair and soft, rhythmic breathing.

Alyssa.

Everything inside him tightened with arousal, anxiety, and confusion.

What the hell had happened yesterday? After they'd had mind-blowing sex, he'd crashed, then awakened abruptly once he'd realized Alyssa wasn't in bed beside him. She'd never picked up his calls to her cell phone, and his anxiety grew. When he'd tracked her down at Bonheur hours later, he'd found her in Tyler's arms. The switch for his possessive instinct had flipped on in a big way. He'd been nearly berserk with jealousy.

Luc didn't understand the instinct for several reasons. First, he hadn't lied when he'd said it seemed unlikely Alyssa had allowed her bouncer to fuck her that afternoon. It had taken Luc a while to reach that conclusion, but he knew it was true. Alyssa was too ambitious to risk Bonheur's opening for a piece of ass.

That still didn't ease his aggravation because he doubted their relationship was platonic. Tyler wouldn't stick around if he wasn't getting any, so likely, on any other day the bouncer would have had Alyssa naked and spread out for his pleasure.

Tightening his grip on her sleeping form, he tried to push the image away.

What Luc couldn't figure out was why he cared who Alyssa fucked. Thinking back through all his relationships in the last dozen or so years—most of them ménage—he'd never once felt an urge to grab the girl and keep her all to himself. Now he could hardly tamp down the impulse.

When you've got feelings for a woman, jealousy comes with the territory.

Feelings, Deke had suggested. And Luc had only a few days left to figure them out. Yesterday, she'd pulled away. He'd actually felt her putting distance between them. That reality had infused him with a vague panic he didn't understand. After this week, he'd likely never see Alyssa again. How could he fit her into his life when she didn't fit into the future he'd envisioned? Nothing about the way she looked or behaved said "mother material," especially her relationship with her own mom. And if he pursued Intracytoplasmic sperm injection or they went to a sperm bank, getting pregnant in her profession would be the kiss of death. Yes, she also had Bonheur, and she could be pregnant and run a restaurant . . . but she still spent a lot of time at Sexy Sirens. Besides, one look at her and artificial insemination was the last thing that came to mind. He didn't see any other option except to fuck her out of his system so that when he returned to East Texas, he could focus on Emily and his dreams of fatherhood.

Problem was, he actually *liked* Alyssa. As a woman. As a person. And whatever they had, it wasn't just sex.

Worse, last night, he'd gotten this odd pleasure in taking care of her. She worked so damn hard, fulfilling the needs of her businesses and her employees before seeing to her own.

Once he was gone, who would take care of her?

Tyler.

God, even the man's name burned like acid in his gut. He squeezed his eyes shut. Why the hell should he be so jealous of another man when he was the one lying naked beside her?

Because it's not going to last.

Shoving the ugly thought away, he propped himself up and looked at Alyssa's clock. Ten eighteen. Wow, they'd both been exhausted, sleeping a good nine hours plus.

Suddenly, she rolled over slowly and opened her eyes. Her lashes batted slumberously, her makeup smudged beneath her eyes. Rather than resembling a raccoon, she looked vulnerable.

Once she saw him, Alyssa glanced away, vague panic on her face. "What happened?"

Damn it, she was pulling away again, and all he wanted was that trusting warmth against him again, her arms around him, her lips raised to his.

He stroked her shoulder with a soothing touch. "Nothing. You were hungry and exhausted. Do you remember eating last night?"

Immediately, she flushed and nodded. "You fed me."

A smile touched his mouth. "Yes. Then I brought you to bed. You fell asleep halfway up the stairs."

She covered her face with her hands, then peeked one eye out. "Seriously?"

Luc nodded. "Dead asleep. You mumbled something about not wanting to ruin your dress just before you conked out, so I took it off and tucked you in."

Alyssa wriggled, blinked. "You took *everything* off."

"I didn't know what you usually slept in . . . and I like you this way."

Sighing, she rolled her eyes. "What time— Oh!" Glancing at the clock, she cursed. "We should be at Bonheur around twelve. I think the others will be there by two."

"Good. Then we have time."

"For what?" Her eyes narrowed suspiciously.

Her body was pressed close to his; she couldn't have any doubts that he wanted her badly. But her expression told him that sex wasn't first on her list, and he supposed she still had questions about yesterday.

"A proper breakfast, for one thing." His tone scolded her.

"And?"

"Whatever else happens."

She sat up in bed and wrapped the covers around her. The sheet hid her lush curves, even as it molded to them. Luc felt nearly dizzy with want.

"In the interest of saving time and bullshit, just answer one question. What is going on between us?"

That was direct. Luc actually admired her for having the guts to ask what she really wanted to, for not taking the easy way out.

"I don't know," he answered honestly. "I like you, I want you, and the thought of you with Tyler rips me to shreds. That's all I know."

She paused. "Uncharted territory for you?"

Luc nodded. He realized that, in all his "relationships," he'd never taken the time to really know a woman unless it suited his purpose. If there was an end to achieve, he figured the woman out enough to manipulate her response in his direction. With Alyssa, he wanted to know her because she fascinated the hell out of him.

"Me, too." She admitted. "I don't . . . do relationships."

He frowned. "You don't get emotionally involved?"

Alyssa raised her knees to her chest and curled her arms around them. "Trust is hard for me. I don't usually let men into my personal space." She tossed him a pointed glare. "This house is supposed to be my Zen retreat, hence the pale walls, the black-and-white nature photos, and water features. I come here to escape, not fuck."

If he was translating her right, she was claiming that she'd never brought another man here. What about Tyler and his house key? For protective purposes only? The fact she'd broken her rule for Luc twice said something about her feelings. The answering leap in his chest scared the shit out of him.

God, could he really fuck her out of his system in four days, or would he just fall in completely?

"Friends with benefits is as far as I ever go. So to actually give a damn at all is weird for me."

So she gave a damn about him. It wasn't huge emotion, but it was a start. Question was . . . where was it leading? He had no clue.

"Any reason you don't get emotional?" He knew from experience that emotion made the sex richer. It was one reason he always tried to feel something for his partners.

"I don't need complication, and happily-ever-after is bullshit.

Every night, I see lots of married men who would give their right nut to fuck me or one of the other girls, wife be damned." She sent him a sad smile. "You're here cheating on a girlfriend. I'm not stupid, Luc. I don't set myself up for heartache."

Had that been why she left yesterday morning without a word, because he'd gotten to her emotionally? And why did he like that thought so much?

"Where does that leave us?" he whispered.

"If we were smart, we'd end this now."

Not until he was good and ready. As miserable as she looked, he didn't think that was what she wanted, either.

So he leaned closer and brushed his mouth over hers. "I don't think I can be smart when it comes to you."

She gasped under his kiss, and he brushed his lips down her neck, letting the sound roll through him.

"Luc . . ." Alyssa put a hand to his shoulder.

He was certain she meant to push him away. Instead, she gripped his hair in her fist and pulled him closer, her lips feathering across his jaw, her teeth nipping at his ear.

A shiver racked him. God, what was it about this woman? Around her, he couldn't keep his head.

Or, he feared, his heart.

Alyssa raised to her knees above him and pushed him to his back. He went willingly, groaning when she ripped the sheet away from his body and fell on top of him, her mouth searing its way across his chest. She did those wicked little tricks with his nipples again, and damn if he wasn't already so hard he couldn't string a thought together.

When her hand drifted down his abdomen and her fingers circled his cock, he cried out.

"You like that?" she asked, all coy vixen as she stroked his length roughly.

"Fuck, yes."

"Everyone else thinks you're controlled. A great Southern gen-tleman." She laughed. "You're so not gentlemanly in the bedroom."

Again, she stroked him up and down, her grasp tight, her pace blistering. When her thumb brushed the crest of his cock, his back arched and his eyes flew wide. *Jesus!*

Alyssa redefined pleasure for him. Virtually every drop of blood in his body had pooled between his legs. The pressure was intense, and every stroke piled sensation on top of sensation.

Then she slid her way down his body.

"Not a good idea," he croaked.

But his hands delved into her hair, holding her between his legs. He guided her to his cock.

At the first touch of her mouth, need spiked. He gritted his teeth. "Oh, God."

Watch her; he had to. Luc didn't want to miss a moment of her mouth on him. She batted her lashes, her blue eyes alive and elec-tric, shocking him down to his core. That sweet red mouth opened, the plump lower lip the perfect resting place for his dick. Her tongue peeked out, swiping his head as if she licked a lollipop. Then she moaned and licked her lips—and he lost his mind.

"Suck it," he demanded. "Put my cock in your mouth and suck hard."

Instead, she raised a brow at him, then licked his balls, running a thumb up the length of his dick. Different sensations—ones that were like adding gasoline to the funeral pyre of his restraint.

"I don't take orders. If I suck you, it will be when and how *I* want."

His fists tightened in her hair. The woman was taunting him. Bad, bad move. His control was shot, body taut, teeth clenched as he tried to get it together. But she drew her tongue up his length again, grazing the sensitive crest with her teeth. He hissed in sizzling plea-sure. He'd never been one for the painful edge of desire before, but the way Alyssa delivered it . . . Damn.

Taking himself in hand, he guided his cock to her mouth.

"Suck it now," he snapped, his voice tight, strained. He'd apologize later. Right now he really needed to feel the wet silk of her mouth heating his cock to a fever.

The moment her tongue cradled his dick, Luc sucked in a sharp breath. The rush of sensation blistered its way through him, darting down his legs. Desire seared his entire body as Alyssa's head bobbed up and down. Gorgeous sight.

She took him to the back of her throat, then eased out with a suction so strong, Luc nearly lost his mind. Her tongue flirted across his head as her fingernails dug into his thighs. Desire swelled, rapidly pushing the limits of his endurance and control. It had taken her maybe thirty seconds to bring him to the edge. *Fuck!* His breathing short-circuited. He fisted his hands in her hair, trying to slow her down. Every flare of sensation and searing tingle worked against him. God, he couldn't last long like this.

No, he wasn't coming in her mouth. Her pussy. It had to be there. Very quickly, that had become his favorite place. As much as he loved her mouth and couldn't wait to explore her ass again . . . he needed to be deep inside the most female part of her, pounding her through multiple orgasms before he finally let go.

But first, he'd repay the brazen witch for her teasing.

Lifting her off his cock, he heard an audible pop when he left her mouth. She reached for him again, whimpering in frustration.

"I wasn't done," she growled.

"You are for now. My turn."

Anticipation scorched his system as he wrapped his arms around her and lifted her up past his hips, over his abdomen, raising her above his shoulders—and settling her thighs on either side of his face.

"Luc!" she protested.

He didn't bother answering her. The scent of her musky tang pierced his system and revved up his desire. Blood sizzled in his veins as he grabbed her hips and lifted his head, swiping his tongue through the wet folds of her pussy until he reached her clit. Wet, swollen, hard. *Perfect.*

When he sucked it into his mouth, she released a high-pitched, ragged gasp and clutched the headboard as if she needed serious steadying. Luc smiled and ran the flat of his tongue over her sensitive bundle of nerves.

"Oh, my— Oh . . . Luc," she panted. "That's so— Damn! It's fast. I can't—"

He scraped his teeth over her clit gently . . . with just enough pressure to prove to her that, in fact, she could. Right that instant.

Alyssa screamed in pleasure, and it was the sweetest sound. Her release filled him with primal need and a satisfaction unlike any other. He'd always insisted on leaving partners sated, but this was both gratifying and frustrating. Incredible . . . but not enough. Not nearly.

Cream flowed from her body, and he was thrilled. She'd need it later, no doubt. But now he wanted more on his tongue. Much more.

Holding her in place with one hand at her hip, he ran the other up the inside of her thigh, then pressed a finger inside her. Her heat enveloped him instantly, her flesh clinging, still rippling with the aftereffects of her climax.

"No more playing around. Just fuck me."

Not until she was good and ready. Not until he dismantled whatever wall she'd erected between them. Not until her body had completely surrendered.

Luc didn't bother with words. Instead, he slid two fingers into her pussy. Tight. God, every time he got inside her it was a delicious struggle he always looked forward to. Today would be even better because she was still swollen from their last encounter.

With a twist of his wrist, he finally submerged his fingers inside her. A few seconds and a bit of fondling later, he found that sensitive smooth spot that drove her mad and rubbed unmercifully as he set his mouth back on her clit.

She gasped, grabbing the sheets around her, her body bowing as she tried to absorb the sensations.

Against his fingers and tongue, he could feel her flesh grow more slick and swollen. Her breath began to catch; then she moaned.

"Luc. Oh, Luc. Please . . . It's too much. Too big. Oh!"

In that moment, he wanted to deliver the kind of pleasure that would devastate her, break her will to resist him ever again.

He rolled her clit around on his tongue like candy, swiping it from top to bottom, side to side. Her sleek thighs tightened, her fists on the headboard grew more frantic, and her folds swelled so beautifully. Luc pulled his mouth away for a moment to look at her. *Yes!* Her flesh throbbed, an angry red that demanded fulfillment.

She breathed a moment of relief—until that itchy, achy feeling caught up to her and made its demands known.

Then she whimpered. "Luc!"

"Don't want me to stop, do you?"

"No. Please, no."

That was all the cue he needed. Grinning, he settled his mouth around her clit once more and sucked in. With teeth and tongue, he worked her, scraping her with pleasure until her whole body tightened, then pulsed. She keened out a release that stripped her throat raw.

Satisfaction spiked through Luc. God, he loved a job well-done.

But he wasn't through with her yet.

He urged her down his body, spreading her legs wider with his knees, holding his waiting cock up with his other hand.

"Wait!" She sounded as though she was trying to catch her breath. "Condom? We . . . forgot last time."

He'd been too busy and overwhelmed to think of it.

Luc hesitated, then finally said, "I'm clean."

"I am, too, but not on birth—"

Surging up, he covered her mouth with his. No need to let her finish that sentence. Didn't matter, and he didn't want to think about it, much less confess his sterility. He probably should wear a condom with her . . . but taking Alyssa bareback was a sublime experience he couldn't forgo.

For a second, she struggled against the kiss, but he persisted, devouring her in a slow fire that soon had her meeting him, melting against him, her mouth every bit as hungry.

Burning up inside, he pushed her down the last few inches, onto his erection.

The slide in was a bit easier this time than last. Still a struggle. Still every bit as hot and devastating as he'd come to expect. The friction made him cross-eyed, ripped a moan from his throat. He gritted his teeth to hold himself together, especially when she gasped and grabbed his hair. Staving off all the sensation became doubly difficult when she writhed on top of him, ensuring that the head of his cock bumped her cervix. He couldn't be in deeper.

It was amazing. No, fucking amazing.

"That good, sugar?"

Alyssa whimpered her answer. He smiled. Then lifted her in a slow withdrawal.

As he thrust into his first stroke, pleasure burned his gut, gripped his cock. Totally overwhelming. He'd wanted this to be yearning and unforgettable. Now she'd overloaded him on desire and he just had to hope he didn't become a battering ram. She must come again. Despite his skyrocketing need, that wasn't negotiable.

Tightening his hands on her hips, he began to fuck her in deep, hard strokes, his entire body tightening, sizzling, with the feel of her all around him. One thrust after another, coming faster . . . faster. He couldn't get enough, feel enough. Being with her . . . The sex was so much more than just sex. Intense, incredible. Holding back the pleasure got more difficult with every lunge inside her lush body, especially as she tightened around him, gasping and mewling.

"Yes!" she cried in his ear as she brought her body flush against his. "Luc . . . Oh, God!"

Hearing her scream his name was killing his self-control. He wanted to lavish pleasure on her for hours, days. But the heat was combustive, burning him up with liquid fire. The pressure, the need, gnawed at his composure. Still, he vowed to take Alyssa with him.

Her breast bobbed in front of his mouth, and he took its tender tip in and sucked. She arched her back, pressing her nipple against his tongue.

Against her flesh, he whispered, "Come for me."

"Yes," she sobbed and clamped down on his cock.

He couldn't hold it in anymore. The base of his spine tingled. His balls tightened. Thankfully, Alyssa was with him, gripping him tight with her pussy, then milking him with hard pulses and desperate kisses across his face, her arms tight around his neck. Luc clung to her while he surged inside her as deep as possible and nudged her cervix.

For a greedy, unguarded moment, he imagined Alyssa wearing his ring, beside him in bed every night, in their house, with *his* child swelling her belly. The thought burst the damn of his self-control and orgasm crashed over him. The vision still dancing in his head, he exploded deep in her body.

After the last shudder, his brain kicked in. What a fucking ridiculous fantasy—for so many reasons.

As soon as Alyssa caught her breath, she slumped against him. Though he shouldn't, Luc reveled in the feel of their heartbeats chugging against each other, the lax, trusting drape of her body over his. He brushed a hand up and down her damp back, soothing.

"You okay, sugar?"

Her head snapped up, and she rolled off him to sit at the edge of the bed. "Fine."

She sounded more exhausted and confused, and he couldn't quite forget that the last words out of her mouth before he'd seduced her were to end whatever was happening between them.

Fat chance, especially now. Luc wasn't done with her. She wasn't out of his system. That sneaky vision of his fantasy future proved it. If anything, she was burrowed deeper, telling him that he'd have to work harder to get over her in three days. Already, his mind turned with ideas. He just prayed they worked.

* * *

INSIDE Bonheur, the kitchen staff bustled with the end of the dinner service. All evening, Alyssa had walked every square inch of the dining room and patio to ensure everything was perfect, her guests satisfied. She glanced at her watch. Less than ten minutes before the doors closed on her first real—and very successful—night of business.

Less than ten minutes left for Luc to keep poking his head out of the kitchen, tracking her down, and murmuring concerned questions about her well-being. His caring was going to be the death of her heart, and if he kept pushing . . . Alyssa didn't know what she would do.

She needed a few minutes to herself. Then she could face him again, armor in place. She hoped.

Closing the door to her office, she flipped on the light and exhaled. Luc just overwhelmed her. Everything about him was so . . . intense, demanding. He had a gentle side; she'd seen it. But something was riding him. He was pushing hard, but for what she didn't understand.

Sighing, she made her way to her new desk. If Bonheur did well, she'd move all her bookkeeping over here, her laptop, her files. She'd elevate one of the dependable dancers like Sadie to manager so she could spend more time here, with her happiness. She'd worked hard for success, to change her life. The thought of never having to take her clothes off in public again was deeply satisfying. And if she succeeded, she could say she'd done it on her own.

For a moment, Alyssa wondered what her mother would have thought of her accomplishments. Then realized that she would have lived in denial about Sexy Sirens and the stripping . . . and everything that had come before it. Good ol' Trisha had always had that Beverly Hills housewife knack for burying her head in the sand, especially if confronted with anything tawdry before her ten a.m. mimosa.

And it didn't matter. Her mom was gone, and her future was on track . . . mostly. Luc aside, Bonheur had done a great business this evening. It was a promising start.

Hope twisted inside her as she pulled her chair away from her desk, glanced down—and screamed.

Chapter Nine

WHORE. The word jumped out at her in big red letters on a stark white page stabbed into the seat of her leather office chair. *Shit!*

More words leapt off the page, swimming into her vision. Trembling, she leaned in, careful not to touch anything, and read:

> *You're fornicating with your chef. With this blade, I will ensure that you never tempt a man again.*

She shook. The sicko behind this meant business. No more pushing that frightening fact aside. This person was also eerily well informed about her relationship with Luc. A scorned woman didn't usually use these scare tactics. So, if the culprit wasn't a jealous female . . . who would do this to her? And why?

A moment later, Luc rushed in, took one look at her face, and grabbed her shoulders. "What is it?"

She pointed down to the chair. His stare followed. A moment

later, his expletives filled the room, and she shuddered. Violence suffocated the air in the small, windowless space. Someone had sneaked into her office this evening to threaten her. For the third time in as many days. Luc looked ready to kill.

"We've got to get to the bottom of this. Whoever is responsible is getting more sadistic and brazen."

Agreed. "I'll call Remy."

Luc scowled. "Is he doing anything to stop this creep? Making any headway in the investigation?"

"They don't even have the results from their investigation of my car yet, so . . ."

With another expletive, he looked back at the empty doorway. "What about Tyler?"

"He doesn't have any theories, either."

"No. I mean, have you thought that, maybe, he might be behind this?"

What? She'd hired Tyler to bounce people out of the club and protect her while she was there. He'd always gone above and beyond the call of duty, hovering overprotectively, putting off a possessive boyfriend vibe. It had worked, too. Since Tyler had come on board a few months ago, the incidences of walking into her office or bedroom at the club and being surprised by a naked man or a would-be rapist had decreased to almost nil.

"Tyler wouldn't do this."

"Who else would be this jealous of our relationship?"

In Luc's mind, were they having a relationship or just fucking?

Let's see . . . He's a famous chef, and, tender care last night aside, you're basically a whore to him. What do you think?

"Any number of people could have done this," she pointed out. "Like Primpton. You've seen what a head case he is. Or Peter. I heard he asked about me at the club last night and was pissed when he learned I hadn't come. Apparently he demanded that someone get me down there ASAP."

"Did you see either of them here tonight?"

She shook her head. "But I didn't see everyone who came. Or it could be someone I've never dealt with, who's just blended in to the club and made up some sick fantasy in his head that I belong to him. It hasn't happened to me, but I've talked to others in the business who say it happens."

"I think we should rule out the more obvious suspects first." Luc swallowed, a fierce, determined expression tightening his face. "I swear if I get my hands on the asshole doing this to you, the police will be lucky if there's enough left of him to identify by dental records."

Alyssa stared. Luc was that outraged on her behalf? Granted, he wouldn't like to see any woman threatened, but . . .

"This is crappy, but he hasn't actually done anything but threaten so far. Hopefully, he never does."

Luc's mouth pursed, and he sent her a grim stare. "I wouldn't bet on that. He's coming for you. Soon. Call Remy. He needs to make this a priority."

Tyler skidded to a halt in the doorway. "Sorry. I was in the can." His gaze bounced back and forth between the two of them. "What the fuck is going on?"

Was it even possible Tyler had it in for her because she'd refused to sleep with him? Was he weirdly obsessed?

Alyssa dismissed the thought almost instantly. He'd done nothing but help her, see to her safety. He'd had a million opportunities to be alone with her and he'd done nothing to hurt or endanger her.

But who else knows for certain that you're having sex with Luc?

"See for yourself," she finally said to her bouncer, then stepped away from the chair. She'd watch his expression, see if he looked surprised . . . or menacing.

He rounded the desk, looking slightly uncomfortable and out of place in a white dress shirt partially unbuttoned and a loose burgundy tie. He'd ditched his suit coat long ago in deference to the heat.

Tyler peered into the chair, stiffening when he saw the note. He scooted closer to read it, then swore profusely. "I'm going to kill this son of a bitch if I get my hands on him."

"You and Luc both. Great. You'll both go to prison for vigilante murder and leave me alone to face the next scum bucket."

Her chef and her bouncer looked at each other, clearly hard-pressed to believe they'd agreed on anything.

"Get Remy on the phone," Tyler demanded. "I want to talk to that lazy Cajun."

"Does he always fail to do his job?" Luc asked.

Alyssa answered before Tyler could. "He's not used to this much trouble from me. He's big into stopping drugs, gangs, and vandals. People he can pound. He's not so great with investigating."

"I'm going to fix it," Luc declared, reaching for the cell phone in his pocket as he headed for the office door.

"Who are you calling?" she asked after him.

He didn't answer.

Muttering under her breath about difficult men, she followed.

"Where are you going?" Tyler demanded of her.

Apparently interested in the answer, Luc turned and stared, blocking the doorway.

The testosterone overload in the little room could seriously go to her head. She could bottle it and women everywhere would pay oodles to feel this ridiculously feminine.

Shaking off the thought, she peered around Luc, down the shadowed hallway, frustrated at the lack of view. "I need to say good-bye to the last of my guests, see them to the door, thank them for coming."

"I'll do it." Luc's offer was more like a demand. "Stay here and call Remy."

"They're *my* guests!"

"They ate *my* food. I'm not playing at semantics when your safety is on the line." Then he turned to Tyler and threw a mean glare the bouncer's way. "Keep her here and guard her. I swear to God if you ruffle a hair on her head, I will split your skull in two and flambé your brain while your heart is still beating."

Tyler grunted. "Notice how none of this shit happened to Alyssa until *you* showed up? Everything was fairly peaceful before you leapt into her life and fucked it all up."

"You get too jealous? Can't stand to see me with her?" Luc challenged.

Oh, dear God. "Can you two refrain from beating the crap out of each other for the next ten minutes? Let's get the doors closed and locked. When the parking lot is empty, you can go out there and have your pissing match."

Luc's gaze touched her; then he glared darkly at Tyler. "I'll be back."

When he'd gone, Tyler's disapproval reverberated through the resulting tense silence. "I don't get it. If you push him out of the fucking door, the threats go away."

"Maybe. Maybe not."

He shook his head. "Probably. But you let him stay. In your house. In your fucking bed! I've only worked for you a few months, but it's not like you to start a fling or wear your heart on your sleeve. Do you . . . love him?"

The question blindsided her. When had Tyler ever really talked about feelings? Almost never, at least before Luc came to town. Was he actually jealous?

Alyssa hesitated. She thought of lying. But if he wanted to hurt her, punish her, why hadn't he done it already?

Finally, she forced herself to look him right in the eye and whisper, "Yes."

* * *

LUC plastered on his most winning smile as he helped the last of Bonheur's patrons out the door. He nodded, smiled, signed autographs, inching them ever closer to the exit. Finally, at just past eleven, he shut them out and locked up, then palmed his phone.

Without hesitating, he dialed his cousin's number. Deke picked up on the first ring.

"What's wrong?"

"How do you know something is?"

Deke snorted. "You'd never call this late if everything was great."

Good point. Nothing was great right now.

Luc sighed. "Whoever broke into Alyssa's club has threatened her—more than once. Tonight, he broke into Bonheur and threatened her again. The locals seem either incapable or unwilling to get to the bottom of this. I need your help."

"I'm leaving on an assignment day after tomorrow. I'll stop in tomorrow with Jack, since I have to confer with him now that he's back. I'll see if I can bring Kimber's brother with me."

"Which one?" Luc swore under his breath. Neither had approved of his brief relationship with their sister and his cousin—and made no effort to hide it.

"Hunter."

Luc swore again. Logan, the younger, was a mean bastard with a temper a mile wide, but he could be reasoned with . . . eventually. Hunter was cold, calculating. Crafty. And as communicative as a brick wall. There would be no talking him out of his dislike.

"Jack and I are trying to convince Hunter to leave the navy. We could use someone like him on our team."

"What can he do here? I need someone able to investigate who's behind these threats."

"Hunter is one of the best. Trust me. You don't have to like each other, just know he's going to solve the issue."

From everything he'd heard, when Hunter was on a mission, he was relentless and cagey. "Whatever keeps Alyssa safe."

"We'll be there before noon so you can brief us."

Luc disconnected the call. Alyssa would not like this; Deke, Jack, and Hunter would insist on controlling her surroundings and re-stricting her movements, but Luc wanted her safe. Period.

When he returned to the little office, Tyler was reaming Remy a new asshole on the phone. Luc almost liked him for it.

Alyssa looked up at his return. "Make him release me."

She held up a wrist shackled to a desk drawer by handcuffs.

Luc turned to Tyler. "You carry those on you?"

The bouncer smiled. "She was going to ditch out and say good night to her guests, then head to Sexy Sirens."

"Like hell!" Luc exploded. Did she have no concept of the fact that if this sick bastard got his hands on her, he'd likely rape her at best, or perhaps torture and kill her?

"I was going to take Tyler, at least until he turned traitor on me. But I have to get to the club. Sadie called and one of the girls showed up stoned. No one can fire her but me. Besides, it's Saturday night, our busiest night of the week. The girls can handle things for one night, but not two in a row."

Luc saw her point, but her business wasn't as urgent as her safety. "The only place we know this freak hasn't invaded is your house. You need to be there. Call the girl who's using and fire her over the phone. Tyler can head over there, be your eyes and ears, but you're not putting yourself in danger."

"It's my club. I can't afford to shirk my responsibility because you don't like it."

His eyes narrowed. "You're *not* going."

If Alyssa had had both hands free, Luc had no doubt she'd tear his head off. "You're not my husband or boyfriend. You said yourself that we're just fucking, so you're not going to stop me."

"I'm not arguing this. What did Remy say?"

Tyler filled him in on a conversation that was a whole bunch of blah, blah, blah as far as Luc was concerned. Bottom line: Legally speaking, other than some vandalism and a little B & E, the culprit hadn't done anything arrest-worthy.

Luc couldn't contain his curse. He'd deal with the lazy sheriff later. For now, he had about twelve hours to keep Alyssa safe. Then Deke, Jack, and Hunter would show up and nail this psycho, and he could concentrate on proving to Alyssa they were more than fucking . . . even if he didn't yet know what.

"Typical Remy." Alyssa shrugged. "Since you pea-brained men are going to sideline me from running my business tonight, will you at least let me hit the bathroom before we leave? I need to change out of my dress."

Luc looked at Tyler, who looked back at him. The silent communication on both parts seemed to ask where she could possibly go without a car. Certainly, she wasn't dumb enough to walk the six blocks to Sexy Sirens near midnight with a stalker chasing her.

"Sure." Tyler finally got to his feet, fished the cuff key out of his pocket, and released her. "Nothing funny."

Alyssa shook her wrist and glared at them both. "Wait here."

* * *

FIVE silent minutes passed. Luc grew antsy, but women and changing clothes . . . He knew from experience that wasn't always a short process. Especially someone who wore stockings and garters and those fuck-me shoes. It all took time. Besides, he and Tyler hovered near the restaurant's front door with an eye on the bathroom hallway. Alyssa had nowhere to else to go.

But Tyler started tapping his thumb on one of the chairs, looking as jumpy as Luc felt.

"If you break her heart, I'll fucking kill you," Tyler proclaimed suddenly into the silence.

"What's between Alyssa and me is none of your business."

Tyler stood, rising to his full height, perhaps a half inch taller and thirty pounds heavier. "Yeah? What's between Alyssa and me is none of your fucking business, either."

Luc gritted his teeth, loath to admit that the other man was right.

"And when you're gone," Tyler went on, "I'll still be here. With her. Every day. Every night. You may be the shiny new toy now, but she'll get over you. I'll help her."

Though he wasn't surprised by Tyler's words in the least, they were like a stab in the heart. To hear his suspicions—fears—about the bouncer's relationship with Alyssa all but spelled out hurt like hell.

He swallowed Tyler's assertion, digested it. In another few minutes, Sunday would begin. Luc had to leave no later than Thursday morning so he could be in L.A. on Friday to conclude final negotiations for his cable cooking show. He also had a cookbook past due, and his editor was probably wondering why the hell he wasn't answering his e-mails.

But even if he could stay, what would he say to Alyssa?

No matter what route he took to fatherhood, he couldn't achieve it without a woman in the picture. Even if Alyssa supported his decision to adopt or undergo surgery or visit a sperm bank, she'd have to agree to go through the process with him, perhaps carry a child. And they'd have to find a way to make their passionate, difficult relationship work.

What kind of mother would she be? Certainly not like his own. And that presumed she even wanted to have children. After trying to warn him this morning that she wasn't on birth control, Luc was fairly sure that motherhood wasn't on her agenda anytime soon. That didn't change the fact the felt something deep and new for her.

So fucking complicated.

Still, he couldn't just leave her to Tyler. "I'll be doing my best to make sure she can't get over me."

Tyler growled at him. "Are you that fucking selfish that you want her heart broken after you're gone? Do you like the thought of seeing her unhappy?"

No. But Luc didn't think Alyssa had many feelings for him that weren't tied to orgasm. And he hated the thought that she likely had the same feelings for Tyler.

"Where the hell is she?" Luc changed the subject and paced, wishing he could hold her now. He needed her, like, five minutes ago, couldn't wait to get her back into her big bed, slide into her body, and forget about everything that was so wrong between them.

Tyler shrugged.

Luc glanced at his watch, then the bathroom door. "Fifteen minutes to change clothes?"

The bouncer glanced at his watch, too, his anger melting into a frown. "It's been that long?"

Yes. And he knew precisely why. "Is there a window in the bathroom?"

Tyler hesitated, body still, mind racing. "Fuck!" He broke into the bathroom with a shoulder to the door. "She bolted."

Luc ran out Bonheur's door. Behind him, Tyler did the same, barely taking the time to lock up.

"Goddamn her. I swear, she doesn't know the meaning of the word 'spanking,' but she will when I'm done with her," her bouncer snarled.

And when Luc was done? She'd know better than to ever disobey him again when he was feeling edgy and protective.

* * *

A few minutes later, Luc stormed into the club, Tyler right behind him. Alyssa wasn't surprised they'd found her quickly. She *was* surprised by how incredibly pissed Luc looked.

"You've got trouble," Sadie pointed out, nodding in the men's direction.

Though it was hard to take someone seriously wearing a thong and pasties, Alyssa couldn't discount the dancer's observation. Her heart raced as if she'd danced two hours straight.

"I'll be upstairs. If either asks, direct them to my office."

"Tyler will know better, but okay." Mouth curling up in a playful smile, Sadie nodded. "You know they're only going to be more angry when they find you."

Alyssa shrugged. "It's going to be a screaming match, no matter what. Thanks again for picking me up at Bonheur so I could let acidhead Jessica go before she made a mess of her act."

"Causing mayhem among the male population is always my pleasure."

Tonight, Alyssa couldn't deny she'd done that, too. Sneaking up the stairs, she eased herself into her bedroom, changed out of her dress, into a short skirt, half shirt. She tugged into thigh-high stiletto boots in red, wondering if they'd be like waving a cape in front of a bull's face when Luc found her, but she sensed she didn't have time for stockings and garters, so this would have to do.

Before she could leave and make her rounds downstairs, Tyler kicked in her door. She looked behind him for Luc. But he was alone. So, Sadie had been right. Luc had believed the other dancer, while Tyler hadn't. Trouble was coming in a one-two punch tonight.

"Goddamn you!" He stormed across the room, and she stood to meet him.

At the fury boiling in his eyes, she backed up. Whatever this expression was on his face, it was beyond normal concern and annoyance. His entire body was taut, wired to explode. A quick dip of her gaze proved he was hard everywhere.

"Tyler," she tried to reason with him. "Stop there. You know you can't—"

"*You* can't! Don't hire me to fucking keep you safe, then run off by yourself when there's danger."

"Sadie picked me up and drove me over here," she placated.

Diffusing his anger was critical. And he was having none of it. He kept coming forward. Prowling toward her. Alyssa stood her ground, refusing to back up any more.

Suddenly, he was against her, panting in her face. He grabbed her by the hair and tugged. Fury and desire were stamped all over his face, and her heart stopped.

"Tyler, n—"

His lips crashed over hers, smothering her protest. She tried to turn away, but he only tightened his grip on her hair and nudged her lips apart with her own. His tongue slipped inside, and still she resisted.

Air. And sanity. She needed both now. Damn it, she refused to be mauled by someone she considered a friend. She had to find a way to pierce his anger.

After examining her limited options, she bit his tongue.

He broke the kiss and backed away. "Fuck me!"

"Not today," Luc growled and charged toward Tyler. "Get your fucking hands off her! Are you the one threatening her?"

"That's it. I'm pounding your pansy ass for asking such a stupid question."

Alyssa stepped between them. They would not fight in her bedroom. "Stop it. Now."

Tyler looked at her, then Luc, before settling his gaze on Alyssa. "We'll talk about this later."

"We will," she vowed. He couldn't possibly think that behavior was acceptable. He'd never lashed out at her, never kissed her like that, against her will. What the hell had gotten into him?

Jealousy. The same expression dominated Luc's face. Her gorgeous chef barely spared Tyler a scowl as the bouncer left the room, slamming the door behind him.

Shutting her alone with Luc in the room. He reached out and, with a single *click*, locked the door. Then he took one look at her cleavage shoved together by the tight white top, barely held together by a little white button, and cursed. His glance scraped over her short black skirt and sexy red boots. Fresh fury crossed his face. Like Tyler, his body was hard—everywhere. Unlike Tyler, if Luc touched her now, she'd go up in flames. And no way was he using sex to manipulate her or curb her independence.

"I was completely safe the whole time. I would never endanger myself. I had a ride from Sadie. I know some self-defense and have pepper spray in my purse."

Luc snorted. "You'd never be safe against a man who could do this."

One minute he was standing three feet in front of her. The next he was invading her personal space, picking her up, shoving her against the wall, and slamming his mouth over hers.

Alyssa wanted to be strong. Really, she did. But Luc had the most amazing effect on her. She couldn't stop herself from opening to him.

The flavor of his kiss, the intensity . . . She didn't feel assaulted when he ravaged her mouth; she felt desired. When he cupped her jaw and groaned, she felt needed. When he ripped the top from her body and wrenched away her bra, she felt shivery and out of control. And she felt his possessiveness down to her marrow. None of that should have made her eager or wet . . . but this was Luc. Everything he did made her want him.

As soon as her torso was bare, he bent to her breasts and sucked them into his mouth, one after the other, hard. She arched toward him, burying her fingers in his silky dark hair. Under his onslaught, her nipples spiked as he feverishly worshipped them.

Blood hummed in her body, and she shifted her hips restlessly, pressing against him, inviting him inside. With Luc, she had no shame; never had. Whatever it took to entice him. Yes, she was furious. And she'd read him the riot act later and make it clear there was no way she'd ever let a man control her. But she couldn't stop him now. His need matched her own, as if they both sensed events speeding out of control and their time together ticking away.

"No more evading me," he gasped as he tore his mouth away, his lips harsh and open as he breathed roughly. "No more being alone with Tyler."

"He wouldn't have hurt me."

Something flared in Luc's eyes. "Maybe not, but he would have fucked you. And goddamn it, I don't share anymore. As long as I'm here with you, you don't give that sweet body to anyone but me."

The words rolled around her brain, both pleasing and disturbing. Before she could process her feelings and respond, Luc felt his way under her skirt and ripped her thong, tossing it to the hardwood floor, then rubbed a finger along her cleft, right over her distended clit.

Sensations pounded her immediately, making her weak-kneed. God, what this man did to her . . . Moments after touching her, she turned dizzy. Her fists clawed uselessly at the wall. An uncomfortable, undeniable need to submit rolled through her. As much as she resented his power over her, she couldn't help it.

"That's it," he crooned. "So wet. Always wet."

Luc plunged two fingers into her pussy. For him, she was always ready. Despite being swollen from all the recent activity, she melted, completely ready for whatever he demanded of her.

He couldn't possibly imagine she was this ready for anyone else. "Tyler doesn't—"

"Not another word about him," Luc roared, penetrating her deeply with a third finger.

She gasped at the fullness, then again when he rubbed her G-spot mercilessly.

"No more Tyler, period. I watched him kiss you . . ." He drew in a deep breath, as if trying to get himself under control.

"Luc . . ."

"No! As long as I'm fucking you, damn it, you don't fuck him."

His words finally pierced her haze of pleasure.

"What are you saying? I can resume my torrid affair with him as soon as my door hits your ass?"

More deep breaths. His chocolate eyes darkened to something nearly black. Dangerous. His cheeks flushed and his expression tightened as he grabbed her hips in a biting grip. Furious and aroused, he looked like a warrior ready to fight, to stake his claim.

God, she wished he'd stake his claim on her permanently, not simply try to hoard her until he left in three days. Was she anything to him beyond a great lay?

He didn't reply, just slanted his mouth over hers again and kissed her with a ferocity that stole her breath. Alyssa tried not to lose herself, but he pressed against her and her mind jetted away in a stream of relentless desire. A moment later, he bent and scraped her nipple with his teeth. She arched and cried out.

"Spread your legs."

Alyssa hesitated. She knew where this was headed . . . but she also knew their time together was limited. Her fantasies of making him fall for her in a week had been wishful thinking. He was leaving soon, and she couldn't stop him. The best she could hope for was to store up memories.

Closing her eyes against bittersweet desire, she complied. He nipped at her other breast with his teeth, then scooped up her legs, one in each arm, and pinned her firmly to the wall. An instant later, his cock probed her folds. She barely had time to wonder when he'd unfastened his slacks before he plunged deep inside her, past swollen tissues and resistance, guided by her wet need and his seeming instinct to conquer.

He probed her for torturous moments, sliding in with toe-curling friction. Panting, Luc finally worked himself balls deep inside her. Now that her wet flesh surrounded him and he had control of their encounter, he trapped her with a wrenching glare.

"God knows, I can't stop you from fucking Tyler again once I'm gone, if that's what you want, but now . . . You're all mine, and I'll make sure you know exactly who's making you scream."

"I don't fuck him," she confessed in a gasp, done playing coy games. "I never have. I hired him for protection. That's it."

Luc sucked in a breath, looking torn. Then he shook his head. "It doesn't matter."

Because they were only fucking. Right . . . His refusal to care about her wasn't really about Tyler; her bouncer was just a convenient excuse. That fact crushed something inside of her.

At the same moment, he sent her body soaring.

Reaching under her thighs, he curled his hands around her hips and pushed up, then plunged back down so fast and deep, her nails bit into his shoulders.

"Luc!"

Electric need sizzled across her skin, bubbled in her blood. He set a lightning-fast pace that had her gasping. His hips pressed against hers, creating a friction on her clit that blew away thoughts, objections, regrets. As soon as the feeling flooded her clit, the ram of his cock through her sensitive channel sparked her desire again until she could no longer catch her breath.

The explosion hit her bloodstream like dynamite—sudden and devastating. She screamed his name, then bit into his shoulder, clamping down on him like nothing she'd ever felt.

"More," he demanded, not missing a beat.

Then he pressed his mouth into hers again, sinking into an endless kiss that hit her in the heart, a mating of mouths that overtook her completely. She didn't know where she ended and he began, and she didn't care. She just knew that she'd given some part of herself to him irrevocably.

And he'd be leaving in a handful of days and would never look back.

The thought skittered away when he jerked away from the wall, holding her body against him, then turned toward the bed. He bent to ease her onto the mattress and slammed deep inside her, all in one motion.

"Spread wider. Bend your knees. Take me deeper."

His voice was almost an unrecognizable growl. He gave her no time to comply before he wrapped his hands around her thighs and opened her to him even more. She moaned as he sank deeper. God, perfect. Luc always knew exactly how to steal her control.

Her limbs heavy, her thoughts scattered, delicious pleasure built in her body again. Urgent pressure filled her clit again as he continued to penetrate deep with every long, hard stroke. Soon she was gasping, constricting around him, nearly bursting with feverish need.

He took her hips in his hands and pushed her down onto his cock as he thrust up. Hard. Directly at the mouth of her cervix. His hips ground against hers and, oh, dear God, the gathering storm swelled inside her, growing beyond her ability to absorb it.

Before she could release, he withdrew, flipped her to her hands and knees, then rammed home again, barely missing a beat. He smacked her ass, leaving behind a hot sting that had her gasping. Then Luc draped his damp chest over her and wrapped one arm around her body. Then he began to torment her clit.

"Does Tyler do this for you?" he whispered against her ear as the explosion brewing inside her gathered, lengthened, multiplied.

His fingers left her clit, and she cried out in protest. He nipped at her neck, eased away, then sank his cock into her pussy at the same time he plunged his wet fingers into her ass.

Sensations sparked as Luc swore and plunged into her again. Alyssa pushed back against him, countering each pounding thrust with her own demand.

A million tingles lit her up like a lightning storm. Orgasm shot from her clit to her toes.

"Oh, God." Alyssa fisted her hands in the sheets and whimpered.

Luc moaned as his climax neared. The sound vibrated through her, making her nipples tingle, her body shudder. His fingers twitched, his cock pulsed, pushing her over the edge again. Rapture crashed and writhed, ripping away her sanity, as the cataclysm coalesced inside her. She screamed with a pleasure so brutal her mind emptied, her throat went numb, and her world nearly went black. A moment later, his seed splashed hotly inside her.

Damn, they'd forgotten a condom again.

Alyssa closed her eyes. She couldn't think about it now. She couldn't think about anything—except the fact Luc had ruined her for any other man and he continued to allow her nonexistent relationship with Tyler to drive a convenient wedge between them.

She had to be the one to stop it. Now. Alyssa couldn't keep "just fucking" him. He'd shatter her heart.

Without waiting for him to move, she wriggled away and, on wobbly legs, stood. Without a word, she crossed the room and searched her drawers for a fresh bra and new shirt, all the while feeling Luc's intent gaze on her.

And the more she thought about this encounter, the angrier she got.

Getting out of this room *now* wasn't a choice but a necessity. She had to think. Alone. Before he clouded her thoughts and made her yearn again. Right now, she felt like a stupid, spineless bimbo. How could she let him have such control over her body when she clearly meant so little to him? What they shared was like a living flame, hot and destructive. She couldn't stand in the middle of the fire and not expect to get burned.

Turning to him, she clutched her clean clothes over her chest, teeth gnashed. "That's it, Luc. That's . . ." She broke off, refusing to cry in front of him. "No more."

"Alyssa, I—I'm sorry. I was angry and I . . ." he croaked into the silence, standing anxiously with pants fastened and shirt buttoned. "Did I hurt you?"

"You think?" she tossed back sarcastically. "This is just a contest to you. Tyler doesn't do *anything* to or for me, and you refuse to believe that. Not that it really matters. You don't want me for yourself, but you don't want him to have me, either. You've chosen to make me the bone between two snarly dogs, not because I'm meaningful, but because you don't have to deal with whatever you might feel for me if you can convince yourself that I'm a whore who's banging some other guy. I won't put up with this shit anymore."

"That's not true. You make me feel things for you that I . . ."

He raked his hands through his hair, looking for words. *Excuses,* she thought. No more.

"Can it. I don't fucking care. I'll have Sadie bring me home around four. You'd better not be there. Since Bonheur and Sexy Sirens are both closed on Sundays, don't make me lay eyes on you until Monday's dinner service. Even then? Don't talk to me. And don't ever touch me again."

Luc didn't say a word as she disappeared into the bathroom. His silence broke her heart all over again. Tears stung her eyes like acid drops. She knew what she'd said, but a part of her wished he cared enough to fight for her. Apparently not. Ridiculous, wishful thinking. She'd learned fairy tales were shit at fifteen. How had she forgotten that valuable lesson?

After cleaning up, she dragged on a new thong and brushed her hair, marveling at the flushed, swollen-lipped woman in the mirror. She'd finally fallen in love for the first time in her life. What a miserable fucking experience.

Turning away from the mirror, she breezed past Luc and headed for her bedroom door. He stood in her way.

"I'm sorry if I hurt you. Don't do this." A battle raged on his face, and he looked both uncertain and contrite.

"Do what? Be smart? Did you plan to ever see me again after Thursday?"

Guilt tightened his face. He looked away. "No."

Pain swelled inside her all over again. "I've been through too much to be your doormat. Since you're so eager to cast me in the role of slut . . . forgetting me should be a snap."

With that, she slid past him and stomped out the door. As soon as she cleared the bedroom, the tears began to fall in earnest. Never again. After he left, she could never again lay eyes on that man. Be alone with him. He'd already crushed her, and she'd crumble at his feet. Beg for his affection.

Damn it, she refused to put herself in a position to be tempted to grovel for anything, especially from someone who didn't value her.

She barreled down the hall, to the stairs, hiding behind the wall of props as she made her way backstage.

"Alyssa?"

She heard Sadie call to her—and she couldn't respond now. She held up a hand and ran to her office where she opened the door, slammed it, locked it, then flipped on the lights.

Closing her eyes against tears, she felt her way to her chair and collapsed in it. A moment and a sniffle later, she opened her eyes to reach for a tissue.

Peter stood there—and he looked beyond pissed.

Chapter Ten

Luc stared at the closed door of the bedroom. He could still hear the slam reverberate in his head.

Her anger had been tangible—and well deserved.

Swiping a hand down his face, he felt exhaustion seep into his bones. Yet . . . deep inside, he itched, wanted, yearned. It had taken everything inside him to be honest about their future and let her walk away.

Seeing Tyler's mouth on Alyssa's had wrung his guts inside out. The beast inside him had screamed, lurching to life, demanding her body and submission. And anything else she'd give him. He couldn't even put a name to everything he needed from her. But it wasn't good-bye.

Yes, she'd let Tyler kiss her, but Luc knew that, of the two of them, he'd fucked up more. After tonight, after losing control with her, he deserved whatever she threw at him.

Now that Alyssa had gone, he had to confront the most basic

question rolling around in his head: Why did jealousy get the best of him whenever he thought for a moment that she might have another lover? He couldn't stay. Why did he take his frustration out on her sexually?

Because you're falling for her, and that scares the hell out of you.

He staggered to the bed, then sank down. Was that even possible? Could he really have fallen for her in a matter of days?

They had as many arguments as they did sexual encounters, both heated. But Alyssa was so much more. Determination, grit. Kind to the other girls. Smart. Pragmatic and unafraid . . . except that vulnerable side she'd let him glimpse only once or twice. There was a part of her she kept hidden that he was dying to know. Everything about her fascinated him. Despite being in a flashy business, Alyssa was so . . . real. More real to him, in fact, than any of his previous lovers.

But she didn't fit in the future he had planned.

Since she wasn't his exclusively and never would be, he had to stop acting like a jackass, even if it killed him. She'd demanded that he leave her in peace until he departed Lafayette. Somehow, he would. It was for the best, and he owed her that. He'd just have to figure out how to forget her. Or learn to live with the open wound.

A moment later, someone pounded on the door. Wincing, he trudged across the room and pulled the door open. Tyler.

Luc had no idea what to think about the man. On the one hand, he acted with the familiarity of Alyssa's lover. The guy had to be one of her friends with benefits, right? But Alyssa had sworn that Tyler wasn't. Luc wanted to believe her so badly.

"Where is she?" Tyler took at the rumpled bed, at Luc's disheveled appearance, at Alyssa's ripped garments strewn across the floor. Then he gritted his teeth. "Goddamn it, did you hurt her? Where the fuck is she?"

How the hell did he answer that? "I didn't hurt her physically."

"But you broke her heart, you sanctimonious bastard."

Tyler hauled back, making a meaty fist. Luc saw it coming a mile away and did nothing. The right cross was a killer, and his head slammed back and pain seared its way through his head, rattling his brain.

He rubbed his sore jaw and glared at Tyler. "If it's any consolation, the minute she left, it was like being hit by a semi. She barreled over me, and I feel like roadkill."

"Good. Alyssa puts on a damn good front, but deep down, she's fragile. She doesn't show her emotions to anyone, but since you came here, she's been wearing them all over her face. And she looks fucking desolate."

Luc hung his head. He'd treated her like a whore, had sex with her to get her out of his system, accused her of sleeping around. He'd been astounded by her intelligence. It had never occurred to him that a stripper could complete advanced degrees. With any other woman, he would simply have admired her accomplishments, not been shocked. He'd all but forced his way into her body and tried to push his way into her heart with no intent to stay around and give himself back to her.

He deserved every bit of his broken heart and more.

"It won't happen again."

"Damn straight!" Tyler snarled. "I love that woman, and you shit on her. Do you know how hard it's been to stand back and watch?"

Incredibly difficult, Luc was certain. He hadn't liked Tyler kissing her, but if he'd been sidelined while being forced to watch another man seduce and mistreat her, he would have gone completely insane and ripped the bastard's head off. Suddenly, he admired Tyler's restraint.

"At this point, I can only say I'm sorry. I'll cook and keep to myself until I leave Thursday."

"Do that. But now we have to find Alyssa. Sadie saw her running backstage a few minutes ago, bawling her eyes out."

Luc closed his eyes. He'd thought he couldn't feel worse. Wrong.

Knowing he'd hurt her—again—was like dragging a sharp, rusty blade through his heart.

Tyler got in his face, clearly not finished with his tirade. "And after we find her, it's open season, asshole. If you cause her another instant of pain, I'm going to enjoy ripping you apart with my bare hands."

Normally, Luc didn't take threats well. This . . . He just nodded. "When she left, did she say where she was headed?"

"No." She hadn't said anything at all.

Tyler hesitated, jaw clenched. "Peter was in the guest area around the stage fifteen minutes ago. He didn't leave; he's not in the john—but he's MIA. So is Alyssa."

Fear jolted Luc from his stupor. He bolted toward the door. "We need to find her."

Giving him a curt nod, Tyler sprinted out of the room and down the stairs, Luc on his heels.

"Could Sadie tell where she was going?"

The bouncer shook his head. "She's checking some of the guest areas now, to make sure Alyssa isn't mingling. We'll check her office."

She would go there, Luc realized. Upset and teary, she'd want privacy, a soundproof room. A door with a lock.

Luc had a bad feeling about this.

"Run!" he shouted at Tyler.

Seconds later, they stood at the door of her office. Closed and locked. Fear clenched Luc's heart. He and Tyler both pounded on the door, shouting her name.

No one answered.

* * *

"WHAT are you doing here?" Alyssa demanded, standing.

Even in her red stiletto boots, she couldn't equal Peter's height, but she wasn't about to give him the psychological advantage of letting him tower over her sitting form. Still, the frat boy was a bruiser, at least six-two, probably a good two hundred thirty pounds of muscle. Young and drunk and horny.

And she'd left her purse with her pepper spray in her bedroom upstairs.

Calm. Reason with him.

Peter just laughed and started shucking his shirt. He looked at her with a lascivious violence that made her flesh crawl.

"Getting some of that ass you're constantly flashing in front of me. You're always letting that bouncer put his hands on you, and I know you're putting out for that chef who's been your shadow this week. Now it's my turn."

Alyssa's eyes widened. "You know about Luc?"

Had he been the one writing the notes?

Peter scoffed. "Hell, yes. The way you two look at each other, it's obvious. Besides, I was upstairs, right outside your door, twenty minutes ago when he was giving it to you good. Baby." He smiled and unfastened his jeans. "I'll fuck you better."

Fear and disgust made her stomach turn. But she had to stay calm. Get herself out of here. She would not be his victim.

"I am not having sex with you. I don't fuck customers, especially not snot-nosed frat boys who think they're entitled to whatever they want. So turn around, open the door—"

He charged her, grabbed her arm, and twisted it behind her back. "I'm man enough to make you cream and scream. I don't take orders from women, especially sluts like you. So shut your fucking mouth, open your pretty thighs, and make yourself useful."

Alyssa's stomach jumped, and adrenaline charged her system. She wriggled to get free, but Peter tightened his grip on her arm and he wrenched it up behind her back. Wincing, she stepped up on her tiptoes. If he forced the appendage up any more, he'd pull her shoulder from the socket or break it. *Shit!*

"Nice boots," he commented. "They'll look hot while I fuck you. Now, what's under that skirt?"

Using her arm to hold her in place, Peter shoved her forward and pushed her face onto her desk. Pain exploded across her cheek when she hit the unyielding surface. Another jab slashed its way across her midsection, on the right side of her rib cage, as the corner of her desk stabbed her. She gasped for her next breath.

While she was still reeling from the pain, Peter used the opportunity to flip her skirt up, expose her thong, and grope her. She shuddered.

"Nice. This is prime, grade-A ass. I know you're going to make the wait worth it."

He ripped her thong off, and the cold air hit her newly exposed skin. She shivered.

This was happening. Really happening. *God. Oh, God.* She had to stop it. She would *not* be Peter's victim. She had to elbow his ribs or stomp on his instep. Something . . . He had her immobilized with his threat to break her arm, and she'd rather let him than submit, but if she was going to sacrifice the use of a limb in battle, she had to make sure her action counted.

Peter bent over her body, curling his fist in her hair and smashing her sore cheek against the desk again. Finally, he released her arm, but kept it wedged between them with his body. Still, it was an opportunity, and she needed to use it.

His hand landed on the small of her back; then he ran a finger down the crack of her ass, lingering on her back entrance. "Ever take a man here? Yeah, I'll bet you have. Whores like you love it kinky and raw. I'm going to fuck you here for sure."

She heard slurping noises; then Peter was pressing a wet finger into her ass. She shuddered, trying to block the reality out, but the biting pain didn't allow that. This was getting serious. Fast.

"Ah, yeah. That's fucking hot. I can't wait to get back here and go for a hard ride." He extracted the finger. "But I gotta see those tits first."

Alyssa expected him to turn her over on her back, give her an opportunity to get her arm free, give her legs more range of motion. Instead, he clenched his fist in the thin cotton at the back of her neck and ripped the garment down and off. To her horror, he aced one-handed bra removal. Once he yanked the garment out from under her, her bare, sore nipples hit the cold desk. She hissed.

He pinned her wrist between their bodies again, and she felt her bra wrap around it. Then he groped around for the other. Damn, he was going to bind her with her own clothing. Hell, no. Never!

Not caring if he broke her arm or slipped it from its socket, she reached back. He had her face turned right, and her left hand was free, so she couldn't see. She'd have one chance to score on this. Thank God she kept her fingernails sharp.

She reached back, aiming high and dead center. On the first try, she grabbed his balls. And squeezed mercilessly.

He grunted and tried to back off, but she held tight, edged off the desk, and turned to him.

"You bitch! I'll fucking hurt you for that."

Alyssa stood over his crouched form, anger pounding her. "I'll hurt you first."

She jammed her heel into his instep. Though he wore tennis shoes, she figured she'd made a bull's eye when he howled and began hopping on one foot. Then, just for fun, she twisted his balls.

He screamed like a little girl. And she smiled.

Suddenly, he reared up and roared, his fist coming at her like a barreling semi. She feinted out of the way and released him, running for the door. He was on her before she could take a step, pulling her by the hair to face him, then shoving her down again. The back of her skull hit the desk with an audible *crack*. Pain exploded through her head, and she gasped.

That wasn't enough for Peter. He made sure her head banged the concrete floor as he dragged her to it. An aching band of abused nerves throbbed across her skull, in her temples. She felt sick. But then he grabbed her hand and took her forearm in the other—and jerked. She heard a snap and felt pain blast down to her hand, radiate through her wrist. She cried out, and he smiled.

"That was for grabbing my balls, bitch. Now, lie still and take it like the slut you are."

Roughly, he grabbed her arms and restrained them above her head. She whimpered against the pain.

Psycho. He was completely mental. And she had no idea how she was going to get free as he pinned her body to the ground and worked his hips between her thighs, his hard cock bare between them. *Oh, God . . .*

Alyssa knew the nightmare she was about to endure.

Despite knowing her office was soundproof and it would do no good, she screamed.

Peter took his cock in his hand and pushed against her swollen opening. "That's it. I like the screamers. You'll scream a lot for me before I'm done."

A moment later, she heard pounding on the door, and Peter stilled. "Fuck!"

Shaking his head, he reared back and tried to stab his way into her body. A moment later, the door burst open.

Tyler and Luc charged Peter like madmen. Her bouncer grabbed him by the hair and the ass of his jeans and threw him across the room. Luc ran after him and kicked the frat boy in the ribs, then followed with ferocious punches that made Peter scream. Tyler joined in, grabbing his hair and slamming his face into the concrete.

She drifted out for a moment until two sets of feet skidded to a stop beside her.

"I'm calling nine-one-one."

Luc sounded concerned. And angry. She frowned. Why? He didn't really care about her. Then again, he wasn't mean. He wouldn't like to see people hurt.

Afraid. And cold. As much as she hated to admit, Alyssa knew she needed help. Someone she *knew* cared about her.

"Tyler," she cried, her voice broken.

"I'm here, baby."

Carefully, Tyler gathered her against his warm body. She choked against the pain when he jostled her wrist, but finally he stilled. *Ah, warmth.*

"Paramedics are on the way," Luc assured her, holding the phone to his ear. "Police, too. Peter is out cold."

"Tell me what's wrong," Tyler demanded softly.

"H-he . . ." She wasn't talking coherently between tears. "Rape—"

"Ah, damn . . . " Tyler pressed his finger to her lips. "Don't think about it now. It's over."

"Not again." Her voice trembled, her insides shredding at the memories of Peter hovering over her, overpowering her, forcing his way inside her. "N-never again."

Identical looks of shock and horror crossed Tyler's and Luc's faces as the edges of her consciousness began to turn black. The truth dawned on Luc's tortured face. She closed her eyes, hating the fact he now understood her eternal shame.

* * *

LUC paced the emergency room's waiting area. Three long hours, and not a word. Over and over in his head, he saw Peter restrain Alyssa's struggling form with his larger body, the promise of violence on his face. For the hundredth time, Luc chastised himself for treating her so badly and letting her walk out of the bedroom alone. No matter how angry she'd been, how crushed he'd been, he should have followed her until she was safe. He hardly needed Tyler's glare to tell him that. Instead, Peter had gotten to her and—

Luc sank into an uncomfortable green chair and buried his head in his hands. God, what had he done? Because of the way he'd behaved, she'd run from him—and straight into Peter's trap.

In the anxious din of the ER's waiting room, the automatic doors *whoosh*ed open, and in walked three familiar figures.

"Deke." Luc rose and accepted his cousin's handshake and hug. "What are you doing here?"

"After I got your call, I figured I was coming tomorrow anyway. I thought you could use the support. Jack insisted on tagging along."

"Thanks for coming." Luc stuck his hand out to Jack. "Especially at three thirty in the morning."

Jack shook it. "Alyssa is my friend, too."

And probably a former lover. Luc couldn't let that matter now. Jack was happily married. Alyssa . . . Luc knew she wanted nothing more to do with him.

Taking a deep breath, he turned to the third man, Kimber's older brother Hunter. To say the soldier had never been a fan of Luc's was a gross understatement.

"How are you, Hunter?" He stuck out his hand.

Hunter Edgington stared pointedly at Luc's outstretched hand until he dropped it. "Fucked up another woman's life, huh?"

Luc sucked in a breath and closed his eyes. Hunter was right and had never been one to pull his punches.

Deke slapped Hunter on the back. "Come on, buddy. Now's not the time."

Mercifully, Hunter dropped the subject. "Who wants coffee?"

Jack was first with an "Amen to that." Deke and Luc both accepted, and Hunter left them to their conversation.

"Any news out of the doctors yet?" Jack asked.

Luc shook his head.

"Tell me what happened." Jack began to pace.

"This bastard who'd been stalking her, leaving her terrible notes, got her alone in her office. He attacked her. We don't know if he succeeded in raping her, too."

"Son of a bitch," Deke spat.

"I hope they put him in County." Jack smiled evilly. "If the boys down there find out he hurt their favorite entertainment, there'll be hell to pay."

Maybe that should have comforted Luc some, but it didn't. He couldn't shake a question that had been haunting him for hours.

"How long have you know Alyssa?" he asked Deke's business partner and self-proclaimed Dominant.

Jack sighed as he clearly sifted through his memories. "About ten years. She started dancing at Sexy Sirens when it was called something else and owned by this bitch named Marquessa. You should have seen Alyssa. Even then, she could light up a room. I was still in the army and on leave when we met. I'd been helping a buddy track down the drug-dealing scum who'd been selling to his little brother in middle school. Apparently, he liked to drop his money on strippers. When Alyssa heard what I was up to, she tracked me down and volunteered to help. I knew she was good people then."

Yeah, that sounded like something she would do, championing the underdog, helping where she could. Her life was far from perfect, but she still found ways and means to assist others. So damn admirable. Why hadn't he focused on that, rather than on her profession and who else might be warming her bed?

Luc swallowed, wishing he didn't have to find a way to get the next words out. "When we pulled this asshole off her, she was sobbing 'not again.' When was she raped previously?"

Jack recoiled. "Raped previously? Not in the last ten years. Alyssa and I are tight. She would have come to me, and even if she hadn't, I would have found out. I know everyone down there. Someone would have spilled."

Horror washed over Luc. "Ten years ago, she would have been, what? Eighteen? Nineteen?"

Jack grimaced. "Yeah."

"Shit," Deke muttered.

Someone had raped Alyssa as a teenager.

The scene with Peter, her in pain and helpless, played over and over in his head. *Goddamn it.*

Luc felt two inches tall. He'd treated her like dirt and judged her.

All this time, he'd been thinking that she didn't fit into his future and may not be good enough to play mother to "his" children . . . Truth was, he was no good for her.

Maybe Tyler had it right; none of this violence against her had materialized until he appeared. God knew, he hadn't looked past her façade to really know the woman underneath until it was too late.

"Who's family here?" the ER doctor, thirtysomething and harried looking, asked in a no-nonsense tone.

"No one," Tyler answered. "She doesn't have any family. I brought—"

"*We* brought her here." Luc raced across the room and cut in.

Tyler shot him a hard look, then nodded. "We brought her in."

Sadie, Jack, and Deke crowded around. The doctor barely glanced at the stripper's brief silk robe and abundance of makeup.

"Ms. Devereaux suffered a mild concussion, multiple contusions, two cracked ribs, and a broken wrist."

With every word out of the doctor's mouth, Luc wanted to thrash Peter all over again. How did that rich little prick dare think he was entitled to hurt Alyssa?

Yet Luc wondered how he'd been different. He hadn't hurt her physically, but he'd treated her as if her profession meant she had no heart, no feelings. He'd trampled all over her. Like Peter had. He was fucking slime.

"She went into shock in the ambulance," the doctor continued. "But we've stabilized her. Nothing life threatening. She will fully recover with time. She's sleeping now. We want to keep her overnight for observation. She'll need a few days of bed rest." He hesitated. "She's refused a rape kit."

"What?" If the rape kit would put Peter away, he wanted her to take it.

"She can't do that," Tyler put in.

The doctor cut a stare in his direction. "I tried to talk her into it.

The vaginal area shows considerable signs of penetration and a cursory exam found traces of semen."

Oh, shit! Luc cleared his throat. "Could be mine."

"You had unprotected sex with the victim?"

Luc didn't look at Tyler; he knew the bouncer was ready to hit him. Instead, he just nodded. "About ten this morning and again around eleven thirty tonight, just before the attack."

"That complicates things. Unless she starts talking, I can't say whether she's been raped." The doctor raked a hand through mussed brown hair. "If she changes her mind about the kit, I'm guessing the police will want you to leave a sample so we can rule out your DNA and see if there are traces of the suspect's."

Luc didn't hesitate. "If she does, I'll do whatever I can to help nail this bastard."

"Well, he's got his own laundry list of injuries, including a broken nose. He won't be hurting anyone for a while."

Luc couldn't feel much triumph. A broken nose? That wouldn't keep Peter from coming after Alyssa again. Only putting him behind bars for a long while would. All those notes the bastard had left her before attacking her would hopefully help put him away for ten to twenty.

"Can I see her?" Luc asked.

The doctor sent him an apologetic stare. "We gave her a sedative, and she's asleep. Before that, she refused all visitors."

Of course. She preferred to suffer in silence. And why would she want to see him?

Tamping down the pain, he turned to Tyler and Sadie. "While she's recovering, can you keep the club going? She'll worry herself sick unless she knows it's being cared for."

"Of course," said the well-endowed brunette.

Tyler nodded. "Part of my job description."

"I'll take care of Bonheur through Wednesday. She'll likely be back on her feet by then." He turned to Jack. "Can you make sure she stays safe for me?"

The Cajun frowned. "You make it sound as if you're leaving."

"I'm leaving her alone."

"The hell you say! She needs you now."

Luc laughed bitterly. "No. I'm the last thing she needs." He spotted Kimber's brother returning with a tray filled with coffees. "Ask him. He'll tell you."

Clapping his cousin on the back, Luc turned and spotted a triage nurse leaving her post to help a woman in labor. He sneaked in the door just before it closed, then wandered down the hall. Temporary rooms were set up in a circle all around the nurses' station. A whiteboard in the middle of the room listed all the patients and their room numbers. Finding Alyssa's room in the corner was easy enough. So was ducking in.

Inside, the thin drape had been drawn. He could see her outline, but nothing more. She didn't want to see him, and he respected that, so he didn't tear it away, as he yearned to. Damn hard. Luc wanted to see for himself that she was okay, unharmed. But she'd made her wishes clear. Now would be his only chance to say good-bye.

Behind the drape, he heard the beep of monitors, the pump of oxygen into her system. An IV stand abutted the wall, only partially concealed. He swallowed, wanting to see her, take her hand . . . something.

She wanted nothing to do with him, and it hurt so fucking bad.

Wishing she wasn't asleep and would hear him, he sighed, his breath ruffling the ugly blue drape. "I'm so damn sorry about so many things. I— Around you, I turned into someone I didn't know how to control, and you were right to dismiss me." He grabbed the curtain, forcing himself to keep it in place, not to rush past it to her bedside and wake her, take her in his arms. "I'm sorry that my behavior drove you away, into Peter's clutches. So sorry. You don't know how close I am to falling completely in love with you. Clearly, it's better for us all if I leave."

The moment was upon him. One word; that was all he had to say. *Good-bye.* Then he could leave, let her rest easier and eventually get on with her life.

Luc couldn't force the word out. Instead, he clenched his fists to hold in what felt suspiciously like tears, then left the hospital room for good.

Chapter Eleven

"Luc?"

He turned toward the familiar voice, swallowing back his annoyance. Emily. She approached him on sensible pumps, looking like something out of a Lands' End catalog with crisp khaki pants, a smart white blouse, and a little red cardigan. The colors suited her pale complexion and dark hair. She was stylishly accessorized, the look modest, understated. When she smiled, the expression reached all the way to her hazel eyes. She really was perfect in so many ways.

The smile he sent in return felt more like a grimace as he waved her over.

Glancing at his watch, he was relieved to see the book signing and cooking demonstration would end in another ten minutes.

Doing his best to meet and greet, pose for pictures, and answer fans' questions, he was conscious of Emily's presence just beyond his left shoulder. He glanced back at her. Damn, she was wearing her purposeful look.

When he'd run out of books and time was more than up, he stood and walked to the portable kitchen area and grabbed the microphone. "Thank you, everyone, for coming. I appreciate the support. Have a great evening."

After a hearty round of applause, people began to file out. A reporter or two milled around, but store personnel escorted them out. Luc braced himself and turned toward Emily.

Everything inside him recoiled. She was lovely, cultured, educated, kind. She loved children, had broadly hinted that she'd welcome a marriage proposal, and wanted to start a family right away. Luc even had the ring in his pocket, a simple two-carat teardrop-shaped diamond—her favorite, according to her—on a thin gold band, just waiting for the right moment.

She was everything he should want. But he'd been waiting for that right moment for three weeks, and the ring was still tucked away in its box in his suit coat.

He sighed, then closed the distance between them to kiss her cheek.

"You look nice." It wasn't her fault that he was dying to see another woman in a sexy short skirt, garters, and a saucy attitude.

Damn! He'd never see *her* again, and Luc knew he needed to get on with his life. Today he'd turned thirty-six. Tonight was as good as any to start embracing his future. If he wanted to have children, he needed to try starting his family soon. It could be a years-long process, but Emily, twenty-eight and ready, would be supportive.

Luc felt guiltily relieved that having children with her wouldn't require sex. She was lovely. And a wonderful person. He'd feel desire for her . . . someday. Maybe.

Emily's smile widened. "You look nice, too. And now I must take you to dinner for your very happy birthday. Where should we go?"

Luc tried to muster enthusiasm for the evening. "What sounds good to you?"

Slowly, her smile fell. "Another headache? Have you been to the doctor yet?"

Since returning from Lafayette six weeks ago, he'd fabricated headaches to explain his lack of interest in their dates and his need to cut evenings short. He hated lying to her. Emily deserved better. Either he needed to actually commit to trying to build a future with her or walk away.

His heart voted for the latter. Logic asked him what the hell he'd do about tomorrow if he left Emily. Alyssa was gone, behind him. No matter how much he wished otherwise, this separation was her wish—and the wise choice he hadn't had the fortitude to make on his own.

He pasted on a smile. "I'm fine."

Emily frowned. "You're not feeling depressed about your birthday, are you?"

Not in the way she meant, but it was a good excuse. "Perhaps a little."

"Then it's my job to cheer you up!" She smiled, flashing dimples, and reached for his hand.

This and chaste kisses. In the last month, he'd managed no more contact with her than that. How could he get through a wedding night when he couldn't imagine ever having sex with her? Worse, what would he do when the need he still felt for Alyssa clawed through his skin, demanding something only she could give? Would his resolve to leave her in peace waver then? Would he disregard his marriage vows? Or would he endure in silence until he grew to resent Emily?

"You don't have to." He gathered his utensils, notebook, and pens, then took a long time arranging them in his backpack—giving himself more time to school his features and erase his hunger for Alyssa.

"Luc." She touched his shoulder. "I wanted to wait until we were alone, but . . . You haven't been the same since you returned from Louisiana. I didn't want to push, but—"

"Then don't," he said quietly. "There's nothing you can do."

The perpetual smile finally slipped from her face. "I'm a good listener."

"I know you are, Emily. I have to work this out alone."

"If you're no longer interested in me and the sort of future we discussed, just tell me."

He closed his eyes. Cling to the past or force out the lie?

"Luc."

He heard another female call his name, this one farther away. But her familiar voice zipped across his senses like an electric charge through his body, spreading chills across his skin. Had he missed her so much he'd dreamed her?

He whirled around, hope spiking inside him. And across the room *she* stood.

"Alyssa?" Shock sucker-punched him. Luc nearly couldn't breathe.

The last time he'd seen her, she'd thrown him out of her club. Out of her life. Why was she here now? Was she okay? Had she missed him, even a bit?

He drank in the sight of her. Despite six weeks passing, Alyssa still took his breath away as she cautiously drew closer. She'd fastened half of her long platinum hair at her nape and let the remaining strands trail down, stopping low on her back. Worn jeans clung to her small figure, looser than he remembered. Somehow the black stilettos made her look more fragile. She wore a tight Sexy Sirens T-shirt with red lettering that invited *Come Live Your Fantasy* right across her breasts. She wore almost no makeup. Even so, her eyes were hauntingly blue. And she looked exhausted.

When she stood a few feet away, Alyssa glanced at Emily, then looked back at him. "Your girlfriend?"

"Yes," Emily answered quickly.

With a raised brow, Alyssa sent him a cold stare. "I'll contact you at a better time."

She turned and walked out the archway, into the main space of the department store. Luc didn't think twice. He dodged around the demonstration table and charged after her.

Just before his approach, she whirled to him, frustration all over her face. Luc stopped in his tracks. He wanted to touch her so badly . . . but she'd told him never to touch her again. Even now, her expression warned him away.

"Don't leave." He heard the pleading in his voice.

God, he'd missed her so much. He'd say anything—do anything—just to spend five more minutes with her. In that moment, Luc feared he knew why.

He'd fallen in love.

She cut a glance over to Emily across the room. Luc didn't have to look at the other woman to feel her confusion and hurt. Some foolish side of him rejoiced. Emily must be seeing where his heart was. So much easier than sitting her down over a civilized dinner to crush her picket fence.

"Your girlfriend doesn't want me here," Alyssa pointed out

"*I* want you here. Don't go." He fastened a desperate gaze on her and willed her to understand.

"Is there someplace we can talk? I won't take up too much of your time."

"Take all you want."

Alyssa bit that lush lower lip, then looked up at him through the veil of her dark lashes. It was a nervous gesture—sexy as hell. But he worried . . . She looked thinner, paler, more vulnerable.

"Are you all right?" He barely stopped himself from wrapping a light hand around her shoulder.

She bit her lip harder. "Not here."

Someplace private. Right. "Wait just a moment."

Luc jogged back to the demonstration room, trying to think of something to say to Emily. He came up blank. "I have to go."

"What about your birthday dinner?" she screeched.

What about it? He opened his mouth, but no words came out. Finally, he shook his head.

Emily examined his face with intelligent hazel eyes. "She's what happened to you in Louisiana."

Perceptive. He sucked in a breath and took the plunge. "Yes."

The woman glanced over at Alyssa. "She's incredibly beautiful."

"Inside and out."

"I never stood a chance." Emily tried to cover her shock and disappointment with a tight smile, but she choked on her words.

Damn, lately it seemed that he hurt people wherever he went, but he had to start being honest with Emily. It was unkind of him to continue this charade with her. He would not make her a good husband. And though Luc didn't know why Alyssa was here, it didn't matter. If she was entering his life again, even for a moment, as long as he had the possibility of being with her, he would grab it with both hands. Maybe the hot flame of their passion would burn out, but he didn't think so. Either way, they weren't done. If she let him in her life again and came to trust him, he'd tell her about his sterility—and let the chips fall.

"You love her," Emily said softly.

It wasn't a question, and Luc refused to insult her with a lie. "Yes."

Her face crumpled. "You're not going to call me again, are you?"

Luc took her hands in his. "Would you really want me to?"

Sighing as a fat tear rolled down her face, she shook her head and pulled her hands free. "I know it's best if you don't. For what it's worth . . . I liked you very much."

Damn, he felt like such a prick. "You're a wonderful woman, and someday, someone will make you very happy because he loves *you*, not the idea of you."

He bent and kissed her cheek. Then with a tight nod, she raced out of the little room, spearing Alyssa with a glance as she exited the department store and out to the crisp autumn afternoon.

The moment she was gone, Luc returned to Alyssa's side. She stepped back as he approached, looking distressed.

"I didn't hear anything she said except . . . it's your birthday?"

Luc smiled encouragingly. "Having you here is a gift I didn't expect."

"I ruined your evening."

No, she'd saved it. "Not at all. Let's grab a bite, and we can talk."

Luc expected her to refuse. Alyssa hesitated, then sent him a nervous nod.

Pleasantly surprised at her agreement, he led her to his waiting car, a new Jaguar he'd purchased after signing the cable TV agreement two weeks ago.

As they approached the vehicle, a photographer race-walked across the sidewalk to reach him, camera flashing. Luc tried to shield Alyssa with his body, thankful that she'd donned sunglasses that hid half her face.

"Emily Adams left alone in tears. Is this your new girlfriend?" the photographer shouted, snapping pictures all the while.

Ouch! "No comment. Please stop."

As they neared the car, the photographer followed, and Luc cursed and ran, urging Alyssa along.

"I should follow you so you don't have to drive me back here . . . after," she suggested, keeping pace with him.

"I don't mind," he insisted.

She sent him a brittle smile. "You will."

What did that mean? Had Peter started misbehaving now that he was out on bail and awaiting his trial? Jack hadn't said a word, damn it! He'd talked to Deke's business partner nearly every day.

"If we want to make a quick exit, it would be best if you just hopped in the car," he pressed, unlocking it with his key fob.

"I insist."

Stubborn to a fault. "Okay . . . Two blocks east there's a quiet little Italian place. I don't think the photographer will follow us there if we're quick."

"They hound you like that a lot now?"

He winced. "Just since I started doing the talk shows. I keep hoping they'll go away. Does Italian sound good?"

"Sure." The word itself was enthusiastic, but the tone was very *whatever*.

Luc gnashed his teeth. The suspense was killing him. Now he added worry to the mix. Something was definitely wrong here.

After she agreed to follow him to the restaurant, he waited for her to pull around. The photographer ran after him until he couldn't jog fast enough to chase their cars anymore.

The drive to Georgio's was the longest five minutes of Luc's life. Why did Alyssa assume that he would mind being with her after dinner? What the hell was going on? Why did she look so thin and tired? Was Bonheur weighing on her? Had she come to him for advice?

Finally, he pulled into a parking spot in the restaurant's lot. The one beside him was empty, but she parked farther down the row. Damn. If Alyssa wanted distance between them, why was she here?

She remained silent until they were seated in a quiet corner. It was early on Saturday afternoon, long past the lunch rush, but well before dinner.

"How is Bonheur?" he asked, hoping to entice her to lift her nose out of the menu and talk to him.

"Fine. I was pleased with the first month's tally. This month is looking even better. Thank you for your help."

Luc smiled for her, though the mystery of her visit chafed at him. "The hard work was yours. I just provided a little name recognition opening week."

"And then some. I saw you on *Ellen* last week."

He winced. "Still getting used to the TV thing."

"You did well."

"Thanks. The network has arranged a lot of these appearances. They want maximum exposure before the show actually launches in January."

The waiter came by and took their drink orders. He ordered a cabernet sauvignon. She asked for water and refused a cocktail. He frowned, and asked the waiter to return later for their dinner selections.

"Let's order now."

This instant? Was she hungry . . . or just didn't want to be in the same room with him any longer than necessary?

Of course the latter. You treated her like a whore.

Reluctantly, Luc agreed, and they placed their orders. The waiter finally left them alone.

Luc turned to Alyssa, willing her to say something. He wanted to touch her so badly, but not against her wishes. He owed her at least that much. She sat in silence for long moments, fidgeting nervously.

"Is this about Peter?" he prompted gently. "Jack told me he didn't rape you. I know he's free and awaiting trial. The DA has a solid assault and attempted rape charge."

She nodded. "Peter still insists he didn't write the notes. I don't think we'll ever know the truth. But that's not why I'm here."

He leaned forward, getting a closer view of just how pale and shaky she was. His worry deepened. "What is it? You can tell me anything."

"Hell of a birthday present . . ." Her eyes closed. Her face tightened as she pressed her lips together, as if looking for strength. Then she stared at him with the deepest regret. "I'm pregnant."

Luc recoiled, blinked, stared. "Pregnant?"

Why tell him? Was she trying to claim the baby was . . . his?

"Are you sure?"

Slowly, she nodded. "I missed my period a few weeks ago and thought maybe it was stress. But days went on, and I noticed changes in my body."

"Like?" He barked the question at her. Maybe she'd made a mistake.

Even if she hadn't, this child wasn't his.

After a horrific teenage illness with a decimating fever, Luc had learned from his doctors that he'd been left with a very low sperm count that made the likelihood of him impregnating someone statistically insignificant. He'd been seventeen then, and his reaction to the news had been mixed, a vague sadness with a whooping cheer that he and his girlfriend of the moment would never have an "oops."

The green light to sex in his late teens and early twenties had given way eventually. He'd returned to his doctor to have a physical for insurance purposes at twenty-seven, and he'd asked to be tested again. Despite having been involved in ménages with Deke for a few years, he'd begun wondering if, maybe, he could find the right woman and have a family of his own. His doctor had quickly squashed that possibility. Luc had even taken a prescription drug, clomiphene citrate, for a few months to see if his sperm count might improve. Further testing revealed his chances of fathering children were slightly better . . . but still virtually impossible.

He hadn't been tested since. Why bother repeating something so humiliating? So devastating?

But Alyssa either thought the child was his or wanted him to believe so. He drummed his fingers against the table, a surge of jealous anger jolting him. Without knowing Luc's secret, she probably thought there was a fifty/fifty chance he had fathered her child. But apparently, that honor was Tyler's. So why track Luc down in Texas to give him the news, rather than name her bouncer the expectant father? Because he'd been on *Ellen*? Because he'd signed a sweet cable deal? That didn't sound like stubbornly independent Alyssa, but he couldn't think of another reason.

Damn her! As lies went, this one hurt so bad, his insides were about to implode. The pain of her rejection six weeks ago had hurt like hell, and she was paying him back in spades.

"My . . . breasts became tender," she continued into the silence. "I—I felt like I had the flu. All of a sudden, I couldn't eat spicy foods. I was—am—tired a lot. I saw my doctor yesterday. I'm pregnant."

Not by me . . . And didn't that reality taste bitter? He drummed his fingers on the table again. What the hell did she want him to say? Congratu-fucking-lations?

"I'm . . . um, due June seventh."

Luc had to give her credit. The math worked in favor of the child being his. Though clearly she'd been fucking Tyler that week as well.

"And . . . you're here because it's mine?"

She rolled her eyes. "Whether you believe me or not, you are the only man I've had sex with in nearly three years. So yes."

Luc resisted the urge to laugh hysterically. It was either that or swallow the reality that another man had impregnated the woman he loved and she now lied to his face. His blood pressure rose, and he drummed his fingers faster.

Luc opened his mouth to tell her the child couldn't possibly be his. Then he stopped cold. *She's having a baby who needs a father.*

He swallowed hard. His thoughts raced. What if . . . he didn't refute her? There must be some reason she'd chosen to pin this on him. Did the why matter?

Once, he'd been eager to marry Kimber, despite the fact he hadn't been in love with her, so he could be a father to the unborn baby she'd thought she was carrying. When Emily departed earlier, yet another chance at fatherhood had walked out the door. Now Alyssa was dropping opportunity right into his lap. And she came with a bonus; unlike Emily or Kimber, he had deep feelings for her. More than he'd ever felt for any woman, lies and all.

Suddenly, he knew exactly what he wanted. He also knew that after the way they'd last parted in Lafayette, he had to play this carefully.

"Say something," she choked.

Luc hesitated, thinking through his strategy. "Have you told anyone?"

She frowned, then started scooting out of the booth. "If you're worried I'm going to mess up your new image or screw up your relationship with your girlfriend, don't be. I don't want anything from you. I thought I'd just be a decent human being and inform you. Duty done."

Interesting tactic on her part. Reverse psychology?

Luc beat her out of the booth and blocked her path. "That's not at all what I meant. I wanted to know if you'd told anyone in Lafayette."

Alyssa bristled. "Like Tyler? Why? There's zero chance this baby is his, so no. I thought I owed you first. When I do tell Tyler, he'll probably come up with some silly scheme to get married . . ."

Luc's guts fell somewhere around his toes. Alyssa married to Tyler? The bouncer playing father to this baby? Over his dead body.

"Now that I've told you about my pregnancy—" She pushed against his chest.

He refused to budge. Finally realizing that he wasn't moving an inch, she flopped back into her seat and glared at him.

"Now that I know, we should discuss our options," he said, sitting again. Luc tried for calm, but his heart raced.

"Options?" she all but shrieked. "I came to inform you in person, instead of taking the chickenshit way out and phoning you. But I'm having this baby. You won't push your money off on me and persuade me abort—"

"That's the *last* thing I want!" The thought horrified him.

"Oh." She looked away. "Look, I'm not asking for anything. It'd be great for the kid's sake if you wanted to be involved, but if not . . ." She shrugged. "Plenty of single moms do it."

She was independent and determined enough to go it alone. He admired her tenacity, even as he wanted to shake her.

Luc chose his words carefully. "So you wouldn't marry Tyler if he asked?"

"I haven't given it much thought. He hasn't actually asked; I'm just guessing he might."

Fairly accurate guess, in Luc's estimation. Tyler loved her and would latch on to any reason to make her his. Besides, the man could argue the child was his. And he'd be right. Luc wasn't going to allow Tyler that chance. He wanted this baby. And despite the lies, he wanted Alyssa, too. So much, the craving was nearly beyond his control. Some part of him was even perversely pleased with this outcome.

This time, he'd be better to her. He'd never let another man touch her. He'd never give her cause for regret.

"Something against Tyler or marriage in general?"

Alyssa frowned. "Tyler's been my rock lately. I don't know much about his life before he showed up on my doorstep, want ad in hand. But he's solid. Marriage . . . I don't think it works. I've seen guys who seem like the most devoted dads come in for a weekly lap dance, looking for something extra on the side."

"Not every man cheats," Luc chided her.

Alyssa raised a golden brow. "Most."

"Some," he corrected. "Women cheat, too." How would she react to that statement? With guilt?

She just shrugged. "I don't see them in my club every night."

The line of questioning had netted nothing. Time to change tactics. "Cheating aside, would you get married? For the baby?"

"To Tyler?" She hesitated a long moment, then sighed. "Maybe."

Luc sifted through the information, still drumming his fingertips. While she didn't seem enthusiastic about the idea, Alyssa hadn't said no. He had to crush that quickly.

"I didn't come to ruin your birthday. I just . . . thought you should know." She rose from the booth again. "I'll call you when the baby is born."

"Wait!" Luc blurted, cursing that she might be playing him like a fiddle. He still didn't know what she wanted, but he had to tip his hand, say or do whatever necessary to keep her and this baby in his life. "Don't go. I'm thrilled you're pregnant."

"Really?" She frowned, looking unconvinced. "You're happy?"

"Ecstatic. The best birthday present *ever.*" He clenched his fists to keep from reaching out to her. "I don't want you to call me when the baby is born. I'd like to be involved in this child's life. I want to be there every step of the way—first tooth, first word, first crush, first date. I also want to be there for you during your pregnancy."

Her eyes went wide. "Wha . . . what do you mean? You want to go to my doctor appointments?"

"Yes. I want to be part of the whole experience. I'm ready to be a father. A great father." *Understatement of the millennium.* "I will not let you down."

Luc hesitated before saying more. Would his enthusiasm lure her in? Or make her run in the other direction? A calculated risk. She was afraid, and he had to be careful.

"Okay." She nodded, looking slightly shocked. "Thanks. That would be . . . helpful."

He planned to be far more than helpful.

"You know, there are advantages to being married," he pointed out. "Financial, of course. But children are a lot of work. Having another set of hands would lighten your load, especially when they're sick or up all night, or you need to work late. And what about safety? It's been a concern for you lately. Having a husband around would add protection for you and the baby. You'd rest easier. The baby would have the stability of a two-parent family, a last name. The love of both a mom and a dad."

Alyssa froze. "You want me to marry Tyler?"

Damn it! Time to stop this verbal poker game and throw his cards on the table.

Luc stood and leaned toward her, risking all and taking her face in his hands. Her gaze bounced up to his, and he felt the zing of that poignant blue all the way to his toes.

When she'd walked back into his life, he'd never imagined it would be to lie to him. Even so, he still wanted her so badly.

"No. I want you to marry me."

* * *

". . . SO that's what's up with me."

It was nearly four in the morning at Sexy Sirens. The club was closed now, and Alyssa faced Sadie and Tyler, nerves jittery in her stomach.

"The fucker got you pregnant and left?" Tyler screamed, his tense body leaving no question that he was ready to hit something—preferably Luc's face. "Where is he? I wanna know right now."

Alyssa sighed. "He didn't 'leave me.' He says he wants to marry me. I don't really know why. The baby, I guess."

Tyler snorted. "You're gorgeous, smart, kind—and you're going to have his kid. Why the fuck wouldn't he want to marry you?"

"He also thinks I'm a whore and may even believe this baby is yours."

"I wish," Tyler muttered under his breath.

Still, Alyssa heard. Could she feel any worse? "His proposal shocked me."

"You're thinking of accepting, even though you threw him out on his ass last time he was here? After the shitty way he treated you?"

Alyssa bit her lip. She'd been thinking through that. Being Luc's wife and having his name on the birth certificate would have benefits. Stability. Money, if anything ever happened to her. Though it might be old-fashioned of her, she'd prefer to raise a child with two parents.

Tyler raised a good point, though. All the volatility and mind games she and Luc had played last time couldn't happen again. If she accepted his proposal, they must be on the same page about that.

But at the end of the day, though it might make her twenty kinds of stupid, she loved Luc too much to say no.

"I'll handle it."

"How?" Tyler snarled. "He practically ran your heart over and left your for dead last time."

"I said I'll handle it."

The possibility of losing Luc to his picture-perfect suburban girlfriend . . . Cold chills didn't begin to describe the feeling. Utter fear. Panic. Jagged, aching sadness.

"This is shit," Tyler yelled. "Given how badly he treated you, what kind of father would he be?"

"I think he'll be a great one," Alyssa answered, going with her gut. "Once he got over the shock of the pregnancy, he seemed really enthusiastic about the baby. Claimed he wants to be *very* involved."

"Maybe that would be enough for him," Tyler argued. "Without marriage."

"And maybe not," Sadie put in. "I learned that the hard way when the courts let my ex, Kenneth, take little Ben from me because of my past."

"You can't marry Luc because you're afraid of what he might do. Hell, I'll marry you. I'd love to."

Alyssa closed her eyes. She'd suspected those words were coming, and she should rejoice. Having Tyler at her side as the other half of a parenting unit would look good to the courts, if it came to that.

But she couldn't deny that even though Luc's proposal had been practical, it had filled her heart with a hope she wished she could deny. Tyler's only filled her with regret.

True, she could wait and see if Luc was vindictive or possessive of this baby. If he was, *then* she could always take him or Tyler up on his offer. But if she was honest with herself, she'd ached for Luc in the last six weeks, as if someone had ripped away a part of her soul. There was a reckless part of her that wanted to see if she could still have that picket-fence dream she'd been clutching to her heart since her world had shattered at fifteen. And have those dreams with the man she loved. The only thing that could make it better was if he fell in love with her in return.

If they had their whole lives ahead of them, rather than just a week, maybe someday . . . If not, they had a child to raise, and that had to be her first focus.

"I appreciate that, Tyler. But I don't want you to sacrifice your life for me."

"It wouldn't be a sacrifice," he said solemnly. "It would be an honor."

"You should find someone who loves you and wants to have your children," she said gently but firmly. Tyler had to understand that she was a dead end for him, especially now.

She tossed back the rest of her water, then stood.

"Where are you going?" Sadie asked.

Alyssa's gaze fell on Tyler, who was clenching his jaw and judiciously not looking at her. She'd hurt him, and guilt hammered her to the core. Why couldn't she love him? He was always there, always kind, funny, interesting . . . A buddy, but not a lover. Luc was sophisticated, complicated—every other sort of -ated she could think of. They shouldn't have anything in common.

Except . . . it was his focus. Alyssa felt special with him. To him. They'd had their share of arguments, but when he took her in his arms or turned on his tender side, something inside her told her it was right.

She caressed Tyler's hard shoulder, a silent apology.

"I'm going to call Luc."

"At this time of night?" Sadie looked at her as if she needed her head examined.

Alyssa shrugged, trying to tamp down her ridiculous giddiness. She may come to regret this decision, but at the moment, she refused. Not only did she have a baby to think about, but this was her last chance at the fairy tale, and she was seizing it. "He said to call anytime. I'm thinking if we're going to get married, I should tell him."

Chapter Twelve

LUC straightened his tie and waited near the wall of Bonheur's windows as the sun streamed in golden and bright on this November noon. The smell of roses and stargazer lilies filled the air, slightly cloying. At the other end of the restaurant, Alyssa emerged from the shadowed hallway in white, looking ethereal, elegant—and very nervous.

"Are you sure you want to do this?" Deke whispered in his ear.

On the other side of Luc, Sadie, dressed in ice blue, shushed him.

Yes and no. He was still thrilled about the baby, but standing beside the justice of the peace as Alyssa walked to him through the hush, it hit him that, as husband and wife, they weren't going to have to merely treat each other with civility, as she'd demanded. They must also get along day in and day out. Balance lives. Find common ground. Get accustomed to sharing space and priorities and feelings. Become good spouses and parents. To make this work, they would have to build trust.

Could they do that with a marriage based on a big lie? He swallowed.

On the groom's side of the room, in the front row, his parents sat, still holding hands after nearly forty years together, looking uncertain. They'd both talked to him about commitment, compromise, honesty, and communication. He and Alyssa might be committing, but so far, they sucked at the other three virtues.

When he'd called to tell his parents that he was getting married in six days, he'd leveled with them about his reasons. Since yesterday, his mother had tried to talk him out of this—twice. He hadn't budged. Now, somehow, he had to make this work.

"I'm good," he whispered back to Deke.

Behind Luc's parents sat his sisters and their families, a handful of aunts, uncles, and cousins, Deke's wife, Kimber, along with her brothers, Logan and Hunter, a few of Luc's close friends and colleagues. His side of the room was full to bursting, and he could have invited more. Alyssa's side was virtually empty.

Tyler sat in the second row, scowling as if he'd like to kill someone. Why the man hadn't tried to stop this wedding, demanded parental rights, or even a paternity test, puzzled Luc. Maybe Alyssa had asked him to step aside, and Tyler's pride kept him from fighting for her. Even so, Luc wasn't sure how the guy was restraining himself. He wouldn't. Then again, maybe Tyler hadn't wanted to shoulder the responsibility for his baby.

Jack and Morgan Cole sat behind the bouncer. Some of the other dancers and restaurant staff were scattered in various rows, dressed in their Sunday best. The first row, usually reserved for family, sat empty.

Until now, he hadn't thought to wonder if her family would be coming. The fact none had made him hurt for her. At the hospital after Alyssa's attack, Tyler had claimed she had no family. Seriously? Not one single blood relation who cared enough to see her on her wedding day?

Luc rolled his shoulders and stared at his bride. God, that sounded odd. But she actually looked bridal, hair upswept, pearls dangling at her ears, sheer tulle trimmed in sparkling beads falling softly down her back, to her hips. Her dress was simple. Cap sleeves clung to her shoulders. A V-neck hinted at cleavage, and the ruched silk cupped her generous breasts. Sparse beading encircled her small waist. The rest of the gown cascaded down to her feet in a gentle fall, a very short train behind her. In trembling hands, she carried a small bouquet of baby red roses that matched her lipstick.

Besides beautiful, Alyssa looked pale and scared. Luc clenched his jaw, resolving to do his best to put the lies behind them and be good to her. She had given him a gift he'd never expected. Despite the enormity of her deception—and his—a part of him still loved her.

As Alyssa neared, he held out his hand to her. She stared, her blue eyes pale, red-rimmed, and swollen. She hadn't slept and she'd been crying. Clearly, second thoughts tortured her. Or was that guilt? Everything inside him tensed.

Luc forced himself to smile. She took a breath, finally putting her cold hand in his. Her gaze asked what her lips couldn't in front of all these people: Why did he want to marry her?

Answering was pointless. The truth would serve no purpose except to expose his humiliation, tear them apart, and send her to back to Tyler's arms. He'd bear the secret. And if the child emerged looking like her bouncer . . . Luc clenched his fist. Nothing to do but cross that bridge then. The best strategy now was to calm his bride and be good to her for the rest of their lives.

Beautiful, he mouthed to her. A smile wobbled across her face.

Then the justice of the peace began the ceremony. The words were short, a blur. He responded when prompted. Alyssa did the same, her voice thin and high and shaking.

Then came time for the rings.

He held out his hand toward Deke, who leaned in and whispered, "You really sure, man?"

Luc merely wiggled his fingers impatiently. With a sigh, his cousin set the ring in the middle of his palm. Then he turned to Alyssa and began to slide it on her finger as he recited his vows.

Love. Honor. Cherish. Until death. Could they make it work? As she looked down at the ring, she gasped. And he smiled.

Earlier in the week, she'd asked him if he wanted one. He'd said a band would be fine. Apparently, she'd assumed he'd get her the same. But when he'd gone to return Emily's ring and find something else, this had caught his eye. Three stones meant to represent their past, present, and future. He'd seen it as their new family. The middle gem was nearly two carats, the stones on either side a carat on their own. Set in platinum. No baguettes, no channel setting, no filigree. Simple sparkling splendor. So Alyssa.

"Do you like it?" he whispered.

Eyes wide, she nodded. A stupidly pleased feeling slid through his gut. This marriage might be a train wreck down the road, but this made her feel special. For now it was enough.

Then the justice of the peace prompted Alyssa. Still shaking, she slipped a ring on his finger, a brushed platinum band. Stylish but not fussy—exactly what he would have chosen for himself.

"With this ring"—she swallowed—"I thee wed. To love, honor, and cherish from this day forward, for better or for worse, in sickness and in health, forsaking all others until death parts us."

Alyssa took a deep breath and met his gaze. Her usually self-assured expression was gone. She looked shaken, anxious. Was she worried he'd discover her lie?

Tamping down the ironic smile, he took her hands in his at the justice's prompting. The older man paused and sent him a weighty stare.

"Kiss your bride."

Now, *this* was something he'd been waiting for since she'd suddenly reappeared in his life last Saturday. Since that moment, they'd talked wedding details by phone and e-mail, the tone infuriatingly businesslike. Earlier this week, he'd had to take a damn PR trip to New York and hadn't returned to Lafayette until yesterday. The simple ceremony hadn't required a rehearsal, so he'd arranged a quiet dinner with his parents last night so they could meet her. He hadn't been alone with Alyssa for a single minute this week. He hadn't touched her since that disastrous night in her bedroom above the club.

He was dying to kiss her.

Luc cupped her face and leaned in. Alyssa clamped her hands around his waist, as if he were her anchor, and waited, breathless. Slowly, he pressed his lips to hers. Soft, a brush. A shared sigh. He lingered, slanting his mouth over hers again, a firmer press. Hunger crashed through him, sharp, fresh, demanding. Beneath him, Alyssa went pliant and opened to him. Luc was so tempted to sink deep into her, drown, guests be damned.

Later. Now was about their first kiss as husband and wife with family and friends looking on. Later, she'd understand exactly what he wanted from her and how badly he wanted it.

After savoring the meeting of their mouths a moment more, Luc eased back and stared down into her flushed, golden face. She sent him a nervous, tentative smile.

"Ladies and gentleman," the Justice said. "Mr. and Mrs. Lucas Traverson."

Their guests politely clapped as the couple walked back down the aisle. Jack Cole reached out to shake his hand. Kimber kissed his cheek, whispering, "Be happy." Sadie hugged Alyssa. Tyler still scowled.

The photographer, a friend of Luc's, awaited them. He snapped a few pictures, posed them close together. Something greedy leapt inside Luc when the man suggested they kiss again so he could get a shot.

Restraining himself this time proved more difficult. The first taste had merely whetted his appetite, made the hungry beast inside him roar to life. Whatever lay between them, this—touching her—

was always gripping and exquisite. To have the right to do it whenever he wished was heady.

The rest of the luncheon passed in quiet festivity. They cut the
cake he'd made early this morning. Simple and all white fondant
with beads of frosting decorating the edge of each of the three
stacked tiers. White ribbons of fondant ran along the sides, so it
resembled an elegant package. Fresh flowers circled the cake on the
pristine white tablecloth.

He and Alyssa hadn't talked specifics after he'd volunteered to
handle this part of the reception. Now Luc was oddly nervous that
she'd had something else in mind.

"You made this?" Her voice was barely more than a whisper. "It's
gorgeous."

"Amaretto with Swiss buttercream filling. I hope you like it."

Together they cut the cake, and flashbulbs went off. Gently, he
fed her a piece and she moaned, to his satisfaction. Then, with shaking fingers, she fed him as well. The desire inside him surged, tearing
at his restraint.

Luc was still grappling for self-control when Deke rose and
toasted them. "After one of the most inauspicious meetings, you've
elected to share a future that I hope will be filled with love and all
the best life has to offer. Congratulations."

Holding her sparkling water, Alyssa leaned to him. "He couldn't
possibly have written that on his own."

Luc laughed for the first time today. "I'm sure Kimber helped."

Then Sadie rose to make her own toast. "To a great boss, friend,
and human being, who's always there for her employees, whether
that's lending a shoulder to cry on or a helping hand. You deserve
great happiness. Luc, I haven't known you long, but I'm hoping you'll
be a strong, positive force in her life and will love her as she is. To a
long and happy life together."

Moments later, the soft instrumental music he'd chosen sounded over the restaurant's speakers. Luc rose and extended his hand to Alyssa. She bounced a surprised gaze up to him.

"Dance?"

She bit her lip, then stood. The guests were dead silent as they watched him take her in his arms. She felt good against him, too good. Hunger kicked up another notch, and Luc buried his face in her neck. Her peaches and cinnamon scent mixed with a light perfume, driving him mad with the need to hold her, strip her, take her.

"I thought the ceremony was lovely," she murmured. "I'm sorry . . . I'm sure your parents would have preferred a fancier wedding."

One that wasn't rushed, in which the bride wasn't a pregnant stripper—Luc heard regret in her voice. He lifted her chin with his finger. "They want whatever makes me happy. Proposing was my choice, and I don't regret it. Sadie wants us to have a long and happy life together. Let's start it by looking forward, not back."

* * *

LUC'S earlier words on the dance floor echoed in her head. Could they really look forward without the past coming back to haunt them?

"What am I doing?" Alyssa asked aloud as Sadie helped her out of her wedding gown in Bonheur's bathroom.

"You asked me this question when you were putting on your wedding dress earlier. The answer is still the same."

"I know I'm providing a more stable home for this baby." She sighed into her hands, regret crashing through her. "But I'm going to fall for Luc completely and utterly, and I'll never be more to him than the great lay whose egg happened to meet his sperm."

"You don't know that. When he looks at you, I see something more."

"Annoyance?"

She knew that wasn't true, but she didn't understand why he'd married her. She'd been perfectly willing to allow him whatever parental rights he wanted. Luc had given her some reasons for the wedding . . . but they all benefited her. What was in it for him?

And the uncertainty on his parents' faces concerned her. It wasn't disapproval . . . yet. But what if that came? What if her job, her life, her past, became a bone of contention between Luc and his family? Or between Luc and herself? There was a whole lot about her he didn't know. And God willing, he never would.

Sadie shook her head. "Annoyance, no. Serious lust, totally. But I think it's even more."

Alyssa was afraid to hope that Luc had genuine feelings for her. Pushing it aside, she stepped out of her wedding dress, then turned her back to Sadie. "Can you take this off?"

Her friend hesitated. "No. That white corset is hot! You'll knock Luc dead with it."

Biting her lip, Alyssa wondered if that was a good thing. She'd tasted the desire in his kiss, felt a surge of her own. Hell, she did whenever he was in the same room. In the same zip code. But they had to start building their marriage on something more than sex and the coming child. They couldn't do that if he kept seeing her as a stripper.

"I'd rather not."

"But it's your wedding night," Sadie reminded.

"Yeah, never thought I'd have one of those." Hoped, maybe, but after fourteen years of pure shit romantically speaking, she'd learned to mistrust men. They'd do or say anything for sex. So why had she tied herself to someone who'd likely become a lying bastard and ruin her life?

Because you were dumb enough to fall in love, and you're still hoping that the baby will round out the perfect family so you can all live happily ever after. Yeah, right . . .

In a million years, she'd never imagined that one man would get under her skin and that she'd be tempted to keep him forever. But she wanted Luc too much to refuse. What if he realized that she loved him? What if he moved on?

"Don't you want to make an impression on your wedding night?"

Alyssa was pretty sure she'd already made it. "Just take it off."

Sadie harrumphed. "You'd better have something sexier in mind."

"Totally," she lied.

With a cackle of glee, Sadie tore into the corset. Alyssa pulled the boning away from her body, then thanked her friend as she waved and exited carrying her dress in its protective bag.

She shoved the corset into her bag, then donned a white lace bra and a matching thong. From a hanger she'd left on the wall, she drew on a chocolate suit with a simple white blouse. After changing shoes, removing her veil, and packing up, she marched outside.

Luc talked in hushed tones with his parents near the door. The few remaining guests milled around outside Bonheur's doors. Beyond the sidewalk, she saw Luc's new Jaguar.

At her approach, he looked up, and her belly pulsed nervously. When she'd merely wanted him sexually, she'd been so full of confidence and swagger. Snaring a man for a night was easy. *Keeping* him when her heart was on the line . . . All her self-assurance had vanished. What the hell did she do now? Tomorrow? And every day after that?

Taking her bag in his hand, Luc guided her back to his parents. They looked somewhere between reserved and resigned. She knew Luc had told them about the baby—and suspected he'd told them about Sexy Sirens. But Alyssa couldn't afford to be embarrassed or apologize. What would it change? Everything probably looked worse because she had no family at the wedding. They likely assumed her family had shunned her. In a way, she supposed they had.

What would her mother have thought if she'd been here today?

Alyssa shoved the thought away. While the woman who had

died just a few months ago had given birth to her, the years and issues separating them had made her a virtual stranger.

"Thank you for coming a long way on short notice," she said to them. "I'm thrilled you could be with us today. I know it meant the world to Luc."

Luc's mother, Clarissa, looked up at his father, Anthony, who sent her a vaguely warm smile. "We wish you and Luc every happiness."

It wasn't exactly *welcome to the family*, but it was a start. "Thank you."

"What time is your flight tomorrow?" Luc asked.

In a few short moments, he made arrangements to pick them up for lunch, then see them off to the terminal. Hugging and kissing their son, they shook her hand politely, then left.

She looked around the room. The guests had all gone now. Inside Bonheur, dirty linens needed washing. Certainly there was a stack of dishes in the kitchen she didn't want to think about now. The floors were a mess and would have to be cleaned. She'd tackle all that in the morning.

First, she and Luc had a wedding night to get through.

"Ready to go?" he asked softly.

No. God, no. What do I know about making a marriage work?

Alyssa drew in a shaky breath. "Absolutely."

* * *

LUC clearly wasn't driving back to her house. As he headed west, beyond Lafayette's city limits, Alyssa hesitated. The silence in the car was thick, expectant. She hated to break it, but . . .

"Where are we going?"

He sent her a black-eyed gaze that scorched her to her toes. Late-afternoon shadows lent an expectant, intimate feel to the car's interior. Alyssa caught her breath.

"It's our wedding night."

Meaning he had something planned? "I—I thought we'd just go to my house."

Luc shook his head. "We should celebrate our first night as husband and wife."

They hadn't talked about this. Being alone with Luc for a whole night—as his wife? Nerves clenched her stomach into a big knot. They'd have sex; that was a given. But he made this sound like . . . more.

Then again, he'd arranged their romantic wedding dance, made the cake, bought her this huge and totally unexpected ring. Why? What did all of this mean to him?

Of course, he'd married her, at least in part, for the baby. And for the sex, too? If so, she knew exactly what would happen once he tired of it. She saw those men in her club every night. So why plan something special tonight? The wedding had been a show for his parents; she understood that. Now that they were alone, what was with all the romance?

"You keep staring at your ring."

His observation startled her. "It's beautiful."

Luc paused. "It reminded me of you."

Alyssa tried not to let his words melt her. "Thank you. You didn't have to—"

"Yes, I did. I wanted to and, while our marriage was quick, that was no reason not to have solid symbols of our union."

She bit her lip. Luc said all the right things . . . but something troubled her, some hint of anger. Or maybe it was just her nerves.

"Where was your family today?" he asked. "I know your mother is gone . . ."

God, where had that question come from? "I'm an only child, and I haven't seen my father since he left. I was four."

Luc frowned. "Aunts, uncles, cousins?"

She shook her head. In truth, she hadn't thought about them in years. She hadn't dared contact them. Her cousins were likely married, had children. Her aunt Anna was probably retired from teaching school.

"None. Could we drop it?"

He looked ready to say something, then closed his mouth. A long, silent minute passed before he finally said, "If you ever want to tell me about your family, I'd love to listen."

"You said yourself we needed to look forward, not back. I think that's an excellent suggestion."

Sighing, Luc gripped the wheel. "Are you hungry? You didn't eat much lunch."

No, but she was starting to feel weak. Since becoming pregnant, she'd noticed that she couldn't skip meals the way she used to. And most days until about two, she lived on crackers and apple juice.

"I should eat."

He smiled. "I'll take care of it."

Like he'd taken care of things this week. Most men would simply have asked when to show up. Instead, he'd arranged the invitations, luncheon, cake, rings, photographer. She'd barely mentioned the things on her to-do list before they were done. Alyssa couldn't fault his taste. Everything had been elegant, likely chosen to please his reserved parents. She'd had only to buy a dress off the rack and order flowers.

She nibbled the inside of her cheek. She'd feel so much better if she could just figure out *why* he married her. Just for the baby . . . or something more.

"We haven't had a chance to really talk about the baby." He broke the silence again. "How has the pregnancy been so far?"

A safer topic. "Other than being really tired, not bad. The vitamins are finally helping. I'm doing better about getting in my fruits and vegetables at dinner. Can't eat much the rest of the day so far. I don't have morning sickness, but food sounds bad until later in the afternoon."

"You'll tell me if that changes."

It wasn't a question, but she couldn't miss the concern in his voice. She should pull back and protect herself . . . but that voice warmed her too much. "I will."

A few minutes later, they reached a bed-and-breakfast in a nearby town. The sun was setting on the grand old brick house and the surrounding cottages that stood in the distance. It was gorgeous, reminiscent of a bygone era. Romantic. Her heart caught.

Theirs was a marriage of convenience and unrequited love. He'd done so much already *and* brought her here for a real wedding night . . . The man overwhelmed her. Which was stupid. He was probably just making the best of their situation. Still, tears stung her eyes.

She breathed, trying to suppress her feelings. "It's beautiful. Thank you."

Luc parked in the driveway. "Wait here. I'll be right back."

When he returned, it was with a big brass key ring; then he drove down the dirt road behind the main house to a little blue cottage with a quaint little porch, complete with rocking chairs. The sign on the door read SWEET SURRENDER.

Alyssa's stomach curled up tighter. Her pulse rocketed.

He unlocked the door and pushed it open. Before she could peek in, Luc swept her up into his arms. She shrieked.

"Tradition," he chided, then carried her in, kicking the door shut behind him.

Inside, the cottage had a homey feel, braided rugs over aged hardwood floors. Wainscoting and cheerful paint covered the walls. Quilts, lacy drapes, and country-style furniture all added charm.

He set her down on a distressed leather sofa, then knelt to remove her shoes, his palms lingering on her calves. She shivered at the heat in his eyes.

"I can tell you didn't sleep much last night. Rest. I'll fix dinner."

No one but Luc had ever taken care of her like this, and it was heaven. She should balk, insist on doing for herself. But this special treatment likely wouldn't last, and leaning on him was so tempting.

"Close your eyes," he demanded.

Finally, she complied. If the past was any indicator, she'd need all the energy she could get for later.

Minutes later, she woke when he set chicken pasta and a salad brimming with vegetables in front of her. As with every day this past week, by dinnertime, she was famished and demolished every bite. "That was incredible."

Luc finished off his own plate. "I have dessert, if you're ready."

Amazing . . . "When did you make all this?"

"This morning. Deke and Kimber delivered it earlier."

He'd thought of everything—and gone the extra mile to make it special. Again, the ever-present question slammed her brain: Why?

Without waiting for her reply, he rose and disappeared to the little kitchen. He returned moments later with a bottle of champagne and one flute, popped the cork, and poured. She supposed he was drinking without her, since she couldn't have the alcohol. Before he took a sip, he disappeared again, then returned with two heaping cups of chocolate mousse and a tray of chocolate-covered strawberries.

"That looks scrumptious. You didn't have to go to this much trouble."

"Since I only plan to be married once, I did." He looked solemn as he picked up the glass to toast her. "To a beautiful bride and the beginning of our lives together."

Ask or leave it alone?

"Do you really believe that, Luc? Other than the fact I'm carrying your child, we have nothing in common but great sex."

Luc raised a dark brow and fingered the rim of the glass for a long moment. "When you were driving to Dallas last week, were you at all excited to see me? Had you missed me even a bit?"

Alyssa hesitated. But why lie when she sought the truth? "Yes."

"I'd missed you, and when you walked through the door, I was damn glad you were there. There's . . . something between us."

Her breath caught. Hope rose. Was it possible he could someday fall in love with her?

What are the chances, really?

Hope crashed. It almost hurt too much, but she couldn't shake the fear. Like a splinter in her psyche, it festered. When had anyone ever wanted her beyond the bump and grind?

She had to stop borrowing tomorrow's trouble and live in to-day's moment. Despite his vows and words to the contrary, all too soon, he could be gone.

Luc raised his glass and took a sip, savoring the champagne. Then he frowned. "This could be better."

"In what way?"

His sensual mouth lifted in a smile. "It would taste better on you."

That was all the warning Alyssa got before Luc dipped his finger in his glass, then traced the liquid over her lips. She barely had a moment to smell the tang, feel the tickle of the bubbles, before Luc rose over her, eyes a blazing black, before he devoured her in a scorching kiss.

Air left her body in a rush of sizzle and need. She swayed toward him, and he pulled her in tighter, slanting his lips over hers again and sinking deep into her. So deep. It was as if the last seven weeks of separation had never happened. Her body *knew* him, dampened, ached, opened, yearned.

Moaning, Luc pressed closer, conquering the last of her resistance and wits with his fervent kiss. Without conscious thought, her hands found their way into his hair, tied neatly at his nape. She needed to bury her fingers in it the same way she needed to bury her senses in his scent.

Suddenly, he pulled away and traced more champagne on her

lips. Now they tingled and trembled, and she couldn't wait to feel his mouth over hers again. Luc didn't disappoint, tasting her, drinking from her as if he'd never get enough.

Alyssa wondered if she ever would.

"I need more of you," he demanded, peeling off her suit coat and attacking the buttons of her blouse. "Now."

His gaze remained riveted on her, a searing promise of ecstasy to come, a silent declaration of his intent to satisfy her until she was boneless and whimpering. Already she trembled. Desire throbbed between her legs. Blood scalded her veins. She couldn't wait to feel him skin to skin, surging deep inside her until she knew nothing but the pounding pulse of desire and the wild surge of climax overtaking her body and inhibitions.

Next, he tore into her bra, yanked away her skirt, and shredded her thong with his hands. Now completely naked and at the mercy of a man who appeared to have none, Alyssa throbbed.

"Undress," she rasped, reaching for his coat.

He shook off her request, then reached for a chocolate-covered strawberry. "Open."

Arguing with that forceful command seemed impossible. As soon as her lips parted, he placed the sweet fruit on her tongue. Flavor burst across her senses, and she bit into its succulence, melting most of the chocolate on her tongue. Sipping champagne, Luc watched, his gaze smoldering.

The second she swallowed, he was all over her again, his mouth forcing hers open under the crush of his. The chocolate met the bubbly wine on her tongue. The flavors entwined to create something irresistible. Pressing closer, she ate at his mouth, needing more, and he gave, delving into her endlessly. She gasped.

Moments later, he was gone, reaching for the nearby table. "Mousse?"

Panting, unable to answer, Alyssa stared as Luc picked up a cup and spooned a bite into her mouth.

Oh, dear God! That man could create the most amazing flavors. She closed her eyes and moaned. When she opened them, he was swallowing another sip of champagne—and swooping down for another kiss.

This time, she anticipated the flavors, the rich, lingering taste, now creamy and smooth and addicting. Every time his tongue brushed hers, the flavor of the bubbly wine added the perfect tang to the sweet decadence of the dessert.

She grabbed his shoulders to rid him of the jacket and pull him closer. He edged away, then grabbed the mousse once more.

He tossed the spoon aside, and it landed with a clatter on the table. Alyssa flinched, but the sound didn't register with him. He simply shoved two fingers into the smooth confection and scooped some out.

"Wha-what are you doing?"

Dizzy, overwhelmed, she could barely catch a breath. He'd kissed her, stripped her bare, and already she was in danger of losing her head completely. And she didn't care. Now she just needed more of this volatile ride to pleasure only he could deliver.

Luc spread her out on the sofa, then smeared the mousse between her swollen folds. She gasped at the icy-hot sensation of the dessert and warm skin against her and struggled to keep her head.

He was having none of that. He grabbed the bottle of champagne and tipped it above her. Cold, bubbly liquid sloshed over her breasts and abdomen, pooled in her navel . . . drizzled into her pussy with a sensation that made her gasp.

Wearing a devilish smile, Luc stared at her wet body and chocolate-covered clit. "Having dessert."

Chapter Thirteen

HIS own personal slice of heaven. Luc speared her pussy with his tongue, chocolate, champagne, and Alyssa's natural taste a flavor that instantly hooked him. Kneeling beside the couch, he lunged for her again, spreading her thighs wider with insistent hands and wedging his shoulders in between.

As he tasted her again, Alyssa's hips bucked as her body thrashed. She cried out, and the sounds drove him up, higher. Closer to that place where he'd lose control.

Tonight, he didn't care.

Another tempting taste of her, another laving of her clit. She gasped and fisted her hands in his hair. The sting on his scalp aroused the hell out of him.

He grabbed the mousse from the table beside him and spooned more right onto the hot flesh of her folds with his fingers, then poured more of the champagne right over that distended bundle of nerves. Her breath caught, a jagged inhalation that thrilled him. Then he swooped in, taking her hard bud in his mouth and sucking, and shoved two fingers inside her weeping entrance. She screamed.

Her body clamped down on his fingers, hungry, demanding, and he couldn't stop imagining exactly how she'd feel on his cock when he got inside her. Everything about this woman, his *wife*, made him feel hedonistic and rapacious. Fuck apologizing for it anymore. She incited him like no other, and it wasn't something he could—or wanted to—stop.

As her orgasm high subsided, he smeared a bit more of the mousse on his fingers, then spread it over her nipple. As he laved it, then sucked deep, she groaned.

"Luc! Oh . . ." She panted, her face and chest flushed and glowing.

Damn, she looked beautiful. As he tore off his clothes and threw them haphazardly over the back of the sofa, he glanced at her left hand, at the sparkling diamond on her finger. She was *his*.

Easing his way up her body, Luc reached out for the champagne flute and tipped it over, above the valley between her breasts. She gasped as he covered her chest with his. The liquid heated between their bodies as they slid sensuously against each other. He grabbed a strawberry and placed it against her lips.

"Eat this," his low voice commanded.

Alyssa stared with wide blue eyes, sparkling with excitement and curiosity, and he felt himself fall for her a bit more. She parted her lush lips, her tongue peeking out to wet them, before she accepted his offering. Luc set the berry in her mouth, chocolate first. As she bit down, she moaned. Her eyes slid shut. His cock jumped as impatience and need thrummed in his blood. He was dying to get inside her.

As she chewed the chocolaty fruit, he tossed back the last of the champagne. The moment she swallowed, he consumed her mouth in a greedy kiss, tasting the sharp swirl of flavors, savoring the way she opened to him, accepted him deep inside her mouth. He wanted to be deeper.

Clutching her hips in his hands, he probed her slick, creamy folds with his cock, then began to push his way in, straight to the haven he'd missed and yearned for over the past seven weeks.

Tight. So damn tight. He always had to fight his way in, and tonight was no exception. One shallow thrust, another, a third . . . Each time he eased in a bit farther, her snug walls created a sinful friction that had him hissing in a breath. Teeth-gritting patience and destructive pleasure—both nearly undid him.

Finally, he sheathed himself completely inside her. With an eager moan, Alyssa rose up to meet both his tongue and his cock. What was it about her? So lush, so perfect, so . . . whatever that he could never get enough?

Under him, her body grew taut. Her fingernails dug into his shoulders, and her legs rose around his hips. She caught his rhythm, and she writhed beneath his increasingly harsh thrusts.

Her breath, hot on his neck, feathered over sensitive skin. An icy-hot shiver nearly undid him. Sex with Alyssa was always more dazzling, more mind-blowing, than anything he'd ever experienced. But tonight, knowing she was his in every way, was killing his control.

"Yes," she murmured. "God, yes . . . Luc!"

"Fuck, you feel so good, sugar. You're shaking."

"I'm close . . ."

A fact he couldn't miss. She kept tightening around him with every second, and he had to anchor his hands on her hips to push his way in. Every thrust became a rich slide into ecstasy that had him panting, growling, needing to empty himself inside her.

"Come for me," he demanded. "Now!"

She tensed even more, gasped. Then the moment was on her, and her eyes flew open. As their stares met, the naked connection smacked him, grabbing him by the cock, tugging at something in his chest. He didn't stand a chance in hell of resisting her.

Pleasure seized his whole body as the climax boiled inside him, then burst wide. He shouted, shuddered, buried himself deep. The sensation was so perfect Luc never wanted to leave.

If he had anything to say about it, he never would.

They were married now. Officially, in every way. Time to put the baby's parentage aside and make this work. At the least, he wanted to earn her trust, be her best friend, the man she turned to for anything.

But deep down, Luc knew he was fooling himself. He wanted much more. Everything she had to give. He wouldn't rest until she was his completely.

*　*　*

MOONLIGHT streamed through the windows as Alyssa stretched, her body aching in a million delicious places. She marveled at how treasured and sated she felt. Every night she spent with Luc ended in mind-blowing passion, but this one . . . She couldn't help but sigh in bliss.

After all but ravaging her on the couch, she'd nearly fallen asleep. Her untimely insomnia the night before, coupled with stress and pregnancy, had shut her body down. He'd said nothing about the interruption to the wedding night he'd so carefully planned. Instead, Luc had carried her to the cottage's huge claw-foot tub and set her in hot water to soak. With infinite care, he washed her body, her hair—even when she'd insisted she could perform the task herself.

She may as well not have wasted her breath.

Afterward, he'd combed her hair, even dried it, then urged her onto the most inviting bed she'd ever seen, firm yet plush, with pillows and fluffy quilts built for comfort. He'd slid her between soft sheets, naked as the day she was born, then followed her down, kissing her lips gently. Alyssa had fallen asleep the moment her head hit the pillow.

Now, a few hours later, she'd awakened, comforted by Luc's deep, even breathing beside her. But then she smelled him. Tempted, she curled up against his body heat and tentatively smoothed her palm down the hard chest, traced his ribbed abdomen, guided soft fingertips over his growing erection.

Flashes of his passion and care bombarded her—the romantic wedding night she'd never expected, the feel of him filling her mouth and body at once, his soothing touch as he'd bathed her from head to toe.

Tears flooded her eyes, closed her throat. And here she thought she couldn't love him more, but tonight his care had expanded her feelings until they nearly drowned her. Alyssa didn't kid herself. Even if this marriage ended badly, Luc would always be in her heart.

From the moment she'd met him, she'd been fascinated. He had intelligence, coupled with a kindness she rarely saw in her customers. When she and Luc had first met, he'd wanted nothing to do with her. He hadn't been rude or disrespectful, but merely stayed away.

Then came the unexpected Sunday morning last summer he'd called her with an outrageous proposition: the favor of fucking him and Deke in exchange for the culinary favor of her choice. He'd known of her restaurant opening soon, just as he'd known she wouldn't be foolish enough to turn him down. Accepting had felt a bit like prostituting herself, but given her past and how much credibility he'd lend to her opening, being squeamish seemed silly.

That wild evening, Deke had departed without touching her—and Luc had been insatiable. Incredible. But he'd never treated her like a whore. In fact, he'd acted as if he'd never been so enthralled with sex, never wanted a woman so much. God knew she'd never burned for any man the way she had for Luc. The next morning, she'd awakened aching for him again . . . only to find the bed empty.

Deep in her heart, she'd hoped that their astounding night might lead to something more. So she'd be lying if she said his desertion hadn't hurt. She'd also be lying if she said it was unexpected.

For weeks afterward, she'd tried to think of something to lure him back, hoping that the memories of their amazing sex would give her a foundation to build on. But she'd seen him again only when she'd forced him to live up to his obligation. The fact he'd resisted her advances and had a new girlfriend had been an ax to her heart . . . but instead of giving up on Luc, she'd seduced him—only to realize he assumed she was fucking Tyler and thought her little more than a whore.

So despite Luc's "explanation," his insistence on this marriage still didn't make sense. She was the same person with the same occupation and the same bouncer Luc believed was her lover. The only difference? She was pregnant. Yes, he'd claimed to miss her in the weeks they'd been apart . . . but enough to marry her?

And now she was in deeper. Last night, with his passion and tenderness, he'd shattered her. No other way to describe it. He'd begun tearing away the walls she never let anyone behind, destroying her defenses. Whether he'd meant to or not, he'd made her irrevocably his. Alyssa hoped that, maybe, at least in part, Luc was hers, too.

"You're thinking too hard," Luc murmured and rolled to face her.

His inky hair tumbled over his shoulder, the ends flirting with his pectorals. His bedroom eyes looked black and smoky in the shadows. Her pulse picked up speed.

It would be so easy to fall into his arms, and let whatever was going to happen between them simply happen. But she'd never had the luxury of wearing rose-colored glasses. Alyssa needed to know why Luc had married her. Asking why had gotten her nowhere. If she wanted to know if he'd married her simply for the baby or the sex, she had to change tactics.

"A lot on my mind," she answered finally.

"Yesterday was a big day."

She nodded. "Getting married is huge, and we really haven't known each other long. I mean, we've spent, maybe, five days together total."

Luc brushed the hair back from her face. "It doesn't sound like a lot, but . . . somehow, between us, it is."

Alyssa understood exactly what he meant. Every moment had been full of discovery and gravity, bringing them together when they were at their best, pitting their tempers against each other when they were at their worst.

"I need—" God, her stomach revolted, and it had nothing to do with pregnancy hormones. What if Luc laughed or scoffed or became angry at her question?

Then you'll know.

"Need what?" he prompted, tracing his fingertips over her bare shoulder. She shivered.

"How do you feel about me?"

Her question clearly surprised him. Luc hesitated, then resumed his brushing caress. "That's a direct question, but I expect that from you."

"I'm pragmatic."

"That, you are."

She bristled. "I've had to be."

As he cupped her cheek, his face softened. "I'm not judging you. In fact, it's part of what I admire about you."

That warmed her a bit. "So you admire me?"

Like a child caught with a hand in the cookie jar, Luc smiled. "You're smart and tough and tenacious. Jack told me the way you rebounded after Peter's attack even impressed the hell out of him."

Great, but none of that added up to love. Though she hadn't expected more, disappointment caved in on her.

Alyssa fought off the feeling. Maybe her love would be enough for both of them.

Then she sighed. She knew nothing about relationships, but

doubted one-sided devotion would work. After last night, she needed to pull back, do her best to rebuild the walls around her heart.

"Thank you," she muttered, rolling away.

He grabbed her arm and turned her back to him, fitting their bodies together. "Where are you going?"

"Get dressed and get to work. I left Bonheur a mess after yesterday."

He pressed her back to the mattress. "The restaurant has been cleaned from top to bottom—dishes, linens, the works. Today's food is already prepped for tonight's opening."

Her mouth gaped open. "Who did . . . ? How do you know?"

"I called a few people and took care of it."

Like he'd taken care of everything else. She just kept falling over and over for Luc, with no end in sight. "Thank you."

He was so thoughtful, good at anticipating her needs and seeing to them. Did that mean he maybe more than admired her? Or was she letting stupid hope talk her into making more of the gesture than she should?

"You work too hard." His thumb traced the arch of her brow as he stared down into her face with an expression she couldn't read. "Like I said, I admire you, but I worry."

"Admiration in a marriage . . ." *Isn't enough.* She choked the words down. "It helps, I'm sure."

Luc took her face in his hands. "I didn't say that was all I felt."

Alyssa's heart skipped a beat. His arm encircled her waist, and he urged her thigh over his hip, opening her to him. He pressed a kiss to her mouth, nibbled at her neck, breathed in her ear. Tingles and goose bumps skittered across her skin. Her body snapped to attention, as if it knew its lord and master, and readied itself in anticipation of his possession.

But the way he looked at her made her breath catch. His expression said she mattered. Very much.

"Oh," she breathed.

"Now that we're married, we must be honest. Communicate better." He slanted his mouth over hers again, and Alyssa had to fight to focus on his words when he pulled back enough to whisper. "The truth is, I've never felt for any woman as deeply as I feel for you."

More than Kimber, even? *Thump, thump, thump.* Her heart threatened to jump from her chest.

"You look shocked."

"I am. I know you've been in relationships before . . ."

"They're behind me." He propped his head on his palm, his gaze delving deep. "How do you feel about me?"

So ridiculously in love it scares the hell out of me. "I care, too. More than I thought possible after a few days."

Alyssa didn't dare confess to more than that. Telling him too much, being too open, she knew from experience gave a man exactly what he needed to make her vulnerable and drop her to her knees— right at his feet.

"Good." Luc smiled, his expression so intimate in the dark, her toes curled. "It's up to us to make this marriage work."

And what did she know about that? "Agreed."

"What do you need from me?" he whispered. "What are you seeking in a husband?"

In truth, she'd never given it any real thought. "Someone who likes and respects me, who understands what makes me tick. I've enjoyed the fact you've taken care of me these past few days, but I don't expect it. I need you to believe that I can stand on my own two feet."

He brushed a thumb across her lips, then took possession of them in a lush but brief kiss that melted her even more. "I believe you can do anything you set your mind to."

Pride filled her. "Thank you. I'm not always good at sharing what I'm thinking. I've lived and worked alone for too long, I guess."

That, and barely surviving the ultimate betrayal of her feelings and trust. But he didn't need those gory details.

"Don't be surprised if I ask you a lot of questions. I like knowing what's going on with you and being involved in Bonheur or anything else you have going on. I'll help however I can. You have only to ask. I won't step in the middle of your business unless something seems dangerous or wrong. I know you've managed just fine for many years without me, and I'd never presume to think that's changed."

God, just when she thought the walls around her heart couldn't crumble anymore . . . "Thank you."

"If you think I've overstepped, we'll talk. In return, I'll ask only three things of you."

Was this the catch she'd been looking for? "What?"

"First, no more stripping. The male population of Louisiana doesn't need to see my wife naked anymore."

"Done." The last thing she wanted to do was take her clothes off for a bunch of drunk, slobbering strangers again. The fact he cared about who saw her body warmed her heart.

"Good. Second, I need your trust. After Peter's attack, it became clear that someone once raped you. I don't need details today or tomorrow. But I want you to know you can trust me with whatever you want to tell me."

She'd figured he'd come to some fairly accurate conclusions, but the fact he wasn't going to push her? Her relief was almost tangible. She'd heard enough from the other dancers whose cavemen husbands thought a piece of paper entitled them to know everything to be afraid. Alyssa didn't think she was wired to share herself that deeply again.

"I appreciate that."

"Hmm." Luc exhaled across her shoulder and pressed his mouth to her collarbone. "I appreciate your skin."

As his palm drifted down to her breast, she caught his wrist and stopped him. Yes, she wanted him again, feeling him deep and strong

and demanding inside her. She was a glutton where Luc was concerned. But this conversation was too productive to stop now.

"And third?"

He froze, except for the clenching of his jaw. "Complete fidelity."

Stinging as if she'd been slapped, she yanked away. "You still
think I'm a whore."

Luc was right on her, curling his arm around her waist and dragging her closer. "No. You don't turn tricks or fuck customers. Before
I got to know you as a person, I believed the stereotype, that a woman
who'd shed her clothes for money would also be willing to spread her
legs for it. But that's not you."

Alyssa pushed back tears, the relief was so profound. Then she
noticed that her husband's carefully crafted reply hadn't included
Tyler.

She'd given Luc a dozen reasons to assume that she and her
bouncer were lovers. Tyler touched her openly in public, had a key
to her house, saw her naked often . . . In Luc's shoes, she'd assume the
same thing. Insisting again that Tyler was only her friend was counterproductive. Luc would learn the truth soon enough.

"I don't know a lot about marriage, but I believe fidelity is important. If you're going to demand it of me, I want the same in return.
When you go to Los Angeles to tape your shows next week, don't
imagine it's okay to hook up with whatever brainless starlet plops in
your lap."

Luc laughed. "Not interested in brainless starlets plopping in my
lap, bed, or anywhere else. I'm completely enthralled by you, and
being with you, inside you . . ."

His voice lowered an octave, his gaze turning dark and forceful.
Intent narrowed his eyes, and before she could think or breathe, Luc
probed between her thighs and pushed inward.

His penetration seared her swollen folds. Not surprisingly, she
was wet for him. Her nipples beaded. He took one in his mouth and
nipped with a stinging pleasure-pain as he forced his cock higher

inside her. Alyssa parted her thighs wider and lifted her hips, desperate to have him as deep as he could go. He pressed at her walls, straining her ability to take him. Accepting all of his length and girth in one stroke was impossible. The ramp up to feeling him deep inside her was deliciously maddening.

Her flesh stung, and the burning behind her clit nearly drove her insane. Luc continued to work her nipples. They were already slightly sore from last night. Now they stood up hard and straight and responded to the smallest lick, even to the feel of his breath on them. But when he sucked them in his mouth and bit gently as he plunged the rest of the way inside her . . .

She screamed.

"Yes," he purred. "Being inside you, making you take every inch of me in this tight, hot pussy. I love sex with you. I'm addicted."

He withdrew slowly, so slowly, she whimpered. As he lingered, his thumbs brushed her tight nipples before he bit at her neck and plunged deep and hard to the hilt, making her gasp again.

"When I don't get to fuck you, I'm shaky and strung out. I ache. I can't think about anything but getting you naked and working my cock inside you, all gripping and scalding. And bare. Always bare. I don't ever want anything between us."

Condoms had always been a way of life for Alyssa. She'd never allowed any man to have sex with her without adequate protection, but what Luc did to her . . . God, there was no description. Even his words made her hot to take him constantly and deeper.

"Your worry, sugar, shouldn't be what I'm going to do when I'm not in your pussy, but how you're ever going to be able to keep me out of it. You make me damn hot, so expect that meals will sometimes get cold before you'll eat them, that your showers won't be solo, that you may not often get a full night's sleep. I love you swollen and wet and ready, and I plan to keep you that way."

Every word out of his mouth melted her into a worthless puddle.

When men had talked to her like that in the past, she'd felt sleazy. But something about Luc and the way he whispered to her, almost reverent and amazed, made her feel both needed and special.

As Luc continued to drag his cock through her sensitive channel, blood heated her skin, rushed to her clit. Sensation flooded her as he drew back with stunning friction. She mewled as he pushed back into her so slowly, she dug her nails into his back, tried to push her heels into his ass. He refused to be rushed. In fact, he refused to allow her any say at all.

"Bad girl," he muttered thickly in her ear. "Impatience will only earn you a slower fucking."

Before her scrambled brain could regroup so that she could figure out what he meant, Luc withdrew and turned her over. Then plunged in deep again, his strokes maddeningly unhurried and torturous.

"Please. Faster."

Luc leaned over her back and kissed the side of her jaw, the back of her neck. "What do you want faster?"

God, he was going to make her say it. They'd played this game their first night together, months ago. She'd resisted, and he'd wrung every begging admission from her eventually, then fulfilled a dozen fantasies. That he might do the same now made her blood thicken like lava in her veins.

Alyssa clenched her jaw to hold the words in, but his unhurried strokes were undoing her. Then he added his fingers to her clit and toyed with the distended button.

"Tell me what I want to hear, and you know I'll give you what you want."

Yes, he would, but he'd also take so much power from her. She'd already handed him her heart. This . . . would be a sign that she'd surrendered the last of her independence. Her soul.

His fingertips dragged over the exposed head of her clit, and she gasped. He nipped in her ear. "I could do this all morning. You're so wet, and I love to keep you on edge. You swell and swell, gripping me so tight . . . *Mmm.*"

Pleasure ripped through her body. Her stomach clenched. The pressure built until it burned and tightened, like hot clamps squeezing at her resistance.

Another dragging withdrawal, another sheet-fisting glide back inside until he bumped her most sensitive spot and pressed. She couldn't breathe. Dizziness encroached. Luc fingered her needy little bud again.

"Luc!" The demanding shout was more like a sob.

"That's it, sugar. Yeah. Keep tightening on me." He clutched her shoulder and used it as leverage as he continued to saw in and out of her body at a molasses pace that made her insane. "Tell me what you want. I can't give it to you until you do."

He was playing her, daring her. Giving in went against her grain . . . but Luc had become so effective at strumming her body for his pleasure. The staggering ache kept crashing in on her until she had no more defenses.

She sobbed again. "Please . . ."

"Tell me. Open that pretty mouth and tell me what you want."

"Faster! Fuck me faster!"

Still he hesitated, his hot, heavy breaths on the back of her neck making her tremble. "Faster? If I do that, what will you do for me?"

He wanted something, and Alyssa had no idea what. If she'd been in her right mind, she would have refused. Who promised something before knowing what it was?

But Alyssa was in no frame of mind to bargain.

"Anything," she gasped, trying to push back on his cock.

Luc clutched her, preventing any movement. "Just anything?"

The pleasure was coalescing inside her, turning thick and sharp and tight. The slightest movement . . . She needed it. Now. Her mind was about to snap, her body already his slave.

"Anything."

"What if I want everything?" he growled.

Alyssa couldn't find her breath, so she gave him a shaky nod.

"Say the words, my little wife." His fingers retreated, tracing the soft pad of flesh above her pussy, denying her that one touch to her clit that would send her into the stratosphere.

God, she had nothing left to fight him with, no way to keep even an ounce of herself hidden. She arched to him, and he slid a bit deeper inside her. And still it wasn't enough.

"Everything!" Her cry resonated in her ears.

Like a predator sensing blood, Luc moved in for the kill. "Absolutely everything?"

"Yes," she breathed. "Please, God, yes!"

"That's exactly what I'll take," he vowed in a snarl, then pounded into her with deep, merciless strokes, fast enough to multiply the friction and still slow enough to savor the mountain of pleasure burying her.

He pressed slick fingers onto her clit again and rubbed in tiny circles. Her blood boiled over, her sanity snapped, and the pleasure burst through her, seemingly bigger than her whole body. It rewrote the definition of amazing sex, became the stick by which she measured encounters with every other man. They all came up woefully short. And still the ecstasy kept piling on top of her, a raging deluge she gladly drowned in.

She'd barely caught her breath and remembered her own name when Luc struck again, this time circulating his slick fingers around the rosette of her back entrance.

Oh, God. He wasn't just trying to tear away her defenses; he was trying to destroy her. "No."

"You said everything," he reminded, his fingers, wet with lubrication still circling the small hole.

"It's too much." Alyssa heard the pleading note in her voice and no longer cared.

"Did I hurt you last time, on our first night?"

He knew better. As often as she'd come for him, he *must* know. But like everything else tonight, he wanted her admission.

"No."

He pressed two fingers deep, his tongue laving her shoulder. "I'm going to make it good, sugar. So good."

Of that, she had no doubt.

Alyssa gasped as his fingers went deep, deeper, as his cock stroked in and out of her pussy, bringing back to life nerve endings she'd been certain were overwrought and dead. They didn't just flicker, but flared, leapt, raced, throbbed.

She was still trying to adjust to the change when he withdrew from her, then angled his body higher over hers. He began pressing his cock into her small back entrance. The stretching bordered pain, and she hissed at the riot of needs flaring to life again as he shoved past her resistance, then pushed in a seemingly endless tunnel inside her until his body pressed completely against her back and she swore she could feel him everywhere.

"Fuck, yes!" He clutched her shoulders, traced her waist with his palms, then grabbed her hips in a brutal, desperate grip. "Rub your clit. This is going to be hard and fast."

Small mercy after all this time, and she should probably tell him she wasn't following his directives. She'd rub her clit if she wanted to and not before. But he'd already made her itchy, edgy, needy.

As soon as she touched herself, Luc set a pounding pace that stole her breath. In seconds, he overwhelmed her. Sensations she hadn't felt in months, wrought by the awakening of greedy nerves and a jacked-up libido, demanded more. She touched herself, dragged up higher and higher by his ferocious strokes into the deepest recesses of her body, igniting the darkest of her fantasies where Luc took her exactly as he wanted, for as long as he wanted, making her climax for him at will.

As he pinched her nipple and tunneled back into the tight channel, he panted at the back of her neck, "Come!"

Her world exploded like a supernova again. Tears of relief and release burst forth. Luc had devastated her, scraped her raw. And still, he kept at her, thick and hard and demanding as tears streamed down her cheeks, until she possessed no more buffers between her husband and her battered heart.

Chapter Fourteen

THE Sunday following their wedding, Alyssa leaned against the doorjamb of the master bedroom and watched Luc pack the last of his suitcase. She'd lived alone for a decade or more. Solitude had always been a comfort. Luc had moved into her house the day after their wedding. It was logical, given that, between his upcoming TV show and his appearances, he'd be traveling, while she was tied to Lafayette by the club and the restaurant. But him *living* in her personal space, her making room in her closet, bathroom, and drawers, all seemed weird. He was neater than her. And he ironed, which was a big bonus. But for the first few days, she'd felt invaded—home, body, and heart.

Now, watching him prepare to leave, Alyssa had to swallow down sadness. She was going to miss Luc, probably more than she should. She'd grown accustomed to seeing him in Bonheur's kitchens, watching over her during Sexy Sirens' wee hours. Two days ago, his publicist had released the news of their wedding. Since then, Luc had whisked her to her car each night, tightly holding her against his side. She'd gotten used to him fixing her a light snack before bed, his comforting presence beside her as she slept, inevitably waking to his delicious, addicting touch and the way he kept her on orgasm overload.

All that would be gone for the next two weeks. Of course it wasn't the end of the world, but somehow being away from him made her jittery and anxious.

"I'll call you when I get in," he promised.

"Thanks."

"You're feeling okay today?"

Alyssa nodded. "A little tired, but that's normal."

"Don't work too hard. Sadie's watching you for me."

"She's a tattletale." She crossed her arms over her chest in a mock pout.

"Which is why I chose her to keep me informed." Luc zipped up his suitcase and set it on the floor. "I'll be back to spend Thanksgiving week with you and go to your doctor appointment the following week."

The first meeting with her obstetrician. The first time to hear her baby's heartbeat. "I appreciate you being here for me to lean on."

He crossed the room and took her face in his hands. Determined dark eyes bored into her. "I wouldn't have it any other way."

God, when he spoke to her, in that voice, with that concern on his face, he absolutely melted her. He must know that.

"Before I go, I have something for you."

She stared, all frowns and confusion as he turned away and pulled something out from behind his briefcase, which leaned against the wall. It was a box roughly the size of a loaf of bread, wrapped in thick foil paper that shimmered with small silver scallops. An elegant white bow topped the gift.

Luc handed it to her. "It's a belated wedding gift."

"A gift? You didn't have to—"

"But I wanted to."

Swallowing down a lump of emotion, she removed the bow and tore through the wrapping paper to reveal a plain brown box. After wrestling with the cardboard, she pulled out the contents and gasped. Inside was a picture frame in the shape of two silver rings entwined. On the left, a picture of her in her wedding dress. On the right, a picture of their wedding kiss. In the middle, where the two rings overlapped, he'd had their first names and their wedding date engraved.

"It's gorgeous!"

She almost choked on a mixture of gratitude and love. Their marriage wasn't perfect. They were still getting to know each other. But Luc was trying. She was still holding back. Then again, sometimes she caught him staring at her, sometimes he thought too long before he answered her, and she sensed that maybe he was too . . .

"You like it?"

Tears threatened, and she tried to blink them away. "I *love* it. Thank you."

Luc took it from her hands. "I thought maybe you could put it here, on the dresser." He set it on the long, rectangular piece on the wall opposite the bed. "That way, while I'm gone, you could look at it."

And think of me. He didn't say the words, but Alyssa heard them. Why would he ask unless he cared, at least a little? How could she refuse him?

"That's perfect," she murmured, making her way to his side and wrapping her hand around the steely strength of his biceps.

He turned her into his arms. Softly, he kissed her mouth, and like every other time Luc touched her, she found her will dissolving. He made her warm and weak, enthralled her completely.

With a grunt of frustration, he pulled away. "If I do any more of that, I won't make my flight. I can just see me trying to explain that I missed the first taping because I couldn't manage to stop fucking my wife."

She laughed. She'd done so little of that in years. Luc was one incredibly sexy man, but living with him now . . . she was beginning to see a whole side of his humor that added a dimension to her attraction.

Every day, she fell a bit more. So damn dangerous, this bottomless pit of feeling. And still, she couldn't stop.

"I don't need anyone blaming me for anything else. I've already got half the women of Lafayette pissed at me. Don't start dragging California bigwigs into the snake pit."

Luc smiled vaguely before his expression settled into something serious. "I have to say something before I go. Peter's been quiet since he's been out on bail."

"I hope his daddy has a tight leash on him now."

"If anything scares you—anything—don't hesitate to call me."

"You'll be two thousand miles away. I'll manage. I'm wearing my big-girl panties."

"For big-girl panties, they always seem very . . . small." He leered, brushing a hand up under her skirt and cupping her bare cheek, then sighed. "And I know you're self-sufficient. Photographers have been a little annoying in the last few days, but I'm sure they'll follow me to L.A., rather than stay here to hound you. Still, if you have any trouble, call me."

"Yes, Daddy," she mocked.

"Am I being overprotective?" He winced.

"A touch."

He sighed. "I'll try to back off. But . . . call me if you need to. Or want to."

"I will. But I'll be fine. The baby will be fine. Bonheur, Sexy Sirens . . . fine. It's only two weeks."

"Right." He ran his hands through her hair, then palmed her nape. "Miss me?"

Like mad. He hadn't left yet, and his absence was already a gaping hole in her heart.

Alyssa didn't trust her voice, didn't trust that she wouldn't reveal too much. She simply nodded.

"And I'll miss you," he whispered against her lips.

Then, after an all-too-brief kiss, he was gone. She was left staring at his incredible gift through her stinging, watery gaze, almost afraid to be this happy. What if it didn't last?

* * *

BY Wednesday at four a.m., she was frazzled. The crowd at Sexy Sirens had been unusually rowdy tonight. She'd fended off more male octopi than she cared to count. Her two blessings were that Tyler never left her side, and Peter, who'd started lurking around the club again on Monday, had apparently been picked up for a DUI early this afternoon so he was back in County—and out of her hair.

Now home, she dragged herself through the front door. After not sleeping well since Luc's departure and the baby sapping all her vitamins, she *needed* a good eight hours' sleep. But damn, it was cold in here. She'd have to turn on the heater pronto.

When she turned to disable her burglar alarm, she saw it had been smashed with a sledgehammer. There was nothing left to disable.

Plastic pieces were strewn across the floor. Wires dangled from the panel. The air in her house felt violated, just like her club and office at Bonheur once had. Why the hell had she insisted to Tyler that she didn't need him to escort her home?

She didn't dare go upstairs alone. In fact, she needed to get out of the house now.

Stepping back out into the dark morning, Alyssa reached for her cell phone. Tyler answered on the first ring.

"What's wrong?"

"Someone broke into my house."

Tyler swore, an ugly string of curses that made her wince. "I'm still in my truck. I'll be there in less than five. Call the police. Now."

Whispering her agreement, she hung up the phone, and shivered in the November chill. It had gotten too cold for her short skirts, and she wished she'd brought a coat. She had wonderfully warm clothes in her closet upstairs . . . but she'd rather freeze than risk going up there alone.

The 911 dispatcher answered quickly, and Alyssa gave her name and address, and described the break-in, at least as much as she knew about it.

Should she call Luc now or wait until a more reasonable hour? It was two in the morning in L.A., and his taping always began so early each morning, he'd be sound asleep.

Before she could decide, Tyler pulled into her driveway with a growl of his engine and threw the truck in park. He climbed out and grabbed her shoulders, dragging her against him. "Are you all right?"

"Shaken. Not hurt."

"And cold."

Swearing, he reached inside the truck, then wrapped his coat around her. Alyssa sighed at the sudden warmth, but her relief was short-lived.

"Show me what you found," Tyler demanded.

"Shouldn't we let Remy and the boys in there for a look first?" Honestly, she just didn't want to see what else the intruder had done to her house.

"You mean preserve the crime scene because they're such fabulous investigators?" Razor blades had nothing on the sharpness of his sarcasm. "I want to see the scene for myself before they fuck it up."

"Did you used to—?"

"Yeah. I won't have time to examine the scene closely before they barge in, but I can look." He pulled out a pair of leather gloves from the truck. "Let's make this quick."

Alyssa's insides shook as she led Tyler back in the house. The questions about his past could wait.

Inside the dim interior, she flipped on the foyer light, as she'd done when she first entered the house. Tyler looked at the alarm panel, studying it with a clenched jaw. "Fuck. Was this as far as you got in the house before leaving?"

"I was too afraid to stay, in case the pissed-off intruder was still here with his friend, Mr. Hammer."

"Especially if he also brought other friends, like Misters Knife or Gun," Tyler muttered grimly. "Good girl."

From the back of his waistband, Tyler pulled out a nasty semi-automatic. Alyssa stared, wide-eyed.

"Where did you get that?"

"My truck. I don't make a production about the fact I have it. Stay behind me," he instructed as he made his way up the dark stairs.

He shouldered open the first door on the left, the guest room, and flipped on the light. "Anything look disturbed?"

Alyssa peeked over his shoulder. Everything looked exactly as she'd left it that afternoon. In fact, it had a vaguely stale smell, as if no one had opened the door in weeks, which was true.

Tyler extinguished the light and rolled his shoulders, as if trying to get calm. He crept toward her exercise room, gun drawn. The door was still wide-open, as it had been after she'd finished her morning workout.

Inside, he groped around for the light switch. A moment later, soft overhead light illuminated the space. Everything was the same: punching bag dangling from the ceiling, stair climber, free weights. Even the remnants of this morning's bottle of water remained on the windowsill.

"Nothing," she murmured.

"Good." He sighed as he switched off the light, clearly trying to find his calm.

"Maybe when the alarm went off, he smashed it in frustration, then took off." But even as she said the words, she *knew* that someone had been up here. She felt it—and the resulting fear.

Tyler just grimaced, as if he didn't want to scare her with the truth.

She chewed on her bottom lip nervously. "I don't know why it didn't alert the police."

"I'm going guess this asshole snipped your phone line before he broke into your house, cutting your connection to the police." Tyler sounded grim. "If you don't have detectors on your windows, he probably cut a hole in the glass and climbed in."

"Which is why it's so cold in the house." Nausea slid through her.

"Exactly. Then he probably disabled the audible alarm system in your attic. That way, no matter what he did next, he never had to worry about alerting your neighbors. Then I'll bet he pounded your alarm panel just for fun."

"Would a run-of-the-mill burglar do all that?"

He shook his head, then turned to trek down the hall, toward her bedroom. "They usually prefer something simpler. Open windows are an engraved invitation. But that's not to say they won't do whatever necessary to get past your fancy equipment if they think you've got something of great value."

"B-but I don't. I never bothered to buy a flat-panel TV. My laptop is at Bonheur. I don't keep cash in the house. I don't have much jewelry."

"And you've been wearing your wedding rock, so it wasn't lying around the house."

So Tyler *had* noticed her ring. And his grousing voice didn't sound thrilled in the least. Then again, she wasn't surprised.

As Tyler opened the master bedroom, he paused. "Light switch?"

"On the wall to your right, closer to the bathroom."

He hesitated, then shook his head. "Too far in the dark. Just in case . . ."

Edging away from her bedroom, he backtracked to the guest bathroom in the hallway and switched on the little room's bright lights. The beam of illumination drifted across the hardwood floor of the hallway and cast gray shadows just inside the doorway of her room.

"Wait here." Tyler's voice made it clear that his demand wasn't up for negotiation.

Terror pulsed in her stomach. She had the worst feeling that whatever she found was going to crush her, scare her in a way that the notes affixed with knives never had. Heart racing, she pressed her lips together so she didn't pant and alert Tyler to the fact she was right behind him.

"You're not following directions."

Alyssa ignored him until he thrust out an arm. "Fucking wait outside the doorway. And get out of my light."

Reluctantly, she stepped aside, peering around the door. A moment later, Tyler flipped the light on.

He revealed complete disaster, and she screamed.

Luc's clothes had been piled in the middle of the bedroom, torn to shreds, then doused in red paint. The linens had been yanked from the mattress and strewn across the floor, again ripped in a fit of fury and drenched in crimson. It was all over her carpet, her bedroom walls. She could *feel* the rage of whoever had done this. The act had been deeply personal, his silent act of war.

"Who would do this?" Her voice shook, and she clutched her stomach, wondering if she was going to lose her dinner.

"Peter would be my first choice."

"He's in County right now."

A grim frown crossed Tyler's face. "Primpton?"

"He just wants to shut me down. For that, he needs to publicly discredit me, not scare me. Invading my personal space doesn't accomplish a damn thing."

"Maybe he's just hoping to run you out of town?"

"I'm sure he'd love that, but he should know better after eighteen months of bitching." She shook her head. Primpton doing this didn't feel right.

"True . . . but he's the only suspect we've got, unless you can think of another slighted customer who would be this pissed at you."

"No."

Alyssa kept taking in the devastation in the room with her mouth agape. Her perfume bottles were everywhere, most broken, and the room smelled like a horrific mix of flowers and chemicals that nearly made her sick. He'd piled a bunch of her lingerie in the middle of the naked bed, and as she approached it, the sight got even more revolting.

"Oh, my God. Th-that's semen."

Instantly, Tyler was at her side, staring at the thick white ejaculate some sick freak had sprayed all over her lingerie.

Alyssa put a hand over her mouth and turned away. Now she really was going to throw up.

But her eyes landed on something silver on the carpet, barely sticking out from under the comforter. Fear and denial turbocharging her heart, she ran to it and reached out to grab it.

"No!" Tyler growled, then pulled her back before she could clutch the object. "You can't touch anything. Let me."

Gingerly with his thumb and forefinger, he lifted the downy comforter enough for Alyssa's worst fears to be confirmed: Someone had destroyed Luc's wedding gift to her. The photo of their wedding kiss had been ripped into little pieces. The terrible intruder had splashed red paint on the picture frame. It dripped down the engraving. She sobbed and reached out for it, wanting the frame restored so badly she ached.

Tyler wrapped his arms around her middle, forcing her arms to her sides. "You can't."

"B-but Luc gave this to me." Sick, shuddering, shaking sobs poured forth and she doubled over, unable to look at the devastation anymore.

Tyler pulled her back against his chest, his palm over her abdomen, his lips at her ear. "It's okay. We'll fix everything. Honey, don't make yourself sick over this. It's not good for you."

Or the baby. She knew that, but the shock and fear crashing through her system, combined with exhaustion and the noxious scents, had her on overload.

"Shh," he soothed.

She just shook her head. "I can't."

"You have to get it together. Remy and the boys will be here soon. Let's go."

Alyssa gave him a miserable nod, and Tyler dragged her to her feet. Her knees nearly didn't support her, but she forced herself to stay upright.

Tyler dropped the comforter, slightly away from the ruined picture frame, revealing the last and worst of the horrors. The picture of her in her wedding dress had been ripped from the frame, and he'd left her a message that made her scream herself into a black abyss.

* * *

ALYSSA was missing. Pacing his Los Angeles hotel room before dawn, Luc tried her house and cell numbers again. No answer at either and no voice mail at the former. Sadie had been unable to locate her at Bonheur or the club. Remy could only tell him that Alyssa had made a 911 call and reported that someone had broken into her house. And that by the time the sheriff and his deputy arrived, her car was there . . . but she was nowhere in sight.

Had someone abducted her? What if someone other than Peter had left those threatening notes and taken her?

The term "cold sweat" had a whole new meaning for him as he shoved the last of his belongings in his suitcase.

An hour ago, he'd called Jack Cole, who had immediately started the hunt for Alyssa. Jack had called a few minutes ago to say that, so far, he'd found nothing. And Luc felt helpless in Los Angeles. If Alyssa was missing . . . The taping of the show was important, but not more than finding her and the baby.

The only other person his wife knew that he hadn't spoken with yet was Tyler. Alyssa would go to him; the bouncer made her feel safe. But what else did he make her feel? Would she really fuck the baby's biological father mere hours after Luc turned his back? He didn't have an answer, but Luc knew Tyler would be only too happy to have Alyssa in his bed again. Still, the jealous clenching of his gut was better than thinking a madman had gotten his hands on her.

But both options sucked.

Swearing, Luc grabbed his phone again and called Jack. "Anything new?"

"Sorry, man." Jack's voice. "I checked the hospitals. Nothing."

Closing his eyes, Luc tamped down panic, fearing that, one way or another, he'd lost Alyssa. "Keep looking. Please. I'm on my way to the airport. I'll call Sadie again, see if she can track Tyler down. I'll catch the first flight back I can."

After more murmured sympathy from Jack, he hung up and made the call to Sadie he dreaded. She answered right away.

"I checked with Brandy," the dancer said. "She hasn't heard from Alyssa."

Luc pinched the bridge of his nose, fighting off the headache he knew stemmed from lack of sleep. When he hadn't been able to reach his wife in the wee hours of the morning, he'd been unable to go to sleep. No way he'd be able to rest until he knew what the hell was going on.

"What about Tyler?"

"I called. No answer. I'd drive by his place . . . but I don't know where he lives. He's never been interested in socializing with anyone but Alyssa."

Socializing? Luc barely held in a grunt. If Tyler had Alyssa, Luc bet the man was doing something far more personal to his wife.

Thanking the dancer, Luc hung up and called Jack again as he grabbed a taxi to the airport. "Can you find an address for a guy named Tyler Murphy? He's new to Lafayette."

"Alyssa's bouncer? Yeah. Give me a few and I'll call you back."

Gratified that Jack was on his side, Luc tried Alyssa again. No response. He left a message on his producer's cell phone, indicating that his wife was missing and he was on his way back to Louisiana.

Traffic was light before six a.m. As soon as Luc hit the airport and cleared security, his phone was ringing. His heart stopped. Hope was a nasty spike of adrenaline. Until he looked at his display. Jack.

"Talk to me."

"There's no record of a Tyler Murphy living in Lafayette. At least no one with a driver's license living in the area between the ages of twenty-five and forty. Checked the surrounding areas, too."

Luc's blood ran cold. "What does that mean?"

"Either Mr. Murphy hasn't updated his license since moving to the area, which he's supposed to do within thirty days, and as a former cop he should know it."

"Yeah, he's been there about four months. What's the 'or'?" But Luc feared he knew the answer.

"Or the man isn't who he claims to be."

Fuck! Maybe her buddy Tyler had been threatening her all along. Getting her pregnant was probably just an added kick on his sick freak agenda.

As Luc boarded the plane, he tried Alyssa one more time. No answer. Luc didn't want to think this but . . . what was he going to do without her?

That question haunted him for the next five hours, along with chilling regret. In that moment, he'd take back the anger, his snide comments, cross words, anything that had made her cry. He replayed their final night at Sexy Sirens, right before Peter's attack, in his head and wondered how the fuck he could have been such a prick while he'd cooked for Bonheur's opening. She'd been nothing but honest about the kind of woman she was, and he'd treated her with contempt. All because he'd been too afraid to admit how much he loved her. Because he'd feared he was forming an attachment to someone who would make him choose between his heart and his dreams—and he'd punished her.

As his plane touched down in Lafayette, Luc had to restrain himself from charging out of his seat as they taxied to the gate. Quickly, he checked his cell phone for messages. Nothing.

But one thought hit him like a ton of bricks: Not once during the long plane trip had he thought of the baby. His every thought, fear, and prayer had been for Alyssa.

* * *

JACK met Luc at the baggage claim, Hunter in tow. A cold sweat flattened him. Had they come to tell him the worst?

"What's going on?" Luc demanded.

"Nothing new has happened." Jack stuck out his hand, and Luc shook it, trembling with overpowering relief. Alyssa might not be safe yet, but at least she hadn't been found dead.

"We're still following clues," Hunter offered. "The sheriff here is an idiot."

Kimber's brother looked as though he might have thawed toward Luc. Maybe. In his assessment of Remy, Luc agreed.

"We came to pick you up." Jack looked at the baggage carousel. "Got bags?"

"Carried on," he told Jack. "You didn't have to come here. I have a car."

Jack raised a dark brow. "Sleep any in the last twenty-four hours? Able to get your mind off of Alyssa at all?"

Luc sent the man a bullish glare. Hell, no, and both he and Hunter knew it. "Then take me to the house. I want to see it."

The two men glanced at each other. Luc saw instantly they were against that plan.

"Unless you have a strong stomach and can absolutely say you won't fly into a rage, I don't recommend that," Jack finally said.

The first . . . usually. The latter, no. He was already pissed.

"Lay it on me straight. Did there look to be signs of a struggle? Remy wouldn't say a damn thing."

"No. At least I don't think so. But the psycho's parting shot didn't leave me with a warm fuzzy."

Luc's heart stopped. "Parting shot? He left something behind?"

Jack grimaced. "Alyssa's wedding photo covered in red paint with the words DEAD WHORE."

Chapter Fifteen

HOPING to find Alyssa, Tyler, or someone who knew something about either, Luc persuaded Jack to run him to Sexy Sirens. It was a long shot, but he couldn't leave any stone unturned.

As soon as they pulled up in front of the aged brick building with its flashy sign, Luc noticed a group forming outside and groaned.

"Primpton? Fuck." Jack sounded as pleased as Luc felt.

Damn, this sanctimonious bastard really pissed him off. Today was not a good day to step on his last nerve.

"And he's got the press with him." Luc cursed. "What the hell does he want?"

"Besides to shut down your wife's club?" Jack stated the obvious.

"Attention," Hunter drawled. "Pricks like him crawl on others' backs with their 'look at me, look at me' mentality. He's a boy in a man's body who wants to be God when he grows up."

Jack nodded. "Yeah, the morality police. Fucker."

As soon as the car stopped, Luc jumped out. He'd have gone

around back to avoid Primpton, but he didn't have a key to the back door. Alyssa had given him one to the front, in case of emergencies. This qualified.

As he approached the club, Primpton blocked this path, his curly gray hair frizzing in the humid afternoon. His jowls shook as he stepped in front of Luc and wagged a finger in his face.

"Stop! Think about your immortal soul before you enter this place where the devil is at work. Where sin is king."

Luc had to clench his teeth and restrain himself to keep from pounding the jerk into the pavement. "Think about the fact you're loitering, and if you take another step, you'll be on private property, and I'll have you arrested for trespassing."

Primpton's rheumy blue eyes went wide. "That's devil's whore has swayed you to the side of sin and fornication!"

"It's not fornication since we're married."

"A pathetic mask! A secular union like yours doesn't change what she is."

"Don't you *dare* talk about my wife that way. She's a taxpaying business member of this community who has never lifted a finger against you. What gives you the right to judge her?"

The councilman puffed up his narrow chest. "It's the job of all of God's true believers to lead others to the path of righteousness."

Vomit. Luc didn't have the time for narrow-minded asses, and today especially, he lacked the patience.

"Then you should be pleased to know that Alyssa is retiring from the stage. She won't be performing again."

Primpton perked up. "She's closing the club?"

"Did your marriage have any impact on your wife's decision to stop performing?" a reporter shouted.

The press. God, didn't these leeches ever get tired of hounding people for nonexistent stories?

No. But in this case, he could give them a *real* one. "Yes. She's devoting more of herself to the restaurant business, with my blessing. We're excited about the next chapter of our life. But last night, someone broke into our house and vandalized it. Terrorized my wife. She's now missing, and I need your help to find her."

"You suspect foul play?" shouted another reporter.

"It's a very real possibility." As Luc said the words, he tried not to think about what he'd do if they were true, if some maniac had actually killed her. It was all he could do now to keep his composure and not panic.

The press asked a few more questions, and Luc provided details about when and where Alyssa was last seen.

Satisfied he'd made the best of a bad situation, Luc turned and stalked toward the door. Again, the councilman blocked his way.

Primpton sniffed and whispered for Luc only, "If someone returned her to her maker, it's no more than she deserves."

Luc fisted his hands. It was all he could do not to strangle the shithead. The fact he felt that way made Luc wonder if Primpton's involvement was more than judgmental gloating.

"If I find out you had anything to do with the break-in at our house and my wife's disappearance—"

"Me?" The older man had a shocked look on his face, yes. But he looked eerily excited, too.

Luc's skin crawled.

"If you thought hurting Alyssa would further your narrow agenda, I know you wouldn't hesitate. You'd say God told you to do it or some such crap. If I find out you've been responsible for harming or terrorizing her in any way, I'll—"

"What?" Primpton barked smugly. "What will you do to me?"

The asshole wanted Luc to threaten him. Luc refused to rise to the bait, no matter how badly he wanted to tell the bastard he'd love to rip him limb from limb and describe it in agonizingly gory detail. But he refused to give the bastard ammunition, especially because he might have Alyssa.

"I'll make sure you're prosecuted to the fullest extent of the law.

And if I can prove you were involved, you *will* need God's help to save you."

The reporters out front left, and Jack called one of his buddies to follow Primpton and see if he knew anything about Alyssa's whereabouts. The guy was on it . . . but who knew how long before he had any answers?

Luc tried not to be disheartened, but worry was an ever-constant drag, gnawing at his stomach, hollow and knotted. What if . . . he didn't find her alive?

Shortly after they left, Remy called to say they'd released the crime scene. Analysis was under way, and Luc could enter the house. Jack made a phone call and arranged for the cleaning service he knew well to meet them at the house in thirty minutes.

Then Deke called. He'd found a contact who might be able to help them locate Tyler. He refused to say much since he needed a few hours to work it.

Fidgeting in the passenger's seat, Luc felt ready to explode.

"I know what you're going through," Jack said quietly.

Luc snapped his gaze around. "Because you fucked my wife once upon a time?"

As soon as the words were out, Luc wished he could take them back. Whatever was between them was ancient history, and Jack had been nothing but helpful today.

"Don't be a dumb ass," Hunter drawled from the backseat of the SUV. "Jack is totally devoted to Morgan."

"It's okay." Jack gripped the steering wheel, then visibly relaxed. "Alyssa was mostly for show on cases."

Mostly, but not completely. Luc didn't miss that distinction.

"It didn't occur to me that you'd worry for a second about shit that went down years ago. Sorry," Jack said. "I'm totally married, man. Shooting straight? You know about me."

The fact Jack Cole was a well-known Dominant, who had bondage down to a fine art? "Yeah."

"Alyssa and I weren't ... compatible. We figured out very quickly that we were better friends than lovers."

Jack couldn't be any more honest, and Luc knew he needed to get over whatever Alyssa had done with the other man before he'd met her. Hell, Luc himself had fucked Kimber after spending an incredible night with Alyssa, so if anyone had done wrong, it was him.

"Thanks. Sorry."

"I understand." Jack smiled ruefully. "I always want to rip the balls off of any man who even looks at my wife. I meant that I understood your concern about her safety. After Morgan was shot, I thought I was going to die. Literally, like someone had opened up a hole in my chest and torn out my guts."

That described Luc's state well. He rubbed a hand across his face. Closing in on three in the afternoon, and he feared information would start to dry up. Now what?

They arrived at the house, and Luc vaulted up the stairs, despite Jack's renewed warnings. The destruction he saw in the master bedroom made him see more red than the paint covering the walls and floors. Alyssa had walked into *this*?

Slowly, he wandered around the room, blinking, hardly able to take it all in. His clothes and the bedsheets were negligible, easily replaced. The damage to the walls and carpet was also fixable. But the rest ... Alyssa's lacy, racy underthings all piled on the bed with some scumbag's come on them sent a fresh blade of panic through Luc. His wedding gift to her destroyed. The beautiful picture of her in her wedding dress, looking elegant and wearing a Mona Lisa smile, desecrated with the bright red threat was another punch to the stomach.

Whoever had done this was serious. And he might have Alyssa in his clutches.

Luc didn't know if this bastard had also written her the WHORE notes with the knives weeks ago. Possible, though this felt far more angry and serious. Either way, whenever Luc found his wife and

whoever was responsible for the violation of their home, he hoped
he got ten minutes of quality time with this asshole.

"I didn't think you should see this. You look somewhere between ready to puke and ready to commit murder."

"Bingo."

"We'll find Alyssa and get this motherfucker."

Not trusting himself to speak, he sent Jack a hard nod.

A moment later, the doorbell rang. Within a few minutes, they'd
escorted the cleanup crew to the master bedroom and instructed
them to toss everything. Luc didn't want any trace of the crime to
remind Alyssa in case he got to bring her home safely.

"In two hours, you'll have no idea this happened," a salty older
woman with peroxided hair assured. "If you've got some touch-up
paint, we'll be in business. Fresh sheets, a little bit of treatment on
the carpets . . . good as new."

After showing the crew where to find what they needed, Luc
followed Jack downstairs. Hunter awaited them, pacing the
kitchen.

"I made a few phone calls to some friends," Kimber's brother
said. "They're working on a psych profile of the perp. But at a glance,
I'd say you're dealing with someone who's obsessed with your wife.
Your wedding seems to have infuriated him, since he stepped up his
game shortly thereafter."

Someone like Primpton? Or Tyler, who had a real reason to be
jealous?

"If it's the same guy as before."

Hunter raised a tawny brow. "How many stalkers can she have?"

"You ever seen my wife onstage?"

Hunter hesitated, then grimaced. "Good point."

Pushing aside the thought that yet another male had seen his wife
close to naked, he focused instead on what to do next. "I can't sit here.
I need to exhaust all possibilities, and that means finding Tyler."

But where was the bastard?

Into the pensive silence, his phone rang. Deke. "Find something?"

"I've got a buddy who knows a guy who works for the electric company there in Lafayette. He's done a cross-reference of the name Tyler Murphy to coincide with an initial service date between May and July. We have three possibilities. There's a Murphy Taylor, a T. Patrick Murphy, and a T. S. Murphy. I'm e-mailing a list of their addresses to your BlackBerry right now."

Thank God. Maybe they were getting somewhere. Luc prayed to God he'd find his wife soon. He hoped she'd simply been scared and gone to the closest person who made her feel safe. That, he understood. Reluctantly, yes, but . . . If she had simply been shaken, why hadn't she called in all these hours?

The three hopped back in Jack's SUV, agreeing to hit Murphy Taylor's house first, since it was less than a mile away. Luc darted out of the vehicle as they rolled to a stop in the man's driveway and pounded on the door. A pretty brunette answered. After they identified themselves, she said that her husband was in the UK on business. Her pretty brown eyes soft with sympathy, she showed them a picture of her husband, just to be certain. Definitely not the Tyler they were looking for.

Cursing, his stomach twisting, they pulled out and headed to T. Patrick Murphy's residence. It was an apartment on the northwest edge of town. Again, Luc knocked impatiently on the door. A moment later a young man answered, maybe all of twenty. Tall, lanky, and exhausted.

After blessing them out for waking someone in the middle of his sleep who worked graveyard shifts, the men muttered their apologies and left. Luc's stomach sank. One more possibility. Luc didn't want to think about what he was going to do if the last lead was a dead end. It almost certainly meant she'd been abducted, and he couldn't think about Alyssa being afraid or in pain at the hands of a madman. Or dead.

In grim silence, the trio made their way to the southwestern edge of town, to an upscale apartment building. It looked new, gleaming. They drove past a sleek new swimming pool that looked more like a tropical oasis than a man-made water hole. Multiple spas, jogging trail, Wi-Fi included. Definitely more upscale than Tyler could afford on a bouncer's salary.

Luc's heart sank, and given Jack's and Hunter's grim faces, they had done the math as well. But they continued on until they reached apartment 314 and knocked.

A scuffle and a grunt and a long minute later, the door opened. Tyler stood there. Shock transformed his square face. "What the hell are you doing here?"

"Do you know where my wife is?"

Tyler raised a brow, then smiled. "Follow me."

Relief crashed Luc's system. "She's here? Is she all right?"

The big tawny bouncer threw a glance over his shoulder, his expression somewhere between confused and annoyed. "Of course."

Biting back his impatience, Luc trailed Tyler, then registered the fact the other man was walking down the hall of a designer-decorated apartment . . . to the bedroom.

At the end of the hall, Luc came to a stomach-lurching stop. There, Alyssa lay sprawled out across the man's bed, curled up with his pillow, wearing one of his T-shirts that rode up around her waist, a thong, and nothing else. She was out cold.

Was this really what it looked like?

What else could it be, idiot? If she'd simply been scared, why hadn't she called to tell him where she was and that she was safe? Why did she need to get undressed and into Tyler's bed?

Betrayal slammed him, so deep he almost couldn't breathe. The sight of her so relaxed and tangled in another man's sheets gouged his heart out of his chest. For a fleeting moment, he acknowledged that her infidelity was better than her death. But they'd been married less than two weeks. What the fuck did he do now?

"You look like I took a battering ram to your stomach."

Luc whipped a glare around to the other man. "Didn't you? How did this work? She came home to find the house vandalized, and called you to protect her, giving you the perfect opportunity to help her out of her clothes? Or did you hit the house to scare her and hope she'd call you, then let you fuck her again?"

"Man, you just don't get it."

What is there to "get" except the fact my wife is fucking another man?

Tyler shook his head. "Take her home; make sure she rests. And get the hell out of my face."

His words were dismissive, as if . . . well, as if Tyler knew he'd see Alyssa—and have her—again. Whenever he pleased. Luc gritted his teeth. He ought to leave her here with her lover. He'd been stupid enough to fall for her—hard—and now he was going to pay the price. He'd married her because she carried this man's child. Now he was getting an inside look at what it had taken for these two to conceive. And didn't it hurt like a bitch?

But if he'd married Alyssa for this baby, then by damned, he was going to take her home for this baby. She might share her body with Tyler, but Luc planned to dig out a place in her heart and make it his, find some way to make her care so that her every betrayal became a rending ache on her conscience.

Gritting his teeth, Luc approached the bed and lifted his sleeping wife into his arms. She barely stirred. "What the hell did you do to her?"

"Nothing out of the ordinary. She's just exhausted."

Meaning Tyler often fucked her into a near coma? The bastard was trying to piss him off.

Luc jerked Alyssa closer to his chest. And he couldn't lie—even knowing what she'd done, he was glad that she was safe and whole and close. "Stay the fuck away from my wife."

"You leave her, then you're leaving someone else to take care of her. And whatever needs she has."

Bullshit. Luc had loved her furiously, desperately, the morning he'd left for Los Angeles. Could she really have had needs so overwhelming in three days that she'd turned to another? Or did she have such feelings for Tyler that Luc's absence made hopping in the other man's bed both more convenient *and* a necessity?

He couldn't stay here and listen to Tyler say another word or he'd turn homicidal. Luc could feel the rage boiling up in his gut, starting to bubble over. As much as Luc hated him, Tyler wasn't worth prison time.

Then again, if Alyssa was voluntarily fucking her bouncer so soon after their wedding, neither was she.

"Fuck off."

Jack and Hunter backed down the hall quickly, leaving a path for him; then they exited Tyler's apartment, emerging into the late-afternoon sun. Luc clutched Alyssa to his chest, purposely avoiding the pitying looks the other men shot him as he climbed into the back of the SUV.

As he settled Alyssa into his lap, he wondered, now that he'd found her, what was he going to do with her?

*   *   *

ALYSSA woke with a headache and a moan. Her limbs seemed to weigh a thousand pounds each. Her mouth felt stuffed with cotton. Putting two thoughts together in her sluggish brain wasn't happening.

Gingerly, she lifted her lids, stunned to find it nearly dark in the shadowed room. *Her* room.

Everything inside her snapped to attention. How had she gotten here? And when? God, it had to be . . . what? Five thirty? Almost six? If Tyler had brought her back, he should know that she should have been at Bonheur hours ago. With a gasp, she rolled over to peek at the clock.

Instead, she found Luc sitting on the edge of the bed, stone still and silent. If his sudden appearance here didn't tell her something was dreadfully wrong, his face said it for him.

"Luc?" She scrambled to sit up . . . and realized she was wearing Tyler's T-shirt.

In fact, now that she looked around, everything had changed. The last time she'd seen this room, it had been all but destroyed. Now the bed was made with fresh sheets and blankets. It smelled faintly like paint. The mess was gone. "What—what's going on?"

He looked grim, and she had the distinct impression he was holding in his fury. "I think it's time I asked you that question. Someone broke in the house, and you didn't call me. You called nine-one-one and Tyler, then disappeared for nearly twelve hours. You never called to tell me you were alive. You never answered your phone."

"I was afraid and . . . I must have left my phone in Tyler's car. I—"

"I assume you've been with him all this time." He fired the question at her, like a well-aimed laser.

Her stomach pitched and rolled when she realized how this must look to Luc.

"Yes. But—"

"In all that time, you never thought to call me to let me know the psycho who'd broken into the house hadn't abducted you? Oh, that's right . . ." He snapped, the sarcasm thick and biting. "You were too busy letting Tyler fuck your brains out to tell your *husband* where the hell you were and that you were alive. I woke Jack up at an ungodly hour, walked away from the taping of my show to hop a plane, and flew across the country. I told the press you were missing. And where do I find you but Tyler's bed." He stood, fists and teeth clenched. "Goddamn you!"

Alyssa closed her eyes. Yes, Luc would jump to this conclusion.

He must have retrieved her from Tyler's apartment. From his bed. She winced.

But why couldn't he get it through his thick head that, despite her "profession," she'd never step out on him?

"It's not what you think. Let me explain," she implored. "I—"

"You're addicted to his cock?"

"No." She sighed. "Luc—"

"You're in love with him?"

She blanched. "No!"

"Then you just get a sick kick out of cheating and making an ass of me?"

How could he believe that for a second? It was probably his anger and residual fear talking, but . . .

Alyssa took a deep breath. Then another. Hadn't they had this conversation—or one remarkably like it—before Luc had left Louisiana and she'd discovered she was pregnant? Yes. He'd accused her of being Tyler's main squeeze and fuck buddy for nearly two months. Couldn't Luc see that she loved *him*? Granted, she'd never said the words, but God, she'd given herself to him in every way, let him into her life, her house. Let him plant his seed in her body. Been thrilled to know she'd always have a part of Luc. And he just kept insisting that she was a whore.

She couldn't keep living like this.

Rolling away from him, Alyssa found the edge of the bed and stood, making her way to the door.

Luc glared at her. "Where the hell are you going?"

Damn it, she wanted to strangle the man for breaking her heart. "Fuck you."

As she stormed out the door, his hand clamped around her biceps and he hauled her back to the bed. "Oh, you fucked me. Totally. You've got me coming and going so much I don't know my name half the time. I'm twisted and tied up in you, so goddamn addicted. And you know the sad part? If you took the other man's T-shirt off your gorgeous body right now, I'd stupidly fall to my knees and be ridiculously grateful for the chance to fuck you again."

His words hit her like a sledgehammer. Luc had feelings for her, but he was terrified to trust her. Because of who she was. What she'd become. If she told him now that she loved him, would he embrace her and tell her that he loved her, too? Or just laugh in her face?

She was too afraid to find out.

Tears flared at the back of Alyssa's eyes, stinging. She blinked them away, refusing to cry over this man again. "No, the sad part is you married me believing the worst about me. You never let me tell you what happened today. And now it doesn't matter. I agreed to this marriage because you seemed to have feelings for me and claimed to want this baby. God, I'm so stupid. You probably even think the baby is Tyler's."

His dark eyes drilled her with anguish and fury. "Is it?"

Two words, and she felt as if he'd punched her in the stomach.

This wasn't going to work. Ever. She'd always believed rose-colored glasses were pointless, but when she'd agreed to marry Luc she'd worn them. At the cost of her heart.

She wrenched her arm away from his grip. "Like I said, fuck you."

Alyssa stormed out the bedroom door and down the hall. Before she reached the stairs, Luc grabbed her from behind and slung her against his chest. He swatted her ass with a broad, hot palm. Fire ran across her skin, down her legs. Why? Even when the man infuriated her, insulted her, her body still responded . . .

"Since you ask *so* sweetly," he growled through clenched teeth.

Before she could absolve him of the notion that she was going to get naked with him, he dropped her to the mattress and ripped Tyler's shirt from her body. Now the only thing standing between him and his angry lust was her lace thong.

As Luc had always done with her barriers, he ripped this one away, as well. The thong fell to the ground.

"You want me to fuck you?" His voice croaked. "I'm all over that."

His control was unraveling. And she knew what would happen then. If she was going to stay, they needed talk now, not sex. She must convince him that the baby wasn't Tyler's. But Luc's demanding stare, the one that told her he was going to fuck her in every way possible, be more thorough than ever, dissolved her arguments. Instead, heat sparked low in her belly. A breathless need to touch him consumed her.

"I don't want this now." She said the words, but they trembled—just like her body.

Luc ignored her, trailing a pair of fingers down her abdomen and dragging them over her hard clit. She tensed and tried to push his hand away. But she was no match for his determination.

His fingers sank deep into her pussy.

"As wet as you are for me," he murmured against her tight nipple, "I think you're lying."

Damn it, he knew her body too well. He took her nipple in his mouth and pumped her full of his fingers. Sensation sparked immediately, and against her better judgment, Alyssa arched to him. She shouldn't, but . . . This was Luc.

"We should talk." Every word came out strained, between pants.

No way was Luc going to take her seriously.

He laved the heavy curve under her breast; then his teeth nipped at the hard tip. "After you come for *me*, and I remind you how hot everything is between us."

As if she'd ever forget. Before she could protest, he plunged his fingers deeper and sought out her G-spot. In seconds, Luc began to ply it mercilessly. *Oh, my . . . Yes!* Grabbing desperate handfuls of his shirt, she moaned.

"That's it. Feel me. You want more, don't you?"

She shouldn't. They should be talking about his assumption that she was fucking Tyler, had become pregnant by him. But damn it, Luc was overwhelming her, her body was on fire, and she loved Luc too much to say no. "Yes . . ."

Luc again rubbed her G-spot, now thumbing her clit. "Who do you want?"

"You, Luc. Always you." She broke out in a damp sweat, panting, mewling for more as pleasure ramped up in her belly. Need burned between her legs, multiplying, building.

How could he alone do this to her, shove her so quickly to the ragged edge of restraint and sanity?

He shimmied down her body and bent to her. Alyssa's anticipation soared as she felt Luc's hot breaths all over her wet, swollen flesh. *Yes, please. Now. Sooner than now.*

"Only me?" he demanded.

"Only you."

His dark eyes blazed across her face, anger warring with lust and possession in a tangle that made her catch her breath. "Make me believe it."

He suckled her clit into his mouth with a hungry snarl, putting his shoulders—his whole body—into it. From his first lick, pleasure seized her unlike anything she'd ever felt. His clever tongue ruthlessly drove her up, along with those long, probing fingers. He pushed her to the brink of orgasm with long, liquid swipes of his tongue on her clit. Then he drew it into his mouth and sucked.

Alyssa arched, grabbed the sheets, and screamed as ecstasy coalesced and exploded, setting her entire body on fire.

God, only Luc could do this to her.

While she still pulsed with aftershocks, he parted her folds with his thumbs and delved inside again with his tongue. She gasped, spread her legs wider. Luc knew exactly how to make her need him again.

He fastened on her clit once more, blowing her mind, ramping her up toward another orgasm that shouldn't have been possible, but was instead imminent. The slope up was faster, steeper, more wrenching.

She was drenched now, dripping. So swollen, she could feel her nipples puckering, her folds engorging. But this time, Luc kept her on the knife's edge, orgasm just a heartbeat away. Arching, wriggling, she tried everything to make his wicked tongue send her straight into bliss, but he anchored her to the bed with a hand on her hip. "I say when."

Everything inside her clenched in denial. She needed it—needed him—now. "What are you doing to me?"

"Making sure you know your body is mine and mine alone." A determined glint smoldered in his dark eyes.

She was no man's possession or toy. But . . . desire racked her. It had become eloquent torture knotting her belly as he plunged his fingers inside her again. Alyssa cried out as he teased her clit with his tongue. The man wanted her to lose her mind. And he was about to succeed.

When he replaced his finger with his thumb and eased his drenched digit into her anus, she clenched around him and moaned.

"You are so fucking sexy." Luc pumped his fingers into her simultaneously. The wild sensation scorched her, and every nerve ending begged for climax.

He sucked on her clit again, this time harder than the last, even as his fingers filled her up. And it was . . . Oh, God, a madness of pleasure that threatened to implode her. Where was her determination to leave now? Her will to resist him until they worked through their issues? Like the perfect storm, demand raged inside her, fueled by anger, fear, love, need. It grew into a fathomless, sucking swirl. His every touch sizzled like lightning. Ecstasy, pure and white-hot, was upon her. Alyssa's eyes flew open wide, connecting with Luc's commanding gaze. Wide shoulders, insistent hands, haunted eyes.

Mine, his stare said.

Yours, her soul silently answered.

The floodgates of pleasure burst open in a torrential flood. As satisfaction crashed over her, she felt dizzy, couldn't breathe. Black spots danced at the edge of her vision. She cried out, thighs tense, womb pulsing. What Luc gave her was brilliant and endless. And should give him absolutely no doubt that he owned her.

Damn him.

And as soon as he let up, eased away, she also realized that what he'd given her was one-sided. As he stood and tore into his own shirt, Alyssa knew that, in his mind, they were nowhere near done.

Now that the need to come wasn't pressing down on her, she saw that he'd derailed their discussion and sought to control her using sex.

Oh, hell, no.

She grabbed the sheet and wrapped it around her. "Stop. We are not doing this now. There's too much to discuss, and I'll be damned if you're going to accuse me of fucking Tyler in one breath, then demanding I fuck you in the next."

"You want to put me off after I just found you in another man's bed?" he snapped, straddling her, flattening her back to the mattress. "Like hell."

Then he ripped Tyler's T-shirt into long strips of material, wrapping them around her wrists and knotting them securely.

What the fuck was he doing? Was he . . . No!

"Luc, let me up!" Fear zipped through her bloodstream, along with a sick spike of adrenaline. "Let me go!"

"You're going to stay here with me until you remember who the hell you're married to. Then we're going to talk until I get the whole goddamned ugly truth."

Scowling, he dragged her wrist to the headboard and grabbed the edges of the cotton bracelet, knotting it around the iron.

He meant to tie her down. Put her at his mercy. *Oh, God.*

"Luc! Don't do this . . ." Icy panic assailed her as she writhed and bucked beneath him. He didn't budge. "Please don't!"

He completely ignored her. His body was an anchor pinning her to the mattress as he reached for her other wrist and tied the material to the headboard. She struggled, but Luc was a hundred times stronger.

Alyssa began to sweat. Cold fear again crashed to her stomach, and she feared she was going to throw up. As he secured her other wrist, immobilizing her arms, pure terror scraped her system.

Alyssa thrashed and screamed, "Luc, please! Don't do this. Don't . . ."

She tried to hold in her sobs, stay calm, but with each second she was immobile and at his mercy, terror grew.

"Don't what? Make sure you stay here long enough to be honest with me? You can't spend the day with your lover, worry me sick, then tell me to fuck myself. Refuse me your pretty body that drives me insane with need every damn day and night."

"Tyler is not my lover! He never has been. I know you don't believe me, but please . . ." That fact, along with her edge of fear, crushed her defenses, cracked her heart open. "Just let me up. Let me go," she sobbed.

"Back to Tyler? No."

Alyssa forced herself to look up into his face and flinched when she saw the barely restrained wrath and bleak determination tighten his angular face. "We can't stay like this. Let me go. Please."

Her pleas didn't affect him. His eyes burned her face, trailed down to her breasts, rested on her abdomen. When his stare returned to her face, he seethed with possessive anger that made her pulse jump with dread and fear.

"I can't." He wrapped his fingers around her wrists and swooped down toward her. "You're my wife, damn it. That's going to mean something to you."

What? That he could force her to have sex anytime he wanted? "Luc, no!"

Alyssa barely got the sound out before he slanted his mouth over hers. His tongue plundered, his lips crushing hers, and she tasted herself on his lips. Desperation, fury, intent all swirled in his kiss. He wanted her. She feared he wouldn't take no for an answer.

His hands tightened on her wrists, his grip biting as he took the kiss deeper.

The defenses she'd built up over the months and years to block out the worst of her memories fell out from under her. She was fifteen again, too trusting. Too innocent to understand that her life was about to change forever.

She shivered and struggled, doing anything, everything, to throw the hard male weight off her, smothering her, hurting her. The agony was coming, she knew. God, how would she survive something that horrific all over again?

Panic chilling her to her marrow, Alyssa bit Luc's lip. He pulled away, clutching his mouth.

"No! Don't do this. Please, God, don't do this. I can't—" Then against her will, she dissolved into sobs. "Don't hurt me."

Her pleas broke through his rage. Luc leapt off her instantly, all lust gone from his face. Concern replaced it. "Hurt you, sugar?"

Tears stung her eyes, scalded their way down her cheeks as she turned herself on her side, as much as her bound wrists allowed, and curled her legs up to her chest. "Please let me go."

She hadn't even finished the plea before Luc's fingers were at the knots, releasing one, then the other. And she was free.

Shooting him a stare full of accusation, and pain, she ran to the bathroom.

"Alyssa!" he shouted, concern urgent in his voice.

When she didn't respond, she heard the frightening rush of his footsteps behind her and kept running.

Finally reaching the bathroom, she slammed the door before he could barge his way in, and she locked it behind her. Safe . . . for the moment. What would she do if he didn't go away?

Leaning against the cold wood, she panted, her past still flashing in her head, reminding her of horror and pain. But this was another day, another man. Would Luc really have hurt her?

Maybe she'd overreacted. She'd certainly shown him her weakness. And if he hadn't already, he'd quickly figure out just how damaged she was.

Sliding down the door until she huddled against it, Alyssa put her face in her hands and sobbed.

Chapter Sixteen

SHE was crying, and not simple tears. Not with mere guilt. Every sob sounded as if it ripped a new piece of her heart out, as if every dream she'd ever had had been crushed forever.

Luc's stomach crashed to his toes.

"Sugar," he implored with a soft knock. "Open the door. I'm so sorry. I lost my temper. I didn't mean to scare you."

No response, just more of the rending cries that clawed his gut with fear and regret. Feeling two inches tall, he leaned against the door, hands pressed to it, wishing like hell that he could reach through and comfort her. How could a few inches of wood separate them so completely, as if a continent of pain and regret stood between them?

"Talk to me, Alyssa."

Under the door's crack, he saw her sitting on the floor, huddled, and ran a frustrated hand down his face. What the hell had he done?

Jack's lifestyle wasn't his. Luc had never felt the *need* to tie up a woman, especially in anger. Whatever she might have done with Tyler, Alyssa had been hurt before. Raped. The terror on her face, the flashback to her past, had been a bitter slap of a reminder for Luc. The fact she could even mentally put him in the same category as the man who hurt her was the worst sort of pain. He felt like a thoughtless snake. Damn it.

"Sugar, please. I won't hurt you. I won't *touch* you. Just come out so we can talk."

Silence. Then a sniffle and a shuffle. She got to her feet. His heart leapt, and hope seized him that she would open the door, hear him out. This time, he'd listen to her explanation about her time with Tyler. Even if it was exactly what he thought it was, he doubted Alyssa meant to hurt him. She had no idea he loved her. Maybe he should confess. Maybe they could talk through their problems and salvage everything.

Instead of removing the barrier between them, she walked away and started the shower.

He knocked again. No answer.

Long minutes passed. The spray of water was loud . . . but not enough to drown out the continued sobs that split the air and tore at his heart.

Calling to her wasn't doing any good, and all this crying couldn't be good for her or the baby. Her home had been viciously invaded and she'd been scared out of her mind both by an intruder and her own husband. He had to focus on that, had to reach her and persuade her to let him help.

Another jagged cry sounded over the water. God, she could hardly catch a breath. The sobs were coming faster now, each sounding more wrenching than the last. Luc couldn't take it anymore.

Thanking God for Deke's insistence that he know forms of self-defense, including martial arts, Luc gathered his energy, centered it, then kicked the bathroom door. With a crash and a splintering of wood, it gave in.

Behind the shower curtain, she gasped as the door lurched on its hinges and crashed against the wall.

Once inside, Luc didn't hesitate. He yanked back the shower curtain. Inside, Alyssa sat on the shower bench under scalding water, steam rising around her. She'd curled her knees up to her chest, her teeth chattering viciously. She looked up at him with haunted blue eyes, mascara running down her face.

The sight kicked him in the stomach.

Swallowing his nerves, he climbed into the shower, clothes, shoes, and all. Hot water pelted him, plastering his hair to his shoulders and neck. He barely noticed. Instead, he lifted his wife into his arms. Thank God, she went without a fight.

Luc sat on the shower bench and set Alyssa in his lap. "I'm so sorry."

She closed her eyes, stiffened. "I came home a little after four this morning to find the house had been broken into, called nine-one-one and Tyler. I didn't call you. It was two in the morning in Los Angeles. There was nothing you could do."

Her monotone voice sounded dead. Luc ached all over again for her.

"I'm listening."

"Tyler examined the crime scene before Remy got there. While Tyler was looking around, I got sick, passed out."

"What?" Luc tightened his arms around her.

"The paint fumes and perfume and shock, I guess. When I came to, I was in Tyler's car and he was taking me to the emergency room. I told him I didn't need to go. I just needed sleep."

"Did he take you anyway?" Luc asked hopefully.

Alyssa shook her head. "I pleaded. He insisted that I eat something, and he can't cook. So we went to that egg place not far from the club. After I'd eaten, I started cramping."

"Like you'd eaten something bad? It usually takes longer for food—"

"No. Like menstrual cramps."

Luc's heart came to a screeching halt. *"What?"*

"I went to the restaurant's bathroom." She began sobbing again, nearly uncontrollably.

He curled her against his chest and kissed her forehead. "Please, take a deep breath. This isn't good for you."

Finally, she managed to breathe deeply; then she swallowed back tears. "I found blood."

Oh, Jesus Christ. His stomach went into a free fall. "Did you go to the emergency room?"

Again, she shook her head. "I was afraid we'd have to wait too long. I called my new obstetrician. She agreed to meet me at her office before hours, so Tyler took me there, waited while the doctor examined me."

And he'd missed all of this. Luc stroked her shoulder, pressed another kiss to her forehead. Not only had he missed it; he'd heaped more shit on her.

Why the fuck hadn't he listened instead of letting his jealousy do the talking?

"Are you okay?" Luc was almost afraid to ask the question. "What did she say?"

"That it's not uncommon to spot if you're on your feet too much or under too much stress."

Without a doubt, Alyssa suffered from both.

"The baby is okay. But she told me to rest. Sleep. I couldn't come here, and Tyler wanted me somewhere he could protect me. So he offered me his place to crash, but when we got there, I was too keyed up and couldn't sleep. I didn't want to worry you. You were so far away. I was too shaken to realize you might be worried. I'm not used to having anyone care . . ."

"Sugar, anywhere, anytime, anyplace, you call me." Luc wanted to growl the words at her. She was so damn independent, and it had probably grated her to even ask Tyler for help, much less call some-one halfway across the country.

"Anyway, Tyler called the doctor again, asked if there was any-thing she could give me. Though she normally wouldn't do this for someone pregnant, she prescribed me a sedative because of my stress and fatigue."

"And you fell asleep." *In Tyler's bed.*

She nodded. "I know I should have called. Everything happened so fast."

Of course she'd been more worried about making sure the baby was okay than soothing his jangled nerves. It wasn't her fault he was a jealous, distrusting bastard.

"I'm so sorry you went through all of that without me. That someone broke in the house. That you spotted. That I scared you." He held her close.

The water began to cool, and Luc reached out to turn it off. Leaning out of the tub, he grabbed her towel off the bar and wrapped it around her small frame, dabbing it across her face and removing the mascara, squeezing the long strands of her hair inside its folds.

She stood docile, almost unmoving. It wasn't like her, and he worried until it was a bleeding hole in his chest.

Quickly, he threw off his wet clothes and left them in the bottom of the shower, then reached for his towel. He didn't bother drying, and his hair dripped thick streams of water down his back and shoul-ders. Instead, he wrapped the towel around his waist and helped her out of the shower.

Alyssa didn't say a word as he steadied her over to the bed. On the way, he grabbed their robes from the back of the door. He helped her into hers, belting it for her as if she were a child, then shrugged into his own. In silence, he toweled more moisture from her hair and stud-ied her face. He still didn't like her expression. Somewhere past shock, it was almost blank.

Luc swallowed down his frustration. Whatever was going on with her was more than someone breaking into the house, more than the fact he'd been angry enough to tie her to the bed. And he had to get her to open up, let it go, if he could.

He pulled her into his lap, gratified that she went trustingly, resting her head on his shoulder. "Alyssa, sugar. Tell me why I scared you."

Her head jerked, jolted, until it finally became a full-blown shake. "It's nothing."

"Please." He grabbed her tighter, then forced himself to let go, afraid he'd scare her all over again. "Someone hurt you."

She closed her eyes. A tear ran down her cheek.

It nearly killed him. "Someone raped you. I did something to remind you of that, right?"

"It was a long time ago. Just forget it. I have."

Luc barely heard her whisper, but he knew it was a lie. She wasn't over it, and hearing the chocked admission heaped in denial crushed him. "You were a teenager."

For a long minute, Alyssa said nothing, but stared at the wall on his right. Finally, she murmured, "Fifteen."

Dear God. Not even old enough to drive. Barely more than a girl, and some asshole had forced his way into her body against her will? Rape was one of the ugliest of crimes, but against one so young?

Stomach turning, Luc hesitated. He had to keep asking questions that would allow her to reveal the ordeal a bit at a time. She wasn't ready to just spill her entire secret in one breath.

"Were you on a date?"

Her whole body tensed. "No." Then she gave a hysterical sob. "I wasn't allowed to date. My mother expected me to be a virgin when I got married."

He wasn't sure he wanted to hear this, truly. But he *had* to. Without this knowledge, Luc sensed that he couldn't truly understand his wife.

"And you were a virgin when this . . . ?" He tensed, swallowed, somehow hoping like hell she'd say no.

But she nodded.

Luc had never been nauseous and angry at once. He wanted to smash this bastard's head, make him feel every bit of the pain Alyssa had clearly felt. But he kept it to himself. No sudden movements, no swearing, no making fists. Instead, he softly stroked her hair.

"A boy from school?" he ventured, his voice as gentle as he could make it.

Alyssa opened her mouth, then closed it. Hesitated. Then she rose to her feet. Luc wanted to keep her in his lap, safe and warm, where he could hold her and soothe her at the slightest tremor. But he didn't dare hold her down again.

She paced to the bathroom counter and braced herself on it. "Not . . . exactly. It's ancient history. Not really important."

Luc stood and slowly, giving her plenty of time to back away, approached her. Relief poured through his system when she didn't pull away, so he loosely placed his hands on her shoulders.

"I think it's very important. If you don't want to tell me, I understand. I haven't done a good job earning your trust today. Or for the past two months. I've been slow to learn, but I want to do better—with your help. Please, I need to know what's going to frighten you so I don't do it again."

Alyssa bit her lip, sighed, looked at the ceiling as if praying for strength. "N-no bondage. I can't . . ." She shivered, wrapping her arms around herself. "I just can't."

Reality hit Luc in the face. What had Jack said? He and Alyssa had realized quickly they weren't compatible. That made complete sense now. "Not unless you're ready. If that day never comes, I'll understand."

She gave him a jerky nod. "Thank you."

Caressing her shoulders, Luc brought her against his body. She wanted to leave the story there. She'd been fifteen, a virgin, and had been raped. But he sensed the story was only beginning.

"It wasn't a boy from school who hurt you?"

Alyssa wrapped her arms around her middle and shook her head. "I—I don't know if I can talk about this. I haven't told anyone this since the night after it happened."

She'd kept this to herself for fourteen years? "You never told Jack? Tyler? A therapist?"

A sad smile crossed her face before it dissolved. "Jack would have hunted him down, and that's the last thing I want. Tyler . . . If I think my past is coming back to haunt me, I'll tell him. Never could afford a therapist until I worked through a lot of this on my own."

Why the hell wouldn't she want Jack to hunt this asshole down? Personally, Luc was *dying* to. But she didn't want to hear that, and he couldn't jeopardize the conversation now that she was talking.

He hugged her back to his chest again. "Who did this to you, sugar?"

"Joshua." She shuddered, closed her eyes. "He's m-my step-brother."

Sick fury assailed him once again. Someone who was supposedly a part of her blended family had violated her trust and body? As much as hearing this killed him, he had to get the full story. But he didn't know what questions to ask from here.

Swallowing, he decided to simply wing it. "Your mother re-married?"

She nodded slowly. "When I was twelve."

Please, please tell me this creep didn't start taking advantage of her then. "Did it start then? Touching? Fondling?"

"No. At first, he was my best friend. My mom remarried someone *very* wealthy. We moved from our middle-class neighborhood to . . . *Lifestyles of the Rich and Famous.* I started a new school. I didn't know anyone. I was shy. I had a hard time adjusting."

And this prick Joshua had used her insecurity against her. "So he said he'd be your friend?"

"Yes, and he made sure I had all the coolest friends in school. And he kept other guys away from me. When I was a freshman, there was a junior—one of Josh's classmates—who decided he wanted to nail me at a party. He got me drunk and cornered me in the bathroom. Joshua and some of his other friends picked the lock and stormed in. Joshua beat this guy ruthlessly; then he carried me out. The next Monday, he told everyone we were dating and not to fuck with me. I thought he did it for my protection." She grunted in disbelief.

"He wanted you for himself." Luc had no trouble picturing that.

"Yeah. He'd fly into a rage if he even thought anyone was looking at me, or if he suspected I liked someone. Shortly after that incident, he started sneaking into my room, said he wanted to make sure I was safe."

When she laughed bitterly, it twisted his stomach. *Safe?* The asshole had taken total advantage of her. How could he couch that as protecting her? "Did he start kissing you or just attack?"

"Oh, there were kisses. Lots and lots of those, and I stupidly encouraged it, thinking that he really cared. That started when I was fourteen."

And this fucking rapist had been . . . what? Sixteen? Seventeen? Old enough to know that he was using a young, innocent girl.

"When did he start touching you?"

"Right before I turned fifteen. That summer."

The way she sighed raggedly told Luc she needed to pause. He stood silently behind her, caressing her arms. It was on the tip of his tongue to tell her they could stop here, talk later. Certainly, it would be better for his stomach and temper. But he knew getting her back to this place would be difficult and painful. Better to get it all out now.

"When did it become more?"

"I found out that he'd been sleeping with this girl in his English class. I was . . . so stupid that I ever believed that he wanted to marry me someday. In my fairy-tale-minded head, I thought he was waiting for me. You know, to grow up, so our first experience could be together. He told me that of course he had to fuck other girls. Our parents couldn't know about us yet. They'd have freaked. So Joshua said he was keeping up appearances, letting his dad know he had a healthy interest in other females."

"Scumbag," Luc muttered. That was actually a lot milder than what he was thinking, but with that pronouncement, she'd know he empathized but wouldn't alarm her with the violence of his fury.

"Then he said that all the waiting for me had been tough on him and that he'd *had* to have other pussy or his human pressure valves got too tight." She scoffed. "So I told him to go away, that I didn't want him anymore. I stopped speaking to him for weeks."

"And he turned violent?"

"Yes. Just after my sophomore year started, he came to my room one night, tied me down, and said he felt cheated that he'd waited around and hadn't gotten any. And he'd so been looking forward to being my first. He'd even gone so far as to plan this elaborate scheme to 'pop my cherry' for my sweet sixteen."

Luc's nausea rose to new levels, as did his need to wipe this asshole off the face of the earth. He wasn't a violent man, but this . . . Unforgivable.

"I'm sorry." He wanted to say so much more, but at this point, words would only placate him. Her damage had been done. He only hoped he could help heal her.

"Oh, God it hurt . . ." Her body trembled, seized up. The sobs started again. "H-he took me every way a man can take a woman."

Joshua had raped her anally, too? Another blow to the restraint around Luc's rage. He grabbed the countertop on either side of her hips and looked at her bowed head in the mirror. Her haunted eyes, squeezed shut tight, dominated her tense, fragile face.

"Sugar, I'm so sorry." He kissed the back of her head. He didn't trust himself to touch her gently in that moment. Too many violent urges running through his body.

"Wh-when it was over, I was sobbing and bleeding. He was angry and said he wondered why he'd bothered. I was just another whore after all." Fists clenched, she drew in a shuddering breath. "I . . . I wanted to kill him."

Luc understood that feeling well.

"In retrospect, I shouldn't have been surprised by Joshua's behavior. All the signs were there."

"My God, you shouldn't have had to know the signs at that age. You told your parents, right?"

Her body wilted then, as if she had no more fight. "I told my mother."

Biting back the urge to prompt her, Luc waited while she closed her eyes, gathered her courage.

"She didn't believe me."

"What the hell? Certainly she could see . . . There was evidence."

Alyssa shook her head. "I was stupid. I panicked and cleaned up. Today, I'd have marched myself down to the hospital and demanded a rape kit and prosecuted the son of a bitch. But at fifteen, all I could think about was 'getting caught.'

"The day after it happened, Joshua was vile to me at school, told everyone he'd nailed me. He called me his convenient pussy and said he was going to get more that night. I was terrified."

Just when Luc thought this prick couldn't get any lower, Alyssa revealed another fact about her stepbrother that enraged him all over again.

"So after dinner, I pulled my mom aside and told her what had happened. She accused me of trying to ruin her life. I was just being petulant because Joshua liked girls his age and lying because I resented her happiness." Alyssa sniffed, pressed her lips together.

Having your own mother stab you in the back the day after suffering the worst physical and emotional trauma of your life? Luc couldn't even imagine the anguish . . . And knowing that Alyssa had never resolved this between her and her mother? No wonder the woman's death had been confusing for her.

"Your mother's betrayal hurt worst of all." It wasn't a question; he *knew*.

She stared at the marble countertop and nodded.

"It's not your fault; none of this was. Your mother should have stood beside you. She was supposed to protect you. I understand why you both loved and hated her."

Alyssa whipped her gaze over her shoulder, clearly surprised that he'd figured that out. "Yeah. But after she married Richard, she became a different person. Absorbed in him. And I knew he'd be no help. Joshua could do no wrong in his eyes. He probably would have applauded his son's behavior. He was a misogynist who objectified all women."

And Joshua followed in his father's footsteps.

Luc didn't understand either the point of view or the horrific lapse in parenting. But he could tell from Alyssa's demeanor that she still had more to tell.

"After I talked to my mom, it was late. Near bedtime. I knew Joshua would come to my room again. I asked to spend the night at a friend's house, but Mom said no. I packed a bag, took the hundred bucks I had in a drawer, and snuck out my window."

"Oh, dear God. Where did you go?"

"At first to a friend's house, but when my mom called in the middle of the night looking for me, saying I'd run away, her parents drove me home and told me not to come back. My stepfather had apparently threatened them with criminal and civil action. He was a big-time lawyer.

"I went home that night. My mom grounded me and sent me to my room. The only saving grace was that everyone was awake, and Joshua couldn't sneak into my room. The next day, instead of going to school, I ran away again. This time, I made it as far as Hollywood."

Horror zipped through Luc. "Did you know anyone there?"

She shook her head. "It was only a couple dozen miles from home, but it might as well have been a world away."

A fifteen-year-old girl in Hollywood? Alone? She would have been preyed upon, unable to support herself unless— Luc didn't even want to consider how she'd eaten and kept a roof over her head.

"You looked for a job," he guessed.

"Fast-food places wouldn't hire me until I was sixteen, and even then, I had to have parental consent. Sixteen was still nine months away, and even if I could ask my parents, they would never have approved." Alyssa gripped the counter tighter. "You can guess what happened next."

Oh, no. That couldn't be. "Sugar . . ."

She bit her lip, then spoke quickly, without inflection. "The first few times were hard. I closed my eyes a lot and pretended I was someplace else. Thank God none of the men were creepy or dangerous. Just run-of-the-mill johns looking to get laid."

Luc was speechless. Fifteen and reduced to prostitution because her family had hurt her in every way possible. Forced to fend for herself because they were too selfish and had all but abandoned her.

A million things clicked into place: the reason she was so touchy about people assuming she was a whore, the reason she insisted that the girls who work for her better themselves, the reason she hated to rely on others unless forced, the reason she wasn't wound up about being nude in public. She'd learned early that her body was a com-modity and that only educating herself would improve her lot. She'd clearly also figured out that her self-worth had nothing to do with her career, but her inner core.

In his head, Luc thought he'd known that her "profession" hadn't fazed her . . . but *he* hadn't behaved that way. It had been a big deal to him. Now it seemed so stupid. He'd bite his tongue off before he ever said anything that made her feel like less than a lady again.

"Did you ever go home?" he asked quietly.

"I thought about it. The first Christmas without family was hard. I spent it alone in an alley with a candy bar and a campfire, hoping that no one would attack me in my sleep. But the week before, I'd seen Joshua. He came looking for me, flashing my picture around and telling all the other girls that my mom wanted me back for the holidays. Most protected me and played dumb, but one of the older women thought she could 'save' me by snitching. I got away with, maybe, three minutes to spare."

"And since Joshua knew where you were, you couldn't stay."

"I had some money saved up. I bought a bus ticket, told the woman behind the counter I wanted to go someplace warm. Joshua always made fun of Southerners, called them stupid rednecks. So I thought heading to the South would be a good idea."

She shrugged. "Bus ticket brought me here. A woman I talked to for part of the trip promised that stripping was better and nearly as lucrative as . . ." She blew out a breath. "I got a fake ID with a fake name to blend in."

"Alyssa isn't your name?" She was *so* Alyssa to Luc. He couldn't imagine calling her something else.

"It's my middle name. My real name is Lindsey."

It didn't suit her at all. Lindsey was a girl. This woman before him was tough, a survivor, worthy of a name with a big, sexy sound like Alyssa. She astounded Luc with her strength, her resilience, her never-say-die attitude. She'd walked through hell and fire, and emerged on the other side a woman of steel. As much as he ached for what she'd endured, he was proud of her.

"Then I knocked on Sexy Sirens' door," she said. "It was called something else then, but Marquessa, while a bitch, saved my life. She let me live at the club until I got on my feet, worked around my school schedule when I started studying for my GED. Her boys kept the locals from hitting on me too much. I kinda . . . grew up there." She shrugged. "I never went home again until my mother's funeral. I saw Joshua—from a distance. He didn't see me, thank God. And to this day, he still doesn't know what became of me. If he had any clue, I don't know what he would do."

Luc knew what he'd like to do to the asshole, but Alyssa needed his understanding and comfort now, not his fury. He'd look up this prick soon and take him down a peg or twenty, but this moment was about his wife.

Guilt crept in that his behavior had caused her grief and forced her to spill her secrets to him. On the other hand, getting her story out in the open, him hearing it, was perhaps one of the best things that could have happened to them.

"I'm so sorry I upset you. Accused you. Scared you."

And let Tyler's smug face dig under my skin when he answered the door. In retrospect, Luc knew her bouncer/bodyguard was in love with her and probably enjoyed watching him draw the worst conclusions, driving a wedge into Alyssa's new marriage. He didn't respect the guy for it . . . but he understood.

She bowed her head. "The funny thing about you accusing me of sleeping around? Until you, I never really enjoyed sex. I mean, at first it did nothing but bring up bad memories. When I got older and figured out that it wasn't my fault and Joshua was nothing but slime, I tried to date, tried to have sex. It just always seemed . . . uncomfortable and embarrassing. You actually cared about my experience." She grimaced. "Until you, I never had an orgasm that wasn't solo. Until you, I never understood how sex connected people."

Seriously? Luc was stunned silent. She'd never enjoyed the lush, sensual intimacies of sex until him? Then again, how could she with such terrible memories attached?

And where did Tyler fit into this picture? Had she slept with him as some form of payment? No, she wouldn't do that anymore. So, had Tyler been an experiment? Clearly, she trusted the man or she wouldn't have taken a sleeping pill and fallen into his bed. Did some part of her love the bouncer? Luc didn't know. He *did* know that, despite her protestations that she'd never had sex with the man, Tyler had to have fathered Alyssa's coming child.

Whatever reason she had for denying that fact they'd tackle later.

Luc wrapped his arms around his wife, who relaxed against him, leaning back into his body. *Safe, treasured, his.* At least in part. At least for now.

He still had to figure out who was terrorizing her. For a while, he'd assumed it was Tyler, but . . . the man had had a thousand opportunities to hurt Alyssa today. Instead, he'd taken her to the doctor, given up his own bed. Granted, he hadn't called her husband, but since he wanted her for himself, why would he?

Peter had been in the county jail when the house had been broken into. Who did that leave? Primpton? Had the threatening vandalism been his work? Or someone else entirely?

Clutching his wife, Luc lifted Alyssa against him, carrying her to the bed. He set her gently on the sheets. "Rest."

She grabbed his arms. "Stay with me."

Hope surged. The fact she wanted him near her was a good sign.

With a nod, Luc lowered himself to the bed, stretching out beside her, stroking her damp hair.

Their gazes met. Telling this story had stripped her soul down to its core and left her bare. Every bit of that pain and fear was in her blue eyes.

He ached to make all that go away.

"Luc?" Alyssa breathed, her platinum hair floating around her shoulders like a temptress. But looking at her sweet oval face, rosy cheeks, and swollen, impossibly blue eyes only reminded him of the girl with the scarred heart that lay underneath that temptress.

"I'm here. Always here for you," he vowed.

"Touch me. Please." She shook as she unbelted her robe. "Be with me . . ."

Her request shocked him. He wanted to, God knew. Her words filled him with joy, made his cock weep with need. But . . . "Sugar, you've been through a lot tonight. I don't think now is the best time—"

"It is." She shrugged her robe off, revealing every bit of her gorgeous golden skin. "I have to replace the memories of Joshua with something wonderful. With you."

How could he say no to wiping away her worst memories? How could he fight something he wanted so damn badly?

Luc rose up on all fours over her, giving her plenty of space to move if she needed, and kissed her belly. "Are you sure?"

Alyssa reached up, curled her arms around his neck, and brought his mouth down to hers for a lingering, desperate kiss that pleaded. Unnecessary. She'd had him at *"Touch me."*

"Completely sure."

Luc tore off his robe and lowered himself over her, cradling himself between her thighs, taking hold of her hips. He rained kisses over her cheeks, her neck, the swells of her breasts, and she softened in his arms. For long minutes, he brushed his palms over her skin, and finally, she sighed.

Needing to know she was ready for him, Luc reached between them and massaged her clit. She drew in a sweet, shuddering breath, and desire gripped him mercilessly.

Cock in hand, he aligned their bodies. "Tell me if I hurt you. Scare you. I never want to do that again."

She swallowed, her solemn blue gaze fastened on him, and Luc felt her pain and need slice clear through to his heart. "I will, but you won't. Just . . . be with me."

The fact she wanted him anywhere near her now made him feel honored. She'd given him a gift. And he intended to treasure it— and her.

She linked their fingers together. The connection was electric and shuddered down his spine. Alyssa's desire to be closer to him touched him deep, stripping away his anger. Having her ask for him, surrender to him, was so much sweeter than tying her to the bed like a caveman. He'd regret that forever and hoped to make it up to her now.

Slowly, Luc began to push inside her. He stopped, retreated, eased in again—a soft glide, a slow dance. As always, she burned him. Luc squeezed his eyes shut, focusing on making this tender for her, making this good.

With every inch he submerged into the scalding clasp of her body, she seared him, especially when Alyssa braced her feet on the mattress and raised her hips up to meet him.

"Luc. *Yes!*"

Damn it. With two words, she nearly unraveled his self-control. She felt so good that it hurt, boiled his blood. As need rocketed, he began to sweat. Luc tried to breathe deep, re-engage his brain. But he needed her touch, needed to know that despite all that had happened today, she was still his.

Luc drew back, then thrust forward to the hilt. "You feel so perfect around me. I want to make you feel good, too."

Alyssa didn't reply, just pressed her mouth to his for a slow, blistering kiss. He tasted her need, her healing. As difficult as hearing about Joshua had been for him, Luc would do it a thousand times over if it would ease her pain and allow her to feel closer to him.

He pulled back, her body clinging to him. Unable to resist her sweet mouth, he kissed her again, deeper, slower, in rhythm with his thrusts. Alyssa tightened her arms around his neck.

Luc swallowed as he thrust his fingers into her hair, his thumb tracing her jaw. Her eyes were closed in impending bliss and she looked beautiful.

"Alyssa," his whispered, his voice husky.

Slowly, her eyes fluttered open, revealing dilated pupils, and she met his stare. Satisfaction hummed inside him. Now he knew that she was utterly aware of who was deep inside her.

His heart jumped as he drove home in one smooth stroke. She gasped, tightening her slick walls around him.

"Thank you for trusting me with your story," he whispered. "Your body."

Alyssa nodded, her gaze never wavering as tears filled her eyes. Her trust and the exquisite feel of her were denting his self-control. He had to find the will, make this about healing her, not about stroking his possessive instinct. Frightening her was the last thing he wanted.

Lowering his hands to her hips, he tilted her toward him and eased into her again. Pleasure transformed her expression. Her mouth gaped open, eyes going wide.

"Come for me."

"Y-yes."

The catch in her voice drove him deeper inside her. He drowned in her blue eyes and dark lashes. He didn't blink; he didn't want to miss a moment between them.

Suddenly, her body tightened, and she whimpered.

"Luc!" Alyssa dug her nails into his shoulders.

He held the pace steady, sweat beading across his body. Seconds later she clamped down on him and cried out, releasing. Satisfaction roared through him as she keened out her pleasure.

His pleasure spiraled nearly beyond his control as her face

revealed her bliss. And trust. She trusted him to care for her. Nothing was more gorgeous or humbling.

He closed his eyes, trying to get a grip, but need shut down his brain. Grasping for self-control was a waste of time. And if he was going over, he wanted to take her with him again.

With that in mind, he plied her with one unrelenting stroke after another and began to rub her clit.

"Luc!" She could barely find her breath now. "I can't—"

"You can. For me."

In the next moment, she clamped down on him again, her explosion of pleasure mere moments away. And still something drove him.

"Who's deep inside you?" he demanded.

"You are, Luc."

"That's right. Always." And her body told him she was seconds from orgasm. "Who is making you come?"

"Luc!"

She bucked and screamed beneath him, and he swore he was even deeper inside her than before.

Damn, it still wasn't enough. But his control was fraying, his body screaming for release.

As he pushed back inside her swollen sex with a steady, urgent stroke, Luc could never remember feeling closer to any woman, ever. Alyssa rose up to meet him. Her stare locked with his. Her growing pleasure and rising need killed the last of his self-control.

Sweat broke out across his back, his forehead, as he pushed his way inside her again. Then she was chanting his name and climaxing so hard, he could barely move. And clinging to him in every way possible. Luc fell deep into her as the last of his resistance gave way, and he soared into a pleasure so intense, it rattled his core, then remade him, cementing his love for her.

Slowly, their breathing recovered, and Luc wrapped her up in his arms, tangling his legs with hers. In that moment, he felt peace with her. With how far they'd come together. He only hoped that all of the difficulty was behind them.

"Feel better?" he asked softly.

She bit her lip, hesitating. "Do you wish you hadn't married me? I mean, after everything I told you . . ."

"Don't *ever* think that I'd judge you for what you had to do to survive. As much as I hate what you went through, I'm incredibly proud of who you've become."

Her smile was as bright as a breaking dawn, and Luc's heart broke all over again.

"Are you going to sell the club?" he whispered.

He hadn't even finished asking the question when she began shaking her head. "Too many memories. Too many other people who might let the wrong things happen under its roof. I'll turn over management to Sadie, if she wants the job. But I'm moving forward in life, hoping that the restaurant allows me a fresh start."

It would. Luc would see to that. He had the talent, connections, and influence.

He kissed her forehead. "Close your eyes."

She shook her head. "Not yet. Since it seems to be the night for truth, why don't you tell me your secret?"

Chapter Seventeen

LUC couldn't have heard her right. "What?"

"Whatever it is you're not saying. I've sensed it."

How had she known he had a secret?

He shook his head. The honesty of their moment was so real, and the truth sat on Luc's tongue. But he stopped. First, Alyssa had endured enough today, and with the bleeding scare, the issue of the baby's parentage and the inevitable arguments were best left for another day. Second, what would telling her that the baby couldn't possibly be his accomplish except to tear them apart?

In the back of his head, he wondered if there was a possibility, even a remote one, that the baby could be his. She kept swearing she and Tyler weren't lovers. Luc understood his wife now in a way he hadn't until tonight. Alyssa wasn't a liar. What if his "virtual impossibility" had indeed become possible?

He couldn't know the answer to that question unless he visited his doctor and submitted to the humiliating battery of tests. Again.

For her and their marriage, he would. But this miracle he didn't dare hope for. He wanted to—desperately. But likely, it would lead only to disappointment. There was probably another explanation for her pregnancy. Maybe Peter *had* actually raped her when he'd attacked, and Alyssa had blocked out the trauma? Perhaps her memory of the event had been muddled by her concussion . . .

But until Luc had answers, he must avoid this dangerous chasm of a topic. He'd tell her the truth soon, when they were a bit stronger. When he could say that he didn't mind that another man had planted his seed inside her and not want to rip the bastard's head off.

Today wasn't that day.

"We've had a big life change, sugar. Neither of us foresaw getting married, me moving here. The new show and Bonheur are added stress. The baby and your health are always huge concerns . . . If I've been distracted, I'm sorry."

Alyssa gave him a doubtful stare, but let it go. "If there's more, and you want to tell me, I want to hear it."

Luc tightened his arms around her. "I'm fine. Sleep. I'll be here as long as you need me."

* * *

AS Monday became Tuesday, it was an unusually rowdy weeknight at Sexy Sirens. The holidays were often insane, and with Thanksgiving right around the corner, the weather had turned too brisk for outdoor activity—so all the rowdies had crowded under her roof. Lucky her.

"Everyone's gone. Doors are locked," Tyler said, peeking his head in her office.

"Thank God we managed to finish the night without a full-out brawl."

"Copy that. Do you need me anymore? I'm beat."

"Go ahead. Hunter is somewhere around here, obsessively checking every door and window, most likely."

Tyler laughed. "Luc got you some real hard-core bodyguards. But Jack and Deke look downright relaxed compared to Hunter. He's a mean motherfucker."

She winced. "Sorry if he's interfered with your routine. I just . . . With Luc back in L.A. taping, I know he'll feel better if I cooperate. Probably better for me, too."

"Probably. I can't fault him for wanting to take care of you. I'd do the same in his shoes."

Alyssa softened. Tyler had feelings for her, and he didn't go to much trouble to hide them. And she felt guilty that she couldn't have reciprocated. He was a good guy who deserved a woman who loved him madly.

"See you tomorrow," Tyler called, then closed the door behind him.

A moment later, Hunter seemed to materialize out of thin air from a shadowed corner. She jumped in her chair, slapping a hand to her chest.

"Oh, my . . . You scared the hell out of me. How long have you been standing there?"

"Long enough to assure you that I've already obsessively checked the doors and windows. Twice." Hunter never wore emotion on his face, but Alyssa thought she saw a hint of a smile. "I'm touched by your buddy Tyler's opinion. 'Mean motherfucker' is actually kinder than most peoples' descriptions."

Alyssa had no trouble believing that. "I probably need to be here another hour or so. Books are a mess. Sorry. I know it's late."

He shrugged. "I'm here for as long as you are."

Yes, he'd become one of her three shadows. Between Deke, Jack, and Hunter, someone had eyes on her twenty-four/seven, at least until Luc returned on Friday night.

He hadn't wanted to leave her and resume taping his show, but she'd insisted. This show was too important to his future. He'd finally agreed to go—if she agreed to his security detail.

"Thanks for understanding."

Hunter drilled her with a flat stare. "I don't, actually. If I was in Luc's place, you'd be in a secure facility with at least double the guards. I'd never let you out of my sight."

She raised a brow. "A tad paranoid."

"Cautious," he corrected

"I think I can manage a trip to the bathroom on my own." One of the downsides of pregnancy.

"I'll follow you." His matter-of-fact expression told her that wasn't up for discussion.

Alyssa sighed and swallowed a quip about his demeanor scaring women away. Just a guess, but Hunter would enjoy the verbal sparring. Or he might just look at her with that dead stare. She wasn't in the mood for either.

The click of her heels on the concrete floors backstage echoed in the eerily silent club. She was so used to the walls thumping, the music blaring, the patrons howling. Being here alone—or mostly so—often gave her a shiver.

"You could step across the hall so I'm a little less sure you'll hear me pee."

Again, that ghost of a smile appeared. "I could."

But he wouldn't. She pitied the poor woman he fell for someday. He'd dig his teeth into her and never let go.

Rolling her eyes, she shut and locked the squeaky door, then set about her business.

Her head was filled numbers and stacks of receipts when she heard a thumping noise. As she washed her hands, sounds outside the little room were muffled. She shut off the water, and heard Hunter's voice clearly.

"Tyler, what the . . ." Another thump, then a scuffle. "Fuck!"

Then a gunshot. Startling, deafening, heart-jolting.

Complete silence.

Shit! Someone was in her club with a gun. And he must have shot Hunter or she was sure the Navy SEAL would be busting here even now and getting her out.

Most likely, she was on her own.

Tamping down her fear, she looked around for escape. The bathroom had no windows, and if the shooter didn't know where she was already, it wouldn't take him long to figure it out. And she'd left her cell phone at her desk.

Stupid!

"Where are you, my temptress of sin?"

That familiar voice scraped down her senses, leaving behind disquieting fear. Primpton? With a gun?

"You may as well come out. Both of your men here are incapacitated and won't be coming to your rescue. I haven't killed your bouncer. Yet. I might spare him if you face me like the Jezebel you are and pay for your sins."

He hadn't killed Tyler but would? Did that mean Hunter was dead? Likely so, or he would have taken Primpton down. *Oh, God.*

Biting her lip, she held in a cry of panic. There was every chance that the zealot would kill Tyler no matter what, but maybe she could buy Tyler enough time to get the two of them out of here. Right now, it was her best hope. She couldn't sneak out, even if the squeaky door let her, and leave Tyler to die.

Slowly, she pushed the door open. Predictably, the creaking alerted Primpton to her presence. He whipped his gaze around. The gun followed.

The councilman stood near the back door. Tyler was lodged just in the open doorway, flat on his back, his entire body boneless and lax. Was he passed out? Had Primpton hit him on the head? Drugged him?

Not two feet away, Hunter lay on the floor, blood pooling under a bullet wound in his shoulder. The red puddle seeped across the floor, spreading across the blue T-shirt that stretched across his wide chest.

Fear gripped her throat, choked her. Dear God, she'd always known Primpton was whacked, but a murderer? He'd truly come here to kill, and she was at the top of his hit list.

"There you are, looking as fetching as always. You're the devil's own, put on this earth to tempt men to sin. But I must stop you. I'm ashamed to admit that I've taken my own flesh in hand with thoughts of fornicating with you. For that alone I would punish you. But now . . ."

Blech. The mental image of Primpton masturbating while fantasizing about her nearly made her ill. Wait! Had *he* been the one to break into her house and ejaculate all over her lingerie?

Likely, but not important now. How many steps to her office? Could she make it and lock the door before he got down the hall? What would he do to Tyler if she tried? What would he do to her if she didn't?

"Now," he went on. "You must be stopped before you ruin more good Christian men and destroy their marriages."

Alyssa eased a step closer to her office, and popped out a hip. Predictably, Primpton's gaze followed the motion. She tossed her hair over her shoulder and crossed her arms across her chest, plumping up her cleavage. "Meaning?"

"My God-fearing assistant, Randall, has spent so much time here and lusted after you so impurely that his wife has filed for divorce. *You* led him astray."

Randall. The one who paid top dollar for the nastiest lap dances every Saturday night, then attended church every Sunday to repent for his sins?

Leaning yet closer to her office, she gave a pouty shake of her head, a moue of disagreement. "God gave these men free choice."

"You're the temptation no man can resist. I cannot allow you to keep luring them into sin." He raised the gun a bit higher.

"You're just going to shoot me? Here? Now?" She ran a hand up her thigh, lifting her skirt a fraction to show off her red garters.

Primpton choked. "I won't fornicate with you, whore!"

His erection made it clear that his urges had other ideas, and somehow she had to use that against him.

She dropped one shoulder, and the strap of her tank fell down her arm, revealing her black lacy bra strap and additional cleavage. An instant later, his gaze was fused to it. "I would never ask you to go against your principles. And I'm a married woman now."

"A sham! I'd stake my life you fornicated with that bouncer of yours and probably this one, too." He pointed at Hunter.

Primpton was fucking delusional, and she had to get to her damn phone fast. Hunter was losing blood every second.

Alyssa edged closer to her office door under the guise of shifting her legs, sticking one out for his visual feast. It creeped her out to have the psycho leer at her, but she'd done worse in the name of survival.

"You're flaunting yourself!" he accused.

"I'm standing here while you hold a gun on me and I plead for my life."

Immediately, he shook his head. "This club needs to end. You must die. These are the missions God has given me. I *am* his Christian soldier."

He was going to strike—at any second. Alyssa would have liked the chance to move a bit closer. As it was now, she had to hope he had no ability to sprint and couldn't hit a moving target.

Behind him, the wind howled and the back door flapped open, crashing against the wall. Primpton whirled to the sound. Using the distraction, Alyssa dashed to her office, running much faster than she ever had on stilettos.

Just before she shut the door and threw the dead bolt home with shaking hands, she heard Primpton yell. "God will damn you, whore, for tricking me. He'll damn you to hell, and I am the sword by which you will be consigned to burn for eternity."

With that pronouncement, he shot the doorknob. The handle jiggled, wiggled—something *clink*ed on the other side of the door.

Had he dismantled the handle on the other side? Carefully, she approached the door and examined the handle. It hung loose and she could see a crack of light through the hole it left in the door.

Then he shot the dead bolt. She leapt away from the door, her heart thumping erratically. A scratching sound reached her ears next. A scrape, followed by his maniacal laugh. What the hell was the psycho up to?

Before she could begin to figure it out, she heard Primpton's rapid footsteps as he prowled up and down the hall, heard a faint splashing sound. *Liquid?*

What the . . . ?

Frowning, oddly terrified with the door separating them, she panted. More of the splashing she'd heard earlier sounded again, this time closer.

Then the smell of gasoline hit—strong—a wave of petrol that burned her nose, her lungs.

"You'll burn, whore. Right now!" Primpton shouted.

In the next moment, she heard an ominous *whoosh*, the sound of starting fire. The bastard meant to fry her alive.

Heart kicking into overdrive, she tried to open the dead bolt and escape the room before the licking flames she heard got any higher. It wouldn't budge. It was jammed. Disabled. Something. How the hell was she going to get out?

Alyssa grabbed the dangling door handle, but the metal was already turning hot, and she yanked her hands away.

She tried not to panic. 911. She'd call them. Her cell phone was on her desk. Hopefully they'd get here in time.

But when she turned to her desk, her phone was no longer there.

* * *

ALYSSA woke by degrees, too afraid to open her eyes to the pounding headache crashing between her temples. She was someplace that smelled like rubbing alcohol. Whatever she was wearing twisted around her. The bed—clearly not hers—had scratchy sheets. Every muscle in her body screamed.

She took a deep breath—and immediately started to cough. Her lungs burned as if she'd smoked a whole carton of cigarettes in a day.

Her eyes flashed open in reflex.

"Easy," Tyler whispered as he reached out to take her hand.

"What . . . ?"

God, was that croak *her* voice?

"You're in the emergency room. You've been here a few hours."

She frowned, trying to sort through scattered memories. It was a jumble of panic and haze.

"The baby?" She coughed. Damn, her lungs burned.

"Fine. Doc checked you out right away. You're fine. Baby is still in there, growing and well."

Oh, thank God. Relief doused her, and she melted into the bed.

"What"—she coughed—"happened?"

"You're being treated for smoke inhalation. Do you remember Primpton being at Sexy Sirens?"

Then it clicked into place. The club. The gun. Hunter lying in a pool of his blood. The councilman threatening to kill her. The fire.

"Hunter make it?"

"He's fine. After Primpton knocked me out, Hunter found me passed out in the doorway. He knelt down to see if I was okay, and the bastard shot him from the alley. Superficial shoulder wound. He lost blood, but the paramedics got to him in time. His sister is down the hall fussing over him now."

She relaxed against the bed, releasing the breath she hadn't realized she'd been holding; then a new fear gripped her. "The club?"

Please God . . .

"Gone." He shook his head, regret settling into his expression. "I'm sorry. The fire department tried . . ."

Anguish gushed through her blood, like sizzling acid destroying her veins. Her club, her refuge, the place that represented her broken past and its bridge to her stronger present, no more. All because of one crazy zealot's delusions.

No, Sexy Sirens wasn't gone forever. Not if she had anything to say about it.

"You okay?"

He held up both hands, stopping her concern. "Bump on the head. As I opened the door to leave, the asshole hit me on the head with the butt of his gun, knocked me out. After he started the fire, he darted out the back door. I came to and saw Primpton was gone, and Hunter had his eyes open, assessing the sitch. I grabbed my cell, dialed nine-one-one, and handed it to him while I got him on his feet. I went to get you, and the stupid SEAL followed me instead of getting out."

"The place must have been an inferno by then!" And they'd both stayed to help her?

"Smoldering wood falling from the ceiling everywhere . . . He'd jammed rock into your dead bolt's casing, but I got it out. I wasn't leaving without you."

Tears stung her eyes, and she held out a hand to him. "You're a wonderful friend to me."

Pain ripped across his features as he shot her a tight smile. "That's me, a real pal."

It had been the wrong thing to say, she realized. He loved her, and she hated in some ways that she couldn't reciprocate. But she'd given her heart to Luc long ago, probably because she'd known from their first meeting that he was the sort of man who wouldn't care about a woman because she looked hot. He would fall only once he knew her deep inside.

Was there any chance Luc had actually fallen in love with her? All his concern, his tenderness, constant phone calls, business help, fabulous home-cooked meals, and everything else had to be based on more than the fact she was pregnant, right?

"You're going to make some girl wildly happy someday," she murmured to Tyler.

"I wanted it to be you." His jaw clenched, and he grimaced with pain.

"I'm not the one, but you'll find her."

The nurse broke in and checked her vitals, asked her if she needed more pain meds. Alyssa shook her head. All she wanted was out of here.

"Did someone call Luc?" She didn't want him to worry unnecessarily, especially after the drama of her last "disappearance."

"Kimber did. He's on his way back. Should be here in a few hours."

Of all people to call her husband but his former lover. She winced. And wouldn't the producers of Luc's show be thrilled? He'd been back for all of two days . . . "He should have stayed there."

Tyler's mouth dropped open. "Are you serious? Though I wish he had. At least then I could make the argument that he didn't give a shit about you."

Still didn't mean he'd come back for her. The baby had to be on his mind, too.

"Did the cops catch Primpton?" Alyssa changed the subject. Any more emotional conversation about Luc, and she was likely break down and cry—and reveal just how scared she was that her husband didn't love her the way she loved him.

At that, Tyler smiled. "Cops nailed him about fifteen minutes after he fled. He was home with his wife, trying to pretend he'd been sleeping the night away. But they found his clothes and shoes with traces of gasoline, along with his gun." Tyler's smile died. "Baby, they also found a nook in the back of his closet. It was like . . . a shrine devoted to you. Sick bastard had fantasies of making you his sex slave. He had all kinds of pictures of you."

Something crossed Tyler's face that seized her heart. "Pictures?"

He shuddered. "Some he'd clearly Photoshopped so they looked like pictures of you bleeding under his whip, bowing at his feet with hands cuffed."

Everything inside her recoiled.

"He had pictures of you the night you stripped for the anniversary bash."

"Pig."

"He'd written WHORE in red paint all over the walls."

She shuddered at his delusion and thanked God that he'd been caught. "Guess we know who wrote all those notes and broke into my house. Fucking bastard."

Tyler nodded. "That's the police's theory. Mine, too. They're going to run forensics."

A technicality, most likely. Alyssa realized how lucky she'd been. She'd never taken Primpton very seriously, failed to see him for the true whack job he was. Underestimating him could have cost her both her own life and the baby's. Thank God for Tyler and Hunter.

And now that Primpton was behind bars, maybe she could rest easier, stop looking over one shoulder, lose the fear of being attacked again.

Tyler tapped his foot on the tile floor, and she recognized the gesture as a nervous one. "What?"

"You ought to know . . . He had pictures of you and Luc in your bedroom at the club. It looks like he took them through the alley window."

Alyssa gasped, shock blanching her with a chill. "Were we . . . ?"

"Oh, yeah. The look on your face . . ." Tyler looked away. "Luc know how much you love him?"

She pressed her lips together. Damn, Tyler was perceptive. And no one had ever accused him of beating around the bush. "No. It's that obvious?"

He scoffed in answer. "That you're wearing your heart on your sleeve? Yes."

Great. She sighed. "I don't know if he feels the same."

"I don't know, either. He wants you. Bad." Tyler shrugged. "I think there's more there, but I'm not the expert on guys' feelings."

"Used to being the heartbreaker, not the heartbroken?"

A sheepish smile crept across his mouth. "Something like that."

"I have a feeling that, deep down, you're a really bad boy."

"Knock, knock."

Alyssa turned to the sound of the female voice coming from the doorway. Kimber. She was very nice, but Alyssa looked at the younger woman with her auburn hair pulled away from her sweet oval face in a wholesome ponytail and tensed. Luc's former lover had a long, lean body, which showed only a hint of a baby bump so far.

Kimber was everything Luc had wanted out of life and lost to his cousin. Yeah, on their wedding night, he'd told Alyssa that he'd never felt more for any other woman. But who knew if that was really his heart talking or just his attempt to make their marriage work?

Resentment toward the other woman flared, and she swallowed to force it down.

"Come in."

Kimber drifted in, graceful in an athletic way, as if comfortable in her skin. "My brother wanted me to check on you. You okay?"

And caring, too. She probably smiled while giving the perfect blow job, kept a gorgeous garden, had been a virgin for her husband, and was looking forward to PTA meetings.

Alyssa released a shuddering sigh. She couldn't be unkind just because her own insecurities were eating at her. She looked deliriously happy with her husband, Deke, and never gazed at Luc like a lover. The problem, Alyssa realized, was all her.

"Fine. Thanks. How's your brother?"

She rolled her eyes. "Macho as always. They wheeled him out of surgery to remove the bullet half an hour ago, and he's already wanting to leave. Idiot. He'll be fine."

"He came in to save me when he could have left me to burn, and I'll always be grateful."

"Saint Hunter, huh?" Kimber shook her head. "No. If there's an adrenaline rush, my brother will run to it. Burning building? Big fun!"

The sarcasm was thick, and made Alyssa smile. She could actually picture Hunter thinking that an inferno was better than a hip party.

"Hey, I resemble that remark!" Tyler protested.

"Yeah," Alyssa shot back. "And we'll have words about it later."

His expression told her she'd be wasting her breath.

Kimber turned to Tyler. "Can you give us a minute?"

Alyssa frowned. What could the other woman possibly have to say that Tyler couldn't hear?

Her bouncer looked between the two women, then shrugged. "Sure. I'll see if the doc is around to examine you so we can get you out of here."

"Thanks," she murmured, her attention focused on Kimber.

The woman moved into the room to occupy the chair Tyler had just vacated and clenched her hands in her lap. "I know I'm not your favorite person and that it's none of my business, but I wanted to thank you for what you're doing for Luc."

Alyssa hesitated, filtered through Kimber's statement a few times, then frowned. "What am I doing? I don't know what you mean."

"You know . . . Marrying him and letting him play father to your baby. He was so crushed when I wasn't pregnant a few months ago . . . when he was still with Deke and me. Luc has wanted a baby for years, and knowing he can't father one has nearly killed him. But you giving him this opportunity—"

"What?" Luc unable to father a child? That didn't add up. Of course he could; she was living proof. But Kimber's expression made it clear that she absolutely believed every word coming out of her mouth. "That's not true."

Kimber raised her brows, then sent her a smile full of pity. "You don't have to pretend for me. Luc has known for nearly twenty years that he can't have children. He's been looking for alternative methods to fatherhood for the last few. That's why he was involved with Deke and me. He didn't love me, you know. He just hoped the three of us . . . Well, that Deke would get me pregnant so Luc could be a daddy."

Alyssa blinked. Blinked again. Stopped breathing. *That* was why he'd been involved in ménages? Luc genuinely thought he was sterile? Oh, my . . . If Kimber could be believed—and why would she lie?—that meant Luc "knew" she wasn't pregnant by him.

Cold nausea rushed all through her, and she set a protective hand over her belly. "This baby is Luc's. I haven't—"

"It's okay." Kimber smiled. "Luc told me how grateful he is that you turned to him, instead of Tyler. I'm sure it would have been easier to marry the baby's father, but Luc needed this so badly."

"He told you that?" she repeated numbly. He'd told Kimber that he believed he couldn't have children, but hadn't told his own pregnant wife?

Pain stabbed her in the chest. Betrayal ripped across her heart. It fucking hurt. How could he deceive her like this? Keep such a monumental secret. She'd *known* he was withholding something since they married and, even when she'd asked, he'd refused to share. Goddamn it! How could he marry her, believing the child was another man's, and play along so masterfully?

How could he be so wrong?

God, she was going to be sick.

Kimber nodded. "We're so thrilled for you both. Luc seems so much happier now. I felt guilty when Deke and I paired off and decided to marry and raise our own family. Knowing that you're giving him what he needs means everything to us. Luc is a wonderful guy and he'll make the best father ever. I have no doubt."

Right. Alyssa suddenly had doubts—many of them. First and foremost that he gave a shit about *her*. Hell, she'd bared her soul to him, told him the most painful, intimate parts of her life, given every bit of herself to him. He'd repaid her with deception.

Tears threatened, and she blinked, holding them at bay. Not until Kimber was gone. Not until she could grieve alone.

Joshua and her mom had drilled into her head that she couldn't trust anyone, no matter how close the ties. Luc's tenderness, hot lovemaking, jealousy, protective streak—all bullshit. All manufactured lies to keep her deluded and by his side.

Fucking bastard.

Just then, the doctor knocked, Tyler in tow.

"Oops, that's my cue to leave." Kimber hopped up from her chair. "Good luck. Call me if you need anything. We can swap baby stories."

The woman left with a giggle. As if she hadn't dropped an enormous bombshell on Alyssa that shook the foundation of her very life.

Luc had married her for this child, which she'd known. She'd had no fucking clue he genuinely thought the child was Tyler's. Or some other man's. His initial reaction to the news of her pregnancy now made sense.

And . . . you're here because it's mine?

She'd heard the doubt in his tone and misunderstood it, written it off to his belief that she was a whore who slept around. Which he still must believe.

But it hadn't taken him too long to sing a different tune with her.

The best birthday present ever. I don't want you to call me when the baby is born. I'd like to be involved in this child's life. I want to be there every step of the way . . .

She snorted. It all made sense now. If he thought he couldn't have a baby and would accept another's as his own, then marriage, even if he had to fake feelings for his new wife, was the price of fatherhood.

A new wave of nausea hit her. From start to finish, this marriage had been about this baby and placating her so that she'd share the child with him. He'd lied to her with every whispered word, every touch. All that jealousy? Perhaps feigned to make her believe that he cared. Or maybe he hadn't wanted anyone touching the woman he'd given his name to or endangering the child to whom he planned to devote himself.

She'd been used for a lot of things in her life, but never her womb. Somehow, this felt like the worst violation of all.

Chapter Eighteen

LUC arrived back in Lafayette as the sun set, tearing into their driveway and barely parking his SUV before abandoning it and sprinting through the door, toward the stairs. He had to see Alyssa now, know she was all right. When he'd received Kimber's phone call, his heart had stuttered, then threatened to beat from his chest. Primpton nearly roasting her alive?

Thank God they'd finally caught the sick freak harassing her. He'd known the city councilman wasn't dipping both oars, but would never have suspected that the divorce of one of his followers would put him over the edge and incite him to murder.

But Alyssa was safe. Luc *needed* to see her unharmed and in one piece. Hold her. Tell her that he loved her.

Inside the foyer, he stumbled over something unexpected and tripped, barely righting himself without falling. He looked down. His suitcases. They were packed.

Could that possibly mean what it implied?

His world tilted upside down. A chill went through him as he skirted the luggage and bounded up the stairs. "Alyssa?"

No answer.

Jogging down the shadowed hall, he stopped in the doorway of the master bedroom. There she sat in bed, hair loose and long. Her wedding ring wasn't on her finger. She wore a big gray T-shirt and stared out the window to her right. She looked a million miles away. No, she looked defeated.

Alarm prickled along his skin. Alyssa was a fighter. She'd survived trauma that would have crushed most—and she'd come out stronger. The woman mentally escaping out the window . . . That wasn't her.

"Sugar?"

"You're a smart man, Luc," she said, without looking his way. "I don't want a confrontation. Just take your things and go."

His guts seized up into a ball. His breath stopped. Shock enough that he'd been awakened to the news she'd been trapped in a burning building and had escaped only with Tyler's and Hunter's help. But now she was kicking him out? Saying they were done?

"Whatever has upset you, we can work it out, sugar. I'm sorry I wasn't here to protect you. I came back to check on you, be with you . . . What happened that would make you pack my bags and—"

"I don't want to argue about it."

Luc crossed the room, approached the far side of the bed, and sat on the edge, beside her. Still she continued to look past him to the window. Frustration rose, but he pushed it down, focusing on his concern for her as he took her hand in his. It was cold.

"That makes two of us. So let's talk instead of fight. You tell me what happened, and we'll talk it through. If you're angry that I wasn't here when that bastard Primpton attacked you, believe me, no one could be more upset than me."

She shook her head, then finally looked away from the window, down to her lap. "You had a job to do and you were doing it. We talked in advance about the fact you needed to be in Los Angeles to fulfill your contractual obligations."

Her voice sounded dead. As the sunlight hit her cheeks, he saw the silvery marks of dried tears, and they wrenched his heart. Upon closer inspection, her red eyes and nose indicated she'd cried hard. Now she had no emotion left to give. That realization kicked him breathless.

Beating back his fear, he clutched her hand. "I'm not worried about my contractual obligations right now. I'm worried about my wife."

Alyssa squeezed her eyes shut and shook her head, platinum hair brushing her shoulders. "You're worried about the baby."

"Of course." Why would that be bad?

Finally, she looked at him. The fury and resolve he saw there stunned Luc. His heart lurched. What the hell had happened since the attack? Had Tyler talked her into leaving him somehow?

"At least you're being honest. Finally," she sneered.

A part of him rejoiced at her show of emotion. The other part . . . Dread injected a new trepidation into his concern. He could think of only one thing he'd been less than honest about.

Oh, God, please no.

"What do you mean?" He forced the words out, hearing his own voice shake.

"I mean, I figured you'd be concerned about the baby. I just never clued in that the concern stopped there. You're always so tender and attentive." She shook her head, scoffing. "I'm so damn stupid that I fell for it. I keep trusting the wrong men."

Had she just lumped him into the same category as Joshua? Fuck if that didn't make his stomach clench and roll. "Alyssa—"

"I should have asked more questions about your reasons for marrying me." Her tone was a verbal lash to her own psyche, and hearing it damn near killed him. "I knew you'd proposed because of the baby. Deep down, I'd hoped that you cared for me, but . . . I never imagined that you actually *married* me believing the baby wasn't yours."

Luc closed his eyes as his world imploded. Someone had told her his secret, his shame. Someone had given her the information and let her draw the worst conclusions. Since only two people knew, and Deke would never spill, he knew exactly who had revealed the truth.

Kimber he'd deal with later. Now he had to talk to Alyssa, make her understand that his reasons for being married—staying married— had everything to do with her, not just the baby.

"I'm sorry that I didn't tell you about my . . . condition. The fact the baby likely isn't mine doesn't change anything for me. I care about you every bit as much as I care about this baby."

Finally, she flashed blue eyes that spit fire at him. "Are you going to try to convince me that, since our marriage, I've come to mean something to you?"

Luc grabbed her shoulders and forced his gaze deep into hers. "You meant something to me even before we married. I was *so* elated and relieved to see you the day you appeared at the department store. I was ready to drop to my knees, say anything, just to make you talk to me. To become engaged to you that night was more than I ever dared to hope for."

She rolled her eyes. "Stop! Be honest! I appeared with the answer to your fertility problem. *Then* I mattered. A woman you like to fuck conveniently got pregnant. Hallelujah! And even if the baby isn't yours—I guess that's a minor detail in your head—why not suddenly heap adoration on her and persuade her to marry you?" Every word dripped scorn. "Why not become her husband under false pretenses and encourage her to bear her soul to you? She's just a fertile womb."

The barrage of accusations pelted Luc, and he winced. He'd have to answer her quickly if he wanted to diffuse this situation. Clearly, he'd hurt her much worse than he'd imagined. She felt used. That, he'd never seen coming. Damn it to hell.

"That is *not* true. I'm sorry I didn't tell you about my sterility. In this moment, I regret it more than you know. Yes, you did come to me with a convenient solution to my problem, but what I feel for you is so much more." He brought her closer, willing her to understand. "I missed you when we were apart. Being separated from you felt like a part of myself was missing, and I had a gaping hole in my chest where you used to be. I'd love more than anything for this baby to be mine, but . . . the odds are against me."

"So, Sherlock, whose baby is it? Tyler's?"

It would be so easy to lie to her—and so wrong. "I assumed that at first. I know how he feels about you, and the way he touches you is so familiar, as if he's done that—and more—a thousand times. But you've said that you aren't lovers, and I've come to know you well enough to know that you're not a liar."

"Wish I had that same sense of security about you," she hurled at him. "So, at the time we married, you assumed Tyler was the lucky sperm donor. Since you've figured out that's not true, who do you assume I whored myself to? Random customers at the club?"

He cupped her face in his hands. "Of course not. Either Peter raped you, and you don't remember the event—"

"I remember everything perfectly. He never penetrated me. This is *your* child."

"His attack was traumatic," Luc hedged.

Alyssa wrenched away from his touch. "I didn't block it out. If I can still remember the smell of the chlorine bleach on my sheets and the fact my childhood teddy bear stared me in the face while Joshua forcibly took my virginity, I think I can remember whether or not Peter succeeded in raping me."

Dear God. Luc fought an urge to clutch her against him, and his stomach turned inside out at her words. She sounded so certain that

Peter hadn't succeeded in violating her, which meant . . . Was it really possible that he'd managed to get her pregnant?

"Or?" she snapped. "What's the 'or'?"

"Or . . . my doctor was wrong about the severity of my condition."

"Someone get the man a prize." She bounded off the bed, away from him.

He grabbed Alyssa and pulled her back into his lap. She struggled and squirmed to get free. He held her firmly, but not tightly. He wanted her to listen, not be frightened.

"God, I wish more than anything that my doctor had been wrong. I'd love to know that the life growing inside you now is one we created together. But understand that, after years of being told that would be more or less impossible, it's hard for me to comprehend."

Her anger slipped into a mask of resignation. "I understand that. If a doctor tells you something is impossible, you believe it. I would. I don't blame you for that at all."

Thank God. Maybe they *could* work through this mess.

Then she worked free of his grip and bolted across the room, fists clenched, and screamed through gritted teeth, "What I can't stand is the goddamn deception!"

Her demeanor shouted, "Stay the fuck away," and Luc respected it. Trying to comfort her would only be counterproductive, and he wanted her to work through her anger. She was definitely entitled to it. Certainly he was questioning his decisions now. Had not telling her the truth been truly been keeping the peace or mere cowardice?

"I can only tell you that, when you informed me you were pregnant, I wanted you and the baby so badly, I don't have words to explain it. Every nerve in my body screamed at me to make you mine forever. I didn't think that telling the truth would serve any purpose except to tear us apart."

"The truth *is* tearing us apart." She shook her head, face tense.

Tears threatened to spill, and Luc hated that he'd put that look on her face. "When we married, it was enough for me that you were the father of my baby. I thought I loved you enough for both of us, and that someday, you might come to love me, too."

She loved him? The elation he should have felt died a quick death, strangled by fear. Alyssa had spoken in past tense.

"You don't have to hope, sugar. I love you. I—"

"Convenient to say now. Do you really think three words will make everything better?"

Luc stood, swallowing down his dread. "No, and that's not why I'm saying them now. I know it will take time for me to prove it to you. But it's the truth, and I'm relieved to finally say how I feel."

Alyssa turned her back on him. "How am I supposed to ever believe you?"

He didn't have an easy answer except trust—the one thing he'd shattered between them. "Please . . . I swear. I'm telling you the truth."

"The same sort of truth you told when you led me to believe you knew the baby was yours?" She laughed. "They're just words and they don't mean a damn thing."

"That's crap! From where I'm standing, they mean *everything*." Luc raked a hand through his hair. How to make her see that his feelings were deep and wide and went on forever? "We married because you were pregnant. You're still pregnant, and I still want to be a husband and father. This could have been any other marriage of convenience . . . except we fell in love. *Love*, sugar. It's too good to just throw away. We have to come together and work through the misunderstanding, even if it takes a while."

"It's not a misunderstanding; it's a *lie*. You can't use those three little words to put a verbal Band-Aid over the fact that you apparently have so little respect for me, you immediately assumed the baby was another man's. You kept critical information from me, seduced me into believing you cared—"

"I do care, goddamn it! Have you been listening? I. Love. You. I never really knew what that meant until you."

Alyssa shot him a disbelieving glare. "You love me so much you never told me the truth, never bothered to get a second opinion about whether you could possibly father a child, just in case your doctor was wrong—"

"Actually, I made an appointment on Friday to be retested at a clinic in L.A. I'm hoping the second opinion will be different and this baby is mine."

"This new doctor will tell you what I already know: You're capable of siring a child. I have no doubt you'll be an incredible father, and I'll never take this child away from you. He or she is half you and should know its father. But none of the rest of this shit matters. For us, your sudden confession and 'I love you's are too little, too late. Good-bye, Luc."

* * *

THE day after Thanksgiving, and Luc stared out the window of his Tyler, Texas, home at the blustery, gray day. He had reasons to be thankful, he supposed. Feeling it was impossible when he was numb to everything but the terrible emptiness inside him, an emptiness he knew could be filled only by his wife.

And Alyssa wasn't talking to him. At all.

He'd left their house in Lafayette after their argument to give her some space, some time. In the ensuing twelve hours, she'd changed the locks at both her residence and the restaurant, as well as her home and cell phone numbers. The next night, he'd waited in Bonheur's packed parking lot like a damn stalker for her to lock up and head home, just so he might steal a few minutes with her, try to explain again that he was sorry and he loved her.

Instead, Tyler had rushed her to her car and curled his arm around her protectively the second they'd seen him next to her car. Tyler had shoved him away just long enough to allow Alyssa to escape. The bastard had paid for it; Luc knew he had a mean right cross. But it was too late to exchange even a word with his wife.

The next night, she'd called him from the restaurant to reiterate her plea to leave her alone. Before he could say much more than he was sorry and that he loved her, she'd hung up.

That had been a long, miserable eight days ago. Earlier this week, he'd gone back to L.A. and finished his taping. He could only imagine what those episodes looked like, since he'd been on autopilot the whole time. No doubt he'd get a call back to reshoot some.

Yesterday, he'd likely ruined Deke and Kimber's Thanksgiving holiday. They had so much to be thankful for and had invited all of Kimber's family. Luc had tried to fade into the background, but Hunter had stared with those knowing eyes as he'd shaken his head and muttered, "Stupid fucker." His younger brother, Logan, had concurred.

"Anything from Alyssa?" Kimber tiptoed up to him, looking so contrite that he could hardly be angry with her. She'd merely assumed that, since Alyssa was his wife, he'd been honest with her about his "condition."

"No."

"I'm so, so—"

"I know." Luc couldn't hear her apologize again. It only reminded him of everything that was wrong and wouldn't change a damn thing. He gouged the heels of his palms into his eyes. "Why didn't I learn the first time? Besides being my cousin, Deke is my best friend. I kept the truth from him, too. It almost cost me our friendship. And I still didn't fucking learn. I wanted her and that baby so badly . . ." He sighed. "I checked my ethics at the door."

"You thought she was lying to you as well, right, about who the baby's father was?"

"Yeah, and at the time, that's how I justified my deception. But damn it, to quote a cliché, two wrongs don't make a right."

"True." Kimber sighed. "What are you going to do? I've never seen you this miserable."

"There are some things I should be elated about, you know? A year ago, when I first started hearing from the cable network, the show was a dream come true. For that to actually be a reality now . . . It's everything I've worked for, one of the goals in the back of my head when I stayed up until all hours cooking the same dish for the tenth time that day and changing just one ingredient to see if I could make it better. It's one of the reasons I broke my back to make so many personal appearances, put out the best possible cookbooks. I wanted this opportunity to reach avid foodies and share my love of sophisticated Southern cooking."

"I'm sure the shows will be great. Your personality will draw viewers in. I just know it."

He shrugged. "Maybe. Thing is, I'm not sure I care that much anymore."

Kimber squeezed his hand. "You're just upset. God, if I'd had any idea—"

"Don't blame yourself for my wrongdoing. If I hadn't married her under false pretenses, I wouldn't be in this mess."

"I know you're hurting now, but there *are* things to be thankful for. You'll find the love of your show again once you're in a better place emotionally. You have your friends and family, a great house, a lot of talent. You have your health."

His health. Luc laughed bitterly. He had more than that.

"Dr. Kimjin called me this morning."

Deke entered the room and stood behind his wife's chair, a casual hand on her shoulder. "Is he the doctor who tested you last week in L.A.?"

Luc nodded. The man's words still rang in his ears.

"And?"

"In his words, me impregnating Alyssa isn't virtually impossible. He classified it as challenging but not impossible at all. Apparently, in the last nine years, my body healed some on its own and my sperm count increased enough to make my chances of impregnating someone much greater. He was still surprised we'd managed it without fertility drugs or surgical intervention. But he affirmed what I'd already figured out: It's entirely possible the baby is mine. In fact, I'm sure it is."

"That's great, man!" Deke enthused. "Wow."

"Dr. Kimjin said that if my previous physician hadn't told me it was possible my body could heal, he'd done me a disservice."

"And I take it he didn't tell you?" his cousin asked.

"Not a word. I wish to hell I'd seen another doctor and gotten tested sooner."

"But now you know." Kimber's face softened. "Are you going to tell Alyssa?"

Luc scoffed. "How? She's changed every lock, every phone number. Even her e-mail account. She won't see me or talk to me. After putting her trust in a lying scumbag when she was younger and experiencing a horrific outcome, I'm not surprised that she wants nothing to do with someone else she sees as a betrayer."

"But you love her," Kimber argued.

Yeah, he did. So much that he knew he'd never be whole without her. But his feelings didn't change a damn thing.

Just then, the doorbell rang, and Kimber jumped up. "I'll get it."

In her ensuing absence, Deke stared. "Man, you got to get it together and go after her. The longer you stay away, the easier it is for her to convince herself that she was right and you don't give a shit about her."

Luc jumped to his feet. "What the fuck would you have me do? The last time I was there, I practically stalked her just to see her face. I didn't even get to talk to her."

Deke scratched the back of his neck. "Did you send her flowers?"

Given the fact he'd sent them to her with a polite note after the first night he'd spent with her, the one in which he was supposed to share her with Deke? "She'd see it as a kiss-off, not a romantic gesture. Besides, I told her I love her. I'm not sure she doubts that as much as she doubts that I want her more than the baby."

"Do you?" Deke's raised brows conveyed his shock without a word.

Luc nodded without hesitation. "For the last few years, I knew my life was incomplete and, not knowing what was missing, I assumed it was fatherhood—the one thing I'd never experience, right? After Dr. Kimjin's call, I tried to figure out why I wasn't more thankful, more relieved. All these years I spent assuming that being a father would complete me, fill the void I was physically incapable of fulfilling. It's human nature to want what you can't have."

"But you realized that what was missing was just a significant someone with whom to share to your life." Deke didn't ask; he knew.

"Yeah. How fucking stupid could I be? Fatherhood will be great, and I'll always love this baby with all my heart. But I'll love its mother until the day I die, and it's killing me that I can't see her one more time and try to convince her that she's my everything. The person I've been seeking for years and I just didn't know it."

"Luc, there's someone at the door for you," Kimber said softly, then bit her lip. "I tried to tell them you were busy, but . . . he's insisting he talk to you."

"Reporter?"

Her gaze skirted away. "No."

Alarm skittered through Luc as he put one foot in front of the other and made his way out of the kitchen. The walk seemed to take forever, and he feared what awaited him at its end. If this was a simple delivery, Kimber would have handled it. Hell, she would have met his gaze.

He reached the door, his movements seemingly in slow motion even though his heart was racing like a maxed-out, turbocharged engine. Finally, he pulled it open and stared at the clean-shaven, fortysomething suit standing in front of him. The man's face was somewhere between businesslike and grim.

Luc swallowed.

"Are you Luc Traverson?" the man asked.

Unable to find his voice, Luc just nodded.

"I've got some papers for you. Please sign here." He thrust a clipboard at Luc.

Papers. Ominous. He feared he knew what kind of papers these were. God, he couldn't even think about them, much less accept them.

Shaking his head, Luc stepped back. "What kind of papers?"

"I'm not privy to that information, sir. My job is simply to deliver them."

"No." Luc didn't want to know what was inside the thick white envelope tucked under the man's arm.

"Sir, you have to take the papers."

Luc couldn't get a grip on his breathing. His heart skittered, stuttered. He shook his head.

Deke approached him from behind and clapped him on the shoulder. "Sign, buddy. We'll deal with whatever's in there. I promise."

Was that even a promise Deke could keep? Luc wasn't sure he *could* deal with it.

"Sir, please." The messenger thrust the clipboard in his direction again.

"It's okay," Deke whispered in his ear.

No, it wasn't, but burying his head in the sand wasn't going to make it go away. Damn it.

With numb fingers, he grabbed the board and pen.

"Sign here." The man pointed.

Luc's heart sank as he did and accepted the big white envelope. Somehow, he just knew his life was over.

Faintly, he heard Deke mutter something polite and shut the door.

Deke grabbed him by the elbow and hauled him up. "Let's go back to the kitchen and sit down."

Luc was stunned to realize he was on his knees. Literally.

As he stumbled to his feet again, Deke guided him back to his chair. The corner of the envelope cut into his palm, and the feeling that he'd lost everything wound through his blood like poison. The pity on Kimber's face was an arrow to his chest. They all knew what he knew. Luc closed his eyes as pain dismantled him one cell at a time.

Finally, he lurched into his chair. Deke pulled up one beside him.

"Open it."

"No." It would hurt too fucking much.

"This may be something from the network."

Luc shook his head. "They'd contact my agent first."

"Maybe it's a written report from Dr. Kimjin."

"He just received the results this morning. Besides, why not just fax them?"

"You still have to open it." Deke's gravelly voice grated on his brain.

"Would you fucking open it if you were in my shoes? If you were pretty sure the envelope contained the end of your marriage and your happiness, would you really just launch into it like it was any other piece of mail?"

Deke shot his wife a glance. His cousin's face was rife with love, and it almost pained Luc to see them so happy. He wanted the best for them, but if even fucked-up Deke had figured out how much Kimber meant to him and managed to share a life with her, Luc wondered why the hell hadn't he figured out sooner that he wanted the same with Alyssa. That he wanted it all with her.

"I'd probably down a bottle of Jack first, but I'd face reality. The Luc I know would, too."

Luc scoffed, trying to hold tears at bay. He didn't succeed. The little drops were like a pickax to the back of his eyes. His throat tightened. "I hate Jack Daniel's."

"Well, since you haven't been around much, we haven't kept any of your fancy cabernet sauvignon on hand. It's either Jack or sober."

"Fuck." Releasing a shuddering breath, he gripped the envelope. "Sober."

With dread sinking his heart, Luc edged his fingers under the sealed flap of the thick envelope and tore it open. His fingers shook as he withdrew the thick document inside. Big words in a fancy script jumped out at him, stabbing him in the heart.

Ending his hopes of happiness forever.

"What does it say?" Kimber whispered.

He swallowed, but his voice was still scratchy and uneven as he read, "Petition for marital annulment."

Chapter Nineteen

Alyssa entered her house with a tired sigh, avoiding her bare ring finger and its meaning, and looked at her watch. Nearly one a.m. Luc should have received the annulment papers by now, likely hours ago. She'd half expected him to call Bonheur tonight and demand to talk to her. Silence. Or be waiting in her driveway when she arrived home. No one. Nibbling on a ragged fingernail, she wondered what that meant. Would he go along with the process and grant her the legal end of their marriage, as if it had never taken place?

She hoped so. Sort of. Well, that was what she *should* want. He'd deceived her and may never care about her the way she cared about him. Granted, his "not caring" always made her feel special, but she had no way of knowing if his tenderness was an act. And she didn't want to blindly trust him, then wake up one day and realize—too late—that she'd put her faith in someone who would rip her world apart and stab her in the heart.

Someone like Joshua.

Telling Luc about her past had been cathartic. And though difficult, it had seemingly brought them closer together. The fact she'd misjudged the situation only made her more determined to end things now. If she stayed, she'd only get in deeper, and that mistake could be catastrophic.

Though it hurt damn bad, it was better this way. Or would be someday, she supposed. Now, drawing another breath, putting one foot in front of the other, was hell. Alyssa wasn't eating as well as she should. What little she managed to choke down was for the baby's sake. And sleep . . . It just wasn't happening without Luc's hot, protective body next to her. Alyssa knew she was burning her candle at both ends, running herself ragged trying to get a restaurant off the ground, deal with the insurance adjusters and contractors to rebuild Sexy Sirens . . . while trying to forget Luc. But the life growing inside her was a constant reminder of her husband. Even without the baby, she doubted she'd ever get over him.

After locking the front door, she turned on a nearby lamp that provided just enough golden glow for her to trudge up the stairs. Her heels clicked on the hardwood floors in the shadowed hallway to her bedroom.

All at once, she remembered that her alarm hadn't sounded when she'd walked in the house. Had she forgotten to set it this morning? And her bedroom door was closed. Alyssa frowned. The lack of sleep and nourishment must be catching up to her. Other women told her that pregnancy had a way of making a girl forgetful.

Still, she never shut that door when she left. She always wanted to know what—or who—awaited her in her room before she walked in. Something else Joshua had taught her.

Was it possible Luc was waiting for her on the other side of the door? He had a way of melting her defenses with his surprises.

The possibility pumped her full of excitement. They were supposed to be ending their marriage, but she'd be lying if she said she hadn't missed him with every breath she took. She wasn't sure how he'd gotten into the house. After all, she'd changed the locks. Then again, he knew Jack and Hunter, and those two could break into Area 51, wrapped inside Fort Knox, surrounded by the White House.

With a sigh and a stomach tightening in knots, Alyssa pushed the door open, hoping to see that Luc had decorated the bedroom like a fantasy honeymoon suite.

But no. Instead, ropes had been tied to the bedposts at each corner, leaving loops at the ends for wrists and ankles. She gasped, bile rising in her throat.

Blinking, her breath thin, Alyssa stared in horror. What the hell? Luc knew better than almost anyone that she could not endure bondage. Why on earth would he put her through this? To prove that she could, in fact, trust him? If he wanted to reconcile, threatening to tie her to the bed wasn't the way to persuade her to give their marriage another try.

Anger set in. Where was the son of a bitch? In the bathroom? Closet? Hiding because he knew she was going to take a strip out of his hide for this shit?

As she turned toward the bathroom, acid nearly dripped from her tongue. Then she caught sight of who awaited her.

It wasn't Luc who leaned against the wall, jacket stripped off, tie loose, smirk firmly in place.

She screamed.

* * *

LUC pulled up in front of the house he had shared with Alyssa. Parked. Stared. She'd beat him home, based on the softly glowing lamp in the living room. Damn. Would she even answer the door at this time of night?

During the long drive, he questioned himself a hundred times, his thoughts an endless loop of logic that always drew him back to one conclusion: He had to talk to her face-to-face, try to reconcile with her again. He wasn't letting Alyssa go without a fight. Somehow, he had to make her believe that he loved her and would never do anything to betray her trust again.

Armed with his conviction, he turned off the car, stepped out to the still night and chilly November wind. His palms were sweating as he approached the door.

A faint feminine scream of terror burst across the night. The sound seared its way down his spine. It wasn't the TV. It was real and human—and familiar.

Alyssa!

Running to the door, he grabbed the knob and wrenched it. But it was firmly locked.

"Fuck!" Windows? Other door? All locked, he knew. Jack had wired her house tight. Which begged the question: Who had gotten to her and how had they broken in? Later. He couldn't worry about details now.

Luc would also have to break in, somehow. He had to make some decisions—and fast—or Alyssa could die.

Nine-one-one was the first logical choice . . . except Remy didn't do his job well and didn't have the means to get into the house. Calling Tyler made more sense.

Ripping his phone from his belt, he hit his speed dial, thankful he'd filched the number off of Alyssa's cell phone just after she'd gone "missing."

Tyler answered before the second ring. "What?"

"It's Alyssa. There's someone in her house. I can hear her screaming, but I can't get in since she changed the locks."

"Don't try to bullshit me just so you can see her again."

"God's truth." Then Alyssa screamed again—loud.

"Shit!" Her bouncer cursed, and his demeanor changed. "I'm at least ten away. You're going to have to get in and handle this until I get there. I'll get you inside."

"How?" They were losing time. Every second, another opportunity to keep Alyssa from harm was lost.

"Go through the gate, around to the side of the house. In the side yard, there's a door that leads into the garage. On the right of the door, there's a holly bush. Behind it is a tiny film canister. It should be half buried."

Luc sprinted around the side of the house and was now directly below Alyssa's window. He heard her scream again, and the sound cramped his gut with fear and dread. Why couldn't he just break the fucking thing down and save her? He *needed* her in his life, damn it.

"Too damn dark to see anything."

Frustration mounting, he ran back to his car and pulled out his emergency flashlight. While there, he also pulled out the semiautomatic he'd forgotten was in his car and tucked it into the waistband of his jeans, at the small of his back . . . just in case.

The seconds back to the side door seemed to take forever, but he quickly located the canister, extracted the key, and shoved it into the lock.

"I'm in the garage."

The stuffy air was dusty and smelled faintly of grass. Luc didn't dare turn on a light, but at least he knew his way around.

"Shut and lock that door behind you in case the assailant isn't working alone. No need to alert anyone to the fact you're there yet. They could kill her before you have a chance to save her."

"Right." He did as instructed.

Edging around her lawn equipment and the front of her little convertible, he sidled up to the door that led into the den.

"Standing in front of the door to the house."

"You can't use it. It should be locked, and I don't know where she keeps a key. And if you open it, the alarm, if it's engaged, will make a sound and alert her intruder. You need to go through the attic."

"Gotcha." Luc eased back around Alyssa's car and pulled on the string hanging from the garage ceiling. A set of stairs emerged

into the empty space beside her car. He climbed up, flashlight leading the way.

Inside the space, he found Christmas decorations in boxes, tax
records boxed up neatly and arranged one year after another, and
virtually nothing else but empty space. Impatience and fear gnawed
at him.

"I see two small doors. They open to crawl spaces?"

"Right. Never knew helping her fix her cable one day would
come in handy," Tyler tried to joke, but the quip came out tersely.

"The one ahead seems like it would lead over the living room."

"Exactly. Take the one to your right. Once you're inside the crawl
space, it will angle up. The exit is at the end, in the hall just outside
her bedroom."

"I know exactly where." He'd noticed the attic entrance as he'd
traversed the hall.

Luc made his way through the door and, on hands and knees,
crawled up into the rafters of the house.

"This will take a few minutes. It's long and narrow, but you'll
keep the element of surprise."

As much as every second apart from her chafed Luc, he agreed
this was the best plan.

"Any idea who the fuck we're dealing with?" Tyler asked.

"No clue."

"Peter was extradited to Florida. He had a pending sexual assault
charge there, so it's not him. But fucking Primpton made bail."

"You think he's that stupid?"

"He's that tenacious. And he ain't right in the head."

Luc couldn't agree more.

Tyler sighed. "There's something else I should tell you, just in
case this asshole is our problem. You've probably guessed that I'm
not a bouncer by trade."

"Yeah." Luc's guts seized up. What the hell was the man saying?

"I'm from California, Alyssa's home state."

Shit. Luc did not like the sound of this. "What the fuck did you do?"

"I used to be a vice detective for LAPD. Now I'm a PI. I was hired at the end of August by a real wealthy prick to find Alyssa. I was given a teenage picture of her and the information that she was somewhere in Lafayette. The asshole told me it was his missing sister."

Luc went cold all over. "Joshua."

"That's him."

"Why didn't you tell me sooner? Or tell *her*?"

"So she could throw me out of her life completely? No. I thought I had the sitch under control."

"So you think Joshua could be inside?"

"I don't know." He sighed. "As soon as I found Alyssa for him, he wired me payment. I flew back to L.A. to give him her information and photographic proof. Son of a bitch asked me a million questions, like did she have a husband or lover, had I fucked her, was I aware of anyone fucking her. He was obsessed, man."

Luc's gut knotted. "Damn it, we all assumed Primpton was the threat."

"The councilman is unhinged, but I don't think he's eager to up his prison sentence with this prank. You almost through the crawl space?"

"It's tight in here, but I'm close."

"I'm about five away."

For once, Tyler's presence would be a huge relief. "Once you figured out that Joshua was a scumbag, you stayed in Lafayette to protect Alyssa?"

"Yeah. I couldn't breach the confidentiality of my client by telling her without risking my license. For all I knew, he just wanted to know where she was and to beat off to her picture every night. Then when things started to get hot, I couldn't prove who'd left her the knives and the threats. So I stayed, called buddies back home periodically to check up on the bastard, make sure he was still in L.A., and I did my best not to let her out of my sight. It would have been a shitload easier to safeguard her if I'd been her lover. Nothing like twenty-four/seven protection."

Jealousy belted Luc. "That's not the only reason you wanted Alyssa."

"Oh, hell, no. I've been in love with your wife almost from day one." He sighed. "But she's always been into you. I never had a chance."

"You led me to believe more than once that you were fucking her."

"I kept hoping you'd get pissed off, go away, and give me a chance. But you were too tenacious, damn it."

And so the truth came out. Tyler had never once slept with his wife. Alyssa hadn't been lying. Luc gritted his teeth. He'd been so fucking stupid to let his jealousy get out of hand.

"Nor am I letting her go now," he vowed. "The trapdoor that leads out of the crawl space is right in front of me. It lowers from the ceiling. Do I just push down and the stairs lower?"

"Should. But you'll have to be very quiet. The wooden stairs will clatter on the hardwood floor if you don't lower them slowly."

Alyssa screamed again, this time a clear, plaintive wail. "No! Don't touch me!"

"Do you hear that?" Luc growled in low tones. "I don't have time for slowly."

"You don't have a choice. I got a call three hours ago from my old vice partner that Joshua left L.A a few weeks ago."

"A few *weeks*?"

Tyler sighed. "I didn't think after all these months he'd suddenly make a move. I wasn't checking up as often . . . My fuckup, I know. Anyway, Joshua told his wife he'd be on business in London, but TSA says he never left the country . . . If that's him in Alyssa's bedroom, he's going to want to mess with her for a while. He's got over a decade worth of hard-on for Alyssa. If he intends to kill her, it won't be quick. Take a deep breath and find some fucking patience."

Tyler's words ate at him. Anxiety scraped him raw. He swallowed it because the PI was right.

"You got a way to fight him off? Any weapon?" Tyler asked.

"I'm licensed for a concealed weapon in Texas, so I had it in my car. It's tucked in my waistband."

"Slightly illegal, Traverson."

"Had more on my mind than technicalities."

"Roger that. We have to end this call now. You'll need both hands to lower the ladder, and once you open the trapdoor, he'll be able to hear you talk."

"Yeah." Luc gripped the phone, trying to calm his erratic breathing and racing heart. This was it. He *must* save Alyssa or die trying.

Deke had done a lot to prepare Luc for this. Hand-to-hand sparring, karate, a near overdose of target practice . . . But the fact was, Luc was a chef and, other than helping Tyler dismantle Peter in Alyssa's office, Luc had never had to mop up an attacker and rescue someone—especially not someone he loved more than his next breath.

"You can do it," Tyler assured. "Keep calm and quiet. Use the element of surprise if you can. If not, just blow the motherfucker's head off. I'm calling Remy now. The cavalry will be there in less than five. Do whatever you have to do to keep her alive that long, and we'll take care of the rest."

"Thanks." Luc may not be as well trained as Tyler, but he'd be damned before he let whoever this was kill his wife. And if it was Joshua . . . Luc would be fucking thrilled to exorcise this ghost for her—for good.

* * *

ALYSSA blinked. Blinked again. Her worst nightmare had come to life—and now stood in her bedroom.

"Hello, Lindsey. Though I guess now I should just call you 'whore.'"

Run! Her brain couldn't make her body obey the commands as shock overwhelmed her system. She stepped back, fear gripping her lungs as she screamed.

"Quiet now. I've looked a long time to find you. Over a decade, in fact. Now that I've succeeded, time to remind you who you belong to. And yes, the ropes are for you. Old times' sake."

Her body trembled. But when she saw the black-handled serrated knife in his hand—the kind that had been stabbed into her belongings—her world shook.

"*You've* been stalking me?" Not Primpton?

His eyes sparkled with sick mischief. "I enjoyed scaring you with all those notes. Trashing your bedroom was fun, too. But you weren't as terrified as I wanted. I'm put out that you're not the same meek virgin, Lindsey."

She wasn't. But in that moment, it was as if she were fifteen again and stunned that her best friend was now her worst nightmare, causing her immense pain as he stripped away her innocence, one forced thrust after another.

"Don't do this, Joshua," she pleaded, willing to do anything to live for her baby's sake.

"Ah, so you do remember my name. How juicy that you haven't forgotten your first. Let's see what else you remember."

"You're going to kill me." It wasn't a question. She knew the answer deep in her bones.

He didn't hesitate. "Of course. I'd keep you alive, but I don't like the idea of sharing you with that chef you married. Besides, my wife hates my . . . little toys."

His wife? She flinched. What he planned was bad enough, but to desecrate his wedding vows, too? Then again, it didn't sound like the first time he'd strayed.

Joshua's eyes flared with the promise of pain as he stalked toward her with a twisted smile. She backed away. "Leave me alone."

"I can't do that. After you left, I was a laughingstock among my friends. They ribbed me that you'd hated fucking me so much that you left home."

I did! But she knew confirming that would be unwise.

"I began to wonder if my friends were right. It might have been a bit painful at first, you being a virgin, but I was sure I fucked you good."

He'd thought terror and anal bleeding were good? "That's all in the past. There's nothing between us now, Joshua."

"*I'm* the one who decides that. When you left, you took that control from me. Then you shared your body with other men. Got married!" He pressed his lips together. "Very unwise, but thankfully, very temporary."

With his implied threat, anger boiled to the surface, rolling over the fear. "Don't you *dare* touch Luc!"

"He's next on my agenda. Now, be the good stripper you are and drop your clothes."

The time for talk was over. Once Joshua decided that he wanted something, nothing deterred him. He could be methodical and patient, if he found the game and sport worth his while. The rest of the time he was a greedy bastard, wanting what he wanted now.

Alyssa refused to play along.

She had to find a way to defend herself and get out the door. If she turned and ran, he'd only catch her. She was wearing stilettos, and he'd been a track star in high school. No contest. Finding a way to even the odds was critical.

Backing away from him, toward the door, she risked a peek over her shoulder. The first thing to catch her gaze was shiny and silver and, she knew from lifting it, heavy.

Thank you, Luc, for the wedding gift.

She turned her back to Joshua and lunged for the frame. As expected, he darted after her. And she was ready. When he approached, she clutched the heavy, scarred photo frame and swung with all her might, clocking Joshua in the face.

He stumbled back, staggering into the wall, clutching his right eye. "Bitch! You're going to fucking pay for that. You don't know how much I've learned about the fine art of making a fucking hurt in the last fourteen years, but I'll be damn happy to show you."

Alyssa didn't stay to hear his disgusting tirade. She kicked off her shoes and darted for her bedroom door. She stopped short when Joshua managed to grab a few strands of her hair in his fist. Then he began to yank back.

If she let him drag her back into that bedroom, she was as good as dead. She might die anyway, but damn it, she wasn't going down without a fight.

Turning her head one direction, she yanked with all her might in the other. Pain seared across her scalp as the strands tore from their follicles, but she was free.

Knowing she was a second or less ahead of him, she darted out the door, into the darkened hall—and crashed into someone.

She gasped. Dear God, had Joshua brought help?

"Shh," he whispered.

Luc!

She wanted to ask a million questions, but there was no time. Joshua's footsteps resounded on the hardwood floor. Luc shoved her behind him, then backed them against the wall, out of Joshua's path. Alyssa prayed that in the dark, he wouldn't see them right away.

Curled up against Luc's back, she was so relieved to see him—and worried for him at the same time. Joshua wanted to kill him, and Alyssa had no doubt her stepbrother meant it.

Luc pressed her deeper into shadow as Joshua approached, his pace slowing. She could almost feel his methodical gaze sweeping the darkened hallway and held her breath, praying she and Luc would come away from this alive. Somehow.

Something gouged Alyssa in the stomach—hard, cold. She squeezed a hand between them and felt around. Luc had a gun!

He tensed as she touched the weapon, then gave her an infinitesimal shake of his head. Alyssa frowned and let go. Guns weren't her favorite, but hopefully Luc had a plan. Wondering what the hell it might be as he pressed her against the wall, Alyssa panted, her heart thumping in a staccato rhythm so loud she feared people in the next county could hear it.

Joshua crept past them, then stopped at the top of the stairs when sirens split the air.

The police are coming! Thank God.

At the sound, Joshua lifted his head, then growled. "Fucking bitch! Where are you? I'd have heard you run down the stairs. And now the fucking cops are on the way. Someone cut my fun short, damn it, but I'm going to end you before they get within ten feet of saving you."

Without warning, he flipped on the hallway light. And he had a gun pointed directly at Luc's chest.

Joshua looked taken aback to see her husband; then he smiled. "Well, talk about an opportunity to kill two birds with one stone."

Alyssa couldn't breathe. Luc's gun was still behind his back. He'd never have time to pull it free and shoot Joshua in return. Her stepbrother was one trigger pull away from killing Luc. And she knew Josh—he'd do it without remorse. Hell, he'd probably laugh.

That could not happen. If she no longer had Luc, she'd crumble, crack . . . die.

She leaned around Luc's left shoulder and glared at Joshua. "Leave him alone. It's me you want. I'll get in a car with you. You can take me wherever you want, do whatever you want, if you'll leave him alone."

"No!" Luc railed. "Absolutely not."

For a second, hope sparked. *Maybe . . .* Then she remembered. His concern was likely not for her but because she was pregnant. "I know you're worried about the baby. You'll find someone else and have another. I know you will."

"Baby?" Joshua shouted, taking a menacing step forward. "You let him fucking knock you up?"

Luc eyed the gun, but otherwise ignored him. "I'm not thinking about the baby now. I'm worried about *you*. If you go with him, I'll never see you alive again. For me, there'll never be anyone else I'll love half as much as you."

His words warmed her, pouring over her shivering skin like melted chocolate. For that one moment—possibly one of their last together—Alyssa hoped he meant that and, aside from their coming child, she mattered to Luc.

Damn it, why did she have to realize that there was a chance his feelings were every bit as real as hers just when their time together was ending?

No. Joshua had taken everything from her once. Never again would she be this asshole's victim. If anyone was going down this time, it was him.

Luc had a gun, and she had gumption. Time to use both.

"I'm going to be sick," Joshua sneered as he stalked closer and closer—until he pressed the gun to Luc's forehead. "Time to end this lovefest."

Alyssa's heart stopped.

The sirens were screaming, coming closer with every second. She saw the panic on her stepbrother's face. He was about to do something rash, reckless, and given the fact he could shoot Luc point-blank at any moment . . . irrevocable. There was no way her husband could reach his gun and fire quickly enough. She, however, might be able to use the element of surprise.

"You." Joshua pointed his gun at Luc, then waved it to the

left. "Lindsey is mine. She's always been mine. For touching her, you'll die."

"It's Alyssa, asshole," she sneered. "And I hate you. Rot in hell!"

While he stared at her in growing anger, she grabbed Luc's gun, then shoved him aside. Vaguely, she heard him stumble. Joshua was distracted by the commotion long enough for Alyssa to grip the unfamiliar gun, point, and . . .

Bang!

As the sound crashed through her ears, Joshua slapped a hand to his chest and staggered back. When he pulled his fingers away from his white shirt, they came away red. A crimson stain began spreading across his shirt.

"Bitch!" Joshua muttered, then staggered.

To her horror, he righted himself and raised his gun again.

Luc jumped in front of her and ripped the gun from her hands. Before she could protest, he'd planted his body in front of hers, aimed, and fired. The loud shot reverberated through the little space, ringing in her ears.

Joshua's head snapped back. As he fell to his knees, blood oozed from the wound right between his eyes.

Alyssa jumped as he dropped into a noisy heap on her hardwoods. His gun fell out of his lax hand and skittered across the floor.

Luc kicked it away from Joshua, until it rested at his feet. Never taking his eyes off of her stepbrother, he steadied his own gun and pointed it again at the sick bastard.

Alyssa took a step toward Joshua and bent.

"No!" Luc insisted. "It could be a trick."

"Then cover me." She swallowed. "I need this."

And damn it, she wasn't at all shaken by the thought she might have helped kill her stepbrother. In fact, she was holding her breath, hoping she had. If so, she'd throw a fucking party.

Downstairs, they heard a commotion, then a loud thump as the front door hit the foyer wall. Footsteps poured inside, pounding up the stairs, just as Alyssa bent to Joshua and put her fingers on his carotid.

"Well?" Luc prompted.

"You okay, Ms. Devereaux?" Remy asked, standing on the stair directly behind Joshua.

"Mrs. Traverson," Luc corrected Remy tersely, then turned back to her. "Sugar?"

She stood and smiled—really smiled—for the first time in fourteen years. "The son of a bitch is dead."

Chapter Twenty

THE blisteringly clear Friday afternoon gusted through Lafayette. Alyssa watched out the living room window as she paced, waiting. Half an hour before she was due at the obstetrician's office. Luc had begged her to let him accompany her to the appointment. No sign of him so far.

She sighed. What was up with that man?

"You have that 'I'm thinking about Luc' look on your face," Sadie teased.

Alyssa rolled her eyes at her own ridiculousness. She'd taken steps to end her marriage to Luc, yet she couldn't stop thinking about him. This morning, she'd fondled her wedding ring, sorely tempted to put it on just to feel closer to him.

"I don't understand Luc," she confessed. "It's been almost a week since we shot Joshua."

"A bastard more deserving of a pine box I've never met." Sadie gripped her hand. "Honey, why didn't you tell any of us about your past?"

Because it had been her shame, and she'd buried it ruthlessly, using it to fortify her iron heart so that she'd never get too close to anyone else again. Luc had melted her defenses and filled her soul. Now she felt incomplete without him.

For me, there'll never be anyone else I'll love half as much as you.

As she nibbled on a fingernail, those words ran through Alyssa's head. Had Luc really meant that or had the possibility of her and the baby's deaths prompted him to say those words?

"I just wanted to keep it behind me," Alyssa said finally. "Besides, I never imagined that Joshua had seen me at my mother's funeral, recognized me, hired someone to hunt me down . . ."

"You mad at Tyler?"

The question rattled around in her head. "Not mad. He was doing a job. Tyler said that Joshua didn't act creepy or obsessive until after he'd located me and turned over the information. He actually put his life on hold to protect me because he feared the worst."

"And because he was hoping you'd give him the time of day."

Alyssa grimaced. "That, too."

"Did he say what he's going to do now?"

After hours on Monday, he'd insisted on seeing her home, making sure all was well and safe since Luc had left . . .

What did you expect a man you served annulment papers to do? Stay so you could throw him out more creatively?

"He wants to remain in Lafayette. Says he likes it here and had no real ties in Los Angeles. Jack and Deke offered him a job. Apparently, they've been turning away business because they're short-handed, and Deke wants to spend more time with Kimber since they have a baby on the way."

"You do, too, girlfriend. When is that appointment? Shouldn't you be leaving?"

Stomach clenching, Alyssa glanced at her watch and winced. "I'll give Luc five more minutes; then if you're still game . . ."

"Absolutely, I'll go with you. A girl needs moral support for these things," Sadie offered, then smiled sadly. "Though I know you'd rather have Luc."

Alyssa couldn't refute that. After Joshua's attack nearly a week ago and after she and Luc had answered all of Remy's questions, she'd expected him to stay, confront her about the annulment. At least voice an opinion. But he'd only stolen a kiss, told her loved her and pleaded to go to her doctor's appointment, then left for Texas. Midweek, her curiosity had gotten the better of her, and she'd called Luc to ask him the million questions floating through her brain. Again, he'd only told her that he loved her and would be there on Friday to pick her up. She tried to put him out of her head and focus on the myriad items on her to-do list, but no luck.

Sadie glanced at her watch. "Why don't you get your purse together? I'll meet you in the car. I'm parked out front."

Alyssa tried to stifle her disappointment at Luc's no-show long enough to smile for her friend. "Sure. Thanks."

As soon as she heard the *click* of the door behind Sadie, Alyssa felt pesky tears sting her eyes. Damn it, she had a doctor to see, a baby to confer about. If Luc had suddenly embraced the annulment . . . well, maybe it was for the best. At least she tried to tell herself that. The last week without him, she'd come to realize that she would never be completely happy or completely whole without him.

But she also knew that she couldn't be married to a man she loved this fervently who remained only to be with the child he'd always dreamed of having. Without Luc's love, sharing a home, a bed, and a last name would be hollow. Eventually, it would tear them apart. If he didn't truly love her *for her*, better that she know now—not when the child was cranky for a nighttime feeding . . . or when he or she began kindergarten . . . or when they had their first sporting event, first crush, first heartbreak . . . or when Luc finally found the woman to whom he could devote his heart—and left her an empty, broken shell.

Even though she was saving herself more pain later, it fucking hurt now.

Swallowing back the tears, she grabbed her purse, set the new alarm, and carefully shut the door behind her. After locking it, she turned toward Sadie's car at the curb.

Except it was gone.

What the devil? Shaking her head, she followed the *L* of her walkway to the driveway.

There stood Luc, looking at his watch.

Her breath caught. Her heart stopped. He'd made it.

Why?

Thoughts racing, she took tentative steps forward. Luc looked up, saw her—and darted her way.

He cupped her cheek and placed a gentle kiss on her lips, over almost as soon as it started. "Hi, sugar. I've missed you."

Those chocolate eyes looked so earnest, so honest. God, why was he doing this to her? If he still wanted her, why didn't he just tell her he didn't want the annulment? Or maybe he did want it? She was so confused . . .

"Hi. Thanks for taking me to the appointment."

"I wouldn't miss it for the world." He opened the passenger door and held it as she slid inside.

So was his affection for her merely that of for the mother of his child? As he hopped in the driver's seat and glanced her way, there was something on his face she'd never seen before. The heat was still there. He *wanted* her, no question. That expression said he wanted to devour her now—and to keep doing it for hours, days. It was tempered by something warm, like sweet sunshine honey. Something like . . . affection. Even hope. His smile seemed to say there was no one he'd rather be with.

How much of that was tangled up in his feelings for the baby?

He grabbed her hand and backed the Jaguar out of the driveway. She knew she should release him . . . but she couldn't find the strength to let go.

"Have Remy or the boys been out to question you again or give you more information about Joshua's attack?" he asked.

"No. Once Remy cleared us of any sort of homicide charge, I just didn't want to talk about it anymore."

"You must be relieved that Joshua is gone. Your past can't come back to haunt you again." He squeezed her hand.

She took strength in his caress. This wasn't a topic she could discuss with anyone . . . but him. He really *knew* her in a way no one else did. For that, she was grateful.

"I still wish I could have reconciled with my mother, but maybe that was impossible. She didn't want to believe me because it made her life too difficult, and I have no respect for that."

"What Joshua did to you was terrible. Tragic. What she did was worse." Luc's warm gaze wrapped her in a soft blanket of comfort.

It would be so easy to sink in . . . get lost. And so painful later.

"I work every day on forgiving her. It's a day-by-day thing."

"Everything that happened made you who you are today— strong, independent, savvy, pragmatic. I wouldn't change a thing about you. You're the woman I love."

Her heart seized. How badly she wanted to believe him. "Luc . . ."

"Shh." He pulled up in front of the hospital complex. "Let's see the doctor now. Later, we'll talk through this."

Damn it, she didn't want to put it off. Alyssa didn't deal well with shoving unpleasant things aside. Why not just get it over with? But they could hardly discuss their marital issues in the waiting room. She sighed.

Within minutes, the obstetrician's nurse called them back and she greeted the pleasant fortysomething woman who examined her while Luc sat in the chair behind her and held her hand.

"Would you like to hear the baby's heartbeat?"

"Please." She smiled.

"Very much."

Alyssa couldn't see Luc's face, but she could hear the sincerity in his voice.

The doctor applied a cool gel to her abdomen, then a plastic wand and . . .

Whoosh, whoosh, whoosh. A little beating heart. The sound filled the room, young, tender yet remarkably hardy. A miracle.

Tears filled her eyes. "Oh, my God."

Luc squeezed her hand even harder. "I've never heard anything so amazing."

She heard the tears in his voice, too.

"Very strong and healthy," the doctor promised. "On the slower side, which could indicate a boy, but we'll know for sure when we do the ultrasound around week twenty."

A boy? Alyssa's heart clenched, then pitter-pattered. She'd love a boy. Or a girl. She'd love this child, no matter what. And she loved that, no matter what happened, it would always be part of Luc.

Finally, the other woman measured her abdomen, chatted a bit about what to expect over the next month, then sent her on her way. As they settled with the receptionist and exited the building, Luc gripped her hand.

They reached his car, and he stopped her, turning her to face him. "Thank you for sharing that with me. I will be forever grateful, no matter what happens in the future. I'd like fifteen minutes more of your time, if you'll spare them. Then, if you still want to proceed with the annulment, I won't stop you."

Denial and fear slammed her at once, and she tried to block them out. The annulment was—ultimately—a good thing, right? So why should everything inside her rebel at the thought that he wouldn't fight it?

She just loved him too damn much.

"All right." Her voice shook.

Without another word, they returned to her house, and she showed him into the living room. They sat on the sofa, less than two feet apart.

Funny, how their relationship had basically started here, on this piece of furniture, when he'd arrived with his cousin Deke last summer for a seductive ménage that had quickly morphed into an explosive pairing when Luc's cousin left. Would it end here, too?

"Do you want something to drink?" What was on his mind? She needed to know . . . yet feared it.

"No, thank you." He pulled a thick, folded document from his jacket pocket and handed it to her. "This is yours, regardless of what happens."

The gravity in his tone crashed to her hollow stomach. She took deep breaths. With shaking hands, she unfolded the crisp white papers and scanned.

"It's . . ." She blinked once, twice. *Seriously?* "A custody agreement? You're giving me sole custody?"

"If you decide to proceed with the annulment, I've asked for one week a year and either Thanksgiving or Christmas. I think it's important for any child to know his or her father. There's a financial support agreement as well. I took the attorney's recommendation for an annual sum and added fifty percent. I hope you think it's fair, but we can talk if you need more. I'll never tell you how to parent. I'll never get in your way. I'll never ask you to share more of the child than this and an occasional phone call."

Tears came again. Not just tears, but sobs. The foundation of her life was falling out from underneath her, crumbling, and the pain was paralyzing. Luc was letting her go and giving her control over the life they had created together—the child she knew he wanted more than anything.

"Why?" she managed to get out.

He closed his eyes, jaw clamped, as he fought his own tears.

"Because I love you, and I want you to know that no one will ever be more important to me than you, not even our child."

"But you've wanted a baby for years and—"

"I have, so badly I manipulated people I love, deceived them—without even thinking how they would be affected. And I regret that so deeply. I never want you to believe that I married you only for the child. I was stupid when I didn't tell you that I believed the baby to be someone else's. I can only say I'm sorry. I know better now." He sighed. "I realized I wasn't lacking a baby, but someone to share my life with. Someone amazing and strong, smart, ambitious, and wonderful. My other half."

Alyssa sobbed harder. He meant her? He wanted her *more* than their child?

Luc eased off the sofa and onto one knee at her feet. "I need *you*."

"And you're willing to give up custody of the baby to prove it to me?"

He nodded, and the agony on his face hurt her in return. "No strings attached. I want to stay married to you more than anything and be a family in the true sense of the word, but not if you'll always have doubts about how important you are to me."

Oh. My. God. Never in a million years had she expected him to give up the child he'd sought and schemed for. And to do it for her.

"Think on it," he commanded softly. "If I don't hear from you before the annulment is final in the next few months, then this may be the last time you see me. And I'll miss you like hell. I'll love you. Always."

He kissed her mouth gently. It lasted for only a heartbeat, felt like a gossamer breath, but it impacted her heart like a battering ram. Then he was gone.

*   *   *

ALYSSA paced her living room, wringing her hands. *Any minute . . .*

After Luc's departure Friday night, she'd longed to call him back immediately. The scared girl-woman inside her shouted for caution and prudence. She'd stayed up late and read the entire custody agreement he'd proposed—and signed—then left in her hands. He'd been more than generous and left himself minimal rights, save those he would exercise in the event of her untimely death. He'd also added a clause for reversion of custody in the event she remarried to someone who turned out to be abusive.

The fact he'd taken her experience to heart touched her.

She'd spent a sleepless Friday night knowing she had only two choices: End the marriage and raise the child alone, always wondering if she'd made the biggest mistake of her life by leaving the man she loved, or embrace the future and do everything in her power to ensure their marriage grew strong.

Luc said he loved her. Since he'd handed her this custody agreement, Alyssa finally more than hoped—she believed—that was true. She loved him so much, getting through a day without him felt unbearable. Nights were even more hellish.

Still, experience had taught her to be cautious. She'd spent all day Saturday thinking about her options . . . and coming back to the same conclusion. How bleak would her future be without Luc? He couldn't have apologized more eloquently, been more contrite. It wasn't as if she'd never screwed up.

Besides, she'd gone into the marriage tentative and afraid. Failing at lifelong commitment was inevitable without giving both heart and soul. She hadn't done that. Yes, Luc had withheld his "sterility" from her, but she'd withheld her past with Joshua. If Luc hadn't accidentally scared her, would she have ever told him her secret, ever?

She winced. Probably not.

Didn't she owe it to them to try this marriage for real, holding nothing back?

She'd called him early this Sunday morning and asked him to come back to Lafayette. He hadn't asked questions, and she hadn't offered information. They both knew that whatever had to be said should be done in person.

The chime of the doorbell interrupted her musings, and she smoothed a hand down her black wrap-around blouse, holding a palm to her trembling insides. Taking a deep breath, she opened the door.

Luc stood on the other side, expression pensive. "I'm glad you called."

Alyssa nodded, trying to calm her runaway heartbeat. "Come in."

When she stepped back, he entered. But his eyes never left hers, as if he hoped to read her decision on her face. She looked away and walked into the living room. Luc followed, and Alyssa could feel him at her back, so achingly close—yet still so far away.

Please God, let this turn out happily.

On the table beside her rested two documents. She picked up both. "I've read your custody document."

He hesitated; then disappointment crashed over his face. He clenched his jaw and finally nodded. "Do you have any objections?"

"Have you read the annulment papers?"

"Yes."

His tone gave her more hope. "You spit that out like a bad word."

Luc anchored a hand around her waist, then brought her closer to him. Their bodies nearly touched . . . but not quite. Then he lay his forehead on hers, his breath tightly controlled. "It is. Ending our marriage is the last thing I want." He took a deep breath and stepped back. "But I'll respect your decision, whatever it is."

He left everything to her, put the power in her hands. If he cared only about himself and his chance to become a parent, he'd never do that. Ever. He'd push and coerce, threaten, cajole . . . anything but let her make the ultimate decision.

"I love you," she whispered.

The next split second of silence terrified her, especially as both hope and disappointment mingled on his face. What was he thinking?

"I love you, too. So much I . . ." Luc sighed and cupped her cheek. "I'm empty without you."

To others, it might sound like a greeting card, but she knew exactly what he meant. He'd helped to heal her past wounds, fill in her tomorrows. Luc had made her whole. If she did the same for him, she'd rejoice and hold him close for the rest of her days.

"Ending this marriage is the last thing I want, too," she confessed.

To prove her point, she gripped both the annulment petition and custody papers, then ripped them both in half. She dropped them to the ground between them.

Luc glanced at the torn documents, then up at her. His eyes flared, burning fiercely, as he grabbed her and kissed her as if nothing would ever mean more to him.

Not opening to him was impossible, and he sank deep into her mouth, the burn between them his own brand of possession. Though it had been less than a month since she and Luc had shared a bed, the ache racing through her after this one kiss made her feel as if it had been forever. She needed this, needed *him*.

Tears burned her eyes as his lips worshipped her. There would be important events in their lives together undoubtedly, their coming child—and maybe others someday—but Alyssa knew deep in her gut that nothing would ever mean more to her than this moment and their love.

When he lifted his head, she looked at him and melted.

"I need you," he admitted hoarsely. "To love you. As much as you'll give me. I need to feel that you're really mine. Please say you want that, too."

Alyssa nodded. "I do."

Caressing his cheek, she pressed her lips to his and swept into his mouth. When he rewarded her with a slow kiss full of devotion, she trembled.

Not even lifting his head, he laid her across the sofa, her back warmed by the buttery leather as he covered her body with his own, wrapping his arms around her. She felt safe, loved, as she sighed against him, desire growing. He compelled her to touch him in return—his face, neck, taut shoulders and back.

Soft demand filled his next kiss, seeming to reach deep inside of her to embrace *all* of her, even the broken parts. Luc brought light to the places in her soul that had been dark since Joshua's attack. He made her whole again.

His next kiss started like gossamer, then grew more urgent with every brush of lips, every swirl of his tongue, until it was deep, hard, burning. Alyssa couldn't breathe, couldn't think of anything but Luc and the silent promise of devotion between them. She opened to him and gave him everything inside her, secure that there were no more secrets between them.

Drowning in Luc's hungry kisses, she trembled as he slowly removed her top, her jeans, her frilly under things, then spread kisses all over her body. He sucked her aching nipples, palmed her hip, stroked her needy clit. She burned. Luc always had that effect on her. From the moment they'd met, Luc had impacted her as no man had.

Alyssa was dying to have the same effect on him.

With a gentle nudge, she persuaded Luc to roll onto his back. Without a word, she removed his shoes, his shirt, his pants, and everything beneath. Then she was staring at his gorgeous, naked body, masculine shoulders, rippling abs, and hard, imposing cock. She shivered, and her mouth watered.

Kneeling beside him, she threw her hair over one shoulder and bent to him. Luc tensed. When her tongue curled around his dick, she tasted him, harsh and hot and so salty male. Then she took him deeper with a moan.

"Sugar, yeah," he hissed, filtering his fingers into her hair and anchoring against her scalp. "Damn, you're incredible."

So was he.

Alyssa savored him, reacquainting herself with his body and the pleasures of feeling him hard in her mouth. He arched his hips, sinking his stiff flesh deeper, and she gladly took every long inch of his urgent thrusts, loving the fact she could make him so hot.

Moments lapsed into long minutes. His need grew, and he began to shuttle into her mouth with deeper, faster strokes, writing, moaning, needing. He pulsed against her tongue.

Then suddenly he cursed and stopped.

"No." He lifted her away from him suddenly, and his expression told her that he refused to take pleasure from her, but insisted on sharing it. "I want to be inside you, sugar."

Yes. The sooner, the better.

When he rose to his knees and eased her to her back, she went more than willingly, parting her thighs for him without hesitation. Luc groaned, then leaned over her, on top of her. But she hesitated, holding him back, pressing a hand to his chest.

They had one more bridge to cross . . .

"Wait. I—I trust you." Her words trembled.

His dark gaze caressed her with gratitude and love. "I wouldn't have it any other way."

As he tried to envelop her in his embrace again, she stayed him once more. "Luc. I trust you with everything that used to scare me. Cure me of it. Replace it with something better."

For a moment, his thoughts raced; then understanding dawned. "Sugar, are you sure? We don't have to do this now—or ever if you don't want."

Alyssa didn't hesitate. "I want to. Please . . ."

Luc reached for his belt and pulled it through the loops of his pants. He secured it around her wrists and pulled tight, then tilted her body down to loop the other end under the leg of the sofa.

Her breath caught. The restraint was more symbolic than binding, but for her, for a first start, it was enough.

"Are you scared?" he asked.

She sent him a tremulous smile. "Not with you."

"I've loved you for so long. I would never hurt you. Ever."

His whispered vow made her heart beat even harder. "I think I fell in love with you that first night. After Deke left, and you made love to me for hours . . . I knew there was something special about you that was meant for me."

His lips skated across her cheeks, her lips. "I probably fell for you that night, too. I was just too damn scared to admit it. I'm so glad you forced me to live up to my obligation, canceled my hotel room, and seduced me. I'm so glad that a miracle happened for us."

As he caressed the tiny baby bulge just starting to grow, she smiled. "Me, too."

In the next moment, Luc lodged himself in the cradle of her thighs and began to plunge inside her slowly, deeply. She was wet, eager to take every hard inch of him now. But he surged in by degrees, maddeningly slow, and she gasped as his cock scraped every sensitive part of her flesh until he finally buried himself to the hilt.

It was impossible to have him so deep inside her and not feel pleasure so extreme, it almost defied words. And what passed between them now was even more breathtaking for its sheer honesty and tender passion. He unleashed a firestorm of need with his slow thrusts that quickly had her gasping and tightening around him. Luc brushed her lips with his own, then melded their mouths together. In its own way, having her wrists bound and being completely helpless to Luc's touch was freeing.

She'd never felt more alive.

Alyssa didn't just feel Luc's passion, but his silent promise to be the best husband possible to her each and every day. It came from his soul as he drove into her with measured, relentless strokes that quickly brought her to the brink of a blinding, breathless orgasm that had her tightening her legs around him and bucking beneath him in exquisite pleasure. Shouting her name, he followed, emptying himself deep into her.

"Please don't ever leave me again," he panted against her lips.

Never. "Whatever happens in the future, we'll work it out. I promise."

Luc unbelted her wrists, then took her hands. "Thank you for your trust."

"Thank you for healing me."

His thumbs caressed across her fingers; then he looked at her hand and frowned. "Where's your wedding ring?"

A glance told her that he'd never taken his off. She bit her lip, then fished around the floor for her jeans. When she found them, she reached into the pocket and pulled out the large, sparkling diamond.

He took it up from her with shaking fingers and a smile. "Mrs. Traverson, would you do me the honor of remaining my wife?"

As he slid the ring back on her finger, tears of joy fell down her cheeks. "I will. Always."

About the Author

Shayla Black (aka Shelley Bradley) is the *New York Times* and *USA Today* bestselling author of more than thirty sizzling contemporary, erotic, paranormal, and historical romances for multiple print, electronic, and audio publishers. She lives in Texas with her husband, munchkin, and one very spoiled cat. In her "free" time she enjoys watching reality TV, reading, and listening to an eclectic blend of music.

Shayla's work has been translated into approximately a dozen languages. She has also received or been nominated for the Passionate Plume, the Holt Medallion, the Colorado Romance Writers Award of Excellence, and the National Reader's Choice Award. RT Book Club has twice nominated her for Best Erotic Romance of the year and awarded her several Top Picks and a KISS Hero Award.

A writing risk-taker, Shayla enjoys tackling writing challenges with every book. Find Shayla at www.ShaylaBlack.com or visit her on her Shayla Black Author Facebook page.

LOOK FOR SHAYLA BLACK'S SEXY BOOK

Surrender to Me

NOW AVAILABLE FROM BERKLEY HEAT